STRAIGHT INTO DARKNESS

A DESERTED LANDS NOVEL

ROBERT L. SLATER

BELLINGHAM, WA

2015 Rocket Tears Press

www.RocketTears.com

Printed in the United States of America

ISBN 978-0-942096-01-6 (paperback)

ISBN 978-1-942096-04-7 (mobi)

ISBN 978-1-942096-02-3 (epub)

First Paperback Edition

Editor: Amanda Hagarty
Copy Editors: Andrea Kinnaman, Elena A. Bianco

Cover design: Pintado. www.pintado.weebly.com
Interior design: Random Max
        Text: Baskerville, Calibri & Arial Narrow

Other Works
by
Robert L. Slater

ALL IS SILENCE: Deserted Lands I

TOILS AND SNARES: A Deserted Lands novel

*OUTWARD BOUND: Science Fiction
& Poetry Collection*

To Shane and Gabe

and all the others taken too young.

PRELUDE

Run, Baby, Run

LIZZIE SAT ON HER FIDGETING hands in the Provisional Utah Government Career Office, waiting with a dozen or more others. Nerves were getting to her. One official was already meeting with her father, Manuel Guerrero. As the receptionist called more people, Lizzie realized they were taking the able-bodied adults first. That made sense —prioritize the most important, most likely to help.

After a bit she wandered over to the receptionist, a brunette a little older than herself, but dressed like an adult in a white blouse with a dark blue skirt and blazer. She smiled pleasantly, "May I help you?"

"How long does this take?"

"It depends." The young woman clasped her hands and her eyes swept the waiting room. "You ought to be called soon. Unless I decide to torture you." Her face betrayed no hint of humor, but her eyes twinkled.

"I hope you don't," Lizzie said, trying not let herself be cheered up by the joke. Her father re-entered, nodded politely to the man who'd taken him inside and hurried toward them.

The man glanced at his clipboard and said a name. A young man across the room stood up and hurried over.

Lizzie wanted to say, 'Hey, I'm older. I should be next," but she also wanted to find out what had happened to her father. "How'd it go, Dad?"

"Fine. I get to do planning work until I'm fully recovered." He made an ugly face. "Organizing supplies and searches. I suggested I could design victory gardens. He said he'd get back to me."

"Doesn't sound too bad," Lizzie offered. "You're not cleaning toilets."

He laughed. "Well, I'd rather deal with real shit than planning and organization."

"Not me." Lizzie grinned. "I'd hate that, too, but not as much."

"Lizzie Gooden-Guerrero?" a female voice called from behind her.

"Coming," Lizzie called over her shoulder. "Wait for me?"

"Of course, I don't have to be to work until tomorrow."

Lizzie spun, hustling to the lady with the clipboard.

The woman, her gray-streaked hair pulled back in a low ponytail, stared over her reading glasses at Lizzie. "Come with me."

Lizzie followed the woman who reminded her of someone; she turned abruptly and motioned Lizzie into her small cubicle.

Lizzie sat. The hand written name tag said Ms. LaFevbre.

"La Fee Bray. Not Lafeeber or La Fever, please."

Lizzie nodded, not trusting her smart-ass mouth. Would she get to be a Collector? Collector was one of those jobs the school counselor told you wouldn't be invented yet. Zach and Duke had been assigned this post-pandemic job of tagging houses for bodies and scavenging for food and resources. No women were allowed outside the walls built out of Semi-Trailers and Panel trucks that had hauled stuff down from Salt Lake City, but there were still some houses to be collected and inventoried inside the walls. The rule wasn't fair, but the council said it was temporary.

She smoothed her jeans like they were a skirt, rather than picking at them with her flitting fingers, and smiled calmly at Ms. LaFevbre.

"Well. You're almost 18?"

"Yes," Lizzie nodded trying to not be too eager. "In January."

"Yes." Ms. LaFevbre's eyes scanned down the chart. "And you're pregnant."

"That's what the doctor says," Lizzie made sure to sound jovial and not sarcastic.

"Married?"

"What?"

"Are you, or were you, married?"

"No. What difference does that make?"

LaFevbre's eyes scrutinized Lizzie's clothes and then narrowed in on her face. "I suppose it makes no difference now."

"Any issues with reading? Glasses? Dyslexia?"

"No. Nothing. ADHD. Not currently medicated."

LaFevbre pursed her lips and glared over her glasses. "You'll be in school. Extra classes for childbirth and child rearing."

Lizzie's heart sank. Classes. That was it. La Fever reminded Lizzie of her stern second grade teacher, Mrs. March. Just the name March made her want to avoid school.

"I'm really good at collecting. Back home in Bellingham, my friend and I saved a baby and got him all situated." School was not a job, Lizzie had never believed that lie. Jess was working with animals, Nev as an administrative assistant and Rachael with kids in a day-care.

"The toddler," LaFevbre said brusquely. "Sebastian A. Jones. Perhaps you'll learn how to raise him and he won't be taken from you."

Lizzie's jaw dropped. Did she really just say that?

"You will report to the Career and Technical Services building."

"But…"

"Since you are already pregnant, you may arrive late and miss the first class on procreation. Report to Room 212 at 8:05 a.m. tomorrow. That is all."

"But, I don't want to. I want a real job."

One eyebrow raised behind the glasses. "Do you wish to eat?"

"Yes, but-"

"The rules are clear, as is your job. No one else can do it for you. Have your baby. Then depending on how you do, you may be allowed to apply for other work."

Lizzie gritted her teeth and stood. "Thank you, madam," she said and left, revving up for an explosion.

By the time she reached her father it must have been fully visible on her face. His hands motioned, Calm down, but Lizzie blew past him when she saw that.

The receptionist called, "Miss? Are you all right?" as Lizzie slammed the door.

PART I

Safety In Numbers

Chapter One

LIZZIE SKIRTED THE CIRCLES OF LIGHT cast by street lamps on the snow-scattered streets north of Provo, now known as *The City* to its inhabitants. Lizzie called it *The Shitty* when she wasn't feeling charitable. The Council had decided to leave the lights on until the Collections were finished, even in areas outside the new city wall.

Avoiding the lights kept her on her toes, and helped her find her escape route.

The January cold bit through her layers of clothing. Some of the Council's rules made sense, but women not being allowed to leave without escort? That was as stupid as they came. What did her gender have to do with it? She'd taken care of herself and Saj crossing the country. But if someone caught her out here, they'd probably lock her up to protect her baby. In order to get out, she had to skip out with only the clothes on her back and hope to get more gear on the way. *Happy Belated-fucking eighteenth Birthday, Lizzie.*

Someone was following her. It could be paranoia, but paranoia had its place in this fucked-up post-outbreak world. Hell, paranoia had its uses in the old world. She ran down the center of the street, her feet stepping where the drifting snow might cover her tracks.

She rounded a corner and then skidded to a stop. In the distance, someone shambled—one of the "dog-people"—she could tell by its loping gait.

It made her think of Spike. The first dog-man she'd known, she'd named Spike. Because he had a spiked collar and the brains of a really smart dog. Her breath caught as she thought of him. He had exchanged his life for hers. His heart was still human in the end, even if the virus had damaged his brain.

This dog-person was a woman. Lizzie ducked behind a car. The dog-woman shuffled along, past her.

The Collectors tried to pick them up whenever they were spotted; Lizzie still wasn't sure why. They were probably taken care of and given menial labor jobs. Some were still capable of doing tasks if given explicit instructions.

The houses stared at her, each like a death mask, the overwhelming costs of the Flu pandemic reflected in their hollow eyes. Behind those empty eyes lay the dead—the hundreds of millions who didn't survive. People like Mama and Jayce. Quiet forever.

The world had gotten more silent. That was why Lizzie had named the outbreak—the Quieting.

Clean up crews and Collectors had been this way already, she could tell by the red and green spray paint tags on the houses. The only dead on this street were in her imagination.

The quiet of the snow was disturbed by a car engine. She slid behind a wooden fence, spying on the street through a knothole. A cop car rolled into view—one of *The Shitty's* finest, out to serve and protect.

One question was on Lizzie's mind: *Is he out here to serve his protection on me?* Only Rachael knew she was gone, because Lizzie had left Saj with her. No one else should notice until Monday morning. They kept a closer eye on the Preggers like her, but all the sleeping and puking she did meant people didn't check too closely. She should have another day. She needed it.

The cop stopped at the next intersection, turned a circle inside it, and stopped, idling.

The door opened and the cop stepped out, dark hair, buzz-cut and a bit of a paunch. He looked like a cop, not just someone who'd been given the job since the Quieting. That might make him better at his job.

Lizzie sidled along the fence, and worked her way around to the back of the house. A car door slammed—the engine revved and moved away. She crossed between backyards to get to the next street over. When she came out from behind the next house, she ran into the cop.

"Where are you going, Miss?" His hands grasped hers.

Act dumb. She stared at him, trying to look confused. She cocked her head to the side and moved her mouth without any sounds coming out.

"Don't know your game, but you're not one of them—"

She twisted and ran back the way she'd come.

"Don't do this, girly." He huffed after her.

In moments her side ached. He was too close, his breath came in bursts. Up ahead she saw the dog-lady. She grasped the simple-minded woman's clothes and spun her into the cop's path. The woman skidded and fell as Lizzie pushed her away hard to get an extra burst of speed.

She couldn't hear the officer's heavy breath, so she hazarded a glance back. The officer was bent over helping the dog-lady stand. A moment of guilt tore at Lizzie's heart as she ran on.

Her mission should have been easy. The night curfew meant no one on the streets, no one but the patrols. Her mistake. She needed to get out of *The City* and into the suburbs quickly. The railroad track cut across her path, so she headed down into the ditch beside it.

Lizzie stumbled along the rocks and discarded railroad ties for a couple miles, her breath coming in ragged puffs, until she came to the next place the tracks crossed a street. She veered off onto the street again, giving up concealment for the luxury of easier travel. These streets were blown clean of snow, and she ran, ignoring the stitch in her side. But the pain grew until she was forced to slow to a brisk walk.

She clutched her side for a few more steps and then her hand slid down to her belly. Maybe the little guy couldn't take all this excitement. She pulled out her phone and checked the directions.

It still amazed her how things like cell signal and GPS worked when there wasn't anyone left running the utilities. Glen had barraged her with techno-talk attempting to explain. It left her with a headache, all she got out of the conversation was that a lot of stuff was automated.

The hill ahead gave a good vantage point to check her path and see if anyone followed. She hunkered down behind a parked car and let her heart and breathing return to normal. Through its snow-dusted windows, she watched for pursuit, checking to see if the car had keys in the ignition. If only she knew how to hot-wire a car, then she could drive most of the way there.

She twisted her scarf one more loop around her neck to keep it out of the slush and scanned the distance. The only thing moving was her shivering self. She would kill for a shot of 151 and a Marlboro Red. It would get her warmed up, and how much harm could that do? But the heat wouldn't be real and she'd probably die out here like the Little Match Girl.

Lizzie pulled out her phone and slid her nose across the screen to unlock it without taking off her bulky gloves. Saj's toddler grin greeted her as it came to life. She would have new baby photos soon too. A new collection of memories—she would not let these ones go so easily.

The phone buzzed and startled Lizzie; it slipped from her fingers. She fought to grab it but only managed to bounce it off her thigh and onto her foot before it skidded across the road and into the snow.

"Shit."

Maybe she better liberate another phone or two from houses on the way, and get Glen to set them up on the cloud. She pulled it out of the snow and wiped it off. The rubber case was scuffed, but the buzzing continued.

"Hello," she whispered.

"Lizzie?" Glen's baritone voice boomed in her ear. "You okay?"

"Yeah, I'm fine," she said in her normal voice. "I think someone's following me. I'm about twelve miles away."

"So you made it three miles since yesterday? That's all?"

"Fuck you. Who's pregnant, freezing her ass off, out here avoiding the Collectors and clean-up crews? Nice and warm where you are, Glen?"

"Uncle!" His breath wheezed out. "I'm just anxious."

"Yeah. I can tell." Lizzie rolled her eyes.

When Glen hinted about this geeky mission, Lizzie had jumped on the chance to leave The City. It was the excuse she had been looking for. The walls closed in tighter and tighter every day as more "sensible" rules came down from Council. According to Glen, she could get to this secret location and back to Provo in a few days, though she wasn't exactly sure she wanted to go back. It was supposed to be something she thought about while she made the trek.

"This place ought to be amazing," Glen's voice raised a notch. "And if it's far enough away from The City," he hushed his voice, "maybe I can move in and get away from these idiots up here."

"Breeders giving you trouble?"

"Daily. But maybe this place will be somewhere I can move shop and escape."

"Escape is a great plan," she sighed. "Look Glen. I gotta go. Do me a favor? Next time I call you, ask if I've got my back-up phone yet."

"Back-up phone?" He chuckled. "Sure, Lizzie. Good luck."

"What's so funny?"

"Nothing. I'll tell you later."

Lizzie hung up. Clearly, no one was following her. She jogged along further, with her paranoia slightly sedated, her mind flitting to other worries. She still hadn't had a chance to think about what she would do when she found this place. Should I stay, or should I go? Everyone who wanted her safe would still be overprotective. The walls weren't going to disappear anytime soon—if anything there would be more and bigger walls as time went on. Did she really want to leave all the safety of The City? Probably not.

When it came time to have the baby, it was the place to be. She envied the hairy-legs, live-in-the-woods type who could just squat and pop out a little bundle of joy, but she wanted a hospital, doctors, and definitely drugs. The movie she'd seen in health class of a live birth had deeply affected her. Not enough to keep her from having sex, but she would never forget it. Having this baby was scary enough without being alone and undrugged when it came. She liked her pain under control.

As the street headed up an incline, Lizzie left it for the cover of a strip mall. She crossed the brightly lit parking lot quickly and turned around the corner of a warehouse.

Something black and solid slammed into her. She screamed, flailing her arms. The blackness screamed back, air whooshing from dozens of wings.

Birds. They took wing, leaving her stunned, staring at a body on the snow in front of her. Male, button-down shirt undone. A bit of snow had blown up against his frozen limbs. His hands were grasping like stiffened claws; they lay at a strange angle against the chest, frozen and contorted like they'd been holding something when he died. His frozen flesh had been pecked apart by countless beaks, determined to get a meal from this meat popsicle. But the birds had not killed him. Neither had the plague. He'd been murdered.

The back of his skull was blown away. The Quieting itself had gotten him—the lawlessness of too few survivors and too many of them thinking they were in charge. His eyes were open, staring at nothing.

Lizzie stumbled back. Tire tracks led away in the packed snow. He'd been murdered and dumped here. Recently.

Her own footprints were all over the scene like an admission of guilt. She spun a full circle, what if the killers were watching her now? *Keep calm, Lizzie.*

She commandeered the lid off a garbage can and wiped out her footprints so they would not be identifiable. Her gloves kept her fingerprints off the lid.

Lizzie walked backwards, carefully wiping the new footprints. When she got to the bare street, she gently tossed the garbage can lid on a snowdrift and tried to renew her focus on her mission, taking a breath and trying to cleanse away yet another gruesome image from her mind. It didn't work, just like every other time she tried to forget.

Further up the hill a flash of light caught her eyes. The cop again? Or somebody else? Before she had time to react, headlights crested the hill and pinned her under their glare.

"Dammit."

Lizzie ran again as fast as she could. She tried to lose her pursuer by crossing parking lots, hopping fences and skittering down icy alleys. She wasn't a champion runner like Nev, but she had street smarts, not like some movie chick who ran down the middle of a straight road. Still, the headlights followed her.

Her foot sank unexpectedly in the snow, and she sprawled forward, her face planting in the powder. Her ankle throbbed as she hobbled in between the houses and then diagonally across a yard. She rolled down behind a snow-flocked hedgerow. The lights splashed across the windows of a house across the street.

Lizzie lay in her cushion of snow as still as possible, hot from her mad dash and the igloo effect of the impromptu snow cave she had nestled into the drift beside the hedge. Her heart pounded in her chest. No one could find her unless they found her tracks. Maybe she was safe.

The quiet of the snow settled back around her. She waited, trying to hold back her breath from billowing out clouds of steam. The car must have gone on past by now.

Lizzie crawled to her knees, peeking over the top of the hedge.

Headlights flashed in her face.

Zach sighed, staring at the cereal in his bowl rather than his girlfriend. "Lizzie will be back."

"She told Rachael to take care of Saj." Neveah's eyes implored him. "What if she meant permanently?"

"Yeah, but—" He was worried, too. Lizzie could be impulsive like no one else, and she wasn't happy being cooped up in The City. "All right. I'll check out her apartment and Mannie's place. She's only been gone a day. Probably needed to get away." At Nev's expression he added, "Temporarily I mean. Burn off some steam; you know Lizzie."

"I better come with you."

"You're supposed to be at work." He didn't want Nev to say the wrong thing at the wrong time. She would never do it on purpose, but that wouldn't stop Lizzie from taking something the wrong way.

Nev seemed to realize it, too. "Fine," she said. "'Cause it's so damn important to count the number of every damned toilet paper roll you Collectors bring in."

"Right!" Zach said, kissing her forehead. "We need to take care of the future, and wiping our asses is part of that future." He kept his expression neutral as Nev rolled her eyes. "I don't have a shift until tomorrow. It's nothing. I'll find her."

"Fine," Nev said, laughing and punching him in the arm. "I know you're just trying to keep me away from your other girlfriend." She winced. "I mean—I don't know what I mean. Please. Call me when you know anything."

"I will." Zach pulled her back into his arms and held her. "I love you."

"Zach Riley. Be careful."

"So you want me not to drive on the wrong side of the street?" He slipped his winter coat on and grabbed his hat and gloves. She shoved him out the door. Outside the air felt too cold to snow. He unplugged the RAV from the charging line and climbed in, manually switching it to gas so it would warm up faster.

He went to Lizzie's place first, and let himself in. Crusts of pizza still lay in a box. Some things never changed, even if the world did. He resisted the urge to clean up, glancing around for a clue as to where she had gone. Her back-pack was missing from the closet, as were her hiking boots. So she planned to be gone for at least a couple days.

In the bedroom, her laptop lay open on the bed. Zach thumbed the power button and got a weak, flashing yellow light. He shoved in the power cable to charge it and pushed the power button. While it came back from the dead, he wandered into the kitchen. Flipping through the cabinets, he found the cupboards were mostly empty, but that wasn't weird. Everyone in The City was on rations.

Lizzie's art-pad lay open on the table. Random song lyrics and weird shapes adorned the page. In the upper corner was one word. 'Glen.' The computer beeped in the other room. Zach pulled out the phone Glen had programmed. The only one Glen accepted calls from. He thumbed through the contacts and dialed Glen as he walked back to the bedroom. Zach typed her password into the waiting laptop, **Bu77$h!t**, while he waited for Glen to pick up.

"Zach? What's up?

"Where's Lizzie, Glen?"

"She didn't tell you?"

"Would I be calling you?"

"Sorry. Of course she didn't tell you," Glen said.

The computer finished booting. Zach hit the history button on the internet and scanned through the list.

"She's doing me a favor."

Google maps. Zach pressed the screen. NSA Data Center. "You sent her to check out the Data Center?"

"Yeah. If I'd known she wouldn't tell you…"

"You can pretty much trust Lizzie's not going to tell anyone anything. Do me a favor, next time you send the pregnant mother of my child out on a secret mission. Drop me a fucking line!"

"Ouch. Yeah. No problem."

Zach let the awkward silence hang for a moment, then said, "You all right, Glen? They treating you well? You seem to be in good spirits."

"Hell, they brought me Mountain Dew!" His tone grew serious. "You're going to go get her, right?"

"Yeah." Zach took a deep breath. Chasing Lizzie was practically a full-time job. "If you don't tell her I'm on to her, I will see what I can do about completing your mission."

"Deal!"

"So tell me, Glen. How good are you at GPS tracking?"

Chapter Two

MANNIE GUERRERO PAUSED, HIS HAND on the cold metal knob of the door to the basement. He should go back, sit down and eat the tamales he'd thawed. The knob turned in his hand and the door opened into empty space and darkness. He maneuvered down the rough wooden stairs. The spiral fluorescent bulb quivered to life. A couple flashes and then a steady glow.

He remembered walking down stairs into basements doing clean up in Kandahar, Afghanistan, never knowing if he was going to find women and children or Taliban. *Cabron. Pinche cabron.* He gritted his teeth and clutched the stair rail.

At the basement floor Mannie glanced around the small space. The pile of blankets by the washing machine looked disturbingly like a woman's body. He shook it off. Metal-framed shelving units lined the bare cinder block walls. He pulled out two of the gallon jugs of distilled water and set them on the ground. A plastic bottle of vodka sat lonely on the shelf. The clear liquid sloshed as he jerked it out, and twisted off the top. He took a strong big swallow. It burned going down. He needed the fuzziness that took the edge off the pain.

His newest wound itched where the bullet had entered near his collarbone and throbbed where it left a bigger hole in his back.

He didn't know why he bothered to hide the bottle, the only person who cared about his drinking was him. Not even Lizzie. Though to be fair, she had bigger things to worry about.

Isabel had cared—and she could always tell. Her sensitive palate made her a brilliant chef, and also able to detect the liquor on his breath.

Mannie willed himself to dump the bottle down the round grate in the floor, but he hesitated, then upended the fiery liquid into his mouth again. It sucked the oxygen from his lungs and he took a moment to recover. He slammed the bottle back on the shelf and replaced the water bottle camouflage before heading back upstairs with heavy feet.

At the kitchen table, he dug into the tamales. Even freezer-burned on the ends they were tasty, but not as good as Isabel's. Zach had found them in a freezer on one of his Collections into Salt Lake City. It was good to have a taste of home in this strange new place, even if it came with its own kind of loneliness.

By the time he'd finished eating, the buzz from the vodka was a pleasant hum at the back of his mind. He tossed the corn husks in the compost bin, washed the dishes and placed them in the drainer.

He had managed to parlay his 'expertise' as a Park Ranger into the job he wanted, producing vegetables next year using The City's park lands. It was mostly busy work right now, with a thick blanket of snow on the ground, but a lot better than sorting and filing.

He pulled his Ranger jacket over his flannel and plopped the comfortable "Smokey the Bear" hat on his head, before heading out the front door. He wore it for work because he got a kick out of the fact that the Forest Service patch said Department of Agriculture. The nearest park, the one he thought of as his, was mostly a kids' playground with a large jungle gym. He had rows marked out, ready for digging in the spring as soon as the ground thawed. He already had plans for the old swing-set, as the perfect support for pole beans.

He checked to make sure all the lines were still tied to their stakes, and wondered if he could start some digging if he got an excavator. The lack of real work was only going to make the bottle in his basement more attractive.

As he rounded the corner of the park bathrooms, closed for the winter and most likely permanently, a small coyote squared on him, growling, and protecting his dinner. Mannie clapped his hands together. "Shoo, Yote!" The coyote hesitated and then loped off sideways. They were getting less and less fearful of the two-legged predators.

He inspected the dinner, a cat, with too much skin. He should pick it up—he was willing to live and let live in the back country, but he preferred to discourage predators from hanging out where humans would be working. Wild Kingdom had become the norm. Eat or be eaten. The next few years would be interesting to watch from a naturalist perspective, but dangerous.

"Hey, Mannie!"

Mannie froze. Not even an encounter with a coyote could compare with the adrenaline rush he felt at the sound of that voice—Jess, Lizzie's best friend.

The glaring lights pinned Lizzie to the spot. Then they snapped off and she recognized the white mini-SUV.

"Fuck you. Zach," Lizzie muttered to herself, clutching her racing heart.

Zach stepped out from behind the door. "Where you going in such a hurry?"

"Fuck you, Zach! You scared the living shit out of me."

"Good," Zach said, pulling a knit hat over his reddish-orange hair. His voice had that edge of anger she'd grown so used to. "Well, it would be good if it did any good."

Lizzie walked to the electric RAV, jerked the door open and slumped in the passenger seat.

Zach got back in, avoiding eye contact. He turned the RAV around and drove in the wrong direction.

"Where are you taking me? Provo's that way."

"Wherever you want to go." Zach's jaw tightened. "As long as you're not going alone."

"I'm not alone. I've got me, myself and my baby." She pulled her gloves off and sat on her cold hands. "How did you find me?"

A hiss of breath escaped from Zach that had nothing to do with the chill of the weather.

"My baby, too, Lizzie." Zach drove over the hill. "I checked out the history on your computer."

Lizzie stared straight ahead.

"Well?" He just couldn't leave it alone. He had to pick at her like his favorite zit.

She kept her mouth shut.

"When were you going to tell me?" He jammed on the brakes and the silent vehicle scraped to a stop. "You remember what you said in the hospital room, not long before you told me I was going to be a father? You remember?"

"I'm not fucking stupid. It was a month ago."

"You promised me you wouldn't go off on your own." He let out an exasperated sigh, and punched the steering wheel. The horn blared briefly and Lizzie jumped.

"Easy," she said, looking out the rear window. "You don't have to alert every cop and Independent to our position."

"Jesus, Lizzie. What the Hell? I am the baby's father—I can't be yours too."

"I never asked you to, Zach. Maybe you shouldn't have saved me back in Bellingham. If you had let the pills do their work I wouldn't be an inconvenience to your wonderful new life."

Zach was silent. Lizzie sat back heavily in her seat and stared out the window, not sure if she really meant what she said.

"Well, I didn't. And now we're here aren't we?" he said, finally. "Yeah, things are sure as shit awkward, but Nev and I want to make this work—we even like having you around."

Lizzie puffed in disbelief.

"Who do you think wanted me to come out here and make sure you were okay? Nev is still your friend, Lizzie."

He took a deep breath, popped the RAV back into gear, and flipped on the GPS. "If you'd told me, we could've done this on my day off. Without stressing me out."

"You're taking me there?"

"Hey, I owe Glen, too. Woulda been nice if you'd let me help."

Lizzie thought about it as the streetlights whizzed by, then she said softly, "I don't get to do anything. Go anywhere. Just sleep, eat and attend childbirth classes. I get so freaking bored hanging out with a bunch of pregnant women. You couldn't possibly understand. You get to be a badass Collector and leave whenever you want."

He shrugged. "No—but Nev might understand. Give her a chance."

Lizzie stared at her hands. It wasn't that she was having the baby of her friend's fiancé that bothered her—they didn't even know Nev was alive when it happened, and it was all a huge end of the world mistake. But despite nobody cheating on anybody and despite the fact she had never had any romantic feelings for Zach, she still couldn't talk to Nev the same way anymore. That killed her.

"Lizzie—"

"Please, Zach. Let me get this out. In this brave fucking new world

I'm an adult and that should mean I get to make my own choices. Having a kid scares the shit out of me. And being treated like I don't get a say about my own life or my body makes me want to run." Lizzie jerked her gloves off and held her fingers together, trying not to let them fidget with each other. She needed Zach to take her seriously—she couldn't fall back into Crazy Lizzie stuff.

"I understand," Zach said.

"I won't jump off a cliff, but I might run away." Lizzie stared at him. He had tears in his eyes. "Sheeze, Zach. I don't want to hurt you. And I won't hurt the baby. It's just the way I am."

"Yeah, I know." He sighed and his foot lightened on the pedal. "Things didn't work out the way any of us wanted."

"You've got Nev. You wanted that." Lizzie regretted how much jealousy she felt at those words. "I'm happy for you guys—I just wish I knew what I wanted."

Mannie turned slowly to Jess. "Hey. How's it going down at the dog pound?"

"It's an Animal Shelter and Hospital, not the dog pound." She cocked her head slightly when she corrected him, then bent to look at what he'd been examining. Her face was a little green when she turned back to him. "Coyote? Or dog?"

"Coyote. Caught him in the act. Right out in the open."

"It's still steaming." Jess turned to him. "Shouldn't we clean it up?"

Mannie sighed. "Yeah. I s'pose. I'll go find a shovel."

"I'll come with you. I can help."

"Fine," Mannie agreed, walking away. He pulled out his keys, opened the tool shed. He had everything laid out like he wanted it. He put his hand on the first two shovels and pulled them out together. He turned to hand one to Jess and nearly hit her in the face with the handle.

She shrunk back, wide-eyed. "Just wanted to see what it was like in here."

"Be careful!" Mannie said. "Looks like a tool shed." He reached over her shoulder and flipped the light switch. "Look all you want."

Why couldn't Jess find herself some young farmer boy and make him a good wife? She was the same age as his daughter, much too young to be waiting around for him. It wasn't right. But he couldn't help appreciating the gentle curve of her smile. He recalled all those nights on the road, when they were making the run from Texas to Washington to find Lizzie. All those nights she spent listening to an old man ramble. She had a spark of genuine kindness in her that reminded him of Isabel. He turned away to inspect the sharpness of a pair of clippers until he could blink away his tears.

"You okay, Mannie?"

Mannie brushed past her. "No. Tired. Sad. Frustrated."

"Need some company?" she asked, quickly stepping out of his way.

"No." *Damn it. Now he was going to feel guilty for being an ass.* He strode to the dead cat and slid the shovel blade under its body. He didn't want to bury it near the veggies, so he walked on until he came to a house with a big red X spray painted on the door. No one would mind the use of the yard. A small plot of roses grown out of control looked like a good spot. It had been a really nice yard. Probably some retiree with a passion for roses. The beds along the fence and against the house were brimming with snow laden rose bushes, not awoken yet from their winter slumber, still frozen in the same state they had been before the end of the world—lucky them.

He plunged the shovel into the hard, snowy ground. He'd intended to throw the body in the trash. Burial seemed like a ridiculous waste of labor. He could have said as much, but he kept digging. He needed something to do anyway.

"I'm sorry, Mannie. Was it something I said?"

"No, Jess. It was nothing you said. I'm not good company, these days. Too much on my plate." His chest spasmed. He grimaced and stood back motioning at the hole. "Dig a bit if you want."

"I think you're good company." Her eyes teased him.

Mannie cringed at the flirtation, and Jess' face fell. He panicked. He couldn't stand the idea of hurting her. "I just feel powerless sometimes," he blurted.

She nodded and stabbed her shovel into the dirt. "I didn't come to bug you, Mannie."

Her smile was gone and its absence made his heart ache.

"I went to see Lizzie." She dug until her shovel hit hard pan.

"That's probably deep enough." Mannie used the shovel to lift the cat's body into the hole.

"Rachael was there with the baby. Lizzie was out. I thought maybe she'd be with you."

He stood out of the way as Jess went to work filling the hole; a girl unafraid of a little work and dirt. "Nope. Haven't seen her."

"I can finish up here," Jess said, "if you want to go back to being alone."

"Thanks." But he didn't leave.

When Jess finished tamping the soil down with her boots, she came around the patch of dirt until she stood uncomfortably close. She pulled his work gloves out of his pocket and slid her hands into them, adjusted the fingers one by one, and turned on her heel and broke off a couple sticks. She tied them into a cross, twisted together with the wire from the plant tag. "There."

"That's nice, Jess."

"Thanks." She picked up her shovel and walked back to the tool shed.

Mannie followed with his shovel. "Look, I didn't mean to be rude," he called after her. "If you're hungry, I've got some leftover tamales. They're pretty good."

"Thanks, Mannie. I'll leave you alone. See you later." She walked off the way she'd come.

Mannie sighed, he missed her already, and for that reason he was relieved she was gone.

Chapter Three

AS THEY ROLLED OUT OF the suburbs and into the hills, the winds buffeted the RAV. Lizzie breathed a sigh of relief. Out here there was only the occasional dark house, and the chance of a patrol encounter was nil. The snow here lay undisturbed across the road like a blanket in the beams of the headlights.

Zach drove on in silence, knuckles white on the steering wheel.

She punched the red button on the dash until the audio to announce the RAV's silent electric motion sounded like a landspeeder from Star Wars. "Trust your feelings, Luke."

Zach snorted, but his grip on the steering wheel didn't let up.

"You want me to text Nev and let her know you found me?"

"I'll do it in a bit. You need anything? We skipped this area on the way to collecting Salt Lake City. These houses are probably gold mines."

Lizzie shook her head. "I'm good. But we should go the last bit on foot, so nobody sees us coming."

"You think there might be people there?"

Lizzie laughed. "Maybe. We'll figure it out when we get there."

The information—or lack of it—did nothing to relax Zach's knuckles. He pulled into a wide street with no snow in the middle.

"It's a military installation," Lizzie said. "If they are going to keep anything manned and operational, I'd guess, it would be the military stuff, but we're hoping that's not the case. Glen says it has the best computers in the country. He's counting on just moving right in to his own personal heaven."

"So, you were going to ring the bell and hide behind a bush?" Zach parked the car.

"Something like that." Lizzie's hands were nearly warm. Just in time to go back out into the weather. "I'm a scout. And so are you, if you are on my mission. Leave the weapons behind. If we get caught, we play dumb."

He handed her leather gloves. "Put these on."

"Thanks, Dad." She slid her fingers into the soft sheepskin. Much nicer than her mittens.

Zach threw up his hands in defeat and chuckled. Finally the old Zach was back—he was over himself and genuinely interested in helping Glen escape the breeders. Mission accomplished, thought Lizzie, or at least one mission. She grinned, "Okay, the base is another mile this way."

"I'm gonna call Nev first. I'll catch up."

Lizzie couldn't resist miming dragging a ball and chain across the snow as she walked on. Zach's glower returned. Lizzie picked up her invisible ball and stomped off toward the base. What was wrong with her, why couldn't she just leave off on a good note for once? "Catch me if you can," she said, sullenly.

She hurried her pace, not wanting to hear what Zach had to say about her. His voice softened as he reached Nev.

Lizzie pulled out her own phone out and dialed, "Glen. Almost there. Zach picked me up."

"Tell him thanks."

"Maybe."

"You two fighting again?" Glen asked. "It's my fault."

"Well, it's my fault you're in the situation with the breeders. But hopefully this mission will fix that. After this we're even."

"Just stay safe. I may need you for more missions." Glen's noisy breathing carried over the call. "I got something for you when the job is done."

"Something for me like a present? I thought I was paying you back."

"Doesn't have to be like that," Glen sighed into the phone. "I can do something nice for you."

"I don't like to feel like I owe somebody." Down the street, Zach walked toward her.

"Besides yesterday was your birthday."

"Don't remind me." Lizzie continued to walk away from Zach,

but not as fast. "Can you give me a hint?"

Glen chuckled. "Let's just say it's data."

"Ugh, really? Well…umm…I look forward to receiving your gift. I know how data is like *your precious*," she said in a Gollum voice.

He laughed. "Maybe you would be more excited if I told you it was a way to get around the traffic shutdowns to external IPs in Provo?"

"Huh?"

"A way to talk to survivors outside Provo—other than my genius self."

"Shit, really?" The explanation in The City was that Internet communications were out due to power issues elsewhere. This kind of bullshit was what made her want to get far away.

"Someone went to a lot of trouble to keep the rest of the world out, but I figured how to circumvent their blocks."

"Glad you're my friend, Glen, the geek god!"

"Let me know what you find out, ASAP," Glen couldn't contain his excitement.

"I will. Talk to you later. Thanks."

"Oh, and don't worry, I already wiped the GPS tracker off of Zach's phone."

"Wait a sec. Did you tell him about the mission? Did you let him track my phone?"

"Ummm."

"What the fuck, Glen. Some secret mission. What kind of a person tracks a friend's GPS?"

"He made a pretty good, though violently paranoid point about you being pregnant and alone out there. Plus he was a good way to get you your present. He is supposed to give it to you after the mission."

As Zach got closer, she hurried her steps.

"Shit, Glen. This is fucked up." Looking at her internet history was probably a lie. Zach was spying on her. Even if the tracker was deleted. He could go to Glen anytime he wanted another one—maybe this wasn't even the first time.

"Sorry."

"So is everybody else. Thanks a lot, Glen."

"Wait up." Zach jogged toward Lizzie. "Hey," he called softly, "what's your hurry?"

She turned and greeted him with a fake smile. "How's Nev?"

"Fine," Zach said, with a hesitant skepticism at the honey dripping off her words. "She's glad you're safe."

"I'll bet."

He stared at her like she was crazy. "What's wrong? I thought we were good."

"Oh, you're good."

"Who were you talking to?" he asked.

Her first response was 'yer mom,' but it didn't come close to dealing with how pissed off she was. "Glen," she said. Let him wonder what Glen had said. She spun on her heel and stalked away from him.

"Lizzie," his voice begged forgiveness.

"Fuck you, Zach." Lizzie walked up a rise toward a glow of bright lights on the horizon. Glen would be happy to hear the base had power. Zach followed close behind her like a chastened pet. She hated that he'd lied to her—even if it was just telling her a part-truth—he hadn't trusted her. With a sigh of annoyance and resignation she realized that he wasn't doing anything she hadn't done first. But it wasn't the lying; this spying shit was messed up. She wasn't sure what to do about that. Should she tip him off that she knew? Or would she have a better advantage if he didn't know she knew? She knew to watch for the signs now. Of course it hadn't been chance that he had found her out here and been able to follow her so precisely.

"I'm sorry, Lizzie."

"Forget it."

When she got to the top she halted. Stunned. A giant conglomeration of buildings sprawled below them, lit by super bright lights and surrounded by a chain link fence with razor wire at the top.

Zach pulled Lizzie's arm.

"What?" she hissed.

"Get down."

She let him pull her down.

"Anybody could be in there. Could be the military. Or could be someone has taken it over. Maybe Utah Independents?"

"Utah Independents wouldn't know what to do with a—what did Glen call it? 'A Lottabyte capacity data storage facility'."

Zach chuckled. "Maybe not, but it doesn't mean they wouldn't want it."

Lizzie glared. "What are you laughing at?"

"A Lottabyte?" Zach leaned up on his elbow, looking down at her like she was stupid. "It's a YOTTAbyte."

"Bite me."

"Byte you?" Zach teased. "It's a million terabytes. Probably could hold everything the human race ever created digitally."

"Thought you didn't know what we were here for."

"I didn't know, but at least I know how to say the word." Zach stared at her, his brow furrowed.

"Well, look who knows everything about everything—and everyone."

"What are you talking about?"

"Nothing. Let's just do this." What if he wasn't just spying because of the baby? Were the Provo people putting him up to it? His boss? Captain Foote? Maybe he couldn't care less about her—it was all just a job to him. He had been enjoying his job way too much ever since they arrived.

"I'm not some stupid hick," he growled.

His anger startled her out of paranoia overdrive. "*You* were the kid in high school stupid enough to cheat off me."

"Things change."

"Yeah. I know they do, asshole." Lizzie punched him in the arm. "I'm not stupid either, and I don't care if it's a yottabyte or just a lotta bytes—I'm here to help Glen. What are *you* here for?" She put her hands on her hips and waited for an answer.

Zach glanced away, "Let's take a look over the hill."

"Whatever." Lizzie crawled away from him along the ridge. She could just see the tops of the buildings and the lights.

Zach knelt beside her, staring over the hill. "It's huge." He whistled softly. "Looks like an entrance over there."

"Looks empty," Lizzie said. "But the gates are up."

Zach hunched down and moved forward awkwardly.

"Can you see anyone?"

"Nope. Seems quiet," he muttered, collapsing to his knees and crawling further up the rise.

"Okay. I don't really want to walk in the front gate, but I want to give Glen something worth our time and his. Do you have fence cutters in your Collector gear?" She shaded her eyes peering along the perimeter. "Wait. I have a better idea. Let's find someplace to keep an eye on the place. We can take turns sleeping and watching. If there's no one here… Well, either Glen gets it, or *The Shitty* or someplace else is."

Zach glared at her.

"Sorry, *The City*," she said softly. "Come on." She was finally starting to get under his skin. Good. Served him right for all his lying and spying. She wasn't sure if it was her dig at his precious Provo or the thought of him spending all night with her and having to explain it to Nev that did it, but she felt some small satisfaction now and could focus on her mission again.

They wandered further around the installation, checking out potential viewpoints, keeping carefully out of view along the ridge where they could just see the tops of the buildings and the lights. About half-way around, they found a large RV parked close enough to see the front gates.

Zach jimmied the window and stuck his nose inside. "Smells stale, but nothing bad."

He helped Lizzie get inside through the open window.

She let Zach in. There was a bunk above the driver's seat that had a window facing out. "I think we can see most of the facility from up there." She pointed to the bunk. "You sleepy?"

"I could sleep," Zach nodded. "But the cold will keep me awake. I'll take the first watch. If I get sleepy I'll wake you." Zach climbed up into the bunk,

"Suits me." Lizzie walked to the back. Through a skinny door there was a double bed, all neat and made up, like it was waiting for some lovely couple to come through the door. Lizzie climbed in, not bothering to take off her combat boots. Sleep ready, she'd decided. The cool pillowcase made her shiver. She lay there thinking. What did Zach want? Did he really want to keep the baby safe?

Lizzie pulled out her ancient iPod. Her father had laughed aloud when she showed him her treasure filled with all of his music from before she was born. He'd said the $300 player had been one of his last ridiculous splurges.

That music had helped her through the rough years. Of course, it had died eventually and one of her techie friends, sort of a mini-Glen-guy, had switched in a solid state drive and new battery.

She stuck in her ear buds, put it on the sleepy playlist. "Free" from the *Empire Records* soundtrack entwined around itself in her ear. She tried to empty her mind and let sleep come.

Her father could fall asleep anywhere. He'd learned in the Army. Zach and Duke could both do it and neither of them were in the army. It had to be a guy thing. She couldn't do it.

She stared up at the funny mushroom-shaped water stain on the ceiling. Kind of like an atomic bomb—kind of like her life. Was it irony that the world ended without any bombs and yet here she was staring at the aftermath of one? She could never remember what was irony and what wasn't—Alanis Morissette was not a reliable resource and no English teacher had ever said anything that stuck.

Obviously, she wasn't going to sleep. If she snuggled next to Zach it would keep them both warmer, but the thought of Nev finding out made her twitchy.

Lizzie's brain flashed back over her new life, the life since everything ended. Telling Zach and Nev about the baby had been the weirdest. The thing with her and Zach had been a drunken mistake, but it still hung over them like a black cloud.

Not for the first time, she wondered if she should give the baby to Nev and make herself scarce. Or Rachael. Everyone would be better off without Crazy Lizzie around, especially the baby.

She threw off the covers, grabbing the heavy top blanket and clumped to the forward bunk. "I can watch if you want to sleep," she muttered.

"Can't sleep?" Zach asked. He didn't get up.

"Nah." She climbed up the ladder and slid in next to him. "See anything?"

"Nothing moving."

Lizzie lay down next to him and stared out the window. "So, can you go to sleep? Like on a whim?"

Zach shrugged. "Sometimes. You can't?"

"Nah. Too many things chase around in my mind. Knock me over the head, exhaust me or get me drunk… That usually works."

"Go out for a run," Zach grinned. "Don't do any of the others."

"Oh sure. Why don't I have a jog up to the gate and jump around naked in front of the guard house? That won't get their attention. Shut up and let me steal some of your warmth." She leaned in with her back against his side and pulled the covers over both of them.

"Don't you be trying anything, Lizzie."

"Fuck you, Zach. Just—just don't say anything to Nev, okay?"

He could not fulfill her needs for anything more than a warm body. Duke, the other male member of her Bellingham transient tribe, had been hinting and flirting for a month, but she'd managed to ignore it. He was hunky and hot, but her track record with boyfriends was pretty bad.

Chapter Four

LIZZIE JERKED AWAKE. ZACH LEANED against the fake wood of the RV's paneled walls. The morning sunlight streaming through the blinds striped dark shadow lines across his face. "Shit. I fell asleep?"

Zach's eyes shot open and tightened at the brightness of the sun. "Yeah. But I woke up after a couple hours and kept an eye out until dawn, then I must have fallen asleep, too."

Lizzie groaned, rubbing her lower back. "Crappy couple of spies we turned out to be."

Zach scowled at her. "I assume you didn't see anything before you fell asleep."

"No." Lizzie yawned and stretched, stepping back down the ladder. "Pretty boring."

"It was quiet on my watch," he said. "Not even a whisper of humanity inside those gates."

Lizzie's eyes sparkled with mischief. "Let's see if we can get in then!"

"Sure."

"Hungry?" Lizzie pulled a silvery pop-tart pack out of her backpack and tore it open. She handed him a few big chunks of the mutilated pseudo-food.

"Thanks." Zach shoved the smaller bits in his mouth and popped the RV door open.

Outside, Lizzie took a deep breath of the frosty morning air. The promise of the sunlight streaming through the windows turned out to be a lie; the pale disc offered no perceptible warmth.

Lizzie sucked pop-tart crumbs from her fingers as they made their way toward the gatehouse.

A weird clacking sound came from the road.

"Car," Zach hissed, tugging Lizzie away from their path. The sound grew, and he broke into a run. He glanced back to make sure Lizzie was keeping up. A cement irrigation ditch angled toward their path, he pointed and changed direction toward it. He jumped in and went down to his butt.

Lizzie plopped down beside him, her breath coming in quick bursts of steam. Zach glanced at his watch and showed it to Lizzie. 5:55 a.m.

The sound of the vehicle sputtered out. Another engine chugged to life in the distance. Lizzie popped her head up over the edge.

"Stay low," Zach ordered.

Lizzie shushed him with a finger to her lips.

She leaned her head sideways so she could see over the edge with one eye. Black smoke floated in a cloud away from an old Plymouth station wagon. A balding, black man stood next to the gate as an armored Humvee drove up from inside the compound. The flashing light on top flickered a pulse of blood red across the snow. Two soldiers with full tactical gear and semi-automatic weapons stepped out of the gatehouse.

Lizzie hit her forehead with the heel of her hand and mouthed the word 'stupid.' They had been watching all night, and assumed it was safe, but they hadn't watched it during the day. Here they were, ready to saunter up to the gate—saved by the putter of a clunker, right before they made a stupid mistake.

Lizzie pulled the white hoodie over her head and rolled to her knees to get a better view.

Zach copied her. The chain link gate slid back and the two soldiers came out. They made a quick circuit of the car, using a mirror on a stick to look under it and flashlights to point inside as they opened each door and the hood.

Two more soldiers waited by the Humvee, armed and alert.

"Shit," Lizzie whispered, "they were there the whole time. You think they saw us?"

"I think we'd be prisoners if they had."

Lizzie glanced at the calculator watch on her wrist. "Maybe. Or they were taking bets on how far we'd come."

The man looked bored. He ignored the soldiers as they completed the inspection and waved him through. The big gate clanged shut and the soldiers returned to the gatehouse. The Humvee escorted the black-cloud-spewing station wagon into the compound.

"They look different to you?" Zach asked.

"From what?"

"From the wanna-be soldiers. Only one I've seen move like that is Captain Foote, everybody else in Provo is just playing soldier. These guys are the real deal—US military. Not just squatters."

"Weird. Think of it. Most of everybody died, and yet they still managed to scrape together enough soldiers to guard this base? Unless somehow the soldiers were all vaccinated against the flu and the government..." Lizzie's brain ticked away running through all the possible conspiracy scenarios.

"I think you're reaching—I saw plenty of the soldiers with FEMA crews dead of the virus."

Lizzie shook her head, as if to get back to the point. "Well, you'd think the few soldiers left in the world would have better things to do. Glen's not going to be happy about this."

"Oh, well." Zach shrugged. "You did him his favor. Mission complete."

"Shit. You're going to drag me back, aren't you?"

"Kicking and screaming if I have to," Zach said, his lips tight. "I think we can continue down this drain until we're out of sight." He slid forward on his hands and knees.

There he went, like she would just give up and follow him. She knew she had to go back. How could she have thought about leaving Saj? Or her father for that matter? Now she had to go back and be protected again.

Going on the mission had been good, freeing. But then why did she feel like shit? "Zach?" Lizzie whispered, moving after him.

He turned back to her.

"Thanks for helping me. Not treating me like a helpless baby."

"You're welcome." He smiled at her, and for the first time in a while it seemed genuine, but still sad. "Let's get out of here."

At least she and Zach were talking. That was something.

Once they were in the RAV, he said, "I've got a surprise for you...from Glen."

The mention of the gift reminded Lizzie's that she still didn't completely trust him. But she was excited about Glen's present. She held out her hands. "Should I close my eyes?"

"Probably not. It doesn't look like much." He pulled a smartphone out of his coat pocket and handed it to her. "Turn it on."

Lizzie pushed the power button. The phone beeped and a Sprint logo with *GlenPhone* underneath it popped up.

"First thing is, I think Glen's more paranoid than you. This phone won't show up on the network the City folks have set up."

"And?"

"And… you'll find out the rest. Some cool things on the phone." Zach's grin made Lizzie a little sad. He used to be so much more cheerful. The last time she had seen him this boyishly excited was the morning she'd accidentally slept with him.

The phone finished powering on and the screen lit up the interior of the RAV with a soft blue glow. "What things?"

"I think the coolest thing is this." He showed her the screen and pressed an icon titled JumpStart. There was a spinning line like a sonar screen and then a beep. A series of numbers and letters appeared on the screen with three choices underneath: lock, unlock and start. He pressed the lock button and the RAV locked, then he pressed start and the engine started. "Glen says it doesn't work on all cars, but most hybrids and 'lectrics had a glitch, if they didn't get the recall fix, it works. He's gonna get me a phone like this, too." He handed it to her.

"Cool," Lizzie said, "for you. So I can steal your car? Why is this one for me?"

Zach beamed like he would burst. "I think Glen left you a voice mail."

Lizzie pressed the 'message' icon and then play when the first message came up. *'Lizzie? Glen. Check out the voice mails after this. Whatever happens in terms of your mission, thanks. Even if it doesn't work out. You still owe me Mountain Dew.'*

Lizzie pressed the 'next' button. *'Lizzie, it's Mama. Please call me and tell where you're gonna be. I tried Chad and he said he didn't see you at school today.'* Tears streamed down Lizzie's cheeks. "Oh, my god, Zach. How'd he do it?"

"He's a fucking genius. Happy Birthday." Zach leaned over and gave her a hug.

"Thanks, Zach." Maybe he was just trying his best to keep everyone safe. "I'm gonna call Glen to thank him. Oh, and tell him the bad news."

"I'll get us back home." He shoved the RAV into drive and headed back toward Provo.

Lizzie was still annoyed about going back, but hearing Mama's voice gave her a resilience she hadn't felt in months. She called Glen who apologized for not being able to get her the videos. He was pretty stoic, and not really surprised, that soldiers were in control of the data center.

She ended the call when she saw how close they were to Provo. "Drop me off at the edge of the city. I need to walk."

"Can I trust to you to be safe?"

"Hell if I know, Zach," she blurted. "Sorry. Let me off where you know it's safe. I'll come home. The truth is, I'm not ready to leave—yet."

"Okay," he sighed. "I appreciate your honesty."

Was he letting her have her way because he could so easily bully Glen into tracking her? She looked at the new phone—both a blessing and a curse.

"This area," Zach said as he pulled over, "has been tagged, but not collected. Do me a favor and stay out of the red ones?"

Lizzie watched the taillights of the RAV as it pulled away, then trudged back towards home.

This area was the edge of civilization now. The City proper, where everyone lived and the amenities and most of the new government offices were clustered, was still a few miles away. But the Collectors had been here, meaning that some semblance of order was being imposed on these streets again. The windows of the houses were marked with green plusses, orange check marks and red Xs. *It's like a giant game*, she thought. *A first person shooter.* No wonder Zach enjoyed his job so much.

Most of the houses had orange checks. The one red X on this block jumped out from the rest. It drew her in, even as she shook her head. *Don't be Crazy Lizzie.*

The door knob was cold and turned easily. For a moment she paused. But after scanning the street in both directions and seeing nothing, Lizzie shoved the door open. The unmistakable smell of death lingered, not as strong as it must have been a month or two ago. Other than the smell, the house looked undisturbed. She stepped forward and flipped on the light. Her eyes caught movement, she spun to see herself reflected in the giant screen wall TV that dominated the living room.

She stepped forward into the kitchen and stopped. Bodies. Not one, but several, slumped over the kitchen table. Bowls of cereal that had soaked up all the milk still sat in dried pools of blood. A rat the size of a cat sat on the kitchen table; it stared at her for a moment and then went back to its feast. Sounds of scurrying around her told her it wasn't the only one.

A man sprawled on the far side of the kitchen, the gun still near his hand. The perpetrator. There was a hole in the ceiling behind him and blood splayed out across the wall.

A whole family. Gone. 'Saved' from dying of the flu—or the world that came after.

Bile rose in Lizzie's throat. She had stopped vomiting from pregnancy and now… She spun to the sink and threw up purple Pop Tart mush. It could have been her brains splattered on a wall—using her mother's jerkwad boyfriend's shotgun. Those first days alone in the house, she had considered her own options many times. If Jayce hadn't already died, would she have considered his options for him, like this guy did for his kids? Was this what parenting was in the end—deciding when it was time to shoot them in the head?

She stumbled back outside, slammed the door behind her, and froze.

A cougar and her kittens padded softly down the street. As the mother saw Lizzie, her lips peeled back to display long fangs; the cubs crowded around her muscular legs. A low growl emanated from the cougar. Lizzie dared not move, pinned by the cougar's fixed stare, but standing still did not seem to be convincing this giant cat that Lizzie wasn't a threat to her young. Muscles rippled under sleek, golden fur as she padded toward Lizzie on massive paws.

Lizzie jumped up on the edge of the faux-stone wall that enclosed the porch, and waved her arms. "Go on. Scat!" she yelled. The cougar stepped forward. Lizzie screamed, windmilling her arms.

The cougar turned around, nudging her kittens along their path, clearly deciding there was easier prey. When the cougar was out of sight Lizzie stepped back off the wall, her pulse pounding and hands shaking.

A sound of soft clapping spun her around. A woman stood on a rooftop with a crossbow held in the crook of her arm and a rifle over her shoulder. "Bravo," she said in a stage whisper.

"Who the fuck are you?" Lizzie growled.

"Nice language." She held her hand up to her lips and pointed past Lizzie. "Wouldn't want to bring the mama cougar back." A smirk teased across her face. "Who the fuck are you?"

"Lizzie. You know, you coulda done me a solid and shot that cougar before she ripped my throat out."

She nodded. "Pleased to meet you, Lizzie. I see no throats ripped out. Besides, this is her land again now, why would I shoot her just for hunting on it? We all have to eat." The crossbow dropped down, hanging from an old leather guitar strap. "My name is Kylie, Utah

Independents."

Lizzie tried to keep her face impassive. *Goddamn Independents.*

"I didn't realize you were so helpless, Lizzie. Want me to walk you home?" Kylie sneered.

"You're not going to kidnap me?" Lizzie gave back as much snark as she got.

Kylie laughed out loud. "Jesus, what do people think we are?"

"Rapists, kidnappers, killers…"

Kylie's shocked expression seemed genuine. "Don't believe everything you hear."

"Didn't *hear* anything. Saw it with my own eyes. We had a gun battle with your boy, Travis—a friend died."

An angry flash of recognition flashed in Kylie's face. "Travis wasn't an Independent." Her pleasant smile disappeared. "He was a Collector. And a killer." There was venom in her comment.

"He had friends in the Independents. I was there."

She spat in the snow and swallowed with a grimace. "He kills his friends. My son," she said, staring at Lizzie, "was one of his friends. The men who helped him were wing nuts. Independents always draw a few, but then so do government factions, right? Most of us are just trying to survive. Like you."

Lizzie stared back at Kylie. Was she telling the truth? "How old was he?"

"Sixteen. Small for his age. He wanted to go into the city, Provo. Be a man. I told him he was too young, but what could I do?" For a moment Kylie looked old and vulnerable, but anger washed it away. "The benevolent government of The City won't bring Travis to trial and convict him. They won't even banish him where I can get to him."

"I'm sorry," Lizzie said. "What was your son's name?"

"Quentin. Quentin Blocker." Kylie forced a smile. "My offer stands. I'll walk you further into town. "

"I've got a friend. He'll come pick me up."

"All right. I'll skedaddle before he gets back."

"Maybe I'll pay Travis a visit. Ask him about Quentin. Let him know you're waiting for him."

"You do that, Lizzie." Kylie's perpetual smirk gave way to teeth. She did a mock salute and disappeared over the roof.

Lizzie pulled out her phone and dialed Zach.

"Change your mind, already?" Zach's voice asked sarcastically.

"Yeah." Lizzie forced a slow breath out. "Cougar. Scared the shit out of me."

"Oh." Now he sounded properly contrite. "How far are you from where I dropped you?"

"About two blocks. One left and a right."

"You know this is going to make me late for work."

"Sorry."

"Yeah. I'll turn on the Harley engine sound in the RAV. Find me. The cougar will avoid the noise."

"Thanks."

"You want to stay on the phone?"

"No. I'm good." She hit *End Call* and stepped tentatively off the porch, keeping an eye on the last spot she'd seen the cougar. She retraced her steps, shivering at the sight of her footprints partly obliterated by a series of paw prints. In the distance she heard the lup lup of Zach's RAV sounding like a motorcycle, and jogged toward it. She'd done more running in the last two days than she'd done in months. Her pregnant body was starting to protest; all of her muscles were sore.

Chapter Five

AS ZACH CROSSED OVER INTO the collected streets, Lizzie stared out the window in silence. He punched the red button in the RAV, switching from motorcycle to landspeeder.

Graffiti and posters plastered the empty storefronts: *The end is at hand* and *BoNZ* were repeated. *What the hell was Bonz?* The latest pro-birth poster was old style, based on the Uncle Sam, *I WANT YOU*, recruiting call. Except they had replaced Uncle Sam with a lovely redhead, in patriotic garb, beckoning: *DO IT FOR YOUR COUNTRY*.

He rather admired the art, but it was all unnecessary. His hormones did not need a poster to encourage him to start procreating. If they should be making posters for anyone, it should be for the women. Nev was still reluctant. Maybe it was her upbringing and she would come around once they were actually married.

Out of the corner of his eye he saw Lizzie holding a hand over her still flat belly.

"Guess we were ahead of the curve," he said, pointing at the poster and trying to get some sort of positive response from Lizzie.

She rolled her eyes.

He let the RAV glide to a stop and then turned off the engine. Lizzie sat, subdued beside him.

"Sorry." She tried to give him a smile.

"Yeah. I know." He was on duty in 20 minutes and he'd barely slept. He turned to her. "Lizzie?" She stared straight ahead. "I don't want you to promise not to do anything this time, if you do you'll be even more likely to do it. But, please think about letting us in on it. Think about the people who love you. None of us want to be your jailor—I know I don't. Hell—I'm starting to feel like my dad and you know I sure as shit don't want to turn into that bastard."

She shrugged.

"Look, I've got 20 minutes to check in with Nev and get to work."

"Call in sick."

"It's all a big game with you, isn't it?" Zach shook his head.

"Fuck you, Zach."

"Grow up," he growled. He reached across and shoved open her door.

"I thought we should talk about stuff." She stepped out onto the pavement. "But I guess that wasn't your plan. You just wanted to talk at me."

Zach slammed his fists on the dashboard. "Why does it always have to be this way with you, Lizzie? Maybe you're right, maybe we'd all be better off with you gone!"

Tears welled in her eyes.

"Shit, Lizzie. I didn't mean it." But it was too late. She ran from the car, across a snowy field to the women's dorms.

Zach sighed and let his head fall toward the steering wheel. He knew he should go after her, but he'd had enough of going after Lizzie for one day. His job—and fitting in here—was the only future he could see for himself, Lizzie, the baby—most importantly, Nev. He wanted to keep her safe.

"Shit," he said again, shoved the RAV into reverse and punched the accelerator. Work needed him; Nev needed him—he couldn't keep giving all of himself to Lizzie.

Lizzie glared as the white RAV slipped out of the parking lot and away, tossing more snow as it fishtailed. "Fuck you, Zach," she whispered. Her voice wavered and she realized she was shaking.

She took a moment to get herself back under control and pulled out her phone. "Rach? Yeah I'm back. I want to see Saj before daycare."

"Sure thing. How soon will you be here?"

"Long enough to walk from the parking lot." Hopefully, she hadn't already gotten Rachael in trouble for not getting to her job on time like Zach. Why did Lizzie have such a talent for complicating lives?

Though Rachael would never say anything—she had too gentle a heart. Since Rachael had helped Lizzie steal Saj away from the Birthers up north, she had never heard an unkind word.

The air was crisp and cold, but the sun already shone off the snow. And the sky was clear and cloudless. The only warmth she felt came from how near she was to Saj. She hadn't allowed herself to miss him. Not until she was sure she was coming back.

At Rachael's dorm room she tapped gently on the door. Its hollow core echoed more than she expected. She winced, hoping she hadn't woken the neighbors or Saj. It was still early.

"Be right there," Rachael's voice called. "Changing a diaper."

Lizzie tried the door. The knob turned. She entered. "Just me."

"Sissie!" Saj's voice conveyed his excitement as he fought against Rachael's hands holding him firm while she placed the velcro tabs.

"Glad those weren't pins." Rachael released her charge to come at Lizzie.

Lizzie's heart melted. She smiled widely. "Saj? You better get ready. Sissie's coming!" She made an airplane sound and entered the bedroom 'flying' at full speed.

Saj squealed, wide-eyed. "Sissie, sissie, sissie."

She couldn't bring herself to have him call her mommy. He was more like a kid brother than her kid and she was happy to be his Sissie. Well, at some point he would probably call her Lizzie like everyone else.

"Welcome home, Sissie." Rachael said softly, a smug look on her face.

"You knew."

"That you were coming back? Sure. How could you leave this little monster?" Rachael scooped up the squirming boy and held her arm out to Lizzie. "Jess and I started a pool on when you would be back. I'll have to see if I won."

Lizzie chuckled and took the offered hug. "You did not!"

Rachael smiled and checked the clock behind her.

"Oh, shit, did I make you late, too?"

"No. I already called in. I wanted to talk. If you've got the time."

"Well, I could use a shower."

"Then take one," Rachael suggested, sniffing loudly in her direction, "please."

"Stinky?" Saj giggled and started sniffing, too. "Sissie, play?"

"Or don't." Rachael grinned as Saj rolled himself over on the bed and slid down to the floor.

He ran to Lizzie and wrapped his arms around her legs.

"Don't, I guess." She tousled Saj's curly hair. She scooped him up, blowing his belly like she used to do with Jayce. "What do you want to talk about, Rach?"

"Never mind." Rachael stood there, watching Lizzie play with Saj. "It was just a thought but I can see it was stupid."

"Out with it!"

Rachael sighed. "Well, you know that back in the breeder compound. They picked me out to be his mom, and then… I thought… Like I said, it's stupid. I'll never have what you have with him."

"I'm going to be a good mom," Lizzie said.

Rachael's face registered shock. "I didn't mean it like that."

"Why not? It's what everyone else is thinking."

Rachael gaped at her.

Lizzie sighed. "But not everyone is as kind as you are."

Rachael's eyes strayed to the carpet. "I wondered if I was I ready to be a mom. If Hank would love me for as long as he said he would." Her bitter chuckle cut short. "Till death do us part."

"Oh, Rachael." Lizzie pulled her close. "Saj. Rachael needs hugs."

The little boy's arms wrapped around Rachael's neck. "Don't cry. 'S'all right. Everything be okay. Sissie's home."

Lizzie laughed. "Yup. It's all going to be fine. Sissie's home." The sarcasm in her voice didn't help.

Rachael laughed through her tears. "I hear my own voice. That's what I told him when he was crying."

Saj's bright chubby face gazed up at her and it pained her to know those cheeks had been tear-stained because of her. She couldn't leave him again—or Rachael.

"Rachael, it's not fair that I should have two kids and you none. We're a family—you, me and Saj. We might not be like 'together' or even live together in the traditional family unit, but f...err, screw traditional. You can be Saj's daddy." She laughed. "Right, Saj? What do you think of Daddy Rachael?"

Snot blew out of Rachael's nose as she snorted. She turned red and dabbed at her nose.

Saj giggled and poked a finger up his own nose.

Lizzie pulled his hand away and laid her cheek on his soft baby head. "We've got each other. That's what counts."

Zach shoved through the door of the apartment he shared with Nev. Fuming, he dropped his backpack on the kitchen table. Why the hell did Lizzie have to be so stubborn? What he needed now was Nev's strong arms around him, and maybe her legs too.

"Nev?"

She appeared in the doorway and his mood soothed. He could count on her calm personality to smooth away his worries. But she wasn't smiling, her serene face was a mask.

She held one of his shirts in her hands. She shook the wrinkles out with a loud snap and proceeded to fold it into a precise rectangle.

"Well?" she asked.

"She's home safe and sound."

Some of the tightness in her jaw eased, but her eyebrows were still knit together. "It took you all night?"

"Come on, Nev. I did what I had to do to get her home. That's what you wanted, right?"

"Hmph." Nev walked back to the laundry room to add his shirt to a tidy pile in the basket. She focused on matching socks and rolling them together as Zach hung back in the doorway, too afraid to speak or offer to help fold.

"I saw some new pro-family signs on the way home." He chuckled, trying to figure out a better direction for this conversation. "They're getting pretty racy. Made me want to come back here and see what we can do about starting one."

"Oh, really?" She jerked a t-shirt from inside out. "I'm surprised. You already started one with Lizzie, what do you need me for?"

"Seriously?" Two strides and he was beside her, blocking the laundry basket with his arm to get her attention. "You're not the only one suffering in all this. What I want more than anything is the woman I love, right here and right now, to be all fat and round with my baby in her belly. But instead Lizzie is having my baby, and to top it off she barely seems interested in keeping herself and my baby safe—or staying in Provo.

She faced him, arms crossed, mouth tight.

Zach wanted to reach out to her. "I don't know what to do about it most of the time, so I just do my best. Yeah, that means I do a lot of shit wrong. I can't help it; that's how I learn. I can't change that. All I can do is love you like my chest is gonna explode and hope it's enough to make up for being an idiot."

"Well, I guess it serves me right for falling for an idiot." Nev sighed and wrapped her arms around him and rested her cheek on his shoulder. "The last thing I want you to do is change who you are, Zach."

Zach let the bliss of her embrace wash over him, at last.

"I guess you're right, it isn't just you and me suffering."

"Yeah," Zach agreed softly. "She's hurting now. She misses you. Why don't you talk to her?"

Nev's eyes glistened with unshed tears. Her words came out in a rush. "I don't know. It feels so weird. I can't decide whether to shout at her or hug her. I know in my brain that it isn't her fault, but my heart feels a million things and none of them are forgiveness or understanding. My parents raised me to turn the other cheek, and 'if you don't have anything nice to say' kind of stuff. I guess I was hoping to wait until I could think of nice things to say… It's taking longer than I thought."

He hushed her and smoothed her hair. Her tears dripped onto his arm and each one stung like a jelly fish.

"You better go to work. You're going to be late. I called in so I could be here."

"I love you, Nev."

Chapter Six

ZACH STRIPPED OUT OF LAST NIGHT'S clothes in the locker room at the Collectors hub. Between already running late, and comforting Nev, he hadn't had time to change or shower. Luckily, he kept a spare set of work fatigues in his locker. In the command room he gulped down a hot cup of coffee and pulled on his Kevlar vest.

Fifteen minutes later Zach crunched through frozen grass. He was front man this morning, and armed to the teeth with an AR-15 rifle, a taser, a hunting knife and a nightstick. Where the Kevlar covered his chest he was sweating but the icy air chilled him wherever it could find a gap. Front man was the riskier position, but it meant he was tagging and finding the new stuff rather than lugging off dead bodies—and that was worth the risk.

The Utah Independents had kept their distance since the shootout; if they were going to retaliate they would have done it by now. He wasn't really worried, but the cougars Lizzie had seen were no longer rumors, so he kept on his toes.

The big green recycling truck rumbled forward to the next red-tagged house a block or so back. Lucky roll of the dice for him. The poor saps who'd rolled bupkis let go of the handholds and went to retrieve their gruesome recycling, tossing bagged bodies of owners and pets together into the truck.

Zach waved at Will, his farm-boy partner across the street, and motioned forward. Then he turned the corner and went up to the first house on the new block. He tried the front door. Locked. He lifted out the screens and tried to slide the front windows. All latched.

The job could be monotonous, but it was better than sitting in an office. Being outside was good duty; he liked the freedom and he couldn't begrudge Lizzie for wanting some.

Zach replaced the screens. No point in making a mess for someone else to clean up. He wandered around the back, trying windows and doors.

He was about to shoot out the lock on the back porch when he saw a partly opened window on the second floor and a ladder suspended by hooks on the side of the garage. At least there would be fresh air inside. Nobody liked the sealed tombs. Even camphor ointment under the nose couldn't make those bearable. He slid the strap of the rifle over his shoulder and lifted the ladder down, pulling it vertical and extending it a few more feet to reach the window.

Zach swung his leg over the sill and stepped into the room—no stench. He took a grateful breath. Water coming in the window had swollen a particle board bookshelf. It collapsed as his thigh brushed it, spilling toys onto the floor. Something crunched under his foot as he stepped down—a flattened pumpkin coach looked like a 3D Pacman chomping at his foot. "Shit." He stepped gingerly into an open spot and surveyed the small girl's room with a pink canopy bed and lots of stuffed animals. He felt bad about the toy, though the little girl who'd left it on the floor was long gone.

Zach sat on the child-sized bed and lay back taking a moment to close his eyes. Would he and Lizzie be having a daughter? What kind of dad would he be? Lately, he'd been hearing his father in his own voice and he hated it. He sat up. Too much negative thinking.

A little snow globe from Disneyland caught his eye. If he had a daughter, he would want to tell her about Disneyland, He glanced around for something to wrap it in. He pulled open the dresser next to the collapsed shelf and picked a pair of Betty Boop socks, wrapping the snow globe inside one then the other before stuffing it down in his pack. What was Disneyland like empty? Would it be awesome, or just creepy?

Zach went through the rest of the house opening closets, rifling through drawers in all the bedrooms. Nothing much worth keeping. The teen boy had hidden an old girly magazine under a pile of clothes in the back of the closet. He smoothed a rock poster on the wall and found a tack to push into one of the corners that was falling down. The motion gave him an unreal sense of deja vu. He knew he'd done something similar in his old life. It was like he was watching a movie—

but which was the movie, his old life or his new one?

Downstairs, he surveyed another bedroom and an office—nothing but the usual leavings of a suburban family. He checked out the fridge and was assaulted by the usual smells. He pulled out a bottle of Squatters, and slammed the door. Not bothering to find a bottle opener, he popped it open with a smack on the edge of the counter top. The cap took a bite out of the edge of the formica. Zach took a swallow. Nice, dark beer, Captain Bastard's Oatmeal Stout. Being a Collector had its perks. As long as he took it easy, nobody cared.

He opened the freezer to find stacks of tidy butcher quality meat. Locally grown by the look of it. Jackpot! He pressed a green sticky note on the outside and flipped open the cabinets—well-stocked. Double jackpot.

He looked for a basement entrance, any sort of hidey hole. A lot of Mormons were preppers, he had discovered since beginning this job. This house didn't feel Mormon, but sometimes looks were deceiving. No bodies.

"Triple Jackpot," he murmured, exiting through the front door, leaving it unlocked. He pulled the green spray can out of his pack and sprayed a green plus sign on the front window.

Will, Zach's self-described, redneck buddy, was sitting on a porch swing across the street, legs dangling as he puffed on a cigar. His house had a red X with a small green plus on its window.

Sometimes Zach came across a house where everything had been cleaned out. All the canned goods, medicine cabinet, most of the clothes and he wondered where had they gone. Like the whole family had taken what they could carry and tried to run. But there was no escaping the Flu. It either killed you or it didn't.

Will nodded as Zach approached. "Want a smoke?" He laughed, but it turned into a hacking cough. "Shit." He ground it out in the metal ashtray beside the swing and handed Zach a flask in a leather case.

Zach sniffed it. "Whiskey?"

"Yup. Water of Life."

"Better not. Already had a beer." He handed it back to Will, who proceeded to take a long gulp. "Hey, take it easy. That stuff'll kill you."

"What've I got to live for?"

"What is it with everyone being so down today?" First Lizzie, now Will. "Take care of yourself so you'll be here when things get better." Did his words sound hollow—like he was just going through the motions?

Will stared at him like he was an alien. "Whatever."

Mannie strode into Provo's City Center Building. Captain Foote had asked Mannie to come see him about a job. They'd come a long way since their first tense meeting at the barricade of the city. Mannie was pretty sure he didn't want any job the older military man could offer him, but he felt he owed it to him to listen.

He knocked on Foote's door.

"Enter."

Foote sat at his desk and a sharp-featured, dark-haired man in civilian clothes perched on the arm of a chair beside him. His hunched shoulders reminded Mannie of a bird of prey. Mannie acknowledged them both and remained standing.

"Guerrero, this is Tony DiSilvio, Mr. Ray's right hand."

"Mr. DiSilvio." Mannie gave the half wave that had come to replace handshakes in this post-pandemic world. You only made physical contact with people you were always around. Everyone knew the virus was gone—well, *knew* might be too strong a word—but people were still cautious.

"Tony. Mannie Guerrero. Mannie's gonna be my right hand."

Mannie's eyebrows shot up. He'd expected a job offer, but not something so high up the food chain.

"Mannie, welcome to Provo." DiSilvio spread out his hands like he was offering him the whole city.

"Not *The City*, sir?" Mannie asked.

"Tony, please." DiSilvio chuckled. "Provo will always be Provo to me."

DiSilvio's eyes raked him up and down. "*Foote's* right hand. Pun intended." DiSilvio leaned back in his chair. "High praise coming from Foote. Mannie, please, have a seat. You are the man I need to talk to."

Mannie sank into the softness of the high backed chair facing the two men. He preferred to stand, to keep his wits about him and not be lulled by the soft comfort of the seating, but DiSilvio didn't seem like a man who enjoyed being contradicted. There was something tight and dark under the twinkle in his eyes.

"What can I do for you, Mr. Di-" Mannie caught a flash of pique, "-Tony?"

"We're in a precarious place here. Surviving long term depends on what we do the next few years. And that depends on what we do now."

Mannie paid close attention to DiSilvio. It was like he was pitching a product on late night TV. *You, too, can create your own country, just like I did. Learn how in these ten easy steps.*

"We don't have to worry about Koreans or the Jihadists anymore," he said, his pronunciation surprisingly accurate." But we've got the Utah Independents. Plus, there are groups, like the folks you met in San Antonio, who are intent on being the new capital of the United States of America—pure arrogance. All we want to do here is survive and maintain our way of life, which is what it really means to be American." He puffed up a bit at the last statement.

Mannie leaned forward in his chair, trying not to give in to its comfort.

"There are already obstacles to that simple pursuit. We're even seeing wildlife push into our borders, which you, no doubt, have noticed in your parks."

"Had a coyote in my garden this morning," Mannie said at DiSilvio's prompt.

"Exactly my point. How long before a coyote makes off with a small child?"

Mannie hadn't seen a coyote that large, but they would only get larger with better food and more territory. Most of DiSilvio's rant stretched the bounds of the truth, but Mannie's input wasn't really being requested.

"What do we need to survive? Defense. Food." DiSilvio tapped his fingers as he counted them off. "How long will our food stores last, Mannie?"

Mannie shrugged. "I have gardens planned for the spring."

DiSilvio waited for Mannie to continue.

"Well," Mannie avoided a name rather than call him Tony. "I'd guess the frozen stuff being collected will be decent for a year or two. *If* we can keep the power on. Canned goods ought to hold out for decades, maybe. Dry goods too. Pickled and home canned?" he smiled, "I had some 20-or-so-year-old pickles *mi abuela* made. A little rubbery, but they tasted good.

"We should have enough food to keep us going while we get the gardens growing. My concerns at this point are electricity, and whether we will be able to grow enough food in this climate. The winters are long and cold, and the summers are hot and dry. We will have to choose the right crops."

Tony nodded appreciatively. "I would add to your list of concerns that we need to be concerned about security and keeping what we have collected and grown. And what if the electricity does go out? We got an engineer to keep natural gas flowing for the power plant. Ought to last us a while, but not years. Did you know we quit all coal-fired power a few years back?"

Mannie shook his head. "No. I've been in Del Rio, Texas for most of the last 20 years."

DiSilvio leaned forward, finally warming up to a point. "There's a solar plant in Delta. Not far south. It could power all of our needs indefinitely. You know where that power's heading?"

"California," Captain Foote supplied when Mannie shrugged.

Mannie feared where this was going.

"We need that power," DiSilvio continued.

Mannie kept his smile in check. "And you think California's not going to care?"

DiSilvio shrugged. "Lake Mead and Hoover Dam produce enough to keep what's left of California fully powered. They won't even notice." His eyes bored into Mannie.

Mannie was tired of playing questions, but he had a few of his own to ask. "So why am I here? And how do I fit in?"

"How do you want to fit in?" Foote asked.

"I don't. I'm not going to war again. Not for Uncle Sam, not for you."

"But you'll fight to keep your family safe, right?" DiSilvio's eyes were dark and intense.

Mannie sighed and looked down at his hands. He would kill for them, his kid, her friends and his future grandkids. He closed his eyes. *For my family.* That was a pretty twisted way to motivate someone.

"That's why we're forming a militia," DiSilvio said, "To protect our families."

Mannie had come here to flat out refuse anything Captain Foote offered him. "From whom, sir?"

"Have you seen the graffiti? BONZ?"

"No," Mannie said. "I don't get out much. What's bones?"

"B. O. N. Z. The Brethren of New Zion, it's a coalition of fundamentalist Mormon's who see the apocalypse as a sign that they were right."

"The members of," Foote said with a pointed glance at DiSilvio, "The Church of Jesus Christ of Latter-day Saints are, shall we say, concerned about their intentions."

"And are they violent?" Mannie asked. Most of Mannie's

experience with church was the nuns at school who smacked his hands when he spoke in Spanish.

Foote lay open his hands like a benevolent grandfather. "We don't know. There is some precedent. Our concern is that some of the bands we call Independents may be connected to the Brethren."

For my family. If he wasn't involved, who would do it, and how would it be done? "I still don't know what you want me to do."

"Will you be a part of our survival, Mannie?" DiSilvio's stare demanded an answer.

"Mannie, we need you," Captain Foote said, laying his hands flat on his desk as though he were resisting the urge to jump to his feet.

"For what?"

"Can you train recruits?" Foote asked.

Mannie sighed again. "No, sir." He didn't want to—he was pretty sure he didn't have the right attitude anymore. "Not well, *sir*. I can run teams, plan for supplies."

"That would be helpful," Foote said.

Make some demands, Mannie told himself. See how serious they are. "Short term only? When I say, I'm done, I go back to playing in the gardens?"

DiSilvio smiled like he was about to whip out a contract and a pen.

"And who is there to help me?" Mannie asked. "I'll need an assistant or twenty."

"You can put a requisition in at the Jobs office. Ms. LaFevbre is the person in charge."

Mannie wasn't sure he wanted the severe woman that Lizzie believed gave out assignments like punishments doing his hiring. "Can I pick my own team?"

DiSilvio smiled. "Nepotism will work for the time being. Make sure you get the job done and we're fine."

"Okay," Mannie said, his body sinking into the chair, "Where do I start?"

Foote grinned and DiSilvio looked satisfied. DiSilvio being here was not a coincidence, it had been the plan all along—a tactical move. Was it Foote's idea or DiSilvio's?

Foote pointed at the hall. "Third door down on the left. Office of Records is all yours. We'll get the sign changed in a few days."

Shit, a desk job. "Yes, sir." Mannie put on his warmest sycophantic smile. Get enough people together and what do you get? A new old boy network like the days of politics when he was a kid: Richard Nixon and his cronies.

"I'll get to work then." Mostly he wanted out of the room. He respected Foote, but he felt like he needed to shower after being in the room with DiSilvio.

Down the hall, Mannie slipped the key into the lock; the opaque glass revealed nothing of the state within. Once he opened the door, he would be back in the army, an army desk-job even—right where he never wanted to be again. He pushed the door open and let it swing wide.

Stacks of paper piled high on an old wooden desk. The stapler and hole punch were of the era to be classed as deadly weapons. Either there hadn't been a budget for office equipment upgrades since Nixon, or the previous occupant had a thing for antiques. Mannie sure as hell hoped the stacks of paperwork were from before the outbreak.

He picked up the top manila folder. "Handwritten inventory lists from houses that had been collected." This stack was already his. How had they known he would take the job? Foote was a hard man to say no to.

He'd assisted several military operations, but mostly his job was had been courier, filer and sorter. This was going to be a lot of work and he would rather be tromping around in the wilderness bringing information to people, collecting data and supplies.

He needed to find an assistant happy to do the desk work to free him up for the field work. Pronto. Someone with some organization skills. Lizzie would love to get out of her pregnancy group, but he was just starting to get along with her, so maybe working together wasn't the best idea. Jess? Hell no. Nev? She'd gone to a university, but it was Evergreen, so how much of a Greener was she? He pulled out his phone and dialed Nev's number.

"Nev, it's Mannie. I've got a strange question."

"Okay. I'll bite."

"You have any experience in organization? I might be able to get you out of your secretarial-pool."

"I'm on the OCD end of organization," Nev warned. "If you can handle that…"

"Well, I'm about as far from that as possible, I need OCD." A part of him relaxed. "I'll put in a request. See if we can do it without driving each other crazy."

"When do I start?" She sounded eager. He hoped that was a good sign.

"As soon as I can get it approved."

"Sounds good. Thanks, Mr. uh, Mannie."

He set the phone down and stared out at the little bit of sky he could see. The light was fading along with his energy. He pulled open the desk drawers: paperclips, post-its, old USB drives, and in the lower right hand drawer, canned soup, boxes of tea bags and a bag of sugar. He smiled as he rummaged through. His hand struck on something cold, glass. He pulled out a slim fifth of vodka. He dropped it back in and shoved the drawer shut.

The pressure had been enough to drive the previous desk's owner to drink at least half a bottle of Smirnoff's. He jerked the drawer back open and pulled out the bottle. He made his way to the lunch room, undid the cap fully intending to pour it into the sink. A new job deserved a clean slate. But he couldn't do it.

He screwed the cap back on and put it at the back of a cabinet with the cans of coffee. At least he hadn't taken a drink.

Chapter Seven

RED-FACE FROM THE BITING JANUARY cold, Lizzie dropped Saj's hand and knocked on the door to the house her dad had claimed. She had her own place, a small apartment she'd been granted due to her status as a pregnant mom, but going back to it right now seemed like admitting defeat. She and Saj had skipped daycare and class to play in the snow and to visit his grandpa.

Snow drifts piled against the garage door so she could tell he hadn't gone in Rubi, his Jeep Rubicon. But that didn't mean he was home. Despite there being plenty enough gasoline to go around on the planet now, he liked to walk most places.

She checked the knob, unlocked. "Dad? You home? You know, just because the world ended doesn't mean it's any safer to leave your door unlocked." She stamped her feet on the mat and stepped in.

"Mampa?" Saj called, stamping his own feet in imitation.

"Mampa's not home yet, Saj." She started unwinding his clothes. "Let's get these off. It might be cold out there, but you, my little steam engine, are hot!" She kissed his forehead. Too hot. "Shit."

"Sit," Saj said with emphasis.

"Don't say that, Saj. Bad word. Sissie shouldn't say it either." She smoothed back his sweaty hair. "How're you feeling, little buddy?"

His dark blue eyes were a little glassy and he sat without fighting the clothing removal. She finished the disrobing down to diaper and changed it while she had access. But it barely needed changing, he must be dehydrated.

"Saj? You want some water?"

"Water," he agreed.

She went to the sink in the bathroom and while she was there pulled a temperature strip from the first aid pack in the cupboard.

Saj chugged down the water as she put the strip on his forehead.

More? He put his thumbs inside his fingers and banged them together, sign language for more…. *Please.* It had been a while since he'd signed for anything; his verbal vocabulary had been growing in leaps and bounds the last few weeks.

Lizzie refilled the cup half-full and handed it to him. He sucked it noisily.

She pulled out her phone and hit redial. "Rach?" Her words tumbled out in a rush. "I'm worried about Saj. He's feverish and drinking water like crazy. And now he's reverted to signing."

"Temp?"

Lizzie looked at the strip. "101."

"Is he lethargic?" Rachael asked.

"No." Lizzie breathed. "A little."

"There's a bit of the sniffles going around daycare right now. That's probably all it is."

"I hope you're right."

"Of course, I'm right." Rachael said calmly, "Lots of liquid and some rest—if his temp hits 103 or higher take him to Doc Wright."

Lizzie hung up the phone and hugged Saj with tears in her eyes. This is what happened when she left, it was her punishment. She collapsed with him into the recliner. She hummed him a lullaby as they both faded in exhaustion.

The front door opening woke Lizzie, soaked in sweat. Between the baby in her belly and the toddler on her chest, it was a toss-up which was the cause.

"*¿Hola?*" her father called.

"*Aqui, Papa,*" she answered softly, hoping she wouldn't wake Saj. Her Spanish skills still lacked depth, but at least she'd learned what the Clash meant in *Should I Stay or Should I Go.* Silly that they repeated the same lines in Spanish.

She leaned forward to touch Saj's forehead with her cheek. It didn't seem any warmer than it had before the nap. That had to be a good sign.

Her father's tired face peeked in the arch between the living room and kitchen. When he saw Saj on her chest his face softened into a smile. "Taking a nap?"

"Yeah. He's a little sicky."

His jaw tensed.

"Rachael says it's just a cold. I pray she's right. He's got a bit of a temp."

He tiptoed over and peered down at Saj's sleeping face, a furrow between his brows. "He looks peaceful." He kissed Lizzie's cheek.

It still felt awkward, having a dad that was around. She wasn't used to the scratchy stubble or the physical proximity.

"How are you? Have a nice trip?" he asked.

"How the fuck does everyone know I was gone?"

"Small town—big family who loves you. Zach, Jess, Rachael. I heard it through the grapevine.

"Jesus. Can't anyone give me a little peace?"

Her father knelt down, still looking at Saj as he spoke softly to her. "I wasn't there when you were growing up. I want to be here for you now. *Si quieres*."

"*¿Si quieres? ¿Cómo se dice en inglés?*" Lizzie asked, changing the subject.

Her father grinned. Kind of like, *As you wish*."

"*Me gusta,*" she responded.

Her father's lip twitched, but he'd gotten better about not laughing at her *Espanglish*.

She laughed at his pained expression. "Okay, how should I say it?"

"*Yo quiero*. I would like that."

"*Yo quiero*." His smile told her she got it right. 'So, did you get it out of your system?" he asked.

"Yeah. Wasn't really planning on leaving. Though, sometimes I think Rachael would be better for Saj. She's stable. Loves him like crazy. And it's not like I'm really his mom. I just found him."

"You're as close to a mom as he's going to get in this world. What happened to all that adoption paperwork they gave you?"

"Paperwork isn't going to make me feel any different. I'm 18, should I really be adopting a kid?" She winced at how ridiculous that sounded, given the baby she would be having before her 19th birthday.

"Haven't you already?"

Lizzie grunted, noncommittally. Saj squirmed, pressing his knee into her bladder, which made her realize how long she'd been sitting there. "Can you take Saj?" she asked, eyes popping at the sudden urgency.

"Yeah. I'd love to." He shucked off his jacket and tossed it toward the coat rack. It fell short. He scooped up the toddler from her arms and pulled him into his chest. "Oh, he is hot."

As soon as she had extricated Saj from her lap, Lizzie leapt up and bolted for the bathroom. "Pregnant girl, coming through!"

Zach groaned inwardly as Nev finished explaining their fun evening, but he kept the pleasant look on his face knowing he'd skated on thin ice spending the night with Lizzie at the N.S.A. facility. First to the Council meeting, then to dinner, that he could go for. Nev wanted to make certain the council was setting up the monetary exchange logically.

"How often do we get to start from scratch on anything," she asked, "let alone something as important as currency?"

"If I can buy beer, food and clothes for myself and you and our future children, I'll be happy."

Nev wrapped her arms around him and snuggled in. "You're such a guy."

"You don't like that?"

"Yeah," Nev tucked herself inside his arms and under his chin. "I like that you're a guy. But sometimes I wish you were a little more worried about what happens outside."

"Dunno if that's gonna happen." She made it sound like what he was didn't make the grade. "Look, Nev, I care about people, and I'm not dumb. But decisions above my pay-grade? Makes no sense to worry about them." *Damn. Pay-grade.* He was sounding like his old man. "But I will support you in taking on the man if that's what you want to do."

"*That'll do, donkey.*"

"You calling me an ass?"

"If the shoe fits…" Nev slipped out from under his arms and slapped his butt. "Let's go. I don't want to be late."

"You da boss." Zach slipped into his sheepskin jacket. Coming home to be with Nev made everything else in between okay. He opened the door for her and patted her butt more gently. "So, why should I be worried about whether or not we use existing American money, ration books or bartering?"

"Not saying you need to worry about it." Nev lifted his arm onto her shoulder as they walked down the steps. "But if we're going to move forward and not back, currency is one way to keep things stable.

We need stability."

"I'll take your word for it. So, you think having a money system will help keep us from slipping back into the dark ages?"

"I think it will help. People need something to put their faith in. Mr. Ray kind of has that wrapped up right now, but once the major crisis is past and we have to move forward with life. In seven years or so, all the food that's stored and canned and saved… Most of it will start going bad. The City is doing a good job of preparing for that."

Zach took in the changes in the city as they walked and she talked. The Collectors had cleared almost all the houses inside the walls and planned walls. The population was stable. People were getting back to getting by. Resilient. The humans that remained, seemed pretty tough. The first month here, there had been a steady rise in suicides, thank god, Lizzie hadn't been successful.

"Come on, they're closing the doors." Nev tugged at his arm.

He broke into a jog alongside her. He loved to run with her, but a better destination would be good. Mr. Ray slammed the gavel down as they slipped into the second to the last row. It was empty, but the council meeting was well-attended.

As someone read the minutes, Nev focused in on the meeting. Who came to these things? He and Nev were the youngest adults by a decade or so, there were a few small children, bounced on laps, but no young people in between. Every one of the twenty-five council members was a man. And all but a few appeared to be well over fifty.

Within minutes, Zach stifled a yawn, their arguments about how to tag the money the Collectors had brought in so that it could be validated as Provisional Utah Government currency made no difference to him. He'd keep bringing it in, and he hoped his pay would continue to provide for Nev. He fondly watched her intensity as she took in every word.

Mannie settled in with Saj still sleeping on his chest. He pressed his lips to the toddler's sweaty brow. He was worried about Saj's fever, but coming home to them lit him up inside. The questions of how his absence from Lizzie life affected her would continue to haunt him, but it was hard for anything to bring him down when she dropped by for a visit with grand-kid in tow. And Rachael was probably right, nobody had seen any sign of the Flu in months.

Lizzie came back down the hall. "When I was still in Bellingham..." her voice was quiet now. "We were talking on the phone. You told me you'd tell me about you and mom."

Well, that did it, he thought as his mood came crashing down. "I could use a drink for that one."

"Sorry."

"No. It's part of your story, of course you want to know. It's part of my story too—and the truth isn't something that can be changed."

"If it helps," Lizzie said. "I forgive you. There may be times I throw things back in your face, but it's just me being nasty. I've done enough to others that I need forgiveness for..."

"Yeah, I understand."

Lizzie gave him a hug, nestling in against Saj.

"You were about this size when I left." He watched Saj's slightly wheezing breath.

She smiled at him, uncharacteristically patient.

He took a breath and continued. "You were older, but you were always on the small side. Meant you were more coordinated, I think. You walked early. You climbed onto things very quickly." He brushed aside the hair on the left side of her forehead. "Here. You've got a scar. Running down a hill. You totally did a header and scraped up your head. Right before family pictures. Have you seen that? You've got a big bandage on." He dug through his wallet and pulled out a photo torn in half leaving just him and Lizzie. He fingered the edge. "Sorry it's torn."

"Some things are hard to take back."

"Yeah..." He slipped it carefully back in his wallet.

He worked up the courage to go on. "I was back from Iraq. Finishing up my Ecology degree at Western Washington University. You were a loveable handful and your mom and I were learning to live together again. I was figuring out how to forget the war, and the desert, and the death. Then—

"Then things happened. The nightmares came. Death in the desert. I started drinking again." He pinched the bridge of his nose to take the sting out of his eyes. "After that, your mom was always screaming." He gave a helpless shrug.

"Her screaming was something else," Lizzie agreed.

"I don't know how I managed to finish my degree. But I did. Then I tried to find work. Got some internships that I loved, being out in the North Cascades with kids... But none of the jobs I got paid the rent, and that just led to more screaming. In the end, I don't even know whose decision it was, I just wasn't part of the family anymore. Eventually I hit the road. And for a good long time after that, all I can remember is drunken brawls or shooting up in some scummy restroom with whatever I was using to kill my pain. Stuff I'm glad you missed."

They sat in silence, until Saj fussed awake. Lizzie stood. "I'll get him some food."

"Good idea." He already missed her warmth, though Saj was more than making up for it.

"Thanks for telling me your side."

Chapter Eight

THE NEXT DAY IN CLASS LIZZIE dragged her chair closer to the exit from the classroom. It also gave her a view of the hills outside. Not much to see but the giant, white cement Y on the hillside. What was the point of the letter? The foliage around it, faded from green to gray with tufts of white snow, held her interest more than these vapid baby-makers.

Saj had to stay home from daycare, and unfortunately, Rachael volunteered to babysit, giving Lizzie no excuse to miss happy, hungry hippo class.

The class sat in a circle on hard plastic chairs that were killer on the tailbone. It was like being back in high school. Many of the giggling gaggle of girls opposite Lizzie looked and acted like they still belonged in high school. The class was divided into two facing semi-circles; one of girls hoping to become pregnant and another of expectant mothers in varying stages of pregnancy.

The mothers to be were a mix of ages. One of them, an older woman that Lizzie had caught staring at her a few times, dragged her chair over to sit beside Lizzie.

When they were all seated, Mrs. Margent spoke, "Who wants to share first today?"

A hand shot up from the excitable wanna-be mothers across the way. "My dad said Jimmy and I can have a pre-honeymoon."

Lizzie almost choked on a laugh, and covered it with a cough. *It's like I'm starring in my very own reality web-show.*

Another hand, this time from the pre-hippo group. "Nate likes that my boobs are getting big." Lizzie wished her boobs would somehow shrink—the last thing she needed was bigger boobs. But she was pregnant. She already had a stock of bulky sweatshirts stashed in her closet in anticipation of the inevitable.

Lizzie stared back out the window as more comments were added to the mix, some less ridiculous.

"I felt the baby move this weekend."

"I can't wait until my baby's in my arms."

Lizzie wrote lyrics on her notebook. Or were they just poetry until she could set them to music? If and when she ever did.

> *Sitting in a circle, spilling all our guts*
> *Never really sharing, never really caring*
> *I see all their faces, but they don't see me*
> *Never really baring souls, always ever staring*
>
> *Smiling happy faces, holding hands and glancing*
> *Saving selves for marriage*

Lizzie scratched a single red line through the phrase. Unless that was ironic.

"Next," the teacher asked. "Betsy?"

"Pass," said the woman next to her.

"Elizabeth?"

Betsy hissed, "Lizzie?"

"Huh?" Lizzie glanced up from writing down *makes my mind start swearing* in her notebook.

Mrs. Margent arched her eyebrows. "Anything you'd like to share, Elizabeth?"

Everyone was watching Lizzie now. Someone tittered. "I stopped puking, I think. Now Saj has got a snot-cold, so he's cough until he pukes. Oh, and his shit is really stinky and blackish green."

The classroom fell silent, and Lizzie delighted in their sudden discomfort. Some of the girls' faces were green tinged. Betsy's mouth twitched.

"Well." Mrs. Margent recovered. "Before I forget, Mr. Ray, our future Mayor, will be visiting us this afternoon."

Ray was running for Mayor of Provo, looking for an official endorsement of his leadership. As far as Lizzie knew, no one was running against him. *How perfectly democratic.*

"Let's get back to our seats and prepare for our quiz on potential pregnancy side effects."

"Pregnancy is an effing side effect," Lizzie muttered as she stood and lifted her chair. Betsy snickered. Lizzie couldn't help but grin as they went back to their tables.

The first thing she did when settled into her seat was to pull out her sketchbook and set it beside her notebook. Her pen etched in the shading around the belly on the pregnant nude she was working on. It was totally on topic for the class.

The clock on the wall was nowhere near calling an end to her misery. Like the world never ended and she was still trapped in high school, forever. She didn't need this stupid class—real life was the only class she needed. Saj and the new baby would teach her everything she needed to know.

"Lizzie?" Betsy whispered, leaning over her desk.

Betsy tilted her head toward the door and spoke more loudly, "Excuse me, Mrs. Margent, could I go to the ladies' room?"

"Certainly, Mrs. Kreig."

Lizzie's hand shot up. "May I go, too?"

The teacher nodded, distracted by a non-cooperative projector. Lizzie jumped up and turned to go, as the projector clicked on and displayed a giant cervix on the screen.

Betsy held the door as Lizzie slid past. Her eyes sparkled with mischief like the giant diamond ring on Betsy's hand. As soon as Lizzie was through the door they both sighed as if they'd timed it.

Lizzie giggled and then slapped a hand over her mouth. "Ugh. Sorry. I am starting to sound like those inane girls—thanks for getting me out of there."

"Why are you sorry? There is *so much to giggle about!*" Betsy pasted on an extra dopey grin.

"Like—I know!" Lizzie said in her best sing-songy airhead voice. "I'm Lizzie by the way."

"I know. What I don't know is how much of this are we supposed to be able to take."

"Yeah. I just keep staring at the Y on the hill and wondering why the hell it's there."

"It was supposed to say BYU, but they ran out of energy. A few years back, some enterprising folks took up seven big buckets of colored paint and poured it down in stripes. It was rainbow colored for most of a week."

Lizzie could see a fire in her eyes. "Was one of those enterprising folks named Betsy, Mrs.—?"

"Kreig, Betsy Kreig, the one and only. But not Mrs. No, definitely not!"

"Okay, Betsy, not Mrs., where to now?"

"Well, I really did have to pee, and I wanted to talk to you. You never stick around long enough to chat. Not many of the others have brains enough for conversation."

"Yeah, I feel pretty much like the only girl in there who isn't ecstatically pregnant."

"Well, I'm not a girl, but ecstasy had very little to do with my pregnancy."

"I'm sorry?"

"No. Don't be. It's just that it was planned. Right down to the smallest detail. My wife's egg, a mutual friend's sperm. All mixed together in a cute little petri dish." Her smile held more pain than Lizzie had noticed before. "A miracle," she said dryly, "or an abomination."

"Well, congratulations. You're giving birth to the new generation," she spouted the propaganda.

"Thanks," Betsy said.

"I kind of wish someone had made a conscious choice to have me. I was the happy accident that paved the highway to hell."

Betsy took Lizzie's arm and led her toward the bathroom. "Are congratulations in order for you?"

Lizzie puffed out her cheeks and told the story of her one night stand with Zach and the current level of aftermath.

Betsy placed a comforting hand on Lizzie's shoulders. "And I thought I had problems."

"I think we're all going to be okay. I mean we go back to middle school as friends."

"And you all survived?" Betsy's eyes pressed into Lizzie. "That is really strange."

Lizzie pushed open the door to the girl's restroom and held it for Betsy. "What's the deal with Mr. Ray? He seems too good to be real."

Betsy chuckled. "Yeah. That's about it. Not sure that anyone has googled him to find out what the skeletons are in his closet."

"Where'd he come from?" Lizzie hopped up on the counter as Betsy found a stall. "Gawd. I could really use a smoke. Trips like this to the school bathroom usually ended with a smoke."

"Oh my god. Please don't talk about cigarettes. I think they execute pregnant women by firing squad for smoking in this town," Betsy said as she peed. "Mr. Ray was a school board member, former city councilman. Before that? I don't know."

"And he really did walk all around Provo spreading calm? The way people describe it, you'd think he was Jesus."

Betsy snorted, coming out and washing her hands. "He was always there. He helped nurse the sick, buried the dead, gave us a plan to collect stuff we needed—he's the reason I put up with all this shit."

Betsy's brow knitted into a frown. "Plus, when someone started making a fuss about my sexuality, he shut it down." Betsy turned away. "We better get back before Margent sends out a search party."

Back inside, the room had dimmed, Margent was showing a film on fertilization. Lizzie slid into her seat.

As the film mentioned menstruation, Lizzie pulled out her red pen. It scraped across the paper of her notebook.

Spewing red ink on to white paper. The blue lines like veins, running, an underground river of blood, waiting to be exposed to the air and make the parchment scarred red with slashes.

The words didn't satisfy her. How could any words do justice to how she felt? Hopeless. Trapped. Despair. All hollow. *Black birds clawing at my eyes. Won't let me see the death around me. Make me blind like the man in the snow.* Why did her family want to stay in this place? Why were they making *her* stay?

As the video ended, Mrs. Margent flipped the lights back on and cleared her throat. "Please, take out a piece of paper for the quiz."

The door opened and a man with thinning gray hair walked in. Mr. Ray. She understood what Betsy was talking about. He carried himself with a good-natured confidence. It was a kind of confidence that crept in and infected anyone in the same room. Even Lizzie was having a hard time shaking off the feeling that as long as he was in charge everything would be okay. She gripped her red pen tightly. It was not okay—would not be okay. Just because her body was capable of producing another human being did not mean they could take away her choices, and her freedom. Everybody is so god-dammed happy to be alive they don't notice.

Mr. Ray swept the room with his gaze, seeing each person. Lizzie lowered her eyes before he made eye contact, scratching a few more blood ink words to her page: *Mr. Ray, I want a say, or I won't play.*

"Well, class. Mr. Ray is here early."

"I try to be prompt," Mr. Ray said, his voice a kind baritone rumble.

"I'm sure they're happy to see you." Mrs. Margent squeezed his bicep. "You're saving them from a quiz. Class, please put everything away."

Dammit. She raised her hand.

"Yes, Elizabeth?"

Lizzie put all her charm into her smile. "Can we take notes, Mrs. Margent?"

"Mr. Ray?" Mrs. Margent deferred to him. "Would you like them to take notes?"

Mr. Ray chuckled. "I wouldn't mind. Though I'm not certain I'll have anything worth taking notes about."

"Oh, I'm certain that's not true," Mrs. Margent said. "Please welcome, Mr. Ray to our classroom."

As the girls clapped; Betsy whispered, "Anyone's better than Margent?"

Lizzie nodded with a grin.

"Thank you all for welcoming me into your classroom. How many of you are 18 or older?"

Several hands shot up. After a moment, Lizzie inched her hand up halfway.

"How many of you have ever voted?"

The hands went down except Margent, Betsy, and a few of the other pregnant women. Lizzie wondered if school elections counted, though she'd never voted in any of those either. She'd campaigned against the Shell Oil Tankers, and promised she would vote against a lot of things. She smirked, but she kept her hand down.

"How many of you would vote if you had the chance?"

Half the girls raised their hands, the other half looked afraid. Afraid to have a say in how things ran, or afraid to admit they wanted it? Lizzie looked down at the red scribbles in her book. Voting was only way she would get any say in a group like this. She stuck her hand up high this time.

Margent's mouth dropped in surprise, but she snapped it shut and beamed a smile of approval at Lizzie. Lizzie pulled her hand back down and rolled her eyes. It wasn't *that* big a deal. How much effect could her one vote have anyway?

"I would like to invite you all to vote. Not for me. But for whoever or whatever you care about. We've decided to lower the voting age to 16."

Excited murmurs spread through the room.

"There will be a number of things to vote on. Our temporary charter for self-governing, officially starting up a militia and of course, government officials. Please, listen to all the people who run. Ask them questions. Vote with your hearts."

Lizzie held up her hand.

Mr. Ray nodded to her. Before she could speak, he said, "Stand up. Stand up. Don't be shy. What's your name?"

"Lizzie."

"Nice to meet you, Lizzie. What's your question?"

"So, Mr. Ray, who is running against you?"

The girls tittered.

"A great question! My assistant, Mr. Tony DiSilvio has agreed to run against me. It took a lot of convincing; he is loyal to a fault. But in the end he agreed that it's important to give people a choice. We were hoping more candidates would step forward, but it's looking like it will just be me and Tony. Any other questions?"

Most of the class just stared blankly at him. Betsy relaxed in her chair, like she already knew everything. Mrs. Margent held her breath, as if a single puff of air might scare off a question.

Crickets.

Lizzie decided to raise her hand again.

Mr. Ray made her stand up again, much to her annoyance.

"Why are there extra rules about pregnant women? Why do I have to stay in city limits? Why do you think I can't take care of myself?"

"Something tells me, Lizzie, that you could take care of yourself better than some of our front line Collectors. It's not that anybody doubts that. But we see you, and the little guy or girl you are bringing into this world, as a very precious thing. We want to keep all of you safe. It's important as well that you feel like you are still in control of your lives. That's why it's important to vote."

Thing? Did he just call them things? Possessions? Lizzie stiffened.

Mr. Ray swept the room again, making eye contact with everyone as if to drive home how much he wanted them to vote—or stay like little China dolls in a glass case. Then he brought his gaze back to Lizzie, still standing with her fists balled up at her sides. "Maybe you would like to discuss this further sometime, Lizzie? My door is always open. We could draft amendments to our charter that make sure our young women's rights and freedoms are protected. I could think of nobody better to do it than someone as intelligent and passionate about the issue as you."

Like he or the council would listen to her, a young pregnant female. Lizzie was about to tell him where he could shove his charter when her phone buzzed.

Mrs. Margent's eyes narrowed.

Lizzie shrunk slightly and pulled out the phone. The rule was no calls unless it was an emergency. She didn't recognize the number and there were a string of texts from Rachael.

"Sorry, I have to. My s—Saj has been sick."

Mrs. Margent relented and gestured to the door. "I am so sorry about that interruption, Mr. Ray. Class, any more questions?"

Lizzie hurried out into the hall and answered the call, "Hello?"

A scratchy voice replied. "Lizzie?"

"Yes. Who is this?"

"It's Rachael."

"Rachael? I barely recognize your voice. Are you sick now, too?"

"Dr. Wright wants to keep Saj and I overnight."

"What? Where are you?"

"In the hospital. I've got what Saj had. He's doing worse. His fever spiked and his little heart was racing so fast."

"I'll be right there."

Chapter Nine

AFTER ZACH'S AFTERNOON SHIFT, HE headed for the
Provisional Utah Government Offices. He stood outside the translucent
glass door for several minutes, steadying his nerves. The gold letters
said the word District. Below Attorney had been scraped leaving a
hollow, sticky shadow. He decided to go in rather than be caught
waiting outside looking stupid. He knocked on the wooden edge of the
door. "Captain Foote, sir?"

"Enter," said a gruff voice.

Zach took a deep breath, and then pushed through, holding
himself straight and in control. "Zach Riley, sir."

"You're not in the Militia, yet, Zach. You can drop the sir." The
gray haired man set down the stack of papers he was reading and took
off his glasses. "What can I do for you, son?"

Zach spoke before he lost his nerve. "Sir— Captain Foote. I've
learned something I think is important. But I was out of bounds,
outside the walls and not on duty…" He carefully did not mention
Lizzie. She would have to find her own way of getting in trouble.

"Well?" The old man stared at Zach, his eyes blue and electric.

"I couldn't sleep. Went for a drive. I get a little stir crazy even with
the 'outings' I get to take as a Collector." Zach detected no change in
the Captain's manner. "Anyway, there were these brilliant lights in the
distance like a football field on a Friday night. I checked them out and
found this series of giant buildings, all fenced in. When I got near, I
heard a car coming and hid. There were flashing lights and soldiers

with guns. *Real* soldiers."

The Captain's eyebrow raised.

Zach's face reddened. "Uh, like you, sir."

If Foote noticed he'd called him sir again, he didn't correct him. "Where was this?"

"I looked it up. Near Camp Williams. Some sort of government data center."

"Hmmm… How many soldiers did you see?"

"Four. And the old guy in the car."

"Did they see you?"

Zach shook his head. "I don't think so. Not with how they responded to the guy in the car."

"What do you mean?"

Zach described the search of the car.

"Thanks. Zach Riley," he said, writing out Zach's name on a paper as he said it.

Zach stood in silence as the captain continued to write.

"I will need a more detailed report for Mr. DiSilvio. Go back to your quarters and write down every detail you can remember. Bring it to me in the morning, before your shift. Dismissed."

"Yes, sir." Zach turned on his heel and shut the door carefully behind him.

Had that been a good idea? What would they do with the info? Lizzie was safe. Nothing Zach said would indicate she was involved. But he was disturbed that the captain had not reacted like these United States soldiers were welcome neighbors. Did Captain Foote think there was a danger? Or was he worried about something else? The men at the facility were, despite the pandemic, still evidently doing their duty, as if somebody was still in charge.

It struck Zach that he might not be able to call himself American anymore. They'd all been operating as though the government had been wiped out. And without government there was no country. It was a strange feeling, and it was suddenly worrisome. If these were U.S. soldiers on the base, America might not be as wiped out as they thought. And Zach just ratted them out to Captain Foote—did that mean he was a traitor or doing his duty?

It was impossible to wrap his brain around it.

When he got back to the house, Nev was sitting at the table staring into a tea cup. She barely acknowledged him. He was dying to ask her what she thought about the soldiers, and whether they were still American—if anyone would be able to help him understand it, she would. Or at least she would listen to his frustrations and then snuggle with him and make everything all right.

"You okay, Nev?" He kissed her forehead.

Her eyes focused on him. "Yeah, just thinking."

He wrapped arms around her, just holding her still for minute. Her hand patted his. He knew she'd tell him about whatever it was when she was ready. He found a notebook in the bedroom and brought it back to the kitchen table. He wrote as quickly as he could all the details that were important while leaving out the details about Lizzie.

After a while, Nev came over to stand behind him. She hugged him from behind and then rubbed his shoulders. "Thanks," Zach said, taking her hand and kissing it.

"Do you mind if I read over your shoulder?"

"No. I've got no secrets from you."

"Careful. You might want to keep some."

Zach paused momentarily. There was no way to tell her he wasn't hiding anything from her without digging a deeper hole. He went back to writing. The pen made a pleasant scratching on the paper that reminded him of high school. *God, things had been so much simpler back then.*

When he finished he sat back. He flexed his fingers as he wrapped his arms backwards around Nev. She bent forward, still reading, and kissed his cheek.

"I'm going to get ready for bed. Someday maybe you can tell me about the missing chunks." She hugged him again and then walked down the hall and into the bathroom. He heard the water run and stared at the paper in front of him. He would tell her everything. She was his partner. And damn she was smart.

He reread what he'd written, making minor changes here and there. About halfway through he realized this was probably the longest thing he'd ever written. And it hadn't been difficult. He could hear his English teacher telling him to paragraph, to expand on the details. He wanted to make it better, not because of a grade, but because he wanted to do a good job. For once he wasn't being treated like another fuck-up in a long line of fuck-ups.

Lizzie alternated running and walking. She thought about calling one of the taxis, but she'd probably end up waiting longer than it would take her to get herself to the hospital. The populated areas of Provo had shrunk drastically since the outbreak. That was one of the legacies of Mr. Ray. At his urging, instead of still being scattered to the four corners of the city, most of the population retreated to the area around the college and the hospital, a few miles from the lake shore. As a result most of the amenities were within walking distance, though some were still a bit of a hike.

The sun had gone down and the light had left the sky. The streetlights popped on as she passed by them. The walk to the hospital seemed to be taking much longer than it should.

Finally, she shoved through the Emergency Room door. The heavy-set matron at the desk yawned a greeting.

"I— My—" It took a moment of leaning against the counter before Lizzie could speak. "My baby!"

"Slow down, miss." the older woman's voice was long and southern.

Lizzie nodded and took a deep breath. "Sebastian Anthony Jones. Admitted with Rachael— Uh, um, Rachael." *Why can't I remember Rachael's last name?*

"And you're his mother?"

"No. I found him. His mother is dead."

"Of course, I didn't mean— Old habits. I've been at this job for 23 years. Yes. Sebastian is here."

The woman's name tag, covered with award stickers and smiley faces, read Flo.

"I'll list you as next of kin. Your name?"

"Lizzie Goodin-Guerrero." She spelled it out as Flo typed it in. "Where is he?"

"Children's ward with the woman who brought him in."

"Rachael."

"Yes." Flo stood. "I'll take you the most direct route."

Lizzie followed Flo, who moved quickly for her age and size. Her long legs probably helped. "Thanks."

They took the stairs. Lizzie shuddered remembering the elevator at the 'hospital of the dead' in Bellingham, where she'd found Mama and Jayce's bodies. She had been to the Provo ER for prenatal check-ups. Most of the hospital had been condensed, like the city, so even non-emergency visits took place in the ER.

"Why is he in the Children's ward? I thought the rest of the hospital was shut down." Lizzie asked, trying to block out the ghosts as they went deeper into the belly of the hospital.

"Specialized equipment, and easier for quarantine."

"Quarantine?" Lizzie's heart jumped.

"This way." Flo's pace increased.

Lizzie's forced her short legs to keep up, her chest tight.

A nurse with her hair pulled back in a severe bun frowned as they entered the children's ward.

"Sebastian's mother," said Flo.

Lizzie took a step down the softly lit hall. Which door were Saj and Rachael behind?

The nurse's face softened. "I need you to wait here for the doctor."

"I can't go in?"

The nurse crossed her arms across her chest. "Not until the doctor talks to you."

Lizzie suddenly hiccupped. *Not Now!* Pregnancy had many challenges, puking was bad, but hiccups were worse. She held her breath, even though it never worked.

"I'll tell Dr. Wright you're here. He should be with you in a few minutes." She pressed the headset microphone on her ear. "Dr. Wright to Children's Ward."

Lizzie felt a hand on her shoulder, Flo rubbed her back and led her to a chair.

"Doctor Wright will take care of Sebastian. Don't you worry."

Lizzie hiccupped in misery. She knew if Flo offered a hug she'd be bawling all over the woman's light blue scrubs. "Thanks, Flo," *hiccup*, "I know. Dr. Wright, he does my prenatal exams."

Flo's face bloomed into a smile. "You're having a baby?"

Lizzie hiccupped helplessly. "Yeah." She pointed at her convulsing ribcage with both hands as she hiccupped again.

"I see." Flo laughed, rubbing Lizzie's back some more, as if she could relax the hiccups away. "Congratulations."

She stayed with Lizzie through a few more hiccups and then said her farewells, she couldn't leave the ER unmanned for too long.

Flo must be a great mother or grandmother, Lizzie thought. Then she realized any children or grandchildren Flo had were probably dead. She hiccupped.

"The doctor won't be long. I'm Nasira," said the nurse from behind her station.

Lizzie plugged her ears and swallowed. "Lizzie," she hiccupped.

"Can I get you some water, Lizzie?"

"Yeah." Lizzie put her head in her hands. She felt flushed. Was it from running here or was she getting sick now? She felt like she'd done enough running to last her a lifetime. Her eyes drooped. She had to be here for Saj. "Are you feeling okay?" Nasira asked, pulling up her mask and offering the plastic cup of water.

"Yeah." Lizzie took a sip, then put her mouth on the opposite side of the rim and tilted the cup to sip backwards. Rachael had come up with at least a dozen different hiccup cures in the last few weeks, none of which worked reliably. She wondered if the nurse had a straw. "Just hiccups, and now I'm feeling a bit dizzy."

"Try putting your head between your knees."

She did as Nasira instructed and felt a little better by the time Dr. Wright hurried in. His hair seemed more gray since her last appointment three weeks ago. "Lizzie, Saj is going to be fine."

Lizzie started to stand, then thought better of it. The hiccups seemed to be gone. Add head between the knees to the list. "Why can't I see him?"

"I've already got Rachael quarantined with him. Just a precaution," he reassured her. "But if I let you in, you'll have to stay."

"I've already been exposed to anything he has."

Dr. Wright's brows creased. "Yes, I suppose you have."

"And if I am sick, shouldn't I be here rather than attending birthing classes?" She couldn't believe she was volunteering to be locked up.

Dr. Wright pulled up his face mask and snapped on gloves before offering her a hand up. "Come on then."

Nasira offered her a trashcan to throw her plastic cup in and immediately dumped it in a bin marked *Bio-hazard*, finishing with a quick pump on the hand sanitizer.

Lizzie used Dr. Wright's arm to help her stand and steady herself. She was still feeling woozy. It couldn't be from running.

He led her down the hall, bumping a plate on the wall to open the double doors at the end. "People are afraid of a second wave. A mutated virus that's more deadly." He guided her to a glass door, where a laminated, bright orange sign read: *Isolation - Gown, Gloves, Mask.* "I can't imagine anything more deadly, or that there is a virus left to mutate. It seems to have wiped itself out from its own virulence, but we can't really afford to take chances."

Rachael and Saj were inside, snuggled in a hospital bed, sleeping.

Seeing the tiny room, Lizzie hesitated. It wasn't just the memory of the Hospital of Death in Bellingham holding her back. Memories of her time on the psych ward flashed in her head. Only for Rachael and Saj would she do this.

Dr. Wright donned a paper gown, helped Lizzie into a wheelchair and wheeled her into the room.

A moment of panic wrenched through Lizzie, but she focused on Saj and Rachael instead of the walls, which already seemed more cramped.

"We'll need to get some blood work on you," he said, strapping on a blood pressure cuff and sticking a thermometer in her mouth. "Anyone else you've been in physical contact with during the last forty-eight hours?"

Lizzie's lips tightened around the thermometer.

"Now, Lizzie, don't think of it as narcing anyone out, we aren't taking the sick away to be shot. Think of it as helping keep your friends and the community healthy."

Doctor Wright must be a mind reader, but he made a good case. Was this how cops got snitches? "Besides Rachael? Zach, my dad and a woman named Betsy in the birthing class."

Wright's eyes widened at the last one. He already seemed to be calculating the hit to the brood mares.

"Other than Betsy, I stay away from the rest of them."

"Good." Dr. Wright's face relaxed. "I'll have Nasira begin the protocols." He walked to the door, stripping off his gloves. "Press the button if you need something. Nasira will be here until morning and then someone else will replace her. You have to stay confined, but you won't be alone."

"Yeah, I've got them," Lizzie said, her gaze resting fondly on Rachael and Saj asleep in the bed. "They're the ones who need me most. Thanks, Doc."

"You're welcome," he replied as he pushed through the doors.

Lizzie climbed into the hospital bed behind Rachael and snuggled in with her arms around them both.

Rachael opened fuzzy eyes and made a smooching sound. "Glad you're here."

Lizzie luxuriated in the warmth, soon it would be unbearably hot, but for now, their warmth was all she needed. "Me, too."

Rachael pulled Lizzie's arm around her, but when Lizzie hugged her back, Rachael squirmed. "Press there and you're gonna make me pee myself." She gently extricated her arm from under Saj and rolled toward Lizzie.

For a moment Rachael lay her head on Lizzie's chest like she was listening to her heartbeat, then as she scrambled over Lizzie to get off the bed, her hospital gown snagged on Lizzie's fingers. Rachael collapsed back into Lizzie, giggling. "Don't want to hurt the baby."

As Rachael's warmth escaped, Lizzie took a deep breath and said, "You won't."

Rachael stood, her face joyful. "I hope not." She lay her hand on Lizzie's belly and then scurried to the bathroom.

Nasira came in with a hospital gown for Lizzie.

"Do I have to?" Lizzie heard the whine in her own voice.

"Yes," Nasira said sternly. "I'll be back to do a blood draw in a few minutes." She pushed the clothing into Lizzie's hands and left the door swishing behind her.

Lizzie undressed to her underwear and pulled on the gown as Rachael returned. "Is there anything less classy than a hospital gown?"

"A paper bag or a burlap sack?" Rachael's face lit up. "I think you look cute. I don't think I've ever seen you in anything floral."

Lizzie stared dejectedly at the pink roses. "And you won't ever again."

"Here." Rachael spun her round. "Let me tie you up in the back so you don't feel too exposed."

At least she felt cooler, but the draft was awkward.

Rachael spun her back around. "Okay, back to bed." She climbed under the covers on the far side and held them up for Lizzie.

Lizzie climbed in beside Saj and squirmed toward Rachael until they were close and not too uncomfortable. Lizzie's arm lay across Saj and rested on Rachael's hip. "Rachael? Thanks. For everything."

Rachael rolled her eyes then let them close. "Like you said, you and Saj are my family." She squeezed Lizzie gently, her hand settling on the curve of Lizzie's waist.

In a few moments, Rachael seemed to be back asleep, but Lizzie was wide awake and hyper. The tension of Rachael's hand, a familiar weight on her barely covered skin, made her warm elsewhere. Lizzie slid her own hand slightly further along the curve of Rachael's hip. It had been a long time since she'd lain so close to anyone but Saj. Desire flushed her whole body and she held her breath, not wanting to wake Rachael, in case her friend could see right through her.

Duke wanted her, had made that clear since not long after they arrived in Utah, but he was also politely respecting her desire for space and recovery. She wanted someone to touch her there without it being an accident. Crimson colored her cheeks as she tried to think of anything else, but nothing helped. She closed her eyes, but sleep would not come.

Chapter Ten

ZACH DUSTED HIMSELF OFF AS HE hopped off the Collector truck to get some lunch in HQ. He felt pretty good about this morning. He'd dropped off his report, and DiSilvio had been there. The man had seemed to be impressed and appreciative. Zach figured when Lizzie found out he'd have to explain why he'd done it, but it felt right that he had.

DiSilvio asked Zach a few questions, and Zach managed to compose what he thought were meaningful answers. Who knew breaking the rules would be such a great career move? He wished Nev had been in a more talkative mood, he could have used advice about the whole betraying U.S. soldiers thing, but so far so good. Nobody was talking about attacking the base, just glad to have the intel.

Inside HQ, a tall, rangy man in a khaki uniform holding a clipboard waited.

"Mr. Riley?" the man asked. "I'm Sergeant Ecklund. Can we talk?"

"Sure." Zach unsnapped the Kevlar vest and his gun belt. He'd seen the man at Captain Foote's office. A cold knot tightened his gut, amplifying how empty his stomach was. Whatever the news was, he wished they'd at least let him eat first.

"We'd like to invite you to join the Provo Militia."

Zach shoved the gear into his locker. Militia meant fighting. "I like collecting."

"Provo needs a defense. You're out there. You know the dangers.

If it isn't the Independents, it's wildlife or one of the brainless roamers. Someone needs to keep the city safe—got a girl?"

"Yeah."

"Someone needs to keep her safe, right? Why not let that someone be you?"

"You don't think the U.S. military will come eventually?" Zach asked. Ecklund was dressed the part, someone had tailored the uniform to fit him.

"I think most of them are dead, Mr. Riley. But if they are out there, they are taking care of their own, and they don't give two shits about the rest of us."

Zach considered his words. None of the soldiers at the installation seemed to care about Provo. They had to know there were people here. He became a Collector because, at the time, it seemed to be the most important job for taking care of Nev and establishing a home here in Provo. But now the stockpile of food was growing, so maybe there were other things that needed doing. "All right, I'm in."

The sergeant cracked a smile and scribbled on his clipboard. "Provided you can pass the fitness test. Which I'm certain won't be a problem. Report to the Edwards Stadium tomorrow morning at 8 a.m. sharp."

"I'll be there, Sergeant." Zach scanned the list, interested to note that one Duke Madison was listed three names above his.

"You're dismissed. I've arranged for you to have the rest of the day off. Go see your girl."

Zach grinned. "Thanks."

As soon as he got outside, Zach texted Nev. **How soon r u off?**

He jogged toward downtown, kicking himself for walking to work this morning; Nev was at Mannie's office in the downtown core and Collector HQ was on the outskirts of town.

His phone buzzed. **I'm off now. Mannie just gave me the day off and told me to find my boyfriend? What's up?**

Tell u when I get there. Maybe they could pick up her gear and then go for a run together. It'd been a long time since they'd done that. This would be his warm-up.

When he got to the downtown office, an ambulance with flashing lights sat outside the building. Hopefully no one was hurt. Then he saw Nev. She stood, arms crossed and not looking very happy.

"Hey, girl. What's wrong? Did someone get hurt?" He opened his arms to pull her into a hug.

She shrank away. "Don't touch me."

Zach took another step toward her. "DON'T. Go to the hospital." She pointed at the ambulance.

"What's going on?"

Nev's mouth was a tight line. "Lizzie's at the hospital with Saj and Rach. They want you in quarantine because of your *close physical contact*."

"Nothing happened," Zach blurted, instantly realizing the way he said it sounded guilty.

A man and woman in EMT gear came around the ambulance. "Zach Riley? We are here to escort you to quarantine."

"Do I get a choice?"

"No. After you've been tested, Dr. Wright is allowing people to be home on their own recognizance." The woman looked expectantly at Nev.

"Oh, no." Nev shook her head, thunderclouds in her eyes. "You're not giving it to me and getting me kicked out of my own house." Her voice rose shrilly. "Go to the hospital." Nev turned away barely holding it together.

Zach stood with his mouth hanging open. This is what he got for covering Lizzie's ass in his report? Ratted out? He felt perfectly fine, except for the knife in his heart from Nev and the one in his back from Lizzie.

"We need you to come with us."

"Can I have a few minutes?"

"No," the man said. "We need you to come now." They both pulled up their masks. "Please." He motioned to the back of the ambulance.

"Go." Nev said. She turned back to him, her face tight, but her eyes softer than they had been a minute ago. "We'll talk later."

Relief crept into his heart, and Zach finally complied, climbing in the back of the ambulance. The female EMT shut the door and Zach watched Nev receding as the vehicle pulled away from the curb. He waved, pasting on a goofy smile.

She didn't wave back, but she stayed there, watching until the ambulance turned a corner and she was out of sight.

The TV was on, and Lizzie lay in the hospital bed hooked up to IV tubes for fluids. Her head tilted toward the screen, but Mannie wasn't sure she was watching. He understood the gist of the broadcast even though the sound was off. It was Election Day. Tony DiSilvio on screen talking, with red, white, and blue blazing behind him. Neither he nor Mr. Ray claimed any party affiliations, but the political spouting was much the same—except it was more civil since DiSilvio was only running to give the people a choice.

Doctor Wright had given Mannie a choice, home quarantine or hospital. It was an easy choice to be here with Lizzie and Saj.

Rachael and Saj snoozed on the fold-out visitor couch. Things were a little crowded.

"Think it'll make a difference?" he asked, watching DiSilvio smile and talk at the same time.

"What?" Lizzie blinked.

"Think it'll make a difference who gets elected?"

"Oh." Her gaze returned to the screen. "I like Mr. Ray, I guess. DiSilvio gives me the creeps, seems like a slimy used car salesman."

Mannie said, "Hhhmmmm… Really? I think Mr. Ray is the one who sold cars." He didn't get a good vibe off DiSilvio either. In his own head he cheered her intuition.

"I thought Mr. Ray was a councilman or something."

"Yeah. I think so, but that's usually a part time job. Probably went well with selling cars."

"He doesn't seem the type."

Mannie shrugged. "DiSilvio is just a stooge anyway."

"Right, nobody will vote for him, if they can pick Mr. Ray. Everyone has some kind of savior complex for him. I want to trust him, but trusting people isn't really my thing."

"Well, if we are going to live in Provo we should learn to trust the people in charge, otherwise why live here at all?"

"Exactly."

Mannie didn't like the look in her eyes. She'd obviously been having problems being confined in the little room, but refused to talk about it with him. It reminded him of the look soldiers got after being pinned down by enemy fire for too long. He should say something fatherly and wise, but all he could think of was: 'Take it easy, soldier.' So he kept his mouth shut.

The numbers filtered in. Mr. Ray's were steady in the 59% range. DiSilvio was at 27%. Wallace Taylor was doing well as a last minute write-in candidate, showing 11% and the rest shared the last 3%. Not everyone was drinking the kool-aid. He smiled at the fact that God beat out Mickey Mouse in the under-one percent category.

Mr. Ray had helped the people of Provo through the end of the world. They would follow him off the edge of it.

Lizzie said, "I'm surprised he's only pulling 59%."

Mannie nodded. "Maybe DiSilvio deserves some support. He's been there the whole time too."

"Nah."

"It's not too late to get you an absentee ballot—if you want to have your say."

"What's the point?" Lizzie asked.

Mannie was never sure exactly what was going on inside her head, but he thought she wanted to vote.

"There are no women." Lizzie made a face. "When Saj grows up, he better respect women and their choices."

Lizzie stared at the ceiling, with Saj sleeping on her chest. The little holes in the ceiling tiles begged her to count them. At the psych ward, that had been one way she passed her time. She'd figured out a way to count so that she could save her place. Sometimes she'd count all of them on one tile and then be bored enough try to do the math in her head even though math was never her favorite subject.

Saj's adoption papers lay in her lap, as filled out as Lizzie could make them. Flo had found the forms and gotten them to her. She wasn't sure it was worth the effort. She might not stay in Provo, and then all this work would be for nothing. But what if she did, and what if next time they didn't let her in to see him?

If she closed her eyes she could hear Saj's slightly raspy breath. She leaned over and kissed his forehead. He didn't feel hot at all any more. She had no idea if that was good or bad.

Her father and Rachael occupied the next bed. Betsy had taken a room by herself. Betsy was fit to be tied about the *incarceration*, as she called it, but admitted that she could use the enforced rest to catch up on her reading.

Zach was in the next isolation unit. He had refused to be in the same space or even acknowledge their presence. Lizzie thought about texting him, but decided to let it rest. Resting. Just like she should be. All the cloying safety she'd been trying to escape could not take away the fact that their immunity from the pandemic might not be invincible. If she left Provo, what hospital would she take Saj to if he got sick?

When Lizzie woke the next morning, Rachael told her that Zach had already been released and that they could go, too. It was just a lower-case "f"—flu. They all tested negative to any new strain of the virus and were recovering and non-infectious now. Dr. Wright said it had been clear within a few hours that it wasn't the same virus that had wiped out the world, but they still had to be confined to keep the rest of Provo from freaking out. Politics, not medicine.

Lizzie barely cared. Her IV was out and freedom was imminent— at least from the hospital.

Dr. Wright was already off facing the next medical emergency, a family with a nasty case of food poisoning.

Saj was up and moving around slowly. Her father was tossing a cloth football to him. It hit him in the chest as his hands grasped for it, then he giggled, picked it up and threw it back.

Flo brought them one last breakfast: scrambled eggs and toast. The bread was freshly baked; Rachael raved about it during the entire quarantine. Lizzie missed the wonderful white pseudo-bread of the pre-pandemic world. That and a good slice of American cheese all grilled up and gooey was like crack to her. She didn't care about artisanal bread.

After breakfast, Flo took their vitals a final time with an admonition to call if anyone else showed additional symptoms. She gave them all doctor's orders for three days of rest, meaning Lizzie wouldn't have to go back to the birth-monster classes until Monday.

When they finally got home, Rachael left only after checking to make sure there was food for Saj. Lizzie resisted the urge to shoo her away, just Rachael being Rachael.

"You want to stay for a bit, Dad? We could check the election results."

"Sure. I could make dinner. One of your abuela's recipes."

"I doubt it."

His face twisted in disappointment and confusion.

"I mean, there's really nothing here, but frozen stuff. I don't have like… ingredients."

"Well, I should teach you to cook before I teach you to drive a manual!"

"Not sure that's possible."

Her father shrugged. "At some point we're going to run out of frozen food and/or electrical power."

"Talk to me again when that happens."

"I'll go to my place and get some ingredients."

Lizzie snapped her fingers over her head like a flamenco dancer. "It would be great to have some *buena comida*."

He winced at her grammar and Lizzie gave him a *whatever* eye roll. She was too tired to worry about his feelings. Either the flu or the confinement had really taken it out of her. Probably both.

Her father remained his good-spirited self despite Lizzie grumping all over him. He kissed her goodbye and shut the door behind him. The noise drew Saj's attention.

"Mampa?" Saj asked, his voice on edge. The ordeal in the hospital had left him a little insecure.

"Mampa will be right back. He's going to make us dinner." Lizzie put on her happiest voice to make him feel safe and secure again. Behind her smile, she wondered if safe and secure were good enough.

Chapter Eleven

LIZZIE ENJOYED HER LAZY DAY alone. After spending the afternoon playing with Saj inside and out, he'd conked out in her lap to the classic kids movie, *A Bug's Life.*

A knock on the apartment door startled Lizzie. She slid out of the recliner and managed to lay Saj in the easy chair.

She peeked through the peep-hole. Duke. Shit. She ran her fingers through her hair and turned the knob, putting her finger to her lips as she turned the knob. "Saj's asleep."

"Oh." He stared at her. "Uh. The other night. Your birthday party. You didn't seem happy."

"Do I need to be?" She reclined against the door jam.

"You don't want to be happy?"

"Happy has consequences, don't you think? I mean, what's going to happen next? It's gotta be bad, right?" Lizzie kicked the door open the rest of the way, inviting him in with a tilt of her chin. "Right now, I'll be happy if you don't wake Saj up."

"Isn't it a little early for him to be in bed?"

"Doctor's orders, and since when are you the expert on child-rearing?"

"Used to babysit my sister's kids. Probably changed more diapers than you."

"I practically raised my little brother single-handedly."

"'Cause this is definitely a competition." He popped his knuckles.

"You wanna arm wrestle?" Lizzie playfully punched him in the gut.

"Actually, I was going to offer to go get you some food. I just got back from collecting in Springville."

"Why does everyone assume I have no food in the house? My dad cooked last night, plenty of leftovers." Her words sounded too harsh. She added in a gentler tone, "But I suppose more is always better. Where?"

"There's this burger joint downtown called Zeke's."

"Oh, the one with the Sharpies? Where you can write on the walls?" Her pregnant chick drive for food shifted into high gear. "Remember, I'm eating for two."

"I'll get enough for four then!" Duke gave her a knowing wink.

As soon as Duke left, Lizzie shut the door quietly. She thought about picking Saj up and slipping back under him, but he'd probably wake up. Instead, she lay a blanket over him and sat on the floor next to the easy chair with her notebook.

She spewed some words onto the paper. Hoping to find something that sounded good or meant something. After five minutes the only one that stuck with her was, "I believe I should be leaving." She flicked to a new page.

Dear baby,

It scares me to think that you may not grow up to read this. Everything seems so tentative. Six months ago I wouldn't have believed I would be here in Provo, Utah, having a baby. Zach Riley is your father. He is one of my oldest friends. He saved me when the rest of the world fell apart. He kept me from falling apart. We are not together as a couple.

"Damn." All her life she'd wanted her dad to be there. And what had she done? Gotten pregnant and practically guaranteed that her child would never get to live with both parents at the same time. Tears fell to the paper. She wiped them away and took a deep breath, trying to get it under control before Duke returned.

The railroad tracks of cutting scars on her arm

reminded her of old pain. Each one tied to a specific memory. The time she'd burnt the linoleum in the kitchen and snuck out a window to escape Mama's screaming. The first time one of Mama's boyfriends visited her bedroom when he wasn't supposed to. The time Doug took Jayce out fishing alone and she screamed in her head not to let him be alone with her little brother. She traced each scar with her fingertip, like a rosary of bad memories.

A gentle knock echoed, and Lizzie started. She flipped her notebook closed and let Duke in.

The aroma of fried food blew into the room as Duke entered. Lizzie dug into the bag, unfurled a greasy wrapper and began shoveling fries into her mouth, making muffled sounds of pleasure. She paused to unwrap a burger and carnivore it.

"You're welcome," Duke said, grabbing a burger as though he had to fight for it. "Probably not good for us either, but, hey. We're not going to live forever."

Lizzie's brain flashed back on her lyrics and dark thoughts from earlier. She crammed more fries in her mouth to crowd out her noisy thoughts. "Oh my God, this place is amazing," she said, once she had swallowed enough to speak. "Best post-outbreak reboot ever."

"Oh, I forgot the drinks in the hall." Duke hustled out into the hallway and came back in with two giant soda cups. "Wasn't sure what you'd like so I got classic cola and a cherry cola. They add the flavoring there. Which do you want?"

"I'll try the cherry, but I'm not sure I can drink either."

"Why not?"

"Acid. My tummy." Lizzie sucked on the straw until it rattled; Saj whined and shifted. "That cherry is really good, but I think I'll have some ginger ale." Lizzie scooped up Saj and brought him over to the table.

Saj rubbed his eyes, still fussing until he saw Duke. "Juke!"

"Sorry. Should have asked."

Lizzie scooped up Saj and brought him over to the table. Duke laid out a pint-sized feast in front of the toddler, tearing open ketchup packets and squirting a little red pile next to the fries.

"Uh oh," Duke said. "Better eat fast, Saj, or Sissie'll eat up all those fries."

She snatched one up and made to chomp it.

"Mine," he shrieked.

She dropped it back in his pile. "Whoa. Peace, lil' dude."

He fed himself, dipping a piece of burger into the ketchup with his chubby fingers.

When the food was gone and Saj had bounced himself back to sleep, there was another knock on the door. "You want to get that?"

"Sure," Duke said, crossing quickly to the door with an eye on Saj's sleeping form. He opened it as Zach was about to knock again.

Zach stood there; his eyes moved from Duke to Lizzie and back. "Oh, hey, I just wanted to talk. But I can come back later."

"I'm about done for the night and Saj's asleep." Lizzie yawned.

"I was just about to leave," Duke said, taking the cue. "I'll help clean up first, though."

Duke piled the garbage from their dinner into the trash while Zach lingered in the doorway. "Thanks for having dinner with me, Lizzie." His smile was warm and sincere. On his way to the door he knelt and ran his hand over Saj's scalp.

He stood and locked eyes with her for just a little too long, then kissed her forehead. After he left, she stared at the door, confused by her feelings. Duke was a good guy and would make a great father. She liked hanging out with him, but she couldn't see herself settling down with him.

Lizzie carried Saj to the bedroom, with Zach trailing after her. The only person she had real affection for these day was Saj...and Rachael. Once the little guy was tucked in, she shooed Zach back to the living room.

"I wanted to say sorry for not talking to you in the hospital," he said, once they were alone.

"It's all good."

Zach shook his head. "No, it's not. That's the problem. You and Nev aren't talking. Now she's barely talking to me. I want both of you to be happy and everyone talking to everyone. Why can't we just be the three musketeers again?"

She wanted to scream at him to stop being such a man, and stop insisting she be happy, but instead she said, "That ship has sailed, Zach. This isn't high school. We're friends—even family—but you can't turn back the clock."

"Okay, well... I wanted you to know that I'm not pissed anymore."

She arched her eyebrows, but he escaped out the door before she could comment on the concept that things were okay now because he had forgiven her.

"Fuck you, Zach," she whispered as the door swung shut.

Zach's biceps strained as he pulled himself up the rope hand-over hand. His feet dangled as his arms worked. Tomorrow morning would be pain, but right now testosterone raged in him as he excelled in every part of his militia training. Besides, Nev would be happy to apply a heating muscle rub later.

When he hit the top of the rope he still had to drag his aching body onto the wooden platform. A few more feet. Spittle flew from his lips. He grunted. He threw his arm over and swung his leg up, levering himself to roll onto the platform. He paused to enjoy the triumph, but he had to know if anyone had beaten him. He peered over the platform. No one. He shoved himself to his feet and raised his arms in the air.

"Yeah!" he shouted, collapsing into a cross-legged posture. He loved the obstacle course, the long runs, and even the endless push-ups. But the best part was the camaraderie. Yesterday he had helped Will make it the last hundred yards after he sprained his ankle. They'd still finished fifth.

His dad had always said the Army would do him good, but he refused to admit his father was right. The Army was nothing like the Provo Militia.

"All right boys," the Sergeant called through a scratchy megaphone. "Come on down the back side once you've made it up. Meet me in the mess hall. Riley, you earned yourself a free drink!"

Zach flexed his hands and started down the other side. The handholds were two by fours, so there was plenty to grab onto. Almost like climbing the rock wall at the YMCA.

After showers they crossed the street to the bar they'd all adopted.

He drank his celebratory beer, wondering if anyone was brewing more yet, and then ordered another. How many things were they still taking for granted because they could scrounge? The clock clicked over to 5:30. Nev was probably waiting for him.

Zach started to stand. He felt good. The buzz of the second beer was taking hold. Damn near invincible. A dark shape eclipsed the light behind him. He swung around. "Duke."

"Zach. Thought I'd try and start over. Don't see how we're going to be able to ignore each other."

Zach's head buzzed. "You better not break Lizzie's heart."

"How is it any of your fucking business?" Duke was still smiling, but there was an edge to the smile.

"Well, let me see. She's my oldest friend, the mother of my baby and she's had a pretty shitty life. Don't make it worse."

Duke grinned and slapped him on the shoulder. "I don't plan on causing her any pain. If anyone's heart is going to be broken, it's probably gonna be mine." His face was somber. "I think I care about her more than she cares back."

Zach's jaw clenched. He didn't want to smile. He didn't like Duke. He certainly didn't want to reassure him. Finally he relented. "That's just Lizzie being Lizzie."

Duke stuck his hand out. "Thanks, man. Good job

today.”

When was the last time Zach had touched anyone? Shaken a hand? He couldn’t remember anyone but Nev. Maybe Lizzie.

“I don’t have the plague. You could kiss me, and still not get sick.”

Zach held up his hands. “No, thanks. You’re not my type.” He grasped Duke’s hand and shook it. “I got lucky today.”

“No, Zach. You beat me. You beat all of us, fair and square. You’ve been training.” Duke said. “But I don’t think I’m cut out for this intensity. Saw a request for hunters. Think I’ll put in for a transfer. Figure we need someone who can shoot outside the walls. That’s my skill. And I’d kill for some venison.”

Zach mentally counted how many days Duke would be out of town with a gig like that. He kept his pleasure a secret. “I’d like some venison, too.”

“Yeah. Your next beer’s on me.” Duke looked like he had something more to say, but instead he leaned on the bar, motioning to the bartender, and walked out without looking back.

Zach sat back down, only then realizing that someone had sat down in his booth across from him. Mr. Ray. “Uh, sorry. I didn’t see you.” He tried to stand, but the booth and table conspired to make it difficult.

Mr. Ray grinned and gestured him to stay sitting. “No. Be comfortable. Wanted to offer my congratulations.” He offered his hand, too.

Zach took this one without hesitation.

“Mr. Ray.”

“Mark, please. I’d buy you another beer, but I also want you in top form tomorrow. So, I’ll give you a rain check.”

“Thanks.” Suddenly self-conscious of the warm stupor he was in, Zach dragged a hand down his face, trying to sober up.

“Interesting fellow you were talking to. Are you friends?”

“Long story.”

“I love long stories.”

"He's the reason I'm here." Zach didn't feel like talking about Duke, or Lizzie for that matter.

Mr. Ray seemed to sense that. "Well, Mr. Riley, you can tell me later. I appreciate a cool head."

"Thanks." Zach was pretty sure that Duke had the cooler head.

"Well, I owe him one, too," Mr. Ray said.

"You do?"

"I appreciate your drive to be the best. We've noticed that the rest of the volunteers get better times when you're on the field. And if he pushes you..."

Zach chuckled. "He just told me he's going to be a hunter."

"Well." Mr. Ray gave him a fatherly smile. "We all have to find our own way. Have a good evening. I'll be watching you tomorrow."

Zach felt a warmth he couldn't entirely blame on the alcohol. It had felt like a long time since he was on top of the world, and now maybe his slump was over and he was in a streak. He didn't want to leave, but he should be getting home to Nev. The bartender caught his eye and motioned to an empty glass. Zach nodded and the bartender put it under the tap. Some of the other boys were motioning him over to their table.

By the time he left, he decided driving was a bad idea. When he got home he ran through the ditch to get to the yard. The snow came up to greet him. At least he'd made it almost home before falling. Upstairs he found Nev reading in bed.

"Sorry, I'm late."

"No worries," she said, not looking up. "How'd it go today?"

"Kick ass," Zach said.

Nev made a noncommittal sound.

"I'm gonna be sore tomorrow, but... it went really well." He stripped off his clothes and slid into bed to kiss her.

When he got close to her face, she turned away. "Maybe brush your teeth first?"

"Real romantic, huh?" He breathed into his hand and inhaled. "Are you mad at me?"

"Should I be? Sorry. That was really an uncool response. I'm not your wife and even if I was, I wouldn't want to be that wife."

Which might mean she wanted to be his wife. But he still wasn't certain whether she was mad or not. "So, you're okay?"

"Look, if I'd had a beer, maybe it wouldn't be so hard to take." She shoved him away, but playfully. "Brush your teeth and then you can come kiss me."

Zach nuzzled his mouth into her neck. "Maybe I just kiss you here." He slid down her breastbone. "Or here."

"Zach!"

"Oh, all right." He tickled her with his chin under her collar bone. She slapped him with her book. He retreated to the bathroom, vigorously brushing his teeth, and gargling quickly with mouthwash.

Top of the world.

Chapter Twelve

MANNIE OPENED THE DOOR TO THE garage with his annoyed daughter behind him.

"Dad!"

He stopped and turned to face her at the bottom of the steps. She glared at him. "You're going out of town?"

Mannie heard the accusation clear as day. "It's for work. Pretty boring really."

"Take this." She handed him a cell-phone and glanced around before speaking softly. "All our numbers are already in there. It runs on the secondary network. Don't call me with the other one."

He put his hand on his daughter's arm. "Why all the espionage?" Mannie whispered back.

"Well, it sounds paranoid, but someone is keeping us from getting information from outside of Utah. They may be listening in on the phone lines, and I don't like being spied on."

Mannie took a deep breath. It made sense. When the shit hits the fan, you want to control the information coming in. One wrong story makes it through and the whole place falls apart in panic. He wished Lizzie hadn't found out. It was tough enough keeping her in Provo for the time being.

Mannie waved at Lizzie as he climbed into Rubi, his Jeep Rubicon. He slid the key in and twisted it. The engine coughed and sputtered, but started. He patted the dashboard gently. "Thanks, old girl. You wanna go for a ride?"

He felt his mood rising. How long had it been since he was alone behind the wheel, heading out on the road? Months. He really did understand Lizzie's desire to get away.

Mannie was on a personal mission to check out the Dugway Proving Ground, something he'd been meaning to do since before he found Provo. Dugway was a center for the military study of biological weapons. It wasn't a place to leave for scavengers, and he'd made a promise to the U.S. soldiers in San Antonio to find out what happened there. A promise he'd bought his life with when he was infected with rabies.

The engine smoothed out to a soft rumble, and Mannie hit the garage door opener, amused at the suburbaness of the activity.

He backed Rubi out and whipped a u-turn, heading for the edge of town. His heart raced. Now that Doctor Wright had given him the all-clear, he needed to exercise and get in shape. He ought to find a pool and start swimming laps again.

The months of enforced rest, interrupted only by physical therapy for the muscles effected by the gunshot wound, had taken their toll and he felt like an old man. His drinking probably wasn't helping. Maybe it was time to get back on the program—would someone in town be his sponsor? Of course, many of the citizens were teetotaling LDS members, he needed someone who had been through

Despite his personal mission, his official job today was to recon the Camp Williams Data Center site, and surroundings, in terms of military exposure. DiSilvio wanted to make sure that it could be kept safe from Utah Independents—or so he said. He planned to post observers nearby to keep the place safe, but he had forbidden direct contact. It didn't feel right to Mannie, but he didn't see what harm it did to play along.

Besides, it gave him a great opportunity to get out of the city and check out Dugway.

He slowed at the Guardhouse on Center and they waved him through. He hit the on-ramp to I-15, the Veteran's Memorial Highway, humming "Knockin' on Heaven's Door."

In about ten minutes he passed the Lehi Main St. exit that would take him to Dugway. He glanced in the rear view mirror. Paranoia was something he shared with his daughter. But that had probably kept them both alive. Was it paranoia when you knew something was wrong without being able to figure it out, or just a sixth sense? Whatever it was, he felt it today. How close are DiSilvio's tabs on me?

He was happy the election had gone to Mr. Ray, and DiSilvio was back to number two.

Mannie tried to simply enjoy the snow on the ground and the crisp clear blue sky. There were no signs announcing Camp Williams or a US Data Center. No Restricted Access. Mannie wondered idly if they'd taken the signs down or if signs had never been put up. Hadn't been hard to find out about the place on the internet. So you either had to be a techno-terrorist or know where you were going. He skipped the innocuous 1200 West Exit. He'd go past and come back, easier to get close without being visible.

He topped the high point of the pass and realized he was close to the site of the skirmish between the Utah Independents and the Collectors.

He pulled off the freeway and onto a road that rolled up a hill; he thought he might be able to see the Data Center from there. Besides, taking the driving in short bursts would be better on his knee.

He pulled on his Ranger hat and a black down jacket. The day looked cold and this was the highest point of elevation around.

Mannie loosed the binoculars from their case and stepped out into the chill. He slogged through the foot deep snow to the highest point he could see, turning from time to time to check out the view.

When he reached the peak, of course he saw further peaks, but this would do. He enjoyed the vista. For a moment he felt the past impinge. On their trips cross country looking for work his mother had always demanded they stop at anything that said view point.

Mannie noticed a slight road. He could have driven around behind the backside of the hill and all the way to here. Well, the easiest way often left something to be desired. He'd enjoyed the short climb and the quickness of his breath told him he needed it.

With a sigh for the job he needed to do, Mannie placed the binoculars to his eyes and stared down at the Data Center. The lights Lizzie and Zach had spoken of were off, probably automatic. He couldn't see the gatehouse clearly from here, but he could see the double high chain-link fence with razor wire rolled around the top.

Mannie scanned the area. The snow covered ground rolled in all directions. Much of the landscape was concealed under a white blanket. He wasn't going to learn much up here. He hustled down the hill to drive out the chill. He hopped into Rubi and fired her up, turning the heat on high.

With no traffic, he drove north on the southbound side of the highway, and came to the spot of the skirmish. He knew it because the van that had taken him there sat still, silent, but with several bullet holes and a broken window as testament to what had occurred.

It already seemed like years in the past, another memory to go with all the others: the scent of gunfire, smoke in the eyes and the horrible sounds of bullets impacting flesh. Mannie crossed himself. He'd lost the belief years ago, but it felt right, being respectful to the dead. "May whatever god or gods you believe hold you and keep you."

He hunted around but couldn't find any sign the Independents had come to or from the data center. He climbed back in Rubi and headed down the hill, tipping his head with respect at the mound and the simple wooden cross with its one word epitaph. Spike.

He came to the Camp Williams sign on the left. The Data Center lay out of sight behind the ridge. He turned off the engine, rolled down the windows and let Rubi coast down the hill. Mannie's eyes and ears were on full alert, but nothing disturbed the vast desert of snow.

When he had coasted past where he could see the tops of the buildings he let Rubi slide over onto the shoulder. He fetched the binoculars from the back seat, and put his white stocking cap on instead of the Ranger hat. He hustled toward the fence by the side of the road and carefully put his foot on the bottom barbed wire near the post and then eased his other leg over the side.

He hustled up the slope and dropped to his stomach in the snow at the top. The sun had traveled halfway up the sky and the chill had receded. He scanned the area with bare eyes and then with the binocs. There was no movement. He waited, rolling to his back and staring at the sky. Blue patches showed through the white. Might burn off and be a decent day. He closed his eyes and breathed deep in the cool air. It felt good to be outside, away from people. Mannie pushed himself back over, and scanned the facility again. Still nothing.

He pulled out his cell-phone and called Captain Foote.

"Guerrero?"

"Yes, sir. On site. It's all silent. No sign of any activity."

Foote was quiet.

Mannie waited.

"Why don't you check back for a few hours at dusk?"

"Yes, sir. May I do additional recon, sir?" Mannie hoped he wouldn't have to be more obvious than that.

Foote chuckled. "Go ahead. Enjoy your freedom."

"Thank you, sir."

Mannie did one last scan with the binoculars and then backed down on his knees toward Rubi. As soon as he couldn't see the buildings standing, he ran through the snow.

He jerked Rubi's rear door open and tossed his jacket inside, and kicked the snow off his boots. Then he climbed into the cab and headed her down the hill. As he pulled onto Utah 73, a thought brought him up short. He actually stopped at the stop sign and sat there to think. What if the provisional government was actually tracking his movements? Paranoid, yes. Or checking the odometer. His cell phone would tell them where he was approximately.

I need another vehicle. He pulled forward slowly glancing around for a likely car to steal. No one was really tracking his movements, where they? Mannie had seen enough people with too much power. And if they were thinking of making a move on the NSA Data Center they had big dreams in a small town.

Mannie pulled out the phone Lizzie had given him—the safe phone. He pushed the power button and drove while it booted. When it came to the home screen he slowed to a stop and pressed the map icon. "Fire Station nearby," he said into the phone. It still felt a little too Star Trek to talk to your phone.

The map spun into a location for the Saratoga Springs Fire Station. 1.2 miles back the way he'd come. He whipped Rubi around and stepped on the gas.

At the station the garage doors were open and an ambulance, a fire truck and a red SUV were inside.

He pulled up to the side and got out. "Hallo?" No answer. He walked to the SUV. The keys were in the ignition. He twisted the key and the engine growled to life. He left it running and returned to Rubi.

He pulled his backpack out and strapped his sidearm on. He pulled his PUG phone from his pocket, plugged it into the cigarette lighter power, and left it sitting inside Rubi. He put his Ranger cap back on.

In minutes, he was back on SR73 and headed west. Switching vehicles had his nerves all wound up. *You're no James Bond, Mannie.*

On the morning of Lizzie's last day of freedom before she had to go back to the hippo class, the doorbell rang.

"Coming." Maybe it was Duke. She looked out the peephole. A man and a woman in business suits. Lizzie stared at them for a moment before she opened the door. "May I help you?"

"Elizabeth Goodin?" the lady asked, her voice sounding like years of cigarette smoke. Her face had that pinched look of leather from too much sun, probably aggravated by the tobacco. Her name tag identified her as Renee Reed, DCFS Liaison.

"Goodin-Guerrero," Lizzie answered. "Lizzie, please." Cold dread crept over Lizzie. We're from the government and we're here to help.

"May we come in?" The young man asked. His name tag said Eric Wallach hand-printed in block letters that reminded Lizzie of elementary school.

"As long as you're not vampires." Lizzie joked, trying to hold onto her nerves. The suits stared back at her. Why didn't people get her jokes? "Yeah, come in. My little boy is sick and sleeping."

"He's actually what we want to talk to you about. I'm Renee Reed. This is Eric Wallach."

"You've put in adoption papers for—" Wallach opened a pocket notebook and looked inside it. "Sebastian Antonio Jones."

Lizzie chest seized and her heart pounded. "Yes, of course." DCFS must be like Child Protective Services back home in Washington State. She motioned them inside. "Can I get you anything to drink?" She walked through to the kitchen.

"No, thanks."

"Have a seat. I'll be right there." She puttered nervously around the kitchen trying to calm her nerves. Finally she poured herself a tall glass of water and went to sit at the table with them.

"What's the next step?" she asked.

"We've done a background check. And now we'd like to interview you. Then we make a report."

"Okay." Lizzie put her hands in her lap where they could not see them wrestling with each other. Flo and Daddy both said it would just be a paperwork slog. Why did have to be so difficult? But she'd do it for Saj. "What do you want to know?"

They asked her a series of questions she thought they should already know from their background check. Who was her mother? What about her father? What was her parenting experience? Then the questions got deeper. Why had she spent time in a psych ward? They asked about Zach's shoplifting. Would he be doing any parenting of Saj, since he was the father of her baby?

Lizzie took a drink of water for that one and tried to explain her relationship with Zach succinctly, but it ended up getting longer and longer until Wallach held his hand up.

"We don't need to know everything. I think you've given us a sense."

"One more question. Last week you didn't show up for your Monday birthing class. Can you tell us where you were?"

Lizzie took a drink of water. What were they getting at? "I didn't feel well. The next day, Saj got sick." She heard herself say it, and it sounded about as unbelievable as she thought it would.

Reed wrote a note in her notebook. "You haven't been out of the city since you arrived?"

"No. Of course not." Lizzie stared at the glass of water. "It's dangerous out there. Zach said there are cougars." Did they know already? Had Zach narced on her?

"That's all we need for now." Reed stood abruptly, and Wallach followed her lead.

Lizzie shook hands with them, hoping the sweat seeping from her palms wasn't obvious.

"Good afternoon," Reed said.

When they were gone Lizzie hurried in to check on Saj. The sick feeling in the pit of her stomach coiled around her heart.

She grabbed her phone off the nightstand and stabbed out a text to Zach. **We need 2 talk. Now.**

Chapter Thirteen

THE MONOTONY OF THE SNOW on the road was broken by the sign for Dugway Proving Ground. Mannie lifted his foot from the accelerator, coming in slow.

Two soldiers, fully armed and armored, came out of the gatehouse and flagged him to halt. He rolled his window down and held his left hand up. A military Humvee of reinforcements whizzed across the pavement toward the gate house.

Mannie announced, "Lieutenant Manuel Guerrero, U.S. Army Reserves."

"Step out of the vehicle."

Mannie kept his left arm visible and opened the door with his right.

"You have ID?"

"Yes." Mannie nodded. "Wallet, back pocket." He turned so they could see him pull it out. Mannie handed his wallet to the first soldier, who took it without looking at it. Two more soldiers hustled out of the Humvee. A tall man with a warm amber skin-tone and casual civilian clothes followed them more sedately. His facial expression was ambiguous, but obvious laugh lines hinted at someone with a ready laugh. A stocky soldier with a Medical Corps insignia pulled a medical kit from the vehicle and hustled to catch up.

The tall civilian gestured toward Mannie's borrowed SUV. "Inspect the vehicle."

The Medic jerked hospital gloves and a mask from his bag and held them out to the tall man, who waved him off and stepped toward Mannie. He took the wallet offered by the soldier, opened it and flipped through it. When he found Mannie's military ID he scrutinized it and then Mannie carefully. "Mr. Guerrero?"

"Yes, sir."

"What brings you out so far into the wilderness?" The man's eyes were amused, but the tension in the rest of his face and posture belied it.

"Duty."

"What duty?" He asked brusquely, returning Mannie's ID.

"Can we go somewhere warmer to discuss it, Mr.....?"

"Dwayne Jones. Welcome to Dugway, Mr. Guerrero."

"Home of the Mustangs," Mannie read the sign on the gatehouse.

"A long time ago, maybe." Dwayne gestured to the passenger seat of the Humvee.

Mannie slid into the seat as Dwayne and one of the armed soldiers got in the back. The vehicle jumped forward and they rolled toward the conglomeration of functional-looking buildings, topped by a water tower.

"I've got to be back near Provo in three hours," he said, hoping they would interpret this as: people were expecting him. "May I speak frankly?"

"I'm all ears."

"I'm living in Provo. But I came up from Texas. On the way, I made a detour through San Antonio, met an Army Captain who thought it would be prudent to check out the status here. It seemed like a good idea." Better keep things to the point right now.

Dwayne nodded, but didn't offer anything in return.

"Allegiance is a tricky thing right now, but something as close to the United States government as can be had seems like the best option." Suggest my loyalties lie with them, without actually saying it. "I'm officially out this way to check on the NSA Data center, for the new Provisional Utah Government." He dropped exactly the information he wanted them to have with each word. These guys might end up being a better option than Provo, or they might not. It was too early to tell. In the meantime he needed to control the situation and the information flow, while still appearing helpful.

Dwayne's eyes lit up and he leaned forward. "And?"

"It's there. Supposedly military inside, but I don't know more than that."

"Who's running things in Provo?"

"Mark Ray was just elected mayor. He seems like a good man."

"But?"

"But, I'm not sure if he's really running things. There's another man, Tony DiSilvio." Make them think they are digging information out of me that I am holding back.

Silence. There was nothing to hear except the whine of the engine as Mr. Jones considered the information.

"So why are you here, Lieutenant?"

"I promised San Antonio I'd try to contact you."

They stopped in front of a rectangular cinder block building. Mr. Jones stepped out and Mannie followed him inside. Mr. Jones sat down in a comfortable chair in what seemed to be a waiting room.

"And report back." Dwayne's eyes glittered shrewdly. He knew Mannie was dancing around the truth, but he was letting him keep his secrets, for now.

Mannie gave a brief nod, more a show of respect for Dwayne's win in their little match of wits than agreement.

"I'm the lead biologist here," said Dwayne, as though explaining he was a brain, not a military man. "Most of our trained personnel are dead. We'd like to be recruiting and retraining, but the consensus is we can't be visible yet. We've been spending our time processing samples from our own people. We want to be sure the virus is really dead, or manufacture a vaccine if it's not. We do valuable work here, and could use more trained military men."

"What do you know about the virus?" Mannie hoped he didn't really sound as desperate and helpless as he felt.

"It has an unusually long incubation period, 10-12 days. Manifests with a stuffy nose and cough like the common cold. Then the patient gradually goes downhill. Seems to be contagious for weeks. Airborne by mucus and also transmittable hand to mouth. A 90-95% mortality rate. Aboriginal peoples in the Americas seem most resistant." He glanced at Mannie meaningfully. "There are two kinds of survivors, those who were immune and never got it, and those who managed to fight it off, but seem to have suffered brain damage in the process."

Mannie nodded, none of this was particularly new information to him. The important questions were: How did it start? Was it natural? Could it happen again? But he contained his questions. "My daughter calls them Dog-people."

Dwayne paused, looking at Mannie thoughtfully, then continued. "The best minds left in the world believe the virus killed itself off by being so virulent."

"You seem skeptical."

"I'm a scientist, that's what we do. Of the 987 people in Dugway when it hit… 92 survived until November 1st. We've had two deaths since then, but both were suicides. Secondary casualties."

Mannie had considered suicide. It was on his mind the week, after Isabela died. Right up until Lizzie had called. "So tell me something? For someone who thinks the virus could still be out there, you don't seem to be taking many precautions."

"Well, we've all been more than exposed. We decided to forgo the bulky equipment a few weeks ago on the assumption that even if the virus is still out there, we are all likely immune. The protocols were inconvenient to the soldiers, and difficult to enforce. Not to mention costly on our supplies of biohazard gear. An executive decision was made to save that gear for lab testing where it was more necessary."

He had a sour expression that made Mannie reconsider whether Dwayne was in charge. Perhaps he wasn't the executive who made the decision.

Dwayne drummed his fingers on the arm of the chair. "You didn't finish telling me what you plan to do, I don't think."

"Don't know really." That was the truth. "If things were simple, I would include you in my report to Provo."

Dwayne's response was immediate. "But things aren't simple, are they? Too much could go wrong in that scenario—people attacking Dugway for a cure, or someone to blame. Medical research facilities are the ones responsible for outbreaks in the movies after all."

"Tend to agree… But—" Mannie stood, getting to the bargain at hand. "If things go south in Provo, I need a secondary location to bring my family."

Dwayne kept his poker face. "We have homes ready for families of new recruits." He wasn't revealing all his cards either.

Lizzie paced the carpet as Zach sat on her couch with his feet up. "Dammit, Zach. That's my story. Glen talked to me. Why'd you narc it out to the Shitty people? You want me to tell you whenever I'm thinking about doing something dangerous and then you pull this?"

Zach stared at her like she was stupid. "This is the opposite of dangerous. It's about safety. We have no idea how many soldiers are at that facility. We don't know who they're loyal to-"

Lizzie scoffed and earned an eye roll. "We don't? It seems pretty obvious to me. They're U.S. Government troops and I expect at some point they'll be able to communicate with the newly re-formed U.S. Government."

"Do you trust the newly re-formed U.S. Government?"

"Do I trust anybody?" She stabbed her finger at his chest, stopping short of actually touching him. "No. But I'm not a traitor."

"A traitor to what? The new U.S. government has no power. You remember what your dad said about San Antonio? That's where the power is. There and in that NSA facility. And here. Here we have a good thing. People are safe. People are taking care of each other. Hell, even you are helping out."

"You say that like I'm some sort of freak who doesn't help people."

Zach didn't say anything. Which was somehow worse. He thought so.

"Whatever. Go be righteous. Believe in your own fantasies."

"You don't trust people with power. You were always spouting off about being spied on. NSA is, or was, Big Brother! Remember the Patriot Act? Being afraid to text naked pics because some NSA guys would probably print it out and pass it around the office for a laugh? Remember being afraid to Google how to blow stuff up because the government might be knocking on your door?"

"I'm more worried about the fact that I can't fucking leave town without a 'may I please thank you' to some man somewhere." Her finger did poke him this time.

"I'm not telling you what you can and can't do."

"Bullshit." She turned and headed for the door.

"Where are you going?"

"Away from you. If I may, please?"

Zach let out a rough breath. "Whatever. It's your place."

"Yeah, no shit. Lock the door when you leave. I've got someone to visit."

Lizzie steadied her nerves as she walked down the cinder-block halls of the Provo Correctional Facility. A second barred door slid aside for her and she stepped through. They clanged shut behind her as she continued on. She shoved her hands in her pockets to keep her from twiddling them. This was far too reminiscent of previous confinements in Lizzie's life.

Most recently it had been Travis on this side of the bars, and her in the cell—when she'd first arrived in Utah. Things were better now. She was a citizen of Provo, and protected. Travis was locked up. He couldn't hurt anybody any more.

The guard behind her said, "Go through the next door when it buzzes. He's the third cell on the right."

Lizzie followed the directions, and each wall revealed more stark emptiness. She shivered as she came closer. At—least there would be metal bars between them.

A speaker in the ceiling crackled as she stepped through the door. "Travis. You have a visitor."

"No shit? Who's trying to save me now?"

"It's me, Travis."

"Lizzie? Wow, to what do I owe this honor?" He sat up from his lounging position.

It unnerved her that he recognized her so quickly. She hardly recognized him. His hair was shaggier, unkempt, and a couple inches longer. And his face was covered by a bushy, blond beard that went from his ears to his shirt collar.

"You look good. Not as good as the first time I saw you going for a walk in the cold—" His leer set her skin on edge.

"You look like shit, Travis." She leaned back against the solidity of the cold cement wall. "I couldn't believe it when I heard you were still in here."

"Yeah. They can't seem to decide what to do with me. I think they're afraid I'll stir up trouble if they banish me."

"Yeah. Sounds like maybe they're smart. Somebody was talking about wanting you released and banished, you know." She kept her voice steady, but just being this close to him was vile—like being too close to a dead rat.

"Oh, yeah? Who?" He actually looked hopeful for a second.

"Quentin Blocker's mom sends her regards." Lizzie enjoyed the momentary deflation of Travis' posture. "She says she hopes you get banished soon."

"Well, you can't always get what you want." He stood and strolled toward the bars. "Why'd you really come? You hot for me? That's it isn't it?"

"Yeah, think whatever you want, mountain man." She turned away and walked to the door. She pushed the button and said, "I'm ready to get out."

"Come back any time you want to see me, Lizzie. Maybe you can wear that hot lil' number you wore when we first met—you know I should've touched those naked tits! When I get outta here, I am gonna come for them. You're mine, bitch!"

She didn't waste another 'Fuck you,' on him, but forced herself to walk, not run away.

The door buzzed and she pushed through back into the lighter and warmer hallway. She shook and rubbed her arms, as if trying to clear away the cobwebs of his nastiness. And it wasn't just seeing him that creeped her out, being on the outside of the prison cell looking in had her feeling claustrophobic. If she never saw another prison cell the rest of her life it would be too soon.

Chapter Fourteen

MANNIE DROVE FASTER ON THE WAY back toward the Data Center, sticking as close to his own tracks as he could. He hoped snow would come soon and obscure them. He couldn't put his finger on anything, but he had a bad feeling about where Provo was headed. And he had a daughter and a new chosen family to care for.

He pulled into the fire station, happy and relieved to see Rubi sitting there undisturbed—though it left an eerie aftertaste in him to see the world so deserted, at least in Provo it seemed like there were still people left. He backed the SUV into the garage and turned the engine off and hustled over to Rubi to check the cell phone. Two messages. Lizzie and Foote. "Shit."

He hit redial. "Captain Foote? Sorry, I forgot my cell on the charger in the Jeep."

"No big deal, Mannie. Just a second."

Mannie could hear muffled voices in the background. He waited impatiently.

"Guerrero? You have anything urgent to deal with back here?"

Mannie chuckled. "Well, sir, I called you first, but I've got a message from my pregnant daughter. I doubt it's urgent. What do you need?"

"I'd like you to dig in and observe the Data Center overnight. We'll check in with you."

"But what about my other work, sir?"

"Mannie, I happen to know how much you hate that desk. Your

new assistant has it handled—some kind of administrative dynamo."

"Respectfully, sir, don't you get any ideas about stealing her while I'm away."

Captain Foote's baritone laugh boomed in the phone.

"Scrounge up some chow and call me when you're in position. If you need us to check up on your daughter, let me know."

"Not necessary, I'm sure." Oh, Lizzie would love that.

"Fine. I'll expect to hear from you in the next couple hours."

"Affirmative, Captain."

After he got off the phone with Captain Foote, he tapped voice-mail to see if Lizzie had left one.

"Dad? This is Lizzie. Just wanted to vent. Call me back if you want. Mostly, I wanted to tell you I love you. Bye."

The negative attitude he got whenever dealing with bureaucracy adjusted itself as the thought about his daughter wanting to share her life with him. She didn't sound too stressed.

He reached into the glove box and dug for the Bluetooth earpiece he'd shoved in there. He put it on as he started Rubi and called Lizzie.

"Hey, Dad—I'm better."

"No need for me, huh?"

"I'm happy to talk. What're you up to?"

Mannie thought for a moment about how to answer.

"Oh. Can't tell me?"

"Not really. Nothing too important."

"Okay. Then I can talk about me."

He pictured her self-conscious grin. "What's up, Lizzie?"

"Not much really. Pissed off about being stuck here, like a prize pig at a fair. I can't even have a fucking PBR, even if liked the shit."

"I'm sorry."

"Not your fault."

"Nobody wants you to feel like a prisoner."

"Are you sure?"

Mannie didn't have an answer. Not a good one. "Have you tried to put in a request?"

"No," Lizzie sighed. "I don't want to talk to the LaFevbre woman. Seems like Le Fever should have killed her. Sorry. Not nice. Sorry to be negative." Lizzie forced cheer into her voice. "Could be worse."

"Yeah." He kept his interjections brief. Years of experience taught him to let a woman get stuff off her chest when she needed to.

"When are you going to be home?"

"Tomorrow, I think. I heard Nev's done miracles in my office."

Lizzie laughed loudly. "Wouldn't take much. She's always been organized. All right. Saj is tugging on my shirt tails. Later, I love you."

"I love you, too, Elizabeth." He watched the phone disconnect. Then his other phone rang. "Hello."

"Daddy," Lizzie whispered. "Are you okay?"

"I'm not in the danger zone, Lizzie."

"You're not in the city."

"No, but I'm safe. And I'm glad you gave me the *GlenPhone*. Tell you more later."

"All right. Take care of yourself. G'night."

"Good night, Elizabeth." The phone faded as she hung up.

It had been a long day and it was far from over for him. Better add caffeine to his grocery list. And a lot of it.

Mannie snuggled down into the sleeping bag, wishing he had someone to hold. And the face he didn't want to see came to him unbidden. Jess had been haunting his dreams since he'd met her. That flash of a pink belly button ring as she stretched, the twisting guilt, and all those other feelings.

He fixed his attention on the Data Center to escape. It didn't work well until an ugly old station wagon pulled out of the gate and a soldier appeared as it passed by. The car weaved around and disappeared over the small hill toward Bluffdale and Camp Williams. Mannie watched until the soldier had disappeared again and the gate closed.

Then he turned his attention to the highway. The station wagon did not come his way. So. The old guy Zach and Lizzie had mentioned came from the north. He made some notes in his waterproof notebook. Finally, some action.

He shouldn't have gotten his hopes up, after that little bit of action the place sealed up tight as a drum once more. After a few minutes his mind drifted back to lonely thoughts. Jess. If it was right, then what was holding him back? He was nothing if not bold, that's what Isabela always said. What he was feeling now was simply physical attraction toward someone who made it clear that she wanted him. As much as it felt good, it would pass.

Lizzie walked out of the classroom and down the hall wishing Betsy had been there to make the day more tolerable. At least Jess was going to meet her for lunch. Outside a crowd of people gathered across the street.

A police car sat with its lights spinning lazily. She stopped at the glass doorway, wondering if the lights were for her. She saw Jess coming up the stairs. She shoved the door open and stepped out into the crisp afternoon.

"What's all the hubbub?" Lizzie asked.

"A banishing." Jess' eyes were wide.

"A banishing?"

Jess pulled her close and whispered in her ear. "There was one while you were still in the hospital.

"Yesterday?"

"No, when you were shot. That one was someone who'd beaten up one of the dog-people. They give them a speedy trial and then the sentence is carried out. They're sent out of town."

The PA started to feedback and then a microphone popped. "Check. Check."

Lizzie heard a scratchy male voice through the speakers mounted on a flatbed truck. It still had some red, white and blue ribbon from a past life in a parade. She was too short to see around the people in front of her.

"Provo Utah Community Court has made its decision. Bring the prisoner forward."

Then she could see the top of someone's bald head, bent over as if its owner was praying.

"Mr. Ray will read a few words before the sentence is passed."

Mr. Ray stepped up to the microphone, she saw a glimpse of a sad-looking gray-haired man in a rumpled business suit. He cleared his throat into the microphone and everyone nearby cringed at the squeal of feedback.

"When the pandemic hit and those of us who were left chose to band together here, it was with the understanding that we would protect the young, the infirm, the sick and downtrodden. It saddens me to send you from The City. But it is by no means a death sentence. Please use this as an opportunity for a fresh start. Judge?"

She saw him walk back the way he'd come. His head, too, was bowed. He looked a lot older than he had a few days ago.

"I am Judge Larry Shoen. Terry Green, a jury of your peers has decided that you did commit the crimes against humanity of which you are accused. Taking advantage of one of the less capable survivors is a moral, ethical and legal crime. The sentence is banishment. If anyone wishes of their own free will to accompany you, they may speak now and share your transport. Are there any such people?"

The silence stilled the cold streets. Lizzie hugged Jess.

Then the voice continued. "As Mr. Ray said, use this as an opportunity to start over. Somewhere else. If you are found within a 25-mile radius of the city after you are released, your life will be forfeit. The will of the people is carried out. Take him away."

Lizzie heard a car start up. Then the crowd in the street parted. A police car with its lights spinning pulled slowly forward. The bald, bearded man glared out the side of the car, catching Lizzie's eye, his face found hers and stared at her even as the car pulled away. An icy, icky chill crept over Lizzie's skin.

Jess grasped her coat and pulled her off the street toward home. "Come on, Lizzie." After a block or so, when they were away from the crowd Jess stopped. "Are you okay?"

"I don't know. The way he looked at me." She shuddered.

"Thank god we're here and safe."

Lizzie pulled Jess to her. "Yes. Safer than out there anyway."

"Hey, you wanna come to work with me after lunch?"

"To cuddle cute animals? Hell yeah."

"Can you get out of class?"

"Do you think I care?" Lizzie smiled.

"All right." Jess grinned. "Let's get lunch then. There's this place called Zeke's. Great burgers."

Mannie heard a low rumble and lifted his head from the snow pillow he'd built under the mummy bag. It had been a couple hours since the station wagon had gone.

A troop truck appeared at the gate; Mannie focused his binoculars and saw a driver and passenger in front both fully accoutered in combat garb. When it pulled up, a dozen or so men circled around the back.

Flashlights swept the interior and then the soldiers waved them through. The gate clanged shut. Mannie kept the binoculars up, scanning back and forth. A squad poured out of the truck, into one of the buildings. The driver and passenger got out and stood around smoking cigarettes.

About ten minutes later another squad came out of the building and loaded into the truck to be shipped off to wherever their replacements had come from. How many months had they been guarding this data center undermanned after the virus wiped out most of them? Were they getting tired? Losing their edge?

The truck, like the station wagon before it, didn't come down the hill. They must be barracked up the road at Camp Williams. The dark had stolen on him without notice.

When all was quiet again he reported back to Foote. A decision was made to post a permanent watch on the facility. His replacement was already on the way. Before he returned to Provo, Foote wanted him to explore Camp Williams.

Mannie wondered what the game was. DiSilvio and Foote didn't have the sort of force that could take out a squad of crack U.S. troops. Mannie pulled his sleeping bag tight around him, hoping to get a catnap before his replacement came.

A shuffle nearby in the snow pulled Mannie from slumber. He drew his sidearm, warm from being against his body. He hesitated; he said he wouldn't kill for Foote or any commander, those days were gone.

His phone vibrated softly. He lay still, trying to see in all directions at once. All was silent. Eyes trained in the direction he thought the noise had come from, he slipped his left hand inside his pocket. He saw a name on the screen, and chanced answering. "Zach," he hissed. "That you?"

"Yeah," a soft reply came back. "I'm here to replace you."

Mannie relaxed, squinting into the snow. "Shit, Zach! I could have shot you."

A white shape in winter camouflage detached itself from a snowdrift. "That's exactly why I called," he said, hanging up the now unnecessary phone.

"You're my relief?"

Zach nodded in the dim light.

"You look like the Abominable Snowman."

"Camo is just a smart clothing option out here—when you don't want to be seen."

Mannie glanced back at Zach. He was a good kid. Too bad things hadn't worked out with him and Lizzie; Mannie wasn't so sure about Duke.

He shoved the sleeping bag in on itself, his task done. He'd given them what they asked for: intel.

Mannie's hands were freezing as he started the engine, turning the heat on. The windshield sparkled with spreading patches of ice. Maybe the desk wasn't so bad. At least it was warm.

After lunch, Lizzie walked through the aisles at the new Humane Society building with Jess. Lots and lots of animals. "I had no idea there were so many."

"Pets now outnumber pet owners by, like, a lot."

Row upon row of cages and carriers, sometimes stacked two high, lined the concrete floors of the converted warehouse. They were filled with dogs and cats, young and old. There was even a row of bird cages, turtle-filled kiddie pools, and aquariums containing all manner of creature from angelfish to iguanas. The noise was unbearable. Meowing, yipping, and screeching. Notes reaching into frequencies that even Lizzie couldn't appreciate.

"And you're determined to stay no kill?" Lizzie couldn't fathom how they were going to find homes for a fraction of these animals.

"Yes," Jess replied, tight-lipped.

Lizzie didn't ask how they would manage once pet food started running out. The people of Provo were not going to give up their own resources to keep this project going. If things got tight, people might start looking at less pleasant protein alternatives.

"Mostly," Jess added as one of the assistants dragged a dog, fighting and growling, into the room with a muzzle tight on his face.

Jess turned away, biting her lip. "That was Gozer. I tried to settle him down. But after three days and this—" She pointed at a broad bandage. "He's too feral and we don't have the manpower or the time to do anything about it." She walked to the window, breathing steam onto the cold glass as Gozer was dragged outside.

Lizzie didn't want to know what happened next.

Jess sighed and turned away from the window. "Most of them warm up to humans pretty quick once they aren't lost and confused anymore."

There had been an uproar about straight up shooting pets. So now they all came through here, and the outraged people had already forgotten. Only Jess and her co-workers, Susan, a vet, and Jen, a former dental hygienist, were left to deal with the fallout. How could Jess wake up every morning to such hopelessness?

"But you can't keep them all here forever, like this."

"We have been trying to figure that out. Obviously we are doing a lot of wholesale neutering, it's like a testicle snipping factory in here most days. Susan taught Jen and I how to do it, it's surprisingly easy. Sometimes we get into competitions to see who can do it the fastest." She laughed with a touch of hysteria. "Tomorrow is our first day of adoptions, but we haven't really had time to get the word out. We have an idea to turn some old dog parks into sanctuaries. I just need to talk to Mannie about building shelters in them and shoring up fences. That is, if he is still in charge of parks."

"I'm not sure; maybe."

Jess dragged a hand through her hair and puffed an exhausted sigh. "I'd hate to have to start all over, dealing with someone new."

Alfred bumped up against Lizzie's leg and she scratched his ruff. The fuzzy cat had been there from the beginning and Jess let him wander around when she was on duty. "Nev would be the one to ask about that. Dad's duties just got a lot more complicated. She's his assistant now, trying to subjugate his job to her organization."

"I would rather talk to him about it personally, but he's been kind of difficult to approach lately."

Lizzie wasn't exactly sure what had happened between Jess and her dad on the road. She didn't want to think anything bad of her father, but there was definitely something awkward hanging between them. Whatever it was, they better deal with it. There were already too many fractures appearing in Lizzie's extended family.

A buzzer rang, sounding more like an alarm, signaling the arrival of another truckload. Hopefully people would be ready to adopt tomorrow.

Chapter Fifteen

MANNIE STARED GROGGILY ACROSS THE snow. He extricated his phones from inside three layers to check for messages. A text from Lizzie flashed on the spy phone. **Let Glen know what ur doing.**

Mannie hated texting, especially with cold hands. **I will. Thanks.** His knee screamed at him for relief from spending too much time in the same position. He popped a few IBs and stretched it out.

He needed to get better clothing if he was going to spend days out in this weather. Some real military gear would be nice and maybe a knee brace. The Militia recruits could probably use the same—minus the brace. That was his job now, if it was anybody's. His job seemed to have morphed into if-we-need-something-ask-Mannie. What other supplies should he be on the lookout for? Hot coffee sounded like heaven. Maybe a mocha.

He pulled his hood up and tightened the drawstring. With regret he shoved Rubi's door open. The cold wind blew in, even more chilling than earlier.

This weather was shit for spy work. For anything, really.

Mannie tromped through knee high snow in the cold darkness on the outskirts of Camp Williams. He'd need to be careful once he got near the street lights.

"Put your hands on the top of your head." Something hard pressed into his spine.

Mannie put his hands on top of his head, cold dread prickling his flesh where the gun barrel rested.

His adversary lifted his hand-gun from its holster, and patted him down.

"Now, turn around really easy."

Mannie turned and faced a short woman clad in gray and white military garb with an automatic weapon. He could barely make out the eyes inside the goggles, her voice was his only real clue of her gender.

"We're going to walk slowly and carefully forward. If you make a move, so help me, I will shoot. I'll be aiming for your knee, but—just so you know—I didn't get a medal for marksmanship."

Some spy he'd turned out to be. "I hope you're taking me someplace warm."

"Cute. Now, walk." She gestured with her weapon, and spoke into her comm. "This is Jefferson. I got a prowler."

A scratchy voice answer, "Roger."

"That building, there."

They walked until they reached a building. The snow had been scraped neatly away from the entrance.

"Open the door and step inside," Jefferson ordered.

Inside was definitely a mess hall. They were met by a young man in fatigues. Another gun and shaky hands. Mannie remembered being that young and that nervous; he raised his hands quickly.

"Welcome to Camp Williams," Jefferson said, pushing him forward. "Get out of the damn door, Hernandez, I want in out of the cold."

Hernandez moved aside, but his gun stayed pointed at Mannie's chest.

Mannie didn't want to be fighting the good guys. Not that the folks from the City were bad.

"I'm not the enemy, guys," Mannie said, keeping his hands high.

"Hernandez, point your weapon down, until you're ready to use it. Don't need anybody going off half-cocked."

Hernandez sheepishly lowered his rifle.

"So why did I catch you skulking around our perimeter?" Jefferson pulled off her helmet and shook her head; dark braids fell down, not quite the typical military standard. "Where's the Captain?" she demanded from Hernandez.

"I think he's sleeping?"

"Then wake him up!"

Hernandez disappeared through two swinging doors.

"You want to sit?" Jefferson offered, motioning to a seat with her rifle.

He remained standing but lowered his hands, keeping them in front of him and visible.

Her eyes swept over him like he was an alien.

A few tense minutes later the swinging doors burst open. A young man with a scraggly beard and captain bars stormed in. If this was their captain, it had to be an in-field promotion.

He sized Mannie up and then jerked his thumb toward the door without a word.

Jefferson prompted Mannie with her gun. They entered an office and this time Jefferson forced him to sit in a chair facing the desk. The Captain took the other side, his chair scraped the floor as he shifted. The bags under his eyes indicated that the sleep he'd been woken from was probably the only rest he'd had in some time.

"I am Captain Pierce of the United States Army—"

"You're a captain?" Mannie interjected, lacing his tone with incredulity to keep his adversary off balance. A good interrogation depended on who was in control.

"Why are you out there spying on us?" Captain Pierce blurted, face red.

"Trying to figure out who you are. What you're trying to do."

"We're the fucking U.S. Army, dipshit. We're protecting national resources for the government."

"Which government?"

"The only one. The one that gave us orders back in October to keep this area safe, out of enemy hands."

"What enemy?"

"Shut the fuck up. I am doing the interrogating."

Mannie gave the captain the genial smile of a man who'd meant no harm.

"Any enemy. You for example. You and your friends."

The captain was tightly wound, so were his soldiers—even Jefferson was picking at her fingernails from nerves. Had they been doing alternating guard shifts with a skeleton crew of survivors and no sign of relief for three months? "Well, I'm not your enemy. The people I currently work for, well, who knows what's in their heads these days. Things certainly have gone to hell in a hand-basket since October."

"Tell me exactly what you are doing, if you ever want to see daylight again."

"Look, have you made contact with the folks out at Dugway? You seem to be in need of a little support."

"Dugway?" Pierce's face flickered with a lost, helpless expression.

"Dugway Proving Ground. In the desert. A U.S. Army research facility." Pierce motioned for him to go on and Mannie continued, "If you don't mind my saying, Captain, you look like you could use some reinforcements."

"No shit." Pierce slammed his palm down on the wooden desk. "My people here haven't had a break in months. They need some time off and some other human beings they're not sick of."

Mannie knew that feeling from his time in the desert. You had to rely on your squad to not get killed, but sometimes you wanted to kill them. He explained what he'd learned about Dugway and San Antonio. He found himself trying to cheer up the dejected young Captain, suggesting that they should work together with the crew at Dugway. Pierce perked up at the suggestion of a partnership with Jones and his people at Dugway.

His interrogation faded into a helpful consultation and finally into a plan. Pierce would call Jones and set up an exchange. They could cross-train the soldiers, so there would be at least a break in routine.

Mannie glanced at the clock. 1500 hours. "If I don't report back, there may be a string of dominoes falling that I can't stop."

Fear and frustration battled in Pierce's face. "You're free to go."

Mannie stood to leave, and Pierce stuck out his hand. "Thanks for the help, sir."

"Take care of yourself as well as your people, or you won't be much good to them."

Pierce let a long breath out, totally deflated from the puffed-up young man who had stormed in all brash and bluster.

Lizzie's head pounded. The stupid birthing class teacher drove her as crazy in her own way as the other pregnant girls did. Margent never gave her a break, every time Lizzie did something that seem to surprise and please her, she came down twice as hard the next time Lizzie mouthed off.

She headed for home, wrapping the scarf around her neck. At least Betsy had been there today. Having someone to share eye-rolls with helped. She'd even shown Betsy her drawings.

Duke stood under the street light, watching the snowflakes coming down. "Fancy meeting you here."

"Can I walk you home?" he asked.

"You are certainly persistent. Are those 'do it for your country' posters starting to get to little Duke?" she said, not sure how to handle him other than with insults and humiliation. "You know you're supposed to 'do it' with a girl who's not already pregnant, right?"

"Look, I don't want to be that guy! If you want to just be friends, I'm cool with that." His smile flattened.

"Ouch. That sets up all sorts of problems, don't you think?" She laughed. "You think we can just be friends?"

"I dunno. Problems can be solved."

"You can walk me to the day care," Lizzie hooked her hand in the crook of his arm. She liked Duke, but she wasn't all about hooking up with him. Maybe it was because things had gotten so complicated. "We'll see how things go until then."

"Sounds fair to me. Keep me around as long as I amuse you."

"Oh, I like that. The Queen's jester."

Duke bowed down. "As you wish."

"Hey, be careful what you say." Lizzie's cheeks warmed.

"I always am, milady." He patted her hand. "It's cold out here and as much as I'd like to be with you anywhere, it would probably be a good idea to keep moving."

"Lead on, MacDuke."

"How are the classes?"

"I am sick and tired of squealing voices. I swear every one of those girls was a cheerleader."

"Hey, I was a cheerleader."

Lizzie laughed out loud, tasting snowflakes as she closed her mouth. "You're shittin' me."

"Nope. Thought maybe if I hung around with girls I'd get over my awkwardness."

"Did it work?"

"Not really." He chuckled. "Believe it or not, I was really shy. And a bit shorter than I am now. Well, a lot shorter. But I was strong and had good balance."

"And the girls weren't all over you?"

"If I had a dollar for every time someone told me they thought of me as a brother..." Duke shook his head. "Sheesh. I got slapped the time I responded with, 'Then incest is best.'"

Lizzie grinned and punched him. "You definitely deserved it."

"Yeah." He offered her a pained smile. "I was desperate."

"Some things never change."

"Ouch."

"Okay, I'll let you walk Saj and I home; you can cheer us on through this miserable snow." She wondered if she could get Glen to find a picture of a cheerleader to paste Duke's face on.

"Thanks. Beat me up physically, then with words and then you offer me a reward."

"Carrot and stick." She leaned into him for warmth and his hand slid down her back, a little too close to her butt for comfort. She jerked away. "Whoa, hoss. Probably better back off."

Lizzie blushed at her reaction and tried to hide her face in the layers of her coat. She hadn't meant to give him the wrong idea, or had she?

"So—question. Does anyone ever know where they stand with you?"

Lizzie stopped pulling him up short. "Do you really want to know? No. Trust me, you don't want to scratch my surface." She grasped his arm, trying to drag him along. "Hell, I don't where how anyone stands with me."

"Well maybe I do," Duke said, refusing to budge.

"I don't think so," Lizzie whispered under her steamy breath. "Come on before we freeze. The daycare is right there at the end of the block, and Saj is waiting."

He relented and let her pull him down the sidewalk.

"You ever feel like the folks here in the Shitty are too paranoid?" she asked, changing the subject.

"You're asking me? I think they're prepared. It's why Provo is doing so much better than anywhere else we've been."

"Guess you're right." Lizzie sighed. "How is it? Collecting?"

Duke's gaze went outward across the city. "It started out pretty cool. But finding the bodies got old really quick. And the weirdness of going into someone's house like we were shopping the apocalypse. Makes Black Friday in the old days seem human. It's why I joined the militia. Now I'm glad to get to hunt. Alone."

Lizzie wished she could go explore. "I loved scavenging, back in Bellingham. Rifling through a person's drawers, seeing what they left behind, what they considered important. What's in that old cottage there, that you Collectors didn't bother with?"

"Lizzie," Duke's voice warned, "you're not going into that house."

"Fine." She gave a pout face and stuck her tongue out. "I know I am supposed to feel sad the people died, but it was kind of like being an archeologist, digging up the remains of a civilization. Plus saving the animals was totally my thing."

"I found a house with a giant Koi pond inside. I guess fish don't need as much food as dogs and cats. They were the first live things I found other than flies." He glanced sideways at her. "Let's talk about something more fun."

"How about music and lyrics? Give me your top five songs of all time." Walking and talking, even about the mundane things felt comfortable. She swung their hands back and forth like they were little kids, cleared her throat and sang. "Here we are, no one else, walked to school all by ourselves."

"Hhmmm… We are gonna be friends." Duke scooped her arm and used the swinging to pull her closer. "Your voice is pretty. You have a list all ready? It's going to take me a while."

"You don't have a list ready to go?" Lizzie put on a shocked expression. She scooted out of his embrace and swung his arm back into a walking rhythm.

"For the next time a cute girl asks me? I must have skimmed over that part of the rule book."

"So I'm cute now?"

He opened his mouth and then closed it.

"For me? Springsteen - Jungleland. Melissa Etheridge - Bring Me Some Water. Collective Soul - December. Nirvana - About a Girl. Petty - Dogs on the Run."

"You don't like much from this century, do you? Cool list. Never heard of the Petty song."

"Yeah. Hardly anybody has. 'Funny how a crowd gathers around anyone living life without a net.'"

"Nice line. I guess all the nets are gone."

Lizzie pull his arm across her body. "Not as many arms to catch you when you fall anymore." For a moment she wanted to freeze time with his arm around her.

"I'll catch you." He wrapped his other arm around her.

Lizzie rolled her eyes. "You're sure you're not the one who needs catching?"

"I'm not falling." He glanced over at her and then his eyes twisted and crinkled up at the corners. "Well, maybe I am. Come on. Don't pick up Saj yet." His face came toward hers.

She could let him hold her, caress her. "Nope."

"You don't have to pick him up?" Duke's excitement grew and he pulled her in closer.

"No. Nope, not going there. Yeah, gotta pick him up now. Sorry."

She pushed him back to arm's length and pulled him forward along the sidewalk. When they reached the brightly illuminated daycare, she let go of his arm. Behind the glass-front children ran, throwing, kicking and riding an assortment of 2-and-up safe toys. Their mouths were open in screams made silent by the glass walls. "You want to come in?" This ought to scare him off.

Duke's eyes widened, but the smile remained on his face. "Sure." He pulled the door open for her. "After you, milady."

Lizzie rolled her eyes at him as she stepped into the warmth of the building. Chaos hit her ears. She tripped on a toy—toddler safe, not grown up safe. Saj broke off and toddled toward the door with a wide grin. She knelt down to his height.

"SISSIE." He howled as he barreled into her, knocking her backwards into Duke. She scooped him up.

"Hey, Saj," Duke rumpled his hair.

"Juke," Saj smiled.

"Yup." Lizzie offered Duke her hand and he helped them stand. "Juke's going to walk us home. Where's Rachael? Give her hugs."

"Rachael go home." Saj explained.

One of the other workers handed Lizzie the sign out sheet. "She's started getting out early." The girl said it as if there was some significance Lizzie should pick up.

Lizzie shrugged at Duke. "Okay. Saj, let's get you bundled up, and we can go home."

With Saj bundled they walked outside into the cold. Lizzie held Saj's hand and Duke walked on the other side.

"One, two, free?" Saj begged.

Duke glanced at her quizzically.

"Grab his hand." She pulled her glove off her left hand and tugged Saj's mittens off and into her pocket. "He wants to fly."

Saj's little body strained to jump up and down. His muscles flexed and his body shook without leaving the earth.

Lizzie snickered. "Wait." She stood and gripped Saj's little hand tight. "Okay, we walk first. We say, 'One, two, three,' then we swing him up. "

"Got it."

They walked along with Lizzie showing Duke how to swing his arms. "Ready? One, two, three!" They both swung Saj up into the air; he squealed with glee.

Saj took a few more steps. "ONE, TWO, FREE."

They spun him upwards again before letting him swing back

down to the ground.

"ONE, TWO, FREE," Saj demanded.

"Wait," Lizzie blurted. "Slow down." She was getting a winded. "This time you've gotta say, Uno, dos, tres, Saj."

His lips tightened and he nodded. "OOnooo, dos, tres," he hollered, giggling as he flew up into the air.

"Catorce," Duke finished, giving her a goofy grin.

"Don't teach him wrong!"

"It's U2. Vertigo."

"Duh."

"That's on my top five list. Call it number, uh, *cuatro*."

"*Unoooo,*" Saj started.

"*Dos, tres,*" all three of them said together.

By the time they reached her house, Lizzie's arm ached, but Saj's flushed face and Duke's rosy cheeks made it all worth it. "You want to come in?"

Duke stopped at the door and leaned against the far side of the door jamb. "Yeah. I do. But I don't think I will. Can we have a date?"

"A date? What decade is this? What century?"

He stood there, looking at her with puppy dog eyes that kind of reminded her of Spike.

Did she like him enough for a date? She had fun with him around. Against her better judgement she relented. "Okay, you can have a date. What and when?" Maybe she could try out being normal.

Chapter Sixteen

LIZZIE THREW THE CLOTHES IN her hands at her image in the mirror. She had kept Duke at bay for a month. First the excuse of being wounded. Then the pregnancy…

And now he was on his way over. For a date. "Fuck." What should she wear? None of her clothes felt right—or fit right—and he was gonna be here any minute. All her jeans were too tight and her collection of baggy t-shirts suddenly looked like tents.

She opened up the duffle from Bellingham. The black skirt, super flexible around the baby bump, and practically the only thing she'd wear that wasn't pants. She pulled it on and looked in the mirror. Maybe too dressy for a first date?

Dammit, this is what Nev was good at.

Lizzie stepped into Doc Martin's for the full effect. She examined her belly in the mirror. Were her boobs already getting bigger? They were kind of spilling over her bra a little. Exactly what I don't need.

Shirt. She pulled on a flouncy thing that Nev had given her. It showed a little more skin than Lizzie was used to, but it minimized her chest. She stared at herself. It was all much too girlie. She didn't want to give Duke the impression that she had dressed up for him. This whole thing was a bad idea. She almost took the whole ensemble off, but not even she could wear sweats on a date.

She glared at her hair in the mirror, seeing the frazzled ends, a blend of platinum and purple, contrasting horribly with her dark roots. It desperately needed a trim. Why did she wait till the last minute?

She pulled it back and stuck out her tongue. It made her look severe. She bent over and shook her hair out, ran her fingers through it. It would have to do. She needed to get away from the mirror before she turned into a narcissistic fuck—she slammed the bedroom door behind her and went to the kitchen for a drink. The apartment layout was decent and the location was handy, but the walls were paper thin. She'd heard the neighbors going at it at least a dozen times. Maybe she should hook up with Duke as revenge. Scream really loud.

She glanced at the clock, chugging her diet coke. She spread her fingers in front of her. Should have done something with the nails. What the hell am I turning into?

She forced herself to stop drinking the coke—she didn't want to have to pee an embarrassing number of times tonight. She put a spoon, handle down, into the can and put it in the fridge. An old trick Mama used to keep drinks fizzy till later, which inevitably led to drinking flat pop. But she didn't want to waste it.

A knock sounded on the door.

"Coming," she called. Hoping her voice sounded relaxed. She paused at the door—her hand on the knob. She pulled back the duct tape over the peephole. Duke. Glancing sideways. She jerked the door opened before she could change her mind.

His eyes traveled from her head to feet and then back again. "Hi."

He had either not gone to as much trouble or had decided to look like he hadn't. She turned to hide her flushing cheeks. "Hi. Come in."

He brushed passed her. Her embarrassment turned to smugness as she smelled cologne.

"You don't seem happy to see me."

Lizzie kept her lips in a straight line. "What if I'm not?"

"Well. Then we go for a walk and pretend we're interested until somebody gets brave and calls the whole thing off."

"Oh." Lizzie closed the door behind him, wondering if the neighbors could hear she had a 'gentleman caller.' "Can I get you something? We've got Coke. Classic and Diet? Water and… well. I could make you tea or coffee or…" her voice fell away. "Is this how you usually do the dating thing?"

"I pretty much suck at the dating thing." He turned to the window and stared at the city like the scenery was interesting. "Coke is fine."

"Great." Lizzie breathed as she escaped to the kitchen. She pulled the Coke out. None of her cups were clean and her ice cube trays were empty. "Just the can okay?"

"Sure."

Lizzie came back into the living room to find Duke perched awkwardly on the arm of the couch. "This is stupid."

"What?" His face fell.

She popped the top on the Coke and handed it to him. "Look. You were over here a few days ago. You sat on the couch. We ate food."

"Yeah. Saj was here."

"Yeah. He was. And you were chill."

"So were you."

"Let's get back to there." She held his gaze. "I'm gonna change and we can just go out. Not 'go out,' but go outside." She spun and walked down the hall.

"You look good in the skirt."

Lizzie paused.

"I don't think I've seen you wear a skirt before."

She turned back to him. "You haven't. Give me shit about it and you never will again."

He held up his hands in defense. "Whoa."

"Sorry." She twisted her skirt, trying to get it to fit right. "Feels weird."

He gestured toward the bedroom. "Change if you want. I don't want you to be uncomfortable. But it does look good—I like it."

She tugged him to his feet. "Let's go." She grabbed a winter jacket off the hook by the door. Throwing it around her shoulders relieved her feeling of nakedness.

"Where do you want to go?" he asked once they were outside.

"You don't have a plan?"

"Told you I'm not good at this dating thing."

"Show me your place?" She instantly regretted saying it. Definitely too slutty for a first date.

"Bachelor's barracks number 12?"

"Sounds pretty horrible."

"It isn't as horrible as it sounds, but let's not go there, okay?"

"Okay," Lizzie agreed, relieved.

They walked. And talked.

"Tell me about your family."

"Ugh, really?" Duke asked.

Lizzie pulled his arm over her shoulder. "Just to keep me warm," she said. "And yes, really."

Duke glanced down at her as if he was trying to see what she was really thinking. "Mom died when I was nine. C.J., my brother, you met him in Bellingham, was five."

She grimaced.

He continued. "Until then, Dad was a pretty reasonable man. But as the cancer took my mom, he dove headfirst into the bottle."

"Sorry."

"It is what is." He continued to look far away. "You don't always realize how bad it is until you're looking back."

"Yeah." Lizzie shifted against him. She looked at him sidelong, trying to decide why she liked him. *He has a cute butt. He was fun to hang out with. And the fact that he found her attractive was what made him kinda hot. Sheesh, Lizzie. She was probably over-thinking it. Did other people go through this or was it just her. Did everyone else just know who they wanted? God, she missed this kind of talk with Nev. Maybe Jess or Rachael could help.*

No, not Rachael. The memory of Rachael's body pressing against her in the hospital made her warm. Hot. Damn. Duke was talking and she wasn't listening. What kind of loser am I? He's baring his soul to me and I'm comparing his butt to hers? She shook her head and focused back on Duke's face. He squeezed her shoulder; it felt nice.

"You ever want to be a father?"

"Maybe. I don't know."

"Having kids on purpose right now seems a little crazy. I mean, I get the whole breeder thing, but we don't really know…" She put her hand on her belly.

"Yeah. I know."

Lizzie wished she hadn't brought up the subject of family. "Did you ever make a bucket list?"

"Well. Kind of. Had a teacher that made me write down 50 goals. Said they didn't have to be real, but the idea was to think of things that would need some time. Some were easy, some difficult, some were even impossible."

"Like what?"

"Well, I wanted to go into space."

"Wasn't that impossible. Might be now."

"To have sex."

Lizzie giggled as a vision of Duke floating toward her in a space suit without pants. "Wow. Weightless? You could have done one of those planes."

"Yeah, but that would be like having sex in public."

"What else?"

"I wanted a Lamborghini Diablo."

"Guys and their cars."

"You didn't ever want a car?"

"Not really. My first driving experiences were not very good. Cars kind of represent stress to me. Besides, I'm one of those hippie dippie environmental types."

"A Greenie? You?"

In Seventh Grade my therapist wanted me to channel my anger into something. I made posters. Went to rallies. Even got in a kayak the next year for the protest against arctic oil drilling."

"Then what happened?"

"Shit happened. High school. Sex, drugs, rock and roll." She hesitated, then peeled back her sleeve to show him her scars. Duke must have noticed them before, but he'd never said anything. "I got lost trying to figure out how to control the pain." She took a deep breath and stopped walking. "My therapist didn't know shit. My problem wasn't anger, it was pain. Too much. Not enough. Whatever the fuck. Out of my control. This gave me a way to control it."

"I'm sorry." Duke pulled her into a hug.

Lizzie breathed deep clamping down on the emotions. She kissed him. He kissed her back. Then she pushed him gently away.

"What's wrong, Lizzie?" Duke asked, holding the edge of her sleeve. "Trust me?"

"I do trust you," Lizzie said sadly, "But I don't trust me." She perked herself up. "Hey, tell me about your cars."

"I had a crappy old Datsun pickup. Dad's old work truck. He kept it running with duct tape, bailing wire and old Coke cans."

"But it ran."

"Yeah, it ran. For me that was freedom. The best present he ever gave me. As soon as I could drive without an adult, I could get away."

"You know how to hot-wire a car?"

"Not like in the movies? It's either easier, or practically impossible. Gotta find the right car. Why do you want to know?"

"If I need to leave, need to get somewhere…"

"Seems like a pretty requisite end of the world skill. I'll teach you what I know."

Mannie arrived home, the lights were on inside, but low. Lizzie had probably come over and fallen asleep. What was he going to do about her restlessness? What could he do? He knew she couldn't stand being cooped up and ordered what to do, but until spring came this really was the safest place for them to be. He turned the knob. "I'm home," he called softly.

"In here." The sound of a movie reverberated in the living room. It sounded like she was watching Stripes. The way Lizzie had enshrined his late 90s musical and video tastes warmed him and confused him. It gave them something in common, but it also felt weird, like his ancient tastes in media defined him.

He hung up his coat and tossed his hat on the rack. He sat and slipped out of his boots. He slid his feet into slippers and shuffled into the kitchen. He grabbed a Classic Coke from the counter. He walked into the living room and collapsed into the recliner. "How's your day, Lizzie?"

"Lizzie went out with Duke," Jess said, turning toward him. "Said she'd probably stop by tonight."

"Oh." Mannie's nerves returned to full awareness. "Thought you were Lizzie."

"I figured." Jess pointed the remote at the TV and hit pause. "I wanted to talk to you about something work related. You've been so busy lately, I had no idea how to catch you otherwise—and how could I resist your movie collection. Want to watch it with me?"

"All you have to do is make an appointment with Nev. Sometime during the day."

"Sorry, I can leave." She started to stand.

Maybe he was being too harsh. "Well, you're here already. No sense going out into the snow before you finish your movie."

"You sure?"

"Yeah. Fair warning though. I'm fried from work, I'll probably fall asleep." He sat down in the other recliner, finally relaxing after his long stressful mission. He had to admit it felt good not to come home to an empty house. He's gotten along great with Jess before things became complicated. And Lizzie would probably be here in a bit anyway. He liked hanging out and watching Lizzie enjoying having friends around.

"Okey, Dokey." She wrapped her arms around the big pillow, flicked the remote and returned her gaze to the television.

Despite his exhaustion Jess' explosive laughter didn't let him sleep. He'd had dreams where a situation like this ended with Jess pressing against him and tearing his clothes off. Having her here was not a good idea.

""Jess?" he asked, his voice cracking.

"Yeah?"

"Can we talk?"

"Of course, Mannie."

"I mean, really talk."

"I'd like that." Jess picked up the remote and flipped the television off. She turned to him, a shy smile on her face.

The room, silent with anticipation, made Mannie stumble. "I can't. Jess. It's not good for me to hang around you."

Her smile faded to a sadness. "Mannie, I know you think you can't. I know you've got twice as many years of experience, and you think I'm too young. But, I'm no kid. I'm older than Lizzie and lived through a tragedy that's taught me some hard lessons." She caught his eye, then glanced down shyly. "Then you came and rescued me. It's some kind of Nightingale syndrome probably, but that doesn't mean it's wrong."

"I didn't rescue you, Jess. You rescued yourself."

"Okay. Maybe that's true. Even then. I fell in love with you."

Mannie shifted, uncomfortably.

'I've tried as hard as I could not to, when it became clear what your feelings were, but I can't—damn your antiquated sense of morality! Life is short." Her eyes burned and her voice became husky, "I want you."

Damn, this was going to turn into one of those dreams. He got up and used the empty Coke can as an excuse to walk toward the kitchen.

When he came back her cheeks were flushed a pretty pink, and her flashing eyes locked with his again. "But if you don't want to—or can't, I won't push you anymore."

Shit. Mannie realized she was waiting for an answer from him. He wished to God he had let her talk to him about work, or let her leave when she had offered. He did want her, but too much chatter bounced around his skull. Better to be alone. He shook his head. "I can't and I don't want to. Sorry."

Tears spilled out her eyes. "Okay."

Mannie sat with his hands in his lap as she stood up and made her way to the front door.

She paused with her hand on her coat. "But I think you're being stupid. This is a new world, a scary world. Life won't be easy, finding happiness won't be easy. Don't throw away too many good chances." Then in a business-like voice with only a hint of the hurt, she said, "I'll make an appointment with Nev."

Mannie nodded. His eyes strayed to her jeans and her slender waist. She zipped into her coat, zipped it up and wrapped a scarf around her neck. Then she shut the door gently behind her.

"Well, that went well." He felt like he'd killed one of her puppies. It was better this way. She needed to find someone who wouldn't look at her like she was sin.

He reached in the fridge for another Coke and tipped it back, wishing it had more of a burn.

He looked toward the door to the basement where he kept his stash. She needed someone who wasn't a no good, washed out, old drunk.

Chapter Seventeen

LIZZIE ZONED OUT AT THE television on the wall of her apartment. The screen showed a fake Salt Lake City skyline and the title. Provo News. Next on Channel 11. She absentmindedly ate Saj's applesauce dessert as the weatherman came on.

Saj whined, "Uh uh." His goopy hands reaching for the food.

She jerked the spoon from her lips. "Sorry, Sebastian. Use your words, please."

"Mo', p'ease?" Saj prodded, making the please sign on his chest.

Lizzie spooned a scoop into his mouth, cleaning off the half spoonful around his lips. "Thanks."

The date with Duke had been a real comedy of errors. Pleasant chit chat in between flirting. Comedy, but not too painful.

He had left her at the door with a quick peck on the cheek, while she stood there bemused, only realizing after he had gone that she hadn't said good night or thanked him.

The weather man said, "Good night." The camera stayed focused on his smiling face as he awkwardly waited for it to fade to black and free him. He made a cut sign with his hand across his neck and a commercial about electrical consumption cut in. Then a cheesy Special Bulletin graphic flashed on the screen. **NEW MAYOR ANNOUNCES TRAVEL PROCLAMATION.** The camera switched to the council chambers and a view of the counselors huddled in a group with their backs to the camera. The screen flipped to an empty office and the camera panned across pleasant rose-brown furniture, bookcases and then focused in on the new mayor and Mr. DiSilvio. DiSilvio was speaking to Mr. Ray, but no sound came through.

A muffled voice said, "We're live."

DiSilvio's face beamed at the television audience. Mr. Ray glanced at the camera, looking startled. A person in black clothes with a headset guided him toward a comfy chair in the center of the screen. He stared out at his people over the airwaves like a friendly grandfather, taking a drink from the glass of water on the table beside him. "Good evening, my friends."

He appeared more weary than he had the last time she'd seen him.

"I had the idea of doing a fireside chat to address you, the people of our fair city. I had hoped my first message would be a comforting one, but our concern over the safety of our most delicate citizens has caused us to make a new proclamation."

He pulled out his reading glasses and placed them on his nose. "Our Council has voted 21 to 4 in support of this new ruling. Proclamation. The Provisional Utah Government. These United States. In light of recent events, the incursion of cougars and the proximity of renegade bands calling themselves Independents. And with the intent of keeping our people safe, travel restrictions have been reinstated. No one under the age of 18 will be allowed to leave Provo.

"Fuck." Had Lizzie hit the jackpot by passing her last birthday?

"In addition, no females of childbearing age will be allowed to leave. Newlyweds and approved pre-honeymoon trips to Salt Lake City will continue, but will require an escort under the protection of the Militia." Mr. Ray removed his glasses and rubbed the spot where they rested. "Thank you and good night."

Mr. Ray didn't look any happier than she felt as the screen faded to the Provo skyline at sunset.

"Fuck you and good night." She tossed the applesauce container at the screen. Saj howled.

"Shit. Sorry, Saj." She hurried to the fridge and peeled the lid off another container and set it and the spoon in front of him.

She flipped her phone on and called Duke. "Can you come over here now?" Saj's howl reduced to a sob.

"Yeah. Take me about 15 minutes."

She sat back down by Saj, sighed and kissed his head. "Sorry, Saj. Sissie's a little stressed."

"Sissie mad," Saj said, his face set in a serious look.

Lizzie's pissy mood cracked at his baby face attempting to be an adult. "Sissie mad. But not at Saj." Rachael did it so much better. She switched out of baby talk. "Honey, I'm not mad at you. Those men made me really mad."

"Okay." Saj slopped most of a spoonful of applesauce into his mouth. A similar amount fell onto the highchair tray.

Lizzie wiped it up with her finger. The description of the proclamation overlay the view of the Salt Lake City skyline. She shut it off. She stomped over to the TV and cleaned up the applesauce with a burp rag.

Saj was falling asleep in the high chair; she extricated him from the seat and lay him on her bed.

By the time Duke's knock came at the door, she felt less like murdering someone. Lucky for him.

"What's up, Lizzie?" Duke said, as she let him in.

Lizzie felt her temper and heat climbing back up. "You haven't heard?" Her voice sounded like mother in a bitchy mood.

His brow creased. Then a light went on. "Oh. The proclamation."

"First guess. Congratulations." She took a deep breath and tried to speak more softly. "Next thing you know I won't be able to walk outside without a male companion. Fucking Neanderthal society."

"I'd be happy to be your escort, milady." He offered her his arm.

"Fuck you, Sir Duke." She strode to the kitchen. She wanted a smoke or a drink and instead settled for some mildly freezer-burned ice cream. "Sorry." She dug a big soup spoon into the chunky chocolate. "Why are we here? Why don't we just leave?"

Duke studied her. "Not exactly a good time for travel. Middle of winter? North we got the birthers, The Brotherhood of Light. Desert to the south. West? You ever heard of the Donner party?"

"The cannibals?" She offered him a bite.

He waved off the spoon. "After the desert, you've got Donner Pass. I know it sucks, but until spring, I think we stay put." Duke opened his arms. "You want a hug?"

Lizzie set the ice cream down and moved toward him, letting his warmth envelope her. "Yeah. Thanks."

"I mean," Duke continued, "how bad can it get?"

Lizzie didn't want to answer that. She knew that the ground could still open up beneath her feet. "Please, don't say that," she whispered and held him tight. His heart pounded in her ear. He wasn't any calmer than she was, but he was faking it better. After a bit she pulled away from him.

"Thanks for coming."

"No problem, Lizzie."

He'd brushed his hair. Maybe it wasn't the proclamation that made his heart pound. *Damn.* How come she always missed those cues? "I'm sorry I had you run over here for nothing."

"It's not nothing if you're worried about it." He hopped onto the soft couch. "Sit down. We can talk."

"Okay." They settled in, one at each end and their feet in the middle. Lizzie put her feet up against his and pushed gently. "You really think it's nothing?"

"It's not nothing. But it's not like we have a lot of choices. I'll take you north in the spring if you still want to leave."

Lizzie ran her foot across his leg and then jerked it back when she thought about how he would interpret it. She pulled herself to cross-legged, the sitting style her body preferred since the baby started pooching. Duke's eyes fell to her stomach. She realized her hand was cradling her belly. She moved it aside self-consciously. "Still not used to it being there."

"May I?" Duke leaned forward.

"If you want to."

He reached tentatively.

"Go ahead already." She relaxed her stomach muscles as his warm hand made contact. She let her eyes close. His second hand joined the first. "Not really kicking yet."

"Got a name?" He poked gently with his finger.

Lizzie squirmed and giggled. "Hey, that tickled. I call her, Carry. Cause I'm carrying her. Or him. I guess Cary's a boy's name, too."

"You think she's a girl?"

"How should I know?" Her belly itched under his hand. She pulled her shirt up and his hands shot away as she scratched.

"Sorry."

"Not your fault. They say it'll itch like crazy sometimes, right now it just tickles." She took his hand and placed it back.

Duke leaned forward. "Are you a boy or a girl? Hey, you in there? Whatcha got worth livin' for?"

"Are you quoting Princess Bride?"

"I found a DVD when I was collecting. I'll have to take you by the house. There's like a million movies." He slid to his knees and moved closer.

"I could use some escape." Lizzie sat up. "Hey, you went and distracted me from what I was pissed off about."

"And that's bad?" Duke pulled her shirt back down over her belly.

A knock on the door echoed. Lizzie pulled aside the tape covering the peep hole. "It's Rachael." She opened the door.

"Thought you might want to talk," Rachael said. "Or get out a bit. I figured after the proclamation—" She saw Duke. "Uh… I see you have someone to talk to." Her eyes avoided looking at either Lizzie or Duke. "I'm here. You two want to go for a walk?"

Lizzie caught Duke's suggestive raised eyebrow and she clamped down on her answering smile. "Are you sure, Rach? Saj is already down. But I didn't get him ready for bed. He was falling asleep in the chair." She was chattering. Feeling guilty.

"Sometimes they go till they poop out. Lizzie, go. I can tell you're stressed." Rachael took Lizzie's coat off the easy chair and held it out for her. "Duke, take her away. I know she probably wants to scream or hit something."

Lizzie let Rachael slide her arms into the sleeves. "I'm that transparent?" Rachael spun her around and zipped it up. "I can dress myself."

Rachael nodded dutifully. "Yes, dear."

Duke laughed. "Let's go." He held the door for her. "Thanks, Rach."

Outside the night was cold, but not windy at least. "Maybe you can distract me again?" Lizzie said.

"I can try," Duke said. "Been thinking about the list. Decided Vertigo isn't my fave U2 song. It's either Stay Faraway, So Close or All I Want Is You." He sang the second song title.

"You can have more than one from an artist. I'm going to tell your secret to the world. Duke Madison is a schmaltzy loverboy! What else?"

"Nothin' yet."

"Oh." She wracked her brain for her favorite U2 song, but it kept going back to the proclamation. "Dammit."

"You wanna talk about-"

"No."

Duke took the full frontal hint and they walked in silence for a time, except for the racket in Lizzie's brain. Lizzie pulled her glove off, reaching for his hand.

Duke squeezed her fingers. "Your hands are this cold with gloves on?"

She didn't respond except to squeeze his hand back.

After walking a while he coughed gently.

"What?"

"This is where I live. Unmarried men's barracks."

Lizzie flicked a bit of rusty paint off the complex gate. "Looks like student housing."

"It was."

"And I can't go in there?"

"Why would you want to?"

"To see where you live."

"I'd have to sneak you in. It stinks in there. Nothing but sweaty young men. I don't even have my own bathroom. Probably should walk you back home. My truck's still there."

"And then?"

"Up to you."

Lizzie took his hand, kissing his palm—not really sure what she was doing or if she should be doing it.

"Just wanted to make sure," he said, his breath catching.

She leaned toward him on her tip toes, pulling his face toward her and kissing him aggressively on the lips. What am I doing? She pulled back. "No." Then she turned on her heel and headed for home.

"Wait," Duke called. "You don't trust me?"

Lizzie laughed and shook his head as she reached up and mussed his hair. "No, silly. I don't trust me. These hormones…"

Duke stared at her blankly and then she saw a realization hit him. "Oh." He glanced away. "Lizzie, you are different than every other girl I've ever met."

"Thanks." She grabbed his hand. "Come on. Just pretend I'm a boy."

"Not a chance."

Duke ran after her and slipped her hand back in his.

This is how it's supposed to be, Lizzie told herself.

But she walked through her front door to find a two-year-old bundle of tears trundling toward her. Saj wrapped his arms around her legs, whimpering.

Lizzie tousled his hair. "Sissie's home, Saj."

Rachael came up behind him, arms crossing her chest. "Sorry. He got scared when he woke up and you were gone. He won't let me hold him."

Duke knelt down. "Hey, Sajimon, what's wrong?"

Saj inched around Lizzie's legs, away from Duke.

"He just wants me," Lizzie whispered, bending over and pulling the crying boy into her arms. "He remembers I was unhappy." Sure enough when he was in her arms, he settled down.

"Well," Duke said, "I, um. Think I'll head back."

Lizzie laughed out loud. "I'm not sure who is pouting more. You or Saj."

Zach flexed in the mirror, rolling his stomach. He pulled on his new uniform. It fit well.

He would need to run across the campus to be on time. The door swung shut behind him as he hit the dewy grass. His legs pumped solidly. He'd been in pretty good shape before the pandemic. Since he'd joined the militia he'd pushed himself into prime shape. He could outrun Nev now.

He skidded to a stop and pushed the glass door open. His breath came in small puffs, but he wasn't winded. "What we got today, Lieutenant Simmons?"

His immediate supervisor glanced up from the video monitors at the clock.

Zach spun to look at it, too; he was on time, 8:00, exactly. "Sir!" He saluted. "Tomorrow, I'll be early."

Simmons picked up a clipboard. "Mr. Ray and Mr. DiSilvio are out inspecting the hydro plant out toward Sundance. You were supposed to be here an hour ago."

"Nobody called my phone, sir." Zach said, biting down on his complaint.

"Here." Simmons handed him a belt with holster and pistol inside —the standard police issue Glock 19.

Zach had trained on it, but didn't like the weight. He wanted something that didn't feel like a toy. He strapped it on anyway, pulled the pistol out and checked the clip.

"Go. Now." Simmons tossed Zach some keys. "Take the jeep. Relieve Reynolds. We'll sort this out later."

"Yes, sir." Zach saluted the Lieutenant, and shoved his way out the door. Simmons barely tolerated him. Zach had never given him a reason that he could think of, but it seemed personal.

Zach flipped on the spinning yellow caution light and set it on top of the jeep. He spun the wheel and gravel spewed as the heavy tires bit into the parking area.

He let up on the accelerator as he pulled off the main highway, and by the time he spun into the parking lot hiding Canyon Hills Drive and the entrance to the Olmsted Power Station, he had talked himself down.

Reynolds waved him in. "DiSilvio and Mr. Ray are walking around the grounds."

"And you're standing in the parking lot? We're supposed to be guarding them."

"From what? If you ask me, DiSilvio is paranoid."

"Because it's our job."

Reynolds snorted. "About as useless as half the jobs the Council's got us doing," he said, climbing into the Jeep.

Zach thought about warning Reynolds about Simmons being on a rampage today, but decided not to. Let him mess up his own assignment.

As the tires chirped the pavement, Zach jogged across the parking lot where Reynolds indicated Ray and DiSilvio were.

They were huddled close together in a grove of trees, talking animatedly. Their conversation got quieter and more tense as Zach approached.

This place was horrible for risk management. A cougar could come out of the woods here. There were plenty of places for Independents to hide if they wanted to kidnap Mr. Ray. "Don't you think you're kind of in the open out here?"

Mr. Ray grinned. "I'm not worried."

"Probably pretty safe." DiSilvio chuckled. "Since we don't have any idea what we're doing from day to day. Hard to set up an ambush."

"It's my job, sir." DiSilvio was partly right, the left hand didn't know what the right hand was doing. Crappy communication. That was why Simmons thought he was late. The whole provisional government ought to have some training and discipline. "I am supposed to keep you two safe. Can we at least go inside?"

Mr. Ray put his arm on Zach's shoulder. "There's nothing to worry about. We'll only be out here for a few minutes."

"Your job, Mr. Riley," DiSilvio spoke, his voice clipped, "is to follow orders."

"Yes, sir." He snapped to attention. If DiSilvio was going to throw the shit he was taking from Mr. Ray at him, he'd take it. "Your orders, sir?"

"Zach," Mr. Ray said more gently. "Go ahead and survey the area. Make certain we're safe."

"Yes, sir.

PART II

Touch Me Fall

Chapter Eighteen

LIZZIE PUSHED OPEN THE DOOR to her father's office. "Dad? Can I talk to you?"

"Of course, Elizabeth."

"I mean as a citizen."

"What can I do for you as-" Her father raised his eyebrows as he spun his desk topper around, "the new Provincial Utah Government Secretary of Resources?"

This Provo government was such a sham, but it was her father's job, so she bit her lip. Then the smirk on his face told her he thought the same thing. She let loose a laugh and he joined in. "How many people are in Provo?"

"Proper? Well, let's see. The last count says 47,734."

"Do they all have names?"

"I'm sure they do. Well, there was a baby born this morning. Might not have a name yet. That baby you're carrying…"

"But do we know the names of all the people alive in Provo?" Lizzie asked, as she sat in his comfy visitor's chair, "Is there a list?"

"I'm sure there are lists, Elizabeth. Maybe if you told me what this was about I could help you more."

Lizzie jerked back up to her feet. "When I ran away last time. I saw a body. It wasn't like the other bodies. Not a suicide. Hands all twisted." Lizzie tried to show him what she'd seen using her own body. "Somebody killed him and dumped his body."

Her father's eyes narrowed. "How do you know somebody

dumped the body?"

"Tracks in the snow, also no snowed on the body."

"Did you tell anyone?"

"I didn't want to report it. What if whoever did it found out?" She shook her head. She was sweating now. "But I can't get his face out of my mind. I keep drawing it."

"Do you have the drawings?"

"Yeah." Lizzie pulled her courier bag onto her lap and undid the fasteners. "What if someone is missing their husband? Their father? Or maybe the guy deserved to die. Maybe he was an abuser, a rapist… Shit. I don't know."

"I wonder if there is a Provincial Utah Government Secretary of Population. I doubt it. Maybe that lady who assigns jobs?" His forehead scrunched as he considered it.

"I don't want to see La Fever again!"

"I don't know if they deal with anybody but the newcomers. What we need is a real census."

Lizzie's brain spun with ideas. "Can I volunteer? It would get me out. Keep me moving like the childbirth classes say I'm supposed to."

"And you wouldn't have to be cooped up with a bunch of squealing pregos, right?"

"Did I say that?"

"No. You didn't have to." He drummed his fingers on his desk. "I think you'll have to ask LaFevbre or her boss. Anyone else you think would want to help—?"

"Who's her boss?"

"Mr. Ray now, maybe. Any of the other 'pregos' that might fit?"

Lizzie shook her head. "I don't think so." Could she stand working with them? They were so earnest. Such desire to procreate, to further the species. And most of them were Mormon to the core.

Lizzie never imagined she would be one of those door knockers. Government census was bad enough, but bringing one of her fellow students around with her—no way. There was a line she would not cross. But at last a useful job, and maybe one that would solve a murder, or at least give someone who was missing the dead man peace.

The silence in the library echoed the silence in Provo after the proclamation. A willing silence. Lizzie carried a small stack of books she had pulled off the shelves and settled into a hideous brown arm chair with frayed orange embroidery. It was comfortable at least. Lizzie wasn't much of a reader, but Betsy had messaged her to meet here and Lizzie thought it best to look like she was here for reading. Maybe seven books was overkill, though.

She sat down in a comfy chair with the stack of books that she'd found interesting. She wasn't sure she'd read any of them. Wuthering Heights lay on the top, a dark gothic book. Lizzie snorted out loud at the first line she read.

"Wretched inmates!" I ejaculated, mentally.

She covered her mouth and looked around, but nobody was anywhere near this section of the library. Wuthering Heights was not for her, she slid it to the side and picked up the next book. The Plague by Camus. She lost track of time as she read. Think what it must be for a dying man trapped behind hundreds of walls all sizzling with heat. Lizzie let her eyes fall closed.

Trapped behind hundreds of walls.

"Lizzie?"

Lizzie jerked upright. "Betsy."

"Find anything good?"

Lizzie held up the book. She pulled a hundred dollar bill her father had given her 'for emergencies' out of her purse and used it for a book mark.

"Ahhh…" Betsy smirked. "Believe it or not, I loved that book in high school."

"Really?"

"Yeah. Dark enough for you?"

Lizzie stuck out her tongue. "Maybe. But not yet. You want to go for a coffee or something?"

Betsy passed Lizzie a note. I'm leaving. Out of town. Not going to live in a place like this.

"Let me put these back." She scribbled an answer on Betsy's note. When?

Betsy shrugged.

Lizzie put everything but The Plague back and took it to the check out. The librarian gave her a knowing smile.

Outside, Betsy put her arm over Lizzie's shoulder and sighed. "I think you're the only person I'm going to miss."

"Don't know how I can stand the birthing classes without you."

"Get out."

"What?"

"Get out of them. Figure it out."

"I wish it was that easy."

"Just say bibbity, bobbity, boo!"

"Thanks, fairy godmother. Can you get me a prince, too?"

"Do you want a prince?" Betsy asked pointedly.

"Actually, I think I already found one."

"Funny, that's not really an answer to my question."

"Isn't it?" Lizzie's fingers twisted together. "I have a better question. Where will you go?"

For a moment Lizzie saw doubt and anxiety behind Betsy's tough exterior. "North Northwest."

"Stay away from Boise and Caldwell."

"Figured I'd go through Oregon, out to the coast. Your description of Bellingham and Seattle sounds pretty nice. Compared to this anyway."

"We're safe here." Lizzie heard the lie in her own voice. "What about your baby?"

"Safe from what?"

Lizzie didn't answer, if she waited would Betsy answer her question?

Betsy reached out to her. "You'll figure it out."

Lizzie hugged her friend. "I don't want you to go."

"Come with me.

"I want to, but..." She slid her finger across the GlenPhone screen and scanned down to Glen. "Take this number. When you get to Oregon. If you need anything, call Glen."

Betsy wrote it on book checkout paper and slipped it in her pocket. "Who's Glen?"

"A life saver most of the time." She blinked back tears. "And call me, too."

She should just go with Betsy. Leave. Rachael wouldn't mind. Not too much. Saj would. But he'd probably forget soon enough. "Take care of yourself."

Zeke's was busy today. People filled more than half the tables and a few were seated on the stools at the counter as well. Her stomach was growling as she smelled the burgers. Lizzie's stomach didn't remember that certain foods gave her pregnant body heartburn, but her brain did. Jess shoved through the door and bells jangled to announce her. She slid into the booth next to Lizzie. "You order?"

"Yup. Your fave—the *Messie Jessie*." She shoved the other pie-shake toward Jess. "So I can have some of your fries."

Jess grinned. "I take it you ordered something healthy?"

Lizzie nodded. "*The Today I'm Vegan*. As healthy as it gets here."

Jess played with her shake. "I got a weird question for you."

"Shoot."

"You won't judge me?"

"No," Lizzie laughed. "I will judge you. I'm human."

"Never mind." Her face glowed pink.

"Come on, Jess," Lizzie whined. "I'm a dick, okay? But don't leave me hanging. You tell me your secret and I'll tell you one."

"It's not really a secret." Jess blew a strand of hair out of her face. "Okay. Shit."

Lizzie's eyes widened at the sound of Jess swearing—about as common an occurrence as Halley's Comet. "Come on. Can't be that bad." Lizzie reached out and squeezed Jess' hand.

"Am I too young for your dad?" Her eyes zoned in on Lizzie.

"What?" Lizzie pulled her hands away. "You're kidding, right?"

Jess' face fell. "Stupid me. Shouldn't have said anything."

Lizzie's heart lurched. How to fix this? "Jess. I love you, 'kay?" She held out her hands for Jess' again. "I mean it's weird, but it's none of my business, really." Keep your face straight, Lizzie. But the picture of Jess and her dad together made it tough.

Jess kept her hands under the table.

"So are you my new step-mom?" Lizzie nudged her.

Finally, Jess cracked a smile and reached out for Lizzie's hands. "Sorry. I won't be the source of an endless running step-mom joke. I don't think your dad likes me back—at least he has made it pretty clear he doesn't want me around."

"You talked to him about it?"

Jess didn't respond.

"Wow." Lizzie pondered. Was it any different now that she knew they'd talked? Lizzie wasn't very good at kind interventions. "Think about this way. How long since you lost your family? We're all still in shock. My dad lost Isabel, the love of his life. Are you done mourning?"

"Maybe that's it." Jess wiped the tears from her cheeks.

Lizzie slid out of her side of the table and slid in next to Jess, holding her as she got composed. Jess returned the hug, clinging to Lizzie before letting her go.

"Thanks." Jess sucked on her shake. "I guess I have been coming on a little strong."

"Jess—ew!" Lizzie wrinkled her nose, but winked at Jess to let her know she was kidding. Mostly. "We're lucky. You and I. Most people hardly have anybody left from before the Quieting." She switched gears before she got started perseverating about her own dead. "I know. We'll find you a nice Mormon church boy."

But Jess didn't respond like Lizzie expected. Instead she got a faraway look in her eyes. "I do kinda miss church. When I was a kid, it always seemed like there was somebody looking out for us." She went back to jamming the straw up and down in the shake. "Okay. Enough. Can we pretend this conversation never happened?"

"Sure." An idea blossomed in Lizzie's head. "We need our own church. Like the church of the left behind."

"Sounds too spooky."

"How about the Church of the Breakfast Club?"

Jess giggled. "Sacrilegious. But fun."

"Perfect."

"When do we meet?"

"Saturday of course." Maybe she could get Nev and Zach on board. She hadn't admitted to anyone how much she missed her other two musketeers. "We could do breakfast for dinner and Zach could cook!"

As soon as Lizzie stepped into the dark wood-trimmed room, she saw Mr. Ray, his pleasant face calm. "Sorry to keep you waiting, Ms. Goodin-Guererro." Mr. Ray stood and met Lizzie halfway across the room, shaking her hand warmly.

"Lizzie, sir." They said he'd never stopped shaking hands.

"What can I do for you, Lizzie?" He motioned her to a cushy chair and he took a seat on the couch, clasping his hands together.

"I'm hoping I can do something for you."

"Well," he said, "that's certainly a switch from what I've been hearing."

"I'd like to have a new job."

"What's your current job?"

"Parenting and child-birth classes."

"Right." His eyes twinkled below his bushy, gray eyebrows. "That's a pretty important job. How is your boy? All better, I hope?"

"You remembered that? He's fine. Just the lower-case f flu."

"Wonderful!"

"Mr. Ray, I mostly raised my little brother when my mom was in rehab. I've been raising Saj since I found him. In my classes they've gone over everything once and are starting on the second time around. Please, save me." Lizzie heard the whine in her own voice.

His lips twitched as he held back a smile. "So what is it you want to do, Miss Lizzie?"

"Your population list is incomplete and disorganized. I'd like to do a census. Find out who's missing. Take their pictures; interview them. Help connect people who might not know they have family and friends that survived." The face in the snow flashed in her mind again. "It's probably not as important as birthing a baby, but I'm confident I can do both."

Mr. Ray chuckled. "I have no doubt about that. You're Mannie Guerrero's daughter?"

"Yeah. I'd like to make sure that no one else misses the chance that we got."

"I'll let Ms. LaFevbre know that you've got a new job. You'll be reporting to Jonah Myles in personnel."

"Thank you" Lizzie stood, awkwardly. "Mr. Ray, can I ask you something?"

"Of course."

"They say you never stopped shaking hands, even when the pandemic was at its worst."

His eyes caught Lizzie's, there was an intensity she hadn't seen. "It's part of who I am. When my god is ready to take me, he will. Until then, fellowship with my fellow beings is my job here on earth."

Lizzie held out her hand. "Thank you, Mr. Ray."

"You're welcome, Ms. Goodin-Guerrero." He shook her hand firmly. "Thanks for your help."

Lizzie hurried out before he had a chance to think she'd might be open to hearing more about his religion. His faith was amazing, but she wasn't ready for that.

With the door closed behind her, she felt like cheering. Instead she took a deep breath and strode down the corridor and down the stairs to her father's office. She opened the door gently and stuck her face in.

"Dad?"

Lizzie's father looked up from the papers he was scribbling on. "You got a long lunch?"

"No. I'm done."

"What do you mean? For today?"

"No, I'm released. No classes."

"Why not?" A worried look crossed his face.

"Don't worry, the baby is fine," she said putting a hand on her belly.

"So, what's going on?"

"I got the census job!" She collapsed on his couch. "I'm going to try and find out who that guy was. She gave him a wink. "And maybe do a little spying on our Mr. DiSilvio and friends."

"Spying isn't part of a census, Elizabeth. I want you to be careful, we're in a precarious situation here."

"You are trying to keep me safe now, too? I'm a grown up. I will decide what is dangerous, and what is worth the risk." He was right. But she wasn't in the mood to take anymore safety talk.

"I'm your father, I can't help it."

Lizzie bit back the comments about how long he had been her father.

"You want to go get a Coke? Or a shake?" Lizzie asked. "There's a cool burger place called Zeke's. Have you been there yet? The burgers are sooo good. Jess and I went there a few days ago."

A shadow crossed his face. "I really need to get back to work. I had lunch."

He was distant all of a sudden—was this thing with Jess that bad? She'd only just mentioned her name and he shut down.

"Why don't you talk to Nev? She can give you the population data we already have."

Now it was Lizzie's turn to be spooked. The last call with Nev had been tentative and awkward. "Not sure that's a really good idea." She'd wait until the Breakfast Club get together.

"Come on, Lizzie. You and Nev—"

"Have been friends forever. Yeah. But we used to gang up on Zach. Now…"

"Look, I know it's weird, but I think both of you want what's best for each other, right?"

"So what?" Lizzie responded a little more forcefully than she'd intended. "Sorry."

Her father shrugged and pulled her into a hug. "Just tell your old dad to butt out if I'm wrong."

"It's not that you're wrong. Just—" Lizzie took a deep breath before continuing. "I'm not sure what to do next."

"Maybe just give in and tell her you love her. Start on the next part of your relationship."

"What?"

"You do love her, right?"

"She's like my sister." A strange thought shot into her brain. "Dad?"

"What is it?"

"Do you… did you have a sister?" She bit the inside of her cheek, as tears threatened to well up at the thought of Jayce. "Brothers?"

His eyes seemed to look right through her.

"Sorry. You don't have to answer. You probably need to get back to work."

He shook loose from whatever thoughts had taken him back. "No. It's okay. One sister. Two brothers. I'll tell you about them someday."

"We're doing a get together. All the old folks," Lizzie said. "Can you come? I could really use you being there for support."

"Will Jess be there?"

"Yeah."

"Not sure that's a good idea."

"It's safe. Start on the next part of your relationship."

Mannie grimaced. "Use my own words against me, huh? Fine. I'll come. Probably cut out early thought. Not really a kid anymore."

Chapter Nineteen

WHEN LIZZIE CALLED, NEV VOLUNTEERED to host the Church of the Breakfast Club gathering at her and Zach's place. It seemed a lot easier to Lizzie than trying to clean up her own smaller apartment. And most of all it seemed like another possibility of a thaw between her and Nev.

"Zach, you've really outdone yourself," Jess sighed contentedly, "I had no idea there was a chef hidden under all those muscles."

Zach's freckled face reddened. "Thanks, I've been collecting stuff for a special occasion." He placed a larger serving tray on the table filled with fluffy pancakes and Belgian waffles. "Sausage and bacon will be out in a few."

Lizzie let each bite rest on her tongue before chewing and swallowing. The silence was broken only by happy sighs and the clinking of silverware. Having her dad and Jess in the same room was a little weird, but they were both acting like Jess had never said anything.

After most of the food had disappeared, everybody helped clean up while Zach brought out his guitar. He handed Lizzie the acoustic bass they'd liberated on their road-trip and she sat on the arm of the couch.

Lizzie's heart leapt at the sight of the bass. "I wondered where that got to."

Duke stood behind the couch, leaning in to look at it. "I didn't know you played."

"Lots you don't know about me, Duke." Lizzie teased.

Zach laughed. "That's for sure."

Duke joined in the laughter, but it sounded forced as he walked around and collapsed onto the couch, his arm near her thigh.

Zach glared at Duke.

"Hey, Zach," her dad asked, "you have another guitar?"

Zach handed his over and disappeared, returning quickly with another guitar.

After tuning they managed to play a few songs together. Mannie played House of the Rising Sun. Lizzie watched his hands to tell her what to play on the bass. By the last verse, she glowed with pride at following along, even managing to find a couple extra notes to toss in for the changes.

Zach played Sweet Home Alabama. Mannie grinned as he followed, his fingers forming chords they had obviously learned before.

Lizzie couldn't decide what to play. She wanted to sing. She turned to her father. "Can I borrow your guitar?"

He handed her the guitar and took her bass.

"This song's Breathe by a band called Greenwheel, but Melissa Etheridge got a hit out of it. The chords are A minor, D minor, G, C and F." She played through the intro once.

"I played the fool today," she sang, glad that for the moment her family and friends were focused on her. When they focused on each other things turned to shit. "And everyday," she muttered. As she played she heard the bass beside her reverberating. She stole a glance away from the strings to grin at her father. He watched her proudly.

At the end she got a round of applause and a whoop from Duke.

"So," Nev said, "Do you—"

"Know anything from this century?" Lizzie finished.

Zach poked Nev in the ribs.

Nev slapped him back. "I don't understand why you both like the old stuff so much."

"Actually that last one is from this century, but I knew you were gonna ask that." She played a few simple chords. "If you ever—" Lizzie flowed into Bruno Mars, Count on Me.

"That's better. Thanks for thinking of me, Lizzie."

Her fingertips were beginning to ache. It had been too long since she'd played. Her calluses were wimpy.

"Lizzie," her father said softly, "I think we've got our first casualty of the evening."

Saj had been playing with some building blocks and collapsed on them, his thumb in his mouth, shiny with drool. Handing the guitar to her father, she rolled Saj gently over into her arms.

Her father's mouth tightened. "You want me to take him home with me? You kids can talk."

"Okay." She released Saj into her father's capable arms.

He kissed Lizzie's forehead. "Have fun."

Rachael came over to kiss Saj. "Thanks, Mannie."

Lizzie watched Jess's eyes follow her father, but she didn't say anything. They were both still shell-shocked, but maybe there was the beginning of acceptance there.

As soon as the door clicked shut behind Mannie, Zach reached into a bag and pulled out a couple of six-packs of micro-brews.

"You were waiting until my dad left to bring out the beer?"

"Yeah," Zach said. "Duh, I'm not a dick."

"Really?" Lizzie asked. "I can't drink either."

"Yeah. No shit, Sherlock. You're pregnant. I was there."

"Can we not talk about this?" Nev stepped in between them. "Zach, do you have to drink?"

"Yup. I drink when I cook. I got one going in the kitchen." He came back with a giant bottle with the remnants of a champagne-style wire cork wrap still around its neck. It was already half empty. "Anybody want to try my trippel?"

"Your triple what?" Lizzie asked.

"Trippel Bock. It's a Belgian beer. Found a stash. Kicks ass."

"Sounds like it's already kicking your ass," Lizzie said. "That's a pretty big beer, Zach. You compensating?"

Zach batted his eyes at her, "As you would say, Fuck you."

"Zach," Nev said sharply, tugging on Lizzie's arm. "Lizzie, come with me. We got you some really cool sodas: Jones, Henry Weinhard's, and Green River."

Lizzie backed away from Zach and followed Nev's boyish form. Lizzie wished she looked more like that. The pregnancy was already bumping up her previous curves.

Nev swung the fridge door open and said, "Ta da!"

"Thanks, Nev." Lizzie grabbed a Weinhard's Orange Cream Soda.

"You're welcome," Nev said. "Zach actually did the legwork."

"But you suggested it?"

"Yeah."

"Thanks, Nev." She thought about saying, 'I'm sorry, about things.' But she couldn't figure out what she was sorry for and she didn't think it would make anything better this time. She pulled Nev into a hug. Nev stiffened and then relaxed in Lizzie's arms.

"Hey, how about some of that for me?" Zach asked, coming toward them with his arms wide open. "My two best girls."

Nev broke away and swung Zach away from Lizzie. "Watch out for number one," she said to Zach as she guided him back into the living room.

Lizzie unclenched her fists. Why the hell had she thought this was a good idea? She went back into the living room and sat down between Duke and Jess. Jess was sucking down an I.P.A. But the face she made as she swallowed didn't look like she was enjoying it.

Duke had picked up one of the acoustic guitars and was playing Dust in the Wind.

"Does everyone play guitar around here?" Nev asked.

"I only play videos on Youtube," Rachael joked.

After a bit Duke sang, "Same old song, just a drop of water in an endless sea."

They sat around talking about music. Would there ever be new releases? Songs to download, to watch on Youtube?

Lizzie nursed her Weinhard's until it was warm and almost empty. "Hey, I'm out. Anybody want anything?"

"There's a ceramic flip top bottle in the fridge," Zach said. "Dirty Bastard Wee Heavy. Here, take this dead soldier," he held out the big bottle.

Jess giggled. "You're a wee heavy! Can you bring me something, too, Lizzie? I don't care what."

"A wee heavy dirty bastard," Lizzie muttered. She grabbed Zach's empty as she walked past toward the kitchen. She saw the bathroom attached to it and decided that a little quiet time alone was in order. She closed the door, not bothering to turn the light on. For some reason the dark was calmer. She sat on the toilet and peed, then pulled up her pants and sat on the lid pondering. Her birthday had been pleasant enough, but things were still awkward. What could she do to make things better between her and Zach and Nev?

The door opened. Zach looked startled. "The light wasn't on. Are you hiding? Sorry if I was being an asshole."

"Whoa," Lizzie said, holding up her hands to ward him off. "I didn't say you were an asshole. You did. But I will accept your apology. I'm sorry if my smart-ass comments hurt your feelings."

Zach stepped closer. "Can I have a hug?"

"Yeah, you big dummy."

She could smell the alcohol as he pulled her in. She tensed and he seemed to sense her reluctance, backing off to a few inches away. "I'm glad you're the mother of my baby. I always loved you and Nev."

"Love you, too, Zach."

He bent in like he was going to kiss her. She turned her cheek and broke into laughter. "Zach, you're drunk." She pushed him aside and stepped out of the bathroom. Duke and Nev were standing next to each other staring. Nev's eyes strafed Lizzie up and down, stopping at her waist.

Lizzie glanced down; her pants were unzipped. She pulled up the zipper.

"What the fuck," Nev screamed. "A little quickie in the bathroom for the mommy and daddy?"

Zach stumbled out of the bathroom. "It's not what you think."

"Get out, Zach Riley."

Lizzie froze as Nev came toward them, then stepped out of the way as she saw Nev focus her vitriol on Zach.

Nev pointed at the kitchen door, "Get the fuck out of my house, right now."

Zach looked like the skinny little runt Lizzie had befriended in middle school, scared and angry. "Nev, I—"

"NOW!" Nev picked up a wooden spoon, brandishing it at him as he scrambled backwards around the kitchen table. She jerked the door open and changed direction. "GO!"

Zach went. "I'M SORRY!" he yelled as he slammed the door.

Nev spun on Lizzie. "Jesus, Lizzie, what the fuck?" Nev bore down on her like she was going to beat the shit out of her.

Lizzie spun away into the living room, her brain twisting, her hands clasping and unclasping in fists. What did I do? "This is not my fault." Thoughts cascaded off each other in her head. I don't want to hit Nev; she's my friend. "Zach's an asshole teen-aged boy." Don't let her hit you, she crossed her arms protecting the baby. "I didn't say or do anything." Did the others think it was her fault? She looked to the others for support, but they were frozen, watching the spectacle. Lizzie started to explain, turning back to Nev. "Zach—" The murderous look stopped Lizzie's voice.

Nev advanced toward her. "You are the most self-centered bitch I have ever chosen to call my friend."

Lizzie backed up until her calves hit the couch and she sank into it. Nev towered over her. Lizzie raised her hands to her mouth, but stopped short of chewing them. She heard her mother's voice. Don't chew your nails. They're so ugly.

Nev ranted on, but Lizzie didn't hear the words. Everything was Lizzie's fault. Maybe it was true. They wouldn't even be here in Provo if Lizzie had been content to wait for her dad and Jess to get to Bellingham. Would Spike be alive? Lizzie's heart twisted. "No."

"What?" Nev stared at her.

What was the last thing Nev had said? Lizzie had no idea. "What what?"

"You said, No."

"No, Spike would still be dead. Zach and I would still have this to deal with." She gestured at her belly.

"What the—" Nev's sentence finished in a growl. She shook her head, menacing. "Don't go Crazy Lizzie on me. The sympathy card won't work on me this time."

Lizzie grabbed the edges of Nev's jacket and pulled her down, spinning her into the couch. "Fuck you. I'm not crazy—and I don't need pity." Lizzie pushed herself up off the couch and stood toe to toe with Nev.

Nev's eyes flashed in fear.

Lizzie compressed her lips, as regret washed over her. "I'm not going to hurt you. I love you." She reached out to stroke Nev's shoulder, but dropped her hand as she saw her friend flinch and shrink into the couch. Lizzie sank to the carpet, shoving aside Jess' hands trying to calm her.

Duke gently cleared his throat. He and Rachael stood by the door. Duke winced. "Didn't really have to happen."

"No." Lizzie said, finally giving up the argument. "It didn't."

"Sorry, Lizzie," Rachael said as she slipped into her coat. "I'm going to go get Saj, I'll bring him to your place."

Duke held the door for Rachael, and looked like he was going to say something to Lizzie, but he kept his mouth shut and left.

When they had gone, Lizzie turned to Jess, her arms wrapped around Nev huddling on the couch. "Nev?" Lizzie offered.

"Get away from me," she growled. "I don't want to see you or Zach."

Jess motioned with her head for Lizzie to go.

For a few minutes she had the old Nev back and now she didn't want to make things any worse. Best thing now was to give Nev space —that's all Lizzie ever did. But she couldn't leave it like that. If she could wave a white flag, she should. "I'm sorry, Nev. I really am sorry."

Lizzie shrugged into her down jacket and pulled the stocking cap over her head, waiting for a response from Nev. Nothing. She chewed on the inside of her cheek as she closed the door gently instead of slamming it. This wasn't her fault. Not really. Or Nev's either, she was just reacting.

Duke stood waiting for her across the street. He didn't say anything, didn't even look at her. But he offered her his arm, she took it and let him walk her home. She watched his stoic face for a clue, but got nothing until he hugged her at her doorstep.

He promised to check on her later and excused himself. Lizzie stepped into her own silent apartment, determined not to cry until Rachael had left and Saj was asleep.

Zach flew outside into the cold. He didn't have the right gear for running in the snow, but he ran anyway—toward the barracks. Where else could he go?

God-damned fucking alcohol and his lack of control. Everything he'd hated about his old man popped out today: sexist, drunken, pig. He sprinted until his feet hurt. The Converse Chuck Taylors were piss-poor for anything active outside of a basketball court and not very good there either. He'd put them on this morning in honor of the Breakfast Club. Flashback. Shit. He jogged on, feeling the pain in his soles, glad that the snow provided a little cushion.

The city was quiet except the old man who wandered the streets offering the same few bible quotes—not a dog-man, but close.

"You want to hear some good news today, son?" asked the simple man.

"Don't think I could take it today, sir," Zach hollered as he ran past.

"John 3:16. For god so loved the world that he gave his only begotten son—"

A bitter laugh escaped Zach's throat. "I'm the fucking begotten son, old man," he muttered in between breaths. He wasn't ready for peace yet. He'd finally started feeling his own emotions, after years of fearing what he would become. He didn't have to turn into his dad because he felt angry. He just needed a way to vent it, other than on the people he cared about. But he'd just done that, screwing up just about every relationship that meant anything too him.

When he reached the barracks, he ran straight to the gym. A

couple of the boys were in the boxing ring, half-heartedly hitting each other. Zach pulled a pair of gloves off the hooks.

"All right," Zach ducked in between the ropes, "which one of you wants a real workout?"

They stared at him. The bigger one shrugged. "I'll take it."

The skinnier guy said, "You need head-gear. And a mouth guard."

Zach shook his head. "Not today, I don't."

"Sergeant's orders."

"Let's just say I'm not taking orders today."

The two kids exchanged looks. Zach was only a year or so older than they were, but they seemed like uncertain children. The big guy was near Zach's weight, maybe a little more, and solid. Zach slapped his gloves against him and asked, "Well, we gonna do this?"

The guy sneered. "You're drunk." He popped a mouth guard in.

"Yeah. What are you gonna do about it." Zach shoved the kid back and started circling. He danced on the balls of his feet and feinted with a few jabs.

The guy threw a couple test punches.

Zach shot in with his right and circled left. The kid's gloved fist hit him on the chin. Zach came in pummeling. The other fighter's glove slammed him straight between the eyes—and everything went red.

The next thing Zach knew, he was being pulled off the kid. The guy sat up spewing spit and blood, mouth guard dangling, headgear askew.

Something dark flowed into Zach's eye. His own blood.

Chapter Twenty

LIZZIE SAT STARING INTO THE cup of coffee on her kitchen table. She hadn't had anything to drink the night before, so why did she feel hung-over? Was there such a thing as an emotional hangover? She felt drugged. And empty. She'd alienated pretty much everyone, except her father. But Zach was the problem, him plus the alcohol equaled instant asshole. What had she done to make it worse? She rewound back to the start of the party, pausing at the moment when she and Nev were okay, a team again. Then he had walked in and made some comment. Things had been shaky from there.

There was a knock on her apartment door. She hustled out of her seat. Was it Duke? She wanted someone's arms holding her and words saying that everything would work out. Lizzie's heart bumped a bit stronger. Or the adoption folks? She put her eye to the peephole. Zach. She opened her mouth to spit obscenities with a "go away" tacked on, but the misery on his face made his usual hang dog look seem pleasant.

She turned the knob and pulled the door open far enough to lean against the jamb, but not to give him any ideas that he could come in. Let him start the conversation.

"Lizzie. I'm an asshole."

Zach was a wreck. A cross-ways rip across his brow had been sewn and taped. A bit of blood mixed with the yellow of iodine.

"Shit, Zach, what the hell happened?" she asked, letting the door swing open more than she intended.

"Can I come in?"

"Are you crazy?" She held the door close to her body again, blocking any possibility of entry. "We're not the three musketeers any more, not even the three stooges. There's only one person you should be trying to talk to."

"I can't talk to her."

"Well, then I guess you're screwed."

"You're my best friend, Lizzie."

Lizzie's lips blew out something between spit and sarcastic laughter. "Was your best friend. When I was the only person you knew still alive. Nev should be your best friend."

"Well, she is. I mean, you're right." Zach paced back and forth. "She treats me better than I deserve. How am I supposed to tell her I'm sorry and convince her to take me back?"

"Maybe start deserving the way she treats you," Lizzie said.

"How? I've got nothing there. Maybe talk to my dad."

"Mannie?" Zach's brows furrowed. "But he left your mom when you were a kid."

"Yeah. Probably has thought for years about what he could have, would have, should have said."

Zach sighed. "I am sorry."

"Hell, Zach. I know that. She knows that. But like you tell me all the time. Stop doing things that mean you have to say you're sorry. Jeez, man, did you jump off a cliff to make people feel sorry for you or something? I thought I was the only suicide-sympathy loser in our crew."

Zach ran his finger gently across the stitches. "Went boxing. It's not at all funny, but you should see the other guy."

Lizzie searched his face for a hint of the humor and found none. "Yeah, I got beat up a little, too."

Surprise flashed across Zach's face, "She hit you?"

"No. And I didn't stomp out on her to go get the shit beat out of me by someone else." Lizzie's laugh came out manlier than she intended. "But you missed the part where she told me off for all of my past sins. Quite the show. I thought she was going to hit me."

"It's my fault," he growled.

Zach's hands were fists. He was going to punch the wall. But instead he sank down and sat on the floor, groaning as he twisted his shoulders, hugging himself. "I don't know how to fix this."

"Me neither. Maybe it can't be fixed. You think I get women any better than you do? Try talking to my dad."

He shoved his legs against the floor and slid up the wall. "Thanks.

I will." He jogged down the carpeted hallway and slammed through the door at the end.

Lizzie closed the door and pulled out her phone. She took a deep breath and called Nev. It rang until it went to voice mail. "Nev. It's Lizzie. Duh. You know that. I'm sorry. Nothing happened yesterday. Shit. Something did happen, but nothing of me and Zach and a relationshit kind of thing. Yesterday for a minute at the fridge I had you back. Like the friend I love. I don't know how to make it better with you. I'd like some time with you without Zach. Anyway. I'm gonna try to not be a selfish bitch. We've lost too much to lose each other. I miss you, sister, ex-lover, partner of the father of my baby and my friend. I love you, Nev. I'll call again tomorrow."

Little feet on pattered on the carpet and Saj's sunshine face, swept aside the cold sorrow of lost friendship. "Hey, big boy. You want some breakfast?"

"B'e'kfast," he agreed, grasping her hand and pulling her toward him.

As she poured him a bowl of cereal and milk her phone buzzed once. When she had him at the table eating she checked it. New text from Nev.

Lizzie, I got your message, Nev.

Lizzie didn't know what the note meant, but Nev could have just ignored her voice-mail. Or she could have said, **I never want to communicate with you ever again**. At least it left the door open. Her phone rang. Duke. Did she want to talk to him? If he was going to go off on the Zach and Lizzie in the bathroom thing, all judging, she didn't need it. Her fingers froze over the phone. But she might also be able to use him to forget about the relationshit. She loved her newest coined word. The phone stopped ringing. That answered that. She turned back to Saj. He had consumed all of the marshmallowy treats and most of the rest of the cereal.

Zach sat on Mannie's couch staring at his hands and waiting for answers. At least he hadn't gone in for boxing without gloves. He would've really messed up that kid.

Mannie sat quietly in his recliner, until Zach felt like getting up and running away.

Finally, Mannie cleared his throat. "Not sure I can help. I don't have any answers. Oh, I can see you screwed up. I've even been there, too. But getting out of it?" Mannie shook his head. "Say you're sorry and hope she forgives you."

"I've tried. She won't answer her phone or the door. What else?"

"I've never figured out anything else."

Zach felt anger, confusion and desperation. He let his head fall into his hands.

"The other thing to do," Mannie continued, "is to give it time. Don't push too hard."

Zach nodded. "I'm not very good at waiting."

"Who is?" Mannie laughed lightly. "But forgiveness takes time."

Zach stood up. "Thanks, Mannie."

"Anytime. I hope it helps."

Zach closed the door and started walking. His brain chased itself in circles, pausing only to chew on the bones of his past activities. The chill of the winter air left him puffing steam. Hunger pulled him back homeward, if Nev wouldn't let him in he'd need to get food somewhere else. For the moment his hunger to see her overrode all other needs.

As he came up the steps of the building, he saw the curtains move. He took a deep breath. Zach stopped outside their door. He knocked. No answer. He knocked again. He was pretty sure Nev was standing on the other side, possibly staring through the peephole.

"Nev? Please, if you're there, please, let me in."

"Give me one good reason." Nev's voice came from inside.

Crap. Zach leaned up against the door and slid down.

"I'm sorry. I'm cold. I'm hungry. I'm sorry."

Silence. And then her voice, quiet. "What do you want me to do?"

"I want you to open the door. Then tell me what I can do."

"What the hell happened?" There was a long pause. "You were so sweet. Until we got really serious. Sit down and get married serious. And you asked me. I said yes. And then you changed."

"You're right. I did. I think I figured out part of why."

He heard movement behind the door and then her voice came from up above. "Why?"

He quickly stood up, too. "I need your help."

"No shit, Sherlock. Tell me why?"

Zach took a deep breath. "I don't like asking for help. That's part of the why. My father never asked my mother for help. My Gramps didn't ask Gramma for help. Too much pride."

The deadbolt slid back. But the door didn't open. The first step.

He opened the door.

Nev had backed up against the wall. Her arms were crossed over her chest and she was wearing pajamas and a robe. Her hair was pulled back into a ponytail that showed her face. He could see she'd been crying for a long time.

"I'm sorry, Nev." He waited outside.

She stared at him. Hurt and angry still. "Sorry isn't enough?"

"No." Zach stepped inside and collapsed to his knees. "It's not." He wrapped his arms around her waist, sheltering his head under her arms.

She loosened her arms and let them fall around his shoulders. "Stand up. I want to hold you."

He did. He cried, too. Which made her cry. He kissed her through the salty tears, repeating, "I'm sorry."

"Shut up," Nev ordered, sniffing back her own tears. "Be sorry. But don't tell me about it. Not for this. Tell me sorry for little things. Be sorry once. Tell me you're sorry even if you don't mean it. But for this…" She sucked in a ragged breath. "Tell me you still love me. Because if it's Lizzie you love…"

"It's you. I love you." He pulled her into his arms as she buried her face in his chest.

They clung to each other until Nev shook. "I need to sit. Haven't really eaten today."

"Me neither."

"Make me something." She punched his arm.

"Anything." He would go to Florida for gator meat if she asked.

"I don't know. Iron chef it with whatever we've got in the house. First job is to come up with an appetizer." She sat on the couch.

Zach knelt at her feet, taking her hand in his. "Will you still marry me?"

"You're pushing it." Her face was stone.

His anger rose. But he shoved it down as hard as he could.

"How does that make you feel, Zach?"

"You really want to know?"

"If I didn't, what would be the point?"

"It makes me mad. I said I was sorry." He slumped onto the floor at her feet. "I don't know if I'm good enough for you."

"I don't know either, Zach."

"I'll go make some food," he said.

"If it makes any difference," she called from the other room, "I don't know if I'm good enough either." Then she followed him into the kitchen. "I'll set the table."

After dinner, she asked, "Why would we get married, even without all that happened last night? There's too much going on. I may marry you. But not now. I know it doesn't sound fair, but…"

"Fair?" Zach kissed her hand. "You've been more than fair to me. I don't know why we should get married, either. I want to be there for you. I want to give you everything you want. If marriage isn't one of those things, I will be happy making dinner every night, until the day I die."

"We need to get out of here. Take one of those pre-honeymoon staycations up in Salt Lake." Zach's face lit up.

Nev continued. "Don't get excited. I'm still not going to marry you. But getting away from everything here. Just you and I. Time to talk. We've got some stuff to talk over. Hard conversations. They don't happen here. Maybe I can figure out where I, we, stand."

"I'll get clearance tomorrow morning," Zach said, pulling her into his arms. Things were going to be okay. Once they cleared the decks. And he had something else he needed to say. He stepped back so he could watch her face. "I don't want to spend our time together talking about Lizzie, but—"

"She called me. Left a voice-mail."

"Good. Last night… She didn't do anything wrong. It was me… And I didn't mean to." His excuses just sounded lame. But he wanted Nev to know that it wasn't Lizzie's fault. "It was me."

Nev waited. "Anything else?"

If I'm going to make it right, then yes. "I don't think I should drink any more. Not sure how to do that. Maybe ask Mannie for help."

Nev's face relaxed ever so slightly. She pulled herself back in close and tucked her head under his chin. He clung to her and the opportunity she'd given him.

Chapter Twenty-One

LIZZIE GLANCED AROUND FLUSTERED, TOSSING garbage into the bin, shoving clothes into the closet.

Rachael had begged to take Saj as soon as she heard Duke was coming over. Can I keep him all night? Duke had left a voice-mail. Do you want to talk? Or do you want to not talk and have someone there to not talk to? Lizzie realized that after her unpleasant chat with Zach and her phone message to Nev that she really did want to be distracted. Needed to be distracted. She said yes and told him she didn't want to talk about last night.

Lizzie heard the knock, but before she could get there, Duke came in the doorway, breathing heavy.

"Did you run all the way or are you just happy to see me?" She pushed him backwards against the wall.

Lizzie felt her own breaths shorten as Duke's face moved toward her. Her heart pounded. She hoped her breath didn't stink. Or anything else for that matter. Was it yesterday she'd taken a shower? Yes, before the Breakfast Club Church had gone to hell.

Duke pulled back right before their lips met. "Close your eyes."

"What? Why?"

"You implied that you trusted me, but could not trust yourself."

"Yeah, but."

"Trust me. Please."

"Okay. Can I have a blindfold?"

Duke laughed. "I thought it might come to this." He whipped a blue bandanna out of his pocket. And spun it around itself.

Lizzie pulled herself into him as he covered her eyes. Her heart beat faster. She felt his hot breath on her forehead as the bandanna tightened and his hands smoothed the hair underneath so it didn't pull. Lips touched her hairline. The lips stayed there for a moment as his hands fell to her back. She couldn't see except for a small glow of light at the edges of her blindfold. She was completely helpless in his arms. Heat raced from her core to the tips of her being. The heat in her groin made her want to touch herself.

"Duke?"

"Yes," his voice floated over her head.

"I trust you."

He released her and stepped back his hands coming down her arms to hold hers in his. "Come with me. We're going somewhere special."

She felt him move to the side and release her hand.

She closed her eyes, despite the bandanna.

He led her outside. "Why the blindfold?"

"If you don't see where I take you, you can't tell anyone where it is."

"Oooh. A secret place."

"My truck is around the corner. You sure you're good with this?"

"Pretty sure."

They drove in silence. Duke reached over regularly to hold her hand. He flipped through music, stopping on We Gotta Get Out of this Place. Finally, he said, "Provo is not home for you, is it? Even if your family is here."

"Yeah. But where else would we go? It's pretty nasty out there."

"It's nasty in here. Even worse for you."

"Thanks," Lizzie said softly. "Really. I mean it. But for now… Shut up. Give me my surprise, let me live in today for a little bit."

"Sounds good. We're almost there."

When the truck rolled to a stop, Lizzie sat still as his door slammed and she heard him run around to her side. The door opened.

"Give me your hand."

"Can't I take this off now?"

"A bit of a step. Here."

His other arm guided her, slipping in around her waist and pulling her close to him as he helped her step down.

"We're going to walk forward and around back, then up some steps."

The heat she'd felt when he kissed her forehead rushed back. His arm was firm on her hip keeping her safe. For the moment she didn't mind. She walked where she was guided. The ground underneath felt like gravel. Didn't seem to have snow.

"Steps. Four, three, two, one. Step forward a few feet and then to the right so I can open the door."

Lizzie did as he told. She heard a series of punches and then an electric lock releasing.

Duke chuckled. "The code is 8675309. I thought you'd appreciate it. And it would be easy to remember."

"Yeah. I suck at remembering number unless I can sing them." She heard the door open and music playing in the background. A Sarah McLachlan song, Good Enough.

The door closed behind her and Lizzie heard the deadbolt flip into place. She let herself be lead forward. The floor under her feet changed from something hard like tile to carpet. She breathed in deeply. Something smelled off, like death but it wasn't strong. A slight scent of wood smoke tickled deep inside her nose.

"Sorry for the smell. The former owner permanently occupies the foyer. Figured it would let people think the house hadn't been explored."

"The next step's a doozy, so I need to take your blindfold off."

"All right." She wanted him to touch her again.

He gently pulled her around to face him. She felt his hands on her shoulders undoing the knot at the back of her head. When the bandana fell she blinked, leaned forward and kissed him. The warmth of his lips on hers made her want to push him against the walls and rip his clothes off. Pregnancy hormones didn't really make sense. Why should she want sex more when she couldn't have any more kids than the one that was already inside her?

She leaned in and pressed against him.

"Wait. Do you like the house?"

Lizzie glanced around. The hallway was lined with doors and ended in a bookshelf.

Duke marched to the end of the hall and began moving books. Then he reached up and she heard a click. He pulled the bookcase toward himself. It was a door, now ajar. A light bulb on a string shown harshly on her newly reopened eyes. "It's a secret passage? How'd you find it?"

"It was open when I tagged the house." His smiled shifted. "Hey, don't you want to still jump my bones?"

"Later. Come on." She reached back and grasped Duke's hand, pulling him forward. The music floating in the air around them switched to Sheryl Crow's Aldous Huxley song. She stepped gingerly into the stairwell. The steps were steep and skinny—almost like a ladder. Lizzie gripped the arm rail for stability. As she descended, the single twisted fluorescent bulb brightened. The walls were lined with shelves: books, food, emergency supplies.

Duke pulled the bookcase closed until it clicked. "The guy who lived here was a prepper, but not the usual."

They were locked in; a moment of panic swept her. She stared at him as he stepped down onto the floor. He grinned at her, not a dangerous grin, but more a 12-year-old's "can-I-show-you-my-awesome-fort" grin.

"What do you mean, 'not the usual'?"

"This one focused on having things to read, things to watch, rather than food, water, and medical supplies." He motioned to a stationary bike in front of a TV. "The bike provides enough power to watch a DVD or listen to music. Solar power on the roof comes down here in addition to the main electrical lines. So, probably don't really need the bike. Most of the movies are from the 80s and 90s. And the music, too."

"Wow. Weird. So he would have his fill of entertainment while he starved to death?"

"Yeah. There are some empty shelves, so maybe he was restocking or something.

Lizzie pushed open the door to the next room. It felt like a cheap motel. A bed, nightstand and a small bathroom in the back. On one wall, a giant poster filled a window with a scene of trees and a marsh. The view would never change, but the art was lovely, it was a poster of an amazingly real painting.

Duke came in behind her and she stopped moving, hoping he would touch her again. The bed, neatly made, had something on the pillow. It looked like a couple of those fancy shiny foil wrapped chocolate balls. Upgrade that to a nicer hotel room.

"Well, what do you think?" Duke's hands settled gently on her shoulders.

"You have anywhere you need to be soon?" She place her hands on his and pulled them forward across her chest as she backed into him.

"No." His voice rattled low.

Lizzie felt his warmth press into her. "Good." She placed his hands on her breasts. Her neck arched. She closed her eyes and dragged his right hand lower.

His left hand slipped under her shirt and caressed the outer circle of her belly bump. His finger found the slight indent of her navel.

His hand strayed from her belly and slipped higher his finger tracing the edge of her breasts, just under the lace of her bra. She moved her hand around his hip, pulling the belt loop on the side of his jeans.

His other hand was kneading her breasts through the bra. "Slow down, they're not bread." His movements became lighter and she guided his hand. "Like this." She pressed his fingers lightly against her nipples as she felt her body responding.

She opened her eyes and glanced around the room. The bed was a little above her knees' height. She stumbled forward out of his grasp, his hand still entangled in her shirt. She climbed up on the bed and crawled to the chocolates. "You?"

"Yes." Duke nodded. "You like?"

"I like. White or regular chocolate?"

"I like 'em both. Take whichever one you want."

"I want them both."

He chuckled. "Why does that not surprise me?"

She tore the wrapper off the white chocolate one. "But I will share. If you play along." She popped it into her mouth, holding half of it in her teeth.

His eyes widened and he grinned. "May I?"

He knelt on the bed and moved toward her. She met him halfway offering her mouth with the chocolate ball in it. His lips touched hers and she bit down on the ball and felt the soft chocolate inside flow into her mouth. Her teeth tapped his their tongues swirled around the soft white sweetness. She pulled him onto the bed, her hands entwining in his shirt as his hand found the small of her back, pulling her hungrily toward him. They fell together, giggling, trying to get the last of the candy off each other's lips.

When they came up for air, Duke gasped, "You want the other chocolate?"

"Not now," Lizzie said. "I want you." She pulled her shirt off over her head.

Duke nuzzled his face in between her breasts as his hands slid into her jean pockets, caressing her backside.

Lizzie reached behind her back and released her breasts from their constraints. She flashed her teeth in a feral grin at his lust-filled face. He pulled his shirt off over his head and her hands moved from his tender spots to feel his chest, slightly hairy in the middle, his muscles hard under her hands. "Boobs." She laughed awkwardly. "I like them, too."

"I'm glad," he said as his hands returned to hers, a big grin on his face.

She shoved Duke backward onto the bed and straddled his belly. She could feel his hardness under her and she wanted him inside. "Is there any reason not to do this now?" But literally, how fucked up was she that she mostly wanted him for the relief it would bring her?

"You want me to have the blindfold now?" he asked.

"I just wonder if sleeping together won't ruin a decent friendship."

"I'm hoping it blossoms into something more."

"Well, shit." Lizzie rolled off of him and lay on her back, her arms across her bare breasts. "Why does it have to be such a big deal?"

Duke rolled toward her, his hands pawing timidly at her arm. "It doesn't have to be."

That was his desperation talking. He didn't mean it. If she fucked him now, he would follow her around like a lost puppy for weeks—even more than he already did.

"I'm really trying to be less impulsive, but, ah-fuck." She climbed back on top of him. "We're probably going to hurt each other."

"We can burn that bridge when we get there."

"Deal." She knelt in close and kissed him gently on the lips. She didn't feel like laughing. The now. It's all we've got.

Zach stepped on the gas and the convertible red sports car surged forward up the on-ramp—north on Interstate 15, the Veteran's Highway. Nev snuggled up against him. The wind whipped at her hoodie, pulled tight over her stocking cap. Her smile above looked like a grimace as she clung to him. "You want me to put up the top?"

"What?" she hollered.

Zach motioned at the back as if flipping the convertible top back up.

"YES!"

The cold air cut through his clothes. He pulled over to the side of the road and hit the button for the top. It popped out of its slot and he watched that it engaged properly. Then he hit the high heat and circulate. He pulled his hat and muffler off and unwound Nev's scarf, kissing her neck until she laughed.

"You're incorrigible."

"Is that bad?"

"It's not generally considered good."

"Sounds kind of like encourageable." Zach found her earlobe.

"Sounds like, but it's not the same. Though, now that you mention it, maybe it isn't so bad." She pulled her scarf back from him and rewrapped it around her neck. "Zach, let's wait until we get there."

"This is foreplay."

Nev's laugh, like a crystal chandelier tinkling, warmed him. "Let's get there first. You said we get a whirlpool tub in the suite?"

"Yeah."

"That's what I want. Not sex in the back of a red convertible. Sounds like a bad classic rock song." She straightened her blouse.

Zach slid the car into gear, spitting gravel and snow. "Room at the top of the world. I can do that." He accelerated toward Salt Lake City.

Pre-honeymoon. If only she'd really agreed to marry him. Three days off. A weekend in Salt Lake City. The Committee for Social Interaction had set up a hotel in the empty city and staffed it. Folks considering marriage as well as promising to procreate got free passes for a decadent weekend. Three days of not being cold, not getting up at the crack of dawn leaving Nev warm in bed. At least since the promotion to Mr. Ray's personal guard he'd had a break from inspecting stinky houses. Collecting had seemed so cool. Being a guard felt like he was doing something more important and the work was easier. Boring, but easy. And he still got to do the physical training he enjoyed with the militia boys.

And his new position had gotten him the unescorted drive, though his romantic convertible idea had been stupid. At least they didn't have to ride the Greyhound with the other love-birds.

Nev snuggled back in next to him, sliding her hand under his shirt and caressing his skin.

Chapter Twenty-Two

IN THE MORNING LIZZIE GLANCED back at the house as Duke drove them back to Provo, with a stash of all the worthwhile DVDs in the back of his truck. Other than the red X painted on the front door it was a white brick, nondescript rambler. Inside, the entryway held something she didn't need to see. She wasn't sure how she'd feel about coming here knowing the body lay just behind the front door. Have to have a really good reason. The only thing to hide from was all the people trying to keep her safe.

She repeated the house number in her head. Then out loud.

"Your secret hiding-place. Call it a belated birthday present. If you want to be alone." Duke grinned. "With or without me."

Where are we going now?" Lizzie asked Duke scooting over so her hip touched his.

"I'm taking you home." He lay his hand on her thigh. "You're dad'll flip if he doesn't know where you are."

"He could call me. The phones work."

"Yeah. You know what I mean."

"Yeah." She watched his face. His cheeks were still a little red from their morning session. She tried to get a sense of how she felt. But her own thoughts flitted around like hummingbirds. "Anything weird, Duke?"

"Nope. You?"

"Nope. Thanks." His glance took her back a few hours. He was by far the most considerate person she'd slept with. He'd given her at least much release as he'd had. "For a few hours I forgot about most everything else. Wish I could've had that forgetting for a birthday present."

"Yeah. I mean. I would have… Your birthday."

"Duke," Lizzie said to his expectant smile. "Shut up."

"I just meant…" His smile turned sheepish. "Too bad that wasn't the usual. I mean normal."

"I'd hate to be anybody's the usual, but if that was the usual, I guess people live with a lot less."

"Yeah," Duke said turning away.

Ahh… she'd managed to embarrass him. "As for normal… I've never been the normal. Never wanted to be. And life always tosses you something."

Duke nodded, solemn for a moment, his mouth a serious line, then it swelled back into a soft, pleasant smile. "Thanks, Lizzie."

"You're going to thank me?" Her voice cut the space between them.

"Why not?" His voice had a pleading quality. "You shared yourself with me."

"That's just fucking weird." Lizzie contemplated. "Literally." Maybe he was right, but it felt more like a transaction than she wanted. "Okay. I won't take it as an insult. Thank you, too, sir," she said in a weird affected accent.

"Milady." Duke matched her joking tone. "May I call you Lady Elizabeth? I'd bow if I wasn't driving."

"Well, I wouldn't curtsy. Don't really know how." She squeezed his thigh. "But sometime later, I might dip downward." The truck veered to the left as her hand slid upward. His hand stopped hers just at the edge of his warmth.

"Probably be better if I'm not driving," he squeaked. "Good thing this street isn't crowded."

"You keep your eyes on the road." She enjoyed the power she had over him as much as she did the easy sex. But it couldn't last. She could tell it was a matter of time before this blew up in her face. She would eventually have to choose between keeping him as a friend and turning what they had into a real romance.

When they got back to Lizzie's place, she gave him a quick kiss, full on, but restrained. As soon as hands moved to pull her in she pushed him back gently. "I'm gonna hang out with Saj. Come over for a movie tonight."

Duke laughed out loud and reached behind the seat to pull out a canvas grocery bag filled with DVDs. "Great minds think alike. I'll get my schedule for the week and then come on over. With food!"

Thirty-two heavenly hours after their arrival at the Grand American Hotel Zach leaned up against the big window looking out as the fading sunlight played over the skyscrapers of Salt Lake City.

Behind him, Nev mumbled, "If your hands get cold, you're not allowed back under the covers."

He was a little chilly, fully exposed to the world. It would be super weird if anyone else could see this naked guy leaning up against the window in a penthouse suite. He glanced southward toward Provo. Lights marched out in lines down the Wasatch Valley. As the moon rose over the mountains Zach returned to the warmth of the bed.

"Ahh!" Nev jumped as he put his cold feet against her legs. "Jerk." But she pressed his feet between her thighs to share her warmth.

He could still see the lights of the valley and the moon and planets. Were there fewer lights than there had been before? His mind was playing tricks on him. He turned over, snuggling up against Nev.

"Hands!" She grabbed his hand before he could put it anywhere sensitive, and squeezed it tightly under the warm flesh of her arms. "G'night, Zach."

When he woke up in the middle of the night, the only light was from the moon. Even the glowing night-light was dead, and he stumbled on his way to and from the bathroom. He went to the window. The streetlights were off all over. "Oh, shit."

"What's wrong, Zach?"

"Not sure. But we may be walking down twenty-something flights of stairs in the morning."

Nev sat up quickly. "What?"

"I think the power's out. Really out. There are only a few lights on in all of Salt Lake."

"Come back to bed. I bet they'll be on in the morning." She yawned and rolled over. "I just got you warmed up."

He climbed back in bed, but sleep would not come. He knew Foote and DiSilvio were planning for such possibilities, but he hadn't expected it to be necessary so soon.

"You still awake, Zach?" Nev whispered.

"Yeah. I'm worried."

"Well, let me see if I can take your mind off of that." Her hand slipped lower as she twisted around to face him. Her lips found his and then worked her way back to his ear and then down his neck.

Tomorrow would be soon enough to worry about it.

Lizzie squinted at the clock through morning eyes. The red numbers were not glowing. It had failed to get her up this time. It wasn't all her fault. She and Duke had stayed up way too late watching Ghostbusters 2.

Amazing that Saj was letting her sleep in. What time was it? She fumbled on the nightstand and twisted the knob on the light. It turned but did not turn on. The power is out. She found her phone and unplugged it. It had all green on the charging bar. Time was 8:54.

Saj whined in his sleep. When she first found him she tried to wake him up when he cried in his sleep, but she found that if she let him sleep through it, he woke up fine. Waking him up usually just made him cranky.

What does a two-year-old dream about? Probably his mommy and daddy. Mr. and Mrs. Jones. She'd forgotten their first names, but she had a Bible, a birth certificate, a photo and a watch.

Lizzie carefully disentangled herself from Saj. Leave him sleeping. She tugged the covers back in place to keep him warm and stumbled toward the kitchen. The floor was freezing. How long had the power been out? Her head hurt. Maybe she just needed caffeine.

She poured herself a big mug of leftover coffee and stuck it in the microwave. When she punched the buttons nothing happened. "Damn, Lizzie, you are stupid." She pulled the coffee cup out and opened the fridge, snagging the container of creamer. How long would this stuff last? Ultra-pasteurized? What the hell did that mean?

The light in the fridge was out. Shit. How was she going to cook? And what about all the crap in the freezer? And how was she going to keep herself warm? Saj popped into her head first. Then Duke. She smiled to herself. At least that was the order she thought of them. It made her feel good to have her priorities in order. Saj needed a lot more of her time and attention.

Time to go back to bed. She drank a good slug of the cold coffee and laughed. Half a lifetime ago she would have paid good money for a coffee that tasted like this at a cool temperature. And it would have had whipped cream on top. But not when it was freezing outside. No. Maybe the caffeine would kick in as she slept and make her head stop hurting. She drank another big gulp as she walked back to the bedroom.

Setting the big mug on the nightstand, she spun the blinds to shut out more light. Then she climbed back into the cooler covers and wrapped herself around the sleeping Saj. He whined again, a quiet little fussiness.

Saj's little hand grasped hers and then his fussing stopped. "Love you, Saj." She closed her eyes and in minutes her consciousness had faded to darkness.

Saj twitched, jerking Lizzie from her dreams. His legs continued to tense and wiggle. Was he running? She tried to go back to sleep. But now the question of what was going on and if the power was out all over the city or just her building or block, kept her mind turning. No power meant no heat, no internet. Not that what they currently called the net wasn't already a slim shadow of its former self.

Glen suspected that someone in Provo had control over what came in. He seemed to have more access to what was happening in the outside world. And the outside world did still exist. The pandemic had not killed off humanity, instead it had thinned it. Like when they logged and left a few trees to naturally reseed the forest. Was that what she was going to be? A fucking tree spreading seeds. She giggled at the picture of her standing naked in the forest.

Saj squirmed and she felt warmth on her growing belly. Saj was peeing. How soon before the disposable diapers were all gone? She better be done having kids by then.

Mama had thought she'd do cloth diapers with her little brother Jason. It had lasted about two weeks. And Lizzie had washed most of the shitty diapers. She understood the environmental impact of the diapers and maybe by the time her baby came, she'd feel different. But for now, disposable diapers were easy. Until they got so saturated that the pee just slipped by when they couldn't absorb anymore.

She sighed and tossed back the covers. If she was lucky the sheets and blankets weren't wet. No power meant no laundry and she didn't really want to sleep in a bed that smelled like urine. Lizzie slid a clean diaper under Saj's butt and ripped the velcro tabs off the wet one. Saj woke when she exposed his skin to the cold air. And he responded again. Lizzie managed to avoid the stream as it arced across the bed and onto the sheets. Damn. She was definitely going to have to do laundry when the power came back on. Then it hit her. What if the power wasn't coming back on? Not this time. Maybe not ever.

She remembered the power going out in Bellingham due to windstorms knocking trees over the power lines, but there were hardly any trees big enough here to knock out the power. She finished cleaning up Saj, who was now wide awake and hungry. She picked up her cold coffee mug and drained it to the bottom. Maybe she was a little hungry, too. Once she had Saj dressed, she could call her father and see what the power forecast was.

Mannie stared at the laptop screen on his desk. How long had he been zoning? He should be maximizing the power, but his brain was going in directions more far reaching than this immediate crisis. Here's where they would see if staying in Provo had been a good idea. When the shit hit the fan. You never knew which way people would go. The strongest, pro-equality attorney and the flakiest homeless bum might easily switch places when it came time to pitch in and help during a disaster.

He opened the drawer to his desk. The flask sat there; its contents clear, pure cheap vodka. He shook himself off and shoved the drawer back in place.

The weather information numbers on the computer screen had not changed. Except as he watched the temperature flipped up a degree to 42. Shit. How far above freezing would it take to lose all the food in the freezers? He needed to plan for the worst case scenario and that meant no power in the near future, except what they could run on generators. He wished he could go to NOAA.gov and get a weather report.

The only thing left of the Internet was the local net that the Provincial Utah Government had set up and it would be down in a matter of hours just like the cell towers. Then people would be limited to communicating cell to cell with BlueTruth until their batteries died. That would be cluster-fun if anything really bad went down. How come they hadn't pursued getting the solar power switched over from the Delta plant? Mannie knew the answer. One of the great laws of human nature: If it ain't broke, don't fix it.

So unopened freezers would keep food safe for a couple days. Get the message out. Don't open the freezers. Eat what's in the refrigerators. Start getting people out to ice-mine the lakes. Get as much solid ice as we can and then disperse it.

The building rumbled as his lights flickered and then came on full. At the same time the heater fan restarted and cool air blew at him. He flipped the switch on the fan to low and the heat up a few degrees. Most people weren't lucky enough to have back-up power like the Government offices.

The intercom blasted. "All personnel report to the courtroom immediately for Emergency session."

"Shit. I don't have time for a fucking meeting." Well, he'd be late. They'd have to come drag him out. He checked to see if the internet was back up. Nope. But the local network was. So he could get to Communications. He opened his chat and typed in Benny.

Benny. Get this out on all channels ASAP. Do not open your freezers. Eat food from the cupboards. Save the food in the fridge for last. Power will be restored. Please conserve power when it comes back. Please. [And thanks. Mannie.]

The phone rang.

"Grand Central Station," Mannie muttered as he reached for it.

Chapter Twenty-Three

THE END OF THE WORLD HAD been going so well. Pounding on the door woke Zach as the sun broke over the hills, reflecting off the other nearby buildings.

"Get up. Message from Provo for you. Everyone's called back. Power's out."

"No shit," Zach muttered. In a louder voice, he answered, "All right. I'm awake. Thanks for the heads up."

Twenty minutes later he and Nev were in the car headed back with two additional passengers, young men, but not any that he had seen training back in Provo. Oh well. Might as well get to know them. "So, Mark and Brian, right."

The bigger one, Brian spoke. "Yeah. And you're Zach and Nell?"

"Nev," Zach replied.

"It's short for Nevaeh," Nev said tiredly.

"What'd you guys do in Salt Lake?" Zach asked.

"Maintenance. Bell hop. Room Service,"

"I was a housekeeper," Mark said softly.

"Didn't really want to join up and it sounded pretty cush when that Lady gave us the choice."

Nev snorted. "Miss Not-La Fever? She could make shoveling manure sound cush."

"Why do you think we all have to go back to Provo?" Brian asked.

Zach figured he knew. Without power Provo was days away from chaos. They needed two things. To get the power back on line and to keep the people in line if it took very long. "I don't know. Figure we all gotta pitch in."

"Yeah, I guess," Brian said, not sounding very convinced.

Zach knew the type. Hell, he was the type a couple years ago, before Mom left and he and Dad moved in with Grandpa. He didn't want to work hard and he had a little bit of an attitude, entitlement and testosterone. Partying was a major focus and school was just enough that he'd be able to graduate on time. But it hadn't worked out that way. The world he knew had ended at the beginning of his senior year. "Could be worse. We could all be dead."

"Hey," Brian placated, "didn't mean anything by it."

"Sorry," Zach said. Brian and Mark didn't deserve his annoyance. "Just kind of bummed about missing my pre-honeymoon." He grinned at Nev and she smiled back.

"Totally, Dude." Brian's face cracked into a big grin. "Hope the power comes back soon and you can finish it."

"Thanks," Zach said.

Nev squeezed Zach's leg and winked at him.

"You sure you don't know what's gonna happen?" Mark asked.

"I don't know enough, except to worry." Zach shrugged.

"Mannie might know," Nev offered. "Do the cell phones work?"

"Didn't even notice." It would be nice to know what was up. "Try him."

Nev held her phone to her mouth. "Call Mannie."

Zach could hear it 'ringing' as he drove the 15 back to Provo. The weirdest thing was the traffic. He had gotten used to no cars on the road and now there were cars in front of him, behind him. Hell, some were even passing him and he was trucking along at 80.

"Mannie?" Nev said.

Zach heard Mannie's calm, loud rumble. "Yeah."

Nev held the phone away from her ear. "Wasn't sure the cell phones would work."

"Most towers have back-up power for a few hours. We'll probably have some service all day. Are you still in Salt Lake?"

"I'm in the car with Zach and a couple hitchhikers. They can probably hear you." Nev glanced over at Zach.

"Hey, Mannie," Zach said. "Wondered if there's a plan yet."

There was silence for a long moment. Nev raised her eyebrow at Zach before Mannie continued.

"Well. Nobody's told me anything official except to figure out what my needs are. Was sort of hoping for a longer time before we had to deal with this."

Zach could hear his sigh through the phone. He was glad he wasn't in charge of anything. Taking orders sounded pretty good compared to giving them.

"I'm guessing they have a plan to get power back on. But until that happens, we've got food that might go bad depending on how warm it gets. Luckily, it's winter and a cold one at that, though if you'd asked me a couple weeks ago I wouldn't have had anything good to say about the weather. Course that means we got to figure out how to keep the people warm. Sort of stuff the National Guard would have done in the old days."

"Thanks, Mannie," Zach pitched his voice a little louder than normal. "Kind of what I figured. We'll be back in Provo in about ten minutes."

"All right, take it easy, Zach," Mannie said. "Nev, you coming to work?"

"You got breakfast, Mannie?"

Zach's phone buzzed against his thigh; he pulled it out of the side pocket in his fatigues.

Mannie chuckled. "Bet I could get something delivered."

"Then sure." Nev laughed. "I'll be there."

Zach thumbed the answer and pushed the volume down. It was Sgt. Jefferson, Foote's assistant.

"Riley?" Jefferson drawled. "What's your ETA?"

"Fifteen minutes. Sergeant." If the Sergeant was sounding southern, the stress was getting to him.

"Hotel said you got two volunteers?"

"Yes. They're with me." Zach glanced in the rear view mirror. Both his passengers had pained and worried looks.

"Bring 'em with you."

"Will do, Sergeant."

"Jefferson out."

Zach hit end call and slid the phone back in his pocket. "Well, gentlemen. I guess that's the plan. You're coming with me."

"I guess we don't have much choice?" Mark asked, as if he hoped Zach could save them.

"Well, I could drop you here, outside the City and you can take your chances. For my take, Provo's the best thing going."

"Yeah," Brian said.

"Let me know. I'll report that you didn't want to help."

"No. No." Mark's voice shook a little.

"We'll go," Brian agreed. "Don't have to be happy about it."

"I recommend not whining about it either."

Nev glanced over at Zach, her eyes playful. "You'll help these boys out, won't you, Zach?"

"Sure," Zach agreed with a smile. "I'll do what I can."

After making sandwiches for herself and Saj, Lizzie realized the lights were back on. How long had they been on? She finished getting Saj ready as they shared a desert snack of pears and grated cheese. Then she took him to Rachael's before heading for the next address on her list.

People to meet, collect data from… It was really nice being her own boss. It was weird she didn't even feel like flaking out and not doing it. She was only expected to do 30 hours a week and had already hit 34 hours and it was only Thursday.

Two hours later she decided she was done. Everyone had been polite, but they weren't happy to see her today. Was it the power outage? Made people fearful again that all they had was a propped up facade of what used to be real. Home was in between her and Rachael's, so she stopped in to change out of her winter clothes. Halfway undressed and there was a knock on the door. She pulled the cold damp clothes back on. Who the hell was knocking on her door?

She pulled the tape back off the peephole. Duke. She opened the door. "Come on in."

"You wanna walk?"

"No. I wanna rock." She banged her head like she was in some heavy metal band.

Duke grimaced at the joke.

"Yeah. I'll go for a walk. I need to go get Saj from Rachael's."

She shoved her arms back into the warm coat and pulled him by the hand as she shut the door behind her. "*Uno, dos, tres—*"

Duke stepped in front of her, wrapped her in his arms and lifted her off her feet. "Catorce!"

When he set her down Lizzie squatted slightly, wrapped her arms and grabbed her own hands right under his tail-bone. She grunted and heaved, managing to get his feet off the ground.

"Arriba! Careful pregnant lady," Duke said as she dropped him back down.

"And *abajo*." He was right. "I was careful."

"Careful for you, maybe." He wrapped his arm around her shoulder and they continued on.

When they got to Rachael's she looked seriously agitated. "Have you heard?"

Lizzie glanced at Duke, who shrugged his shoulders. "No. I guess not. What's up?"

"The new council is trying to pass a selective service for the girls."

"You mean they're going to send us to war, too?" Lizzie put her hands together to form a gun and pointed it at Duke. "I don't get it. It's about time."

"No. Selective service for girls. To do our part for our country."

Lizzie's brain flashed. "No. You're kidding."

"Nope. Young women of child-bearing age who have not conceived a child or are not currently pregnant will be tested for fertility and must become pregnant within the next 12 months."

"That's bullshit," Duke growled. "What the hell is this place? Communist China?"

"It's not going to happen," Lizzie said. "They've lowered the voting age and given us the right to vote."

Rachael deflated a bit. "Yeah. I suppose not. Mr. Ray said he would veto it."

"See," Duke agreed. "Nothing to worry about."

Lizzie wasn't used to having to prop Rachael up.

"Juke?" asked a little voice. Saj burst into the room. "Juke and Sissie!" He ran to them. "Unodos?"

"Okay. We'll do *Uno, dos, tres* while we walk."

On the way home, between swinging Saj in the air, she and Duke continued the conversation. By the time they'd gotten home, she'd decided that there was no way it would happen. People wouldn't stand for it.

Mannie's head jerked at the sound of the door knob being turned. He held himself back from standing to see who it was. Instead he continued to search for the data he needed.

Nev walked past the cubicle wall. "What can I do to help?" she asked, a pinched smile on her face.

Mannie could see the stress outlined on her jaw. "I need a priority list for power. I'm betting we can keep generators running here. We need to get people to shut down all non-essentials in the building so the power we've got lasts. They've called me to a meet-"

"I heard the announcement." Her fake smile had faded to a tight frown. "Figured you needed me quick. What else?"

"I don't know. Watch your phone. Hopefully I can text you during the meeting."

Another knock on the door and it opened even faster. "Mr. Guerrero?" A hefty young man in fatigues who'd obviously run the whole way came in and bent over immediately. "They want you now," he gasped.

"Tell them I'm on my way. Setting up systems to get started." Mannie gestured to Nev.

"All right. I'll tell them you're on your way." The runner sighed as he opened the door. His footfalls faded as he ran back.

Nev chuckled dryly as the door bounced back into place. "I do believe that boy needs to get in shape."

Mannie smiled. "Yeah. This time next year maybe he'll be in shape."

"What are you going to tell them? The good news or the bad news?"

"Is there any good news?"

"We're not dead yet?"

He liked her sense of humor. "Well, the good news is we're not dead. And we've got plants coming along in the green houses. We won't go too hungry. I have no bleeding clue how long it'll take to restore power."

"You better get going."

"Said I wasn't going to do this shit again."

Nev shrugged. "Yeah. Lot of that going around."

Mannie shoved himself vertical. His knee told him he'd been sitting in one place too long. He stretched it for a moment. "Sorry you and Zach didn't get your vacation."

"Oh," Nev's pale face reddened, "we got a little."

Mannie laughed. "Good. See you in a bit." At least some things never changed despite the world around them. Kids would still find time to fall in love.

He swung open the door and stepped into the hall, limping as fast as he could toward the courtroom. When he arrived he shoved both doors open. Everyone turned to look at him. There was one space left, right next to Foote, near DiSilvio and Ray. Shit. Well, he sure as hell wasn't going to take on fourth in the line of succession. "You waiting for me?" he asked to the room as the pain in his knee slowed him down to a shuffle.

"Frankly, we decided you probably have a better handle on this than any of us."

Mannie slid into the seat. "When do we get power back?"

DiSilvio cocked his head to the side. "How long can we last without it?"

Mannie harrumphed. "At what level of comfort?" he retorted.

"We figured we had months of natural gas." DiSilvio placed his fingertips together and looked into the space he'd created. "We need more."

"This building's generators run on gasoline. We've been collecting it. But how many other buildings have generators? How soon can we switch over the solar plant in Delta?"

Foote was shaking his head. "We don't have an engineer to tell us how it works."

"Well, we better find one." Mannie immediately regretted the tone of his voice. Foote stared reproachfully at Mannie over his glasses.

Mannie continued in a more respectful voice. "Unless somebody has an extra supply of natural gas, solar is our best bet. What happened to the natural gas supply?"

DiSilvio glanced at Foote and then to Mr. Ray. Then he shrugged. "Somebody measured wrong."

"It happens," Mr. Ray said.

"Well, I want to know why," Mannie said. "What do you need from me?"

Mr. Ray and DiSilvio exchanged a glance. DiSilvio spoke. "We need to know how bad things are in terms of supplies."

"Then why did you pull me in here?" Mannie realize the edge on his voice was not going to win friends and influence people. "Let me get back to my office. I'll send updates as soon as I have solid info." He shoved himself to his feet.

"Mannie?" Foote asked. "Is it outside influence? Did someone shut down the natural gas?"

Mannie shrugged. "No fucking clue, Sir." His glare and comment were met with hard, pissed off faces. "Sorry. I'll tell you if I figure it out." He stamped out the door and back down the hall to his office. He could hear voices in the room he'd left, angry voices, but no one came after him.

He was talking to Nev before he made it all the way into the room. "Okay. I want all the collectors out getting ice. Put it on the emergency bluetooth to all phones."

Power. To think that yesterday he'd been so concerned about the power of the people, the power of the government. He hadn't even entertained the idea that the power for the people would fail. How long before the people were pissed off that the governmental offices still had power? Their generators and power would only work as long as there was fuel. Provo's now 60,000 plus people were too many to be able to move in. But most sure as hell weren't ready to start homesteading. Too many people who would normally be able to take care of themselves, were about to become utterly helpless. That's what happens when people hand over responsibility for their lives to government.

Mannie muttered to himself. "Why the fuck is this my responsibility?" He knew the answer. A responsibility became one's own as soon as it became obvious that it existed. At least that was the case for him. He'd screwed up too many of his other duties and responsibilities. Now he had to suck it up and take care of people who should be taking care of themselves.

He opened his door and slumped back against it.

He got a thin smile from Nev.

"That good, huh?"

"I want to lock the door and keep everyone out that wants something. But I'm pretty sure that isn't a good idea."

"Here's what we've got. Glen got me a bigger weather report than I was able to get here. Who the hell is squeezing our internet?"

Mannie glared at her.

"I know," she whispered. "Big Brother is watching? What the fu…?"

"And the weather is?"

"Nice. Cool, but not cold. No new snow."

"Damn."

"You want it freezing?"

"Yeah. People can stay warm with hats and coats, but keeping food from spoiling…"

Nev nodded. "What do we do?"

"Well, we get an army of ice collectors." Mannie sighed. "I wish I had a fucking clue when the power might be back for the city."

As if in response the lights flickered and went back to steady. "Nev, check to see if the power is back on."

A second later, a whoop echoed through the room. "We're back!"

"*Ojala que* it stays back."

"What's that mean? My Spanish is by the book."

"Means God willing essentially."

"Didn't know you were a believer, Mannie."

"I'm not. It was beaten out of me by the school nuns... But the words of *mi abuela* sometimes come out."

Chapter Twenty-Four

INSIDE LIZZIE'S PLACE THE HEAT had returned. She fed Saj and then read some Camus while Duke and Saj played with Duplos on the floor.

"Psst," Duke whispered, "Lizzie."

Saj had crashed out, falling asleep on the floor, a Duplo person in each hand.

"I was building him a house and next thing I know…" Duke picked him up and gently deposited him on the couch.

"Glad I fed him. I'm hungry." She slid her hundred dollar bookmark into the book and stood. Her left leg zinged from falling asleep as she hobbled over and opened the freezer, relieved to have the light come on.

"The Last Decent Almost Frozen Pizza," Lizzie said with a flourish.

"How do you know it's the last one?"

"There are lots more pizzas, but I'm not sure they're gonna stay frozen and/or decent for long. I figure we better cook all of them now that the power is back on.

"Damn," Duke said. "Shouldn't we say a Eulogy or something?"

Lizzie pulled open the fridge and grabbed a champagne bottle. "We should toast it," she said with a pose she thought might entice. "Course, you should drink most of it, me being pregnant and all."

"I will sacrifice myself at that altar, milady." He took the bottle from her like a sacrificial sword, stripping off the foil and the wire cage and pointing the bottle at her like it was a weapon.

"Be careful where you point that thing, sir knight." She grasped it around the neck and pulled it back from him. She went to work on the cork working it back and forth aiming it at his chest.

"Whoa, your highness. 'There's a shortage of perfect breasts in the world'" He grabbed his own chest and squeezed. "'It would be a pity to damage these.'"

Lizzie snorted. "'I do not think that means what you think it means.'"

"'Incontheivable,'" he muttered as the cork flew out of the bottle and champagne followed it onto the floor. "Hey, don't waste that." He managed to get a glass under the flow from the bottle. She returned it to vertical and handed it to him.

"You may pour, sir."

By the time they had eaten everything but a few crusts off the last of the pizza, Duke had finished off much of the champagne.

As they were sitting watching *A Knight's Tale*, Lizzie couldn't get Rachael's concerned look out of her head. What she was talking about was practically sex slavery. This was the United States, or had been until recently. They couldn't do it. But with a sinking feeling she knew they could.

When Duke slipped out from under Saj and knelt before her on the couch. His face tilted as his boisterous grin grew. "Hey, you wanna get engaged?"

"What the fuck, Duke? Are you kidding me? Where the hell did that come from?"

His face sobered. "It gets you a free weekend in Salt Lake City to get engaged. You don't even have to get married. Ever."

"I don't plan on getting married EVER. And getting engaged for a 'pre-honeymoon' to give The Man his babies like Zach and Nev are doing…"

"The Man?" Duke slumped in front of her. "Is everything political?"

"Yeah. Political or personal or both." Shit. She could really use the distraction. If only for a while. "We can get engaged right here," Lizzie growled, pulling him up toward her.

Duke reanimated, climbing up on top of her with his legs straddling hers. "Here and now is fine."

She glanced over at Saj sleeping. "Maybe not here and now." What would he think waking up to Sissie and Juke groaning and naked? "Definitely not."

"Maybe tomorrow?" Duke said hopefully, "The stars are much prettier away from the city lights. There's this place up on the hill…"

"Tomorrow." Anyplace outside of The City was better than inside. "Maybe," Lizzie said, pulling his face toward her and kissing him, let her tongue find his, promising that the maybe would be. Maybe her father would like to have Saj for the evening.

As the twilight faded, the little boy on Mannie's chest was still except for breathing. Saj, the energizer bunny toddler, had finally run his batteries out of juice. Mannie was glad. He'd gone about as far as he could go. The last two days at work, responding to and recovering from the power scare had knocked him out, too, but he'd agreed to let Lizzie have her night out with Duke.

When Mannie felt his own eyes closing, he'd fed the kid and held him in the recliner while the television droned in the background. A glance at his watch told him it was later than he thought. If he moved the kid would probably wake up.

He stared at the picture in the frame on the end table. He reached out, sliding carefully to the side until he could pull it into his hands. Then he turned it over and slid the metal swivels aside. He flipped it and the bottom came open, releasing several more pictures he'd collected, all were of Isabel. Some included him.

There had been a very long time when he wasn't sure he could love again. Then she found him, befriended him and eventually brought that part of him back to life. When she'd died in the pandemic, he'd given up. Seriously thinking of killing himself or drinking until the pain went away. But she'd loved him enough that he knew he'd be letting them both down if he went out that way. And as much as he didn't believe in heaven, hell or purgatory, he wasn't going to blow the chance of never seeing her again.

When Lizzie called, he had another proof that he had made the right choice. Now here he'd become Saj's, Mampa. And soon enough Lizzie's baby would arrive. Isabel would have loved being *una abuela*.

He would get some more frames. Maybe some candles. Isabel would want him to try to date again. To live a full life. But not yet. For now, being a grandpa was enough. He didn't relish Lizzie and Zach the complications that kids brought. And the complications they'd chosen, but he figured they were young; they'd work it out. Hopefully the three of them didn't make it too rough on everyone else around them.

There was a knock on the door. Lizzie? Nah. She wouldn't knock.

He covered Saj's ear with his hand. "Come in." Another knock. "Come in," he hissed a little louder. Finally, the knob turned. Rachael. A smile lit up her face when she saw the small sleeping shape on his chest.

"Lizzie texted me," she whispered. "Said she was going to be out late again. I'm so glad she and Duke connected. You want me to take Saj?"

Mannie shrugged. "I don't know. Yes, I'm too hot. No, I'm liking this feeling right now. Maybe, because if he wakes up and I can't get him to settle down."

Rachael giggled, suddenly seeming younger. "Yeah, that's the thing with kids, you never know what to expect." A sadness crossed her face, but her smile forced the joviality back.

"How do you like working at the child-care? Is it easier or harder with a bunch of kids?"

"Oh, I like it fine. It's different. Like having parents who can tag-team. It's hardest when you're alone and they're inconsolable."

"Yeah. That's what worries me. I like being the grandpa. I get to give him back."

"Well, I'd like one of my own, but I'm not sure I'm ready for a new relationship."

"That thought makes me pretty sure you're not ready." Mannie's hand strayed through Saj's soft blonde hair. "I think I'm only ready for this one, being a grandpa."

"Yeah. I hear that. Saj'll take all the love I have to give without asking for more." Rachael pulled Saj's winter coat off the back of the couch.

"You ever think there isn't enough of you left to go around?"

Rachael moved to take Saj. "What do you mean?"

"Well. Falling in love. New relationships. Being alone."

"I'm not following you, Mannie." Rachael's face pinched with concern.

Mannie tried to replay his thoughts, make it make sense so he could say it. "Never mind. Just rambling, I guess."

"Sure you don't want to keep him tonight?" Her hand caressed Saj's cheek. "He's quite the cuddler."

Mannie thought about it. He was better off alone. "Yeah. I'm sure. If Lizzie thinks you'll have him…" A yawn escaped. "And I'm fading. Old soldier and all."

"Okay. Let's see if we can get him in his coat without waking him up." She maneuvered one arm in, then tucked it and rolled him onto his side.

Mannie watched the activity on his chest with amusement.

When Rachael had Saj all but zipped she rolled him into her arms.

"You're really good at that."

"Thanks. People at the daycare say I have the touch."

"You sure do. Thanks for relieving *el abuelo*." Mannie flipped the recliner lever down and pushed himself up. His leg felt like it might not hold him, so he sat back on the arm of the chair.

"No problem." Rachael swung the diaper bag strap over her shoulder. "Can you get the door for me?"

Mannie nodded and pushed himself back to his feet. A sharp pain shot through his leg, but he shook it off with a grimace. He opened the door and used it to take some pressure off his leg. As Rachael went by he kissed Saj's forehead. "G'night."

"Good night, Mannie." Rachael pulled Saj in a little closer as she set off down the sidewalk.

The night was clear and cold, not freezing, but chilly. Mannie watched them go. You can't choose who loves you, but you can choose who you love and how. He could love Jess like a daughter and someday, she'd find somebody, maybe when the grief had been able to play out.

He shut the door and leaned against it, shaking out his leg. Physical pain jabbed at his knee. He felt tears in his eyes. Should do his damn physical therapy exercises. Isabel could always get him to do them. He walked toward the bedroom, but stopped at the basement door.

The next night up at Squaw Peak Overlook, Lizzie decided Duke was right. The stars were lovely. In the days before the Quieting there would have been too much light pollution from the city, but tonight was clear and cold. Lizzie shivered as a wind picked up.

Duke pulled her toward him. "You cold?"

"Yeah. Not used to this weather." Lizzie let him. "Aren't you cold?"

Duke shrugged. "Used to spend a lot of time up at Mt. Baker.

Snowboarding. Go until you couldn't feel anything on the ends of your extremities. I'll get the blanket out of my truck."

"Wait," Lizzie said, but his warmth had already left her.

He returned with a big wool blanket labeled ARMY in faded letters. He spun it around her back and sat down next to her.

"How come you're so nice?"

"Having the Dad and brother I had? I had to be nice. But I'm not. Not really nice. Not always. It's not like I never get mad. It's just takes so long that it seems like it. When I do? I really let loose."

He pulled her back toward him. The blanket fell off as he nuzzled into her chest.

After he held her for a while he pulled her shirt back and his finger traced the outline of the tribal inspired sun and moon tattoo around her belly button. She'd designed it in her high school drawing class and managed to find a tattoo artist who would accept Nev's note from her 'mom.' That was the last time Lizzie had been successful in convincing Nev to break the rules. Well, except for the post-apocalyptic shopping trip to the mall. Lizzie let her eyes fall shut as a vision of Nev posing in a push up bra and lace panties played out in her head.

Lizzie squirmed as a shivering yawn shook her whole body. She tugged the blanket up. "Gonna have to check it out by braille or use a flashlight. It's cold."

Duke's breath escaped in a big burst and then he took another back in. It seemed as if he'd forgotten to breathe.

Duke grinned up at her and pulled out his cell phone. He flipped on the light and with a lascivious grin he pulled the blanket over himself. She could feel his warm breath on her leg as his finger tickled again. She shuddered again, as his fingers slipped further. The stars up above held her attention as she warmed up under the blanket. Thoughts of Bellingham and the reasons she'd left crowded out the pleasantness of other sensations. Duke's brother C.J.s body, naked and bloody on the bath mat blocked out any change of warming up today.

"Let's go back to the city. We're gonna freeze out her." She tossed the blanket aside and shoved her shirt down.

Duke stared at her, confusion clouding his face. "Okay."

Chapter Twenty-Five

WHEN THE GO TO THE safe house, Lizzie let Duke lead her downstairs. He put on some mellow music, and pulled his shirt off, moving in to kiss her.

She let her lips move against Duke's as her brain worried about the new ruling. In a way she was lucky to already be pregnant, but that didn't help Rachael, Jess or Nev. Betsy had been the smart one. She was probably out on the coast by now. Duke's body and how he used it usually helped her forget some of the shit she didn't want to think about. It wasn't working now.

"Lizzie?"

"Yeah?"

"You're someplace else."

Lizzie wanted to lie, to kiss him and then push him further down under the covers. "Yeah." She pulled away from him and pulled her legs up as near to her chest as she could and wrapped her arms around herself. "Sex is better than cigarettes."

"For what?" Duke snagged the comforter from the foot of the bed and wrapped it around the two of them.

Lizzie tugged it in close. "For nerves. Anxiety."

He chuckled. "I'd have to agree."

She bit her lip until it hurt. "But it only does so much."

Lizzie relaxed as his arms wrapped around her, leaving his shoulders exposed. "Aren't you cold?"

"No. But you are."

"Ouch."

Duke held his hands up. "Hey. I didn't mean that way. You're all wound up, aren't you?"

"Yeah." She lay back and stared at the popcorn textured ceiling.

Duke wrapped her in his arms, his warm hand slipping onto her belly.

"Thanks for being here for Saj. Last week, taking him to the park when I had had too much. That was life-saving. For me and him!"

"He's a great kid." Duke squeezed her gently. "You ever think about his parents?"

Lizzie nodded. "Yeah. And all the other kids like him who weren't as lucky."

"Shit. That's a downer."

"Yeah. Sorry. I'm a barrel of laughs this evening." Lizzie pulled the comforter up over her head and straddled him. "Shall we go tenting?" She pulled her own shirt off as the comforter shut out the light.

"Yes," he answered. Then they stopped talking.

A while later, lying warm in his arms, Lizzie zoned.

A buzzing brought her back to full consciousness. What time was it? Her phone was in a pile by the door. With a sigh of regret she pulled herself from Duke's warmth and slipped out from under the covers. He shifted to his side, his eyes still closed. She wrapped the comforter around herself and stumbled toward the phone. The little toe of her foot caught on the foot of the chair. "God-damn it!"

Duke shot up. "What happened?"

"I think I broke my damn toe on the chair." She hopped over to her jeans and pulled the phone from the back pocket.

Missed call. Rachael. The screen shifted. New voice-mail. Her heart stopped. She tapped the icon and collapsed onto the carpet. Was it Saj? Or Rachael?

The voicemail hummed. "Lizzie? Sorry to bother you." Rachael's voice seemed loud. Then a pause. "I picked up Saj from your dad. Your dad was kind of... I don't know... weird. Talking like falling in love was the worst thing that could happen. He seemed almost broken. Anyway. You can come get Saj. Or not. Let me know."

The throbbing in Lizzie's toe had subsided. It felt hot, but not broken. Like her. She had taken a beating since the outbreak started, but surprisingly she wasn't broken. All this talk of needing Duke as a distraction wasn't really true. And even if it was, she was using him. She could tell him it was a simple friendly arrangement all she wanted

—he played along because he loved her. She stood and walked back toward the bed.

"What's up?" Duke held the covers up for her.

"I'm not getting back into bed."

"You need to go get Saj? I can come with you."

"I'm sorry."

"What? You're sorry? For what?"

"I'm going home. I can't do this to you."

Duke stared at her, looking confused. "Do what?"

"I can't stay. I can't sleep with you. You're my friend. You're lovely. But, I..."

"But you what?" Duke sighed and propped himself up on his elbows.

"I need to end this. While we're friends."

"What?" Duke's voice raised.

Lizzie could hear the hurt she'd caused. "Duke. It's not you; it's me."

"That's such a fucking cop-out, Lizzie. And it doesn't matter. I fell in love with you. Now, you want to just be friends."

"But that is the problem isn't it. Don't pretend not to remember that I told you this was not about love. It was only ever supposed to be an arrangement between friends. You swore that you wouldn't make it about love."

"I'm sorry I can't be an unfeeling machine like you." He turned away to hide his tears.

"That isn't fair," Lizzie whispered.

He wiped his cheeks quickly. "No. But it isn't fair to expect me not to feel like we had something growing, when you seem to be so happy with me. None of this was fair, right from the start was it?" He looked at her, red blotches spreading across his face. "Why am I not good enough? What is it you are looking for, Lizzie?"

"I'm..." Lizzie started speaking, but she didn't know what to say. "Duke..."

His head dropped into his hands.

"You're right. It's fucked up. It's not fair." She slipped out of the bedding and pulled her underwear and bra on. Why couldn't she be happy with this amazing guy and his love for her? Would she ever find someone she wasn't just settling for? Or using to scratch an itch. It hurt her to hurt him. But she had warned him, so it was all his fault. He had ruined a great thing. If anything she was less attracted to him now, since he'd started looking at her with his love goggles on.

"Don't get me wrong, Duke," she said, steeling herself. "The sex was great. You should make some other girl very happy one day." She stepped into her flannel lined jeans and the ugly snow boots she wore outside.

He stared at her. His still naked body was chiseled and muscular like a sculpture. He wasn't cold and hard like marble, though, he was warm and soft (mostly) and fun. But he wasn't for her.

She clenched her jaw and pulled her T-shirt on over her head. "I said I was sorry, what more do you want?"

Mannie tried to raise his head off the floor. He could hear knocking. He pushed himself to his knees and the world spun. The couch spun up to hit the side of his face. He felt a scraping of skin on the rough cloth of the couch.

The banging grew louder.

"Dad!"

Shit. Lizzie. Your father's a fucking drunk.

He heard a key in the lock. The knob turned, but the door didn't open.

"Undo the deadbolt." Lizzie yelled. "I need you."

¡Dios mio! He pushed himself forward toward the door. His arms barely obeyed. The carpet slammed into his face where he'd scraped it on the couch.

"Lizzie. Coming." Just a few more feet and then he could pull himself up on the knob.

It took all his control to get his hand onto the knob. Then he pulled himself up. He slid his other hand up the door to the deadbolt. He slipped down the textured wall tearing skin off his shoulder. The floor stopped him as the door shoved passed him. His stomach churned and his body clenched. Trying to throw up what wasn't in his stomach. Lizzie rolled him over on his side and then things went black.

He woke in a rainstorm, leaning against a wall. When he managed to open his eyes, he realized that Lizzie had hauled him into the shower with his icky clothes on. The bathroom lights burned his eyeballs and he closed them.

"Lizzie? You there?"

"Yeah. I'm here. Are you?"

He tried to laugh but the acid taste in his mouth made him gag.

He opened his mouth to the water pouring down.

"Jesus, Daddy. You don't do much half-way."

After a minute he turned to the wall, grabbing a towel as he pushed himself up. He spit in the shower and stepped out onto the bathmat.

"You said you needed me?" he asked, scrubbing his face on the rough towel.

"Yeah. Evidently, not as bad as you need me." She laughed. "There's a line and I crowded to the front. When I'm done with you, the office wants you."

"Ay, dios mio." He wasn't in any state to go to the office. But it wasn't like you could call in sick to the end of the world.

"Yeah." Lizzie handed him another towel. "I figured it was important if they'd call me. I'll be outside if you need anything. Coffee? Ibuprofen?"

Mannie almost nodded, but then thought better of it. "Yeah. Both. Thanks."

She pulled the door shut behind her and Mannie collapsed onto the toilet. *"Maria, madre de dios."* After a minute of eyes closed grounding, letting himself feel all of the pain and discomfort, he took a deep breath and reached for the cup by the sink and filled it. Water was the first thing he needed. He stood, steadying himself on the sink and drank it down slow. Then he refilled it and had another sip.

He climbed back in the shower without clothes.

Ten minutes later he heard a knock at the door. "Coffee's hot and sugared. I think the ibuprofen is in there." Lizzie handed him the coffee with an amused look on her face.

"I know. I'm paying for my sins," he said.

"I just hope I don't have to pay for the sins of my father."

"Just pay for your own." He pulled the painkiller from the cupboard and popped a few in his mouth. He downed the rest of the water and then followed up with some coffee.

"You want me to drive you to work?" Concern shadowed her face.

"You think you're up for that?" he asked. "How are you doing on stick shifts?"

"Ouch. I've been practicing. The stick shift is still a little challenging. I figured I could give you some laughs."

"Not sure my head can stand much jostling, but thanks."

"I'll ride with you to work. I need to talk."

His body and his mind protested as he climbed into Rubi. Work was the last place he wanted to be.

Lizzie watched him carefully as he turned the key, though she didn't say anything.

"I'm fine to drive," he said. "Hung over maybe, but not drunk."

"I'm not judging," she said, but her twitchy fingers stilled.

They rode in silence for a few minutes, but it was clear that something else was bothering her. "You seem a little perplexed."

"Perplexed?" Lizzie took a deep breath in and then let out in a whoosh. "How'd you know mom was the one? Or did you? How about Isabel?"

Isabel—like a punch to the stomach. He gripped the steering wheel tighter, but held it together. "Just a little question, huh?" He thought about it for a while. "I thought I knew with both of them. And others. It felt right. But it's not something I can explain. I would say if you really think someone is the one, then they are. No need to overthink it." It grated on him to tell her to go for it with whatever guy she was talking about—probably Duke. But he wasn't going to be the dad who hated all the boyfriends.

Lizzie didn't say anything.

Mannie glanced across at her. "You okay?"

"Yeah. Probably." She gave him a tight smile. "No worse than usual."

When they arrived at the government offices, his head felt closer to normal. He hopped out and opened her door for her. "I love you, Elizabeth. I wish I had better advice in the relationship department. Pretty ironic if I'm the relationship expert for the next generation." He pulled her into his arms and held her until she released him.

"I love you, too. I think I want to go home. But I don't know where that is."

"Well, if you figure it out, let me know. I'll come with you."

"Go. Get to work. I'm going for a walk."

"Good idea. Come by later if you want to talk more."

"I will." She walked away down the snow-lined sidewalk.

He wished he could just go for a walk with her, but people were counting on him. He sighed at went inside.

Nev glanced up, as he walked through the door to his office. "They want you now, Mannie."

"Thanks. I just need to get my thoughts in order. Any hints on what's going on?"

"Power, of course. They've got somebody else waiting to meet with you, too. An engineer."

"Good." Mannie sifted through the notes on his desk. "Hopefully he can help with the Delta solar plant." His hands stacked the notes into one rectangular pile and placed them in the middle of the desk facing the chair. "Okay. I'm going in."

Nev smirked. "Am I supposed to say, 'I'll cover you,' or what?" She put her hands together like a gun, pointing her index fingers at the ceiling.

"Could you bring me in this pile of paperwork and coffee in about fifteen minutes if I'm not out of there?"

"That's more my style. Good luck." Her eyes went back to her paperwork.

Mannie felt dismissed. Nev was a great asset in the office. Too bad she and Lizzie couldn't grow up and get over their relationship garbage.

Mannie swept into the conference room. "Sorry. Babysitting last night and a rough morning. What have we got?"

DiSilvio motioned toward a nervous looking man, who was squinting at Mannie over his reading glasses. "This is Dr. Packard. He helped us switch over systems to the natural gas. He can bring you up to speed on the recent outages. And he's agreed to try to help with the Delta switch-over."

"You're the engineer?" Mannie asked.

Dr. Packard glanced back down at the papers in front of him. "Theoretical until now. Geologist mainly. Underground research: aquifers, mines..."

"We need a power man," Mannie said, "who knows how the electrical power grid works."

Dr. Packard shrugged and shuffled his papers. "I'm what you've got. Let me tell you what I do know. The first power outage occurred when the Chalk Creek basin was depleted. Not a big surprise, it was tiny. Now that the Coalville basin is empty, we've got Leroy and Clay Basins. Leroy is about as big as Coalville was. Clay is about 10 times. So, we should still be fine for the time being."

"'Should still be fine' does not offer me much comfort," Mannie said, trying to keep his voice low.

Mr. Ray nodded. "That's why we need to flip over the solar plant in Delta for our electrical needs. The sun's not going out anytime soon."

Mannie shivered at that thought—after everything else, why not?

DiSilvio stood, leaning forward on the table. "We need to make sure we've got control of it there and can manage it here." He spun on Foote. "How many troops do we have and how ready are they to be deployed?"

Foote chuckled humorlessly. "What do you want me to say?"

"The truth, Foote." DiSilvio's face reddened. "Are you making fun of me?"

"No, Tony." Foote raised his hands in mock defense. "We've had 3 weeks of training. Basic Training in the U.S. Army takes ten weeks and that's working with kids who want to be there, or who have at least passed MEPS tests." He shook his head grimly. "My men are entirely ready to capture an empty solar plant. But not more than a dozen are ready to face an armed enemy."

"Luckily," Mr. Ray's grandfatherly calm interjected, "I don't think that's likely. The only place we've felt any heat is up north."

Foote sat back. "Yes. If our luck holds."

Mr. Ray smiled gently. "The harder we work the luckier we get."

"Mr. Ray," DiSilvio pushed his seat back and sat on the front edge. "Will you give the order?"

"If Mr. Foote agrees, but I want to go on record that this is a peaceful mission. We will send out militia, but we will not fire unless fired upon. And we will abort if we find the plant defended."

Mannie scrutinized Foote; he had trusted him since Foote let him go find Lizzie, but he still wasn't sure where he stood in terms of the new nation state forming around them.

Foote took a breath and blew it out. "Yeah. Let's do it." He stood. "Mannie, come with me."

"Yes, sir," Mannie said automatically.

"One more thing, Foote," DiSilvio said. "Mr. Ray and I would like to make you our general."

Foote's jaw clenched. "I am not your fucking general."

Mannie looked to Mr. Ray and DiSilvio. Couldn't they see how bad an idea this was? Mr. Ray had the class to be shocked. DiSilvio's eyes narrowed, but he did not look appeased.

"If and when we have 5,000 troops," Foote said in low measured tones. "I may consider accepting the position." He collapsed into the chair. "However, since I want to promote the men below me who have earned it, I had better let you promote me first. Colonel would be appropriate considering our level of enlistment."

"Very well," Mr. Ray said, "Colonel Foote, thank you for accepting the promotion."

Foote turned to Mannie. "Sorry, Mannie. Your first promotion. Gentlemen, please approve a rank increase for Major Guerrero."

Shit. Mannie straightened. "Yes, sir, Colonel Foote."

"Let's go, Mannie."

Mr. Ray waved them off as he turned back to DiSilvio, "Well, Tony? What did I do wrong this time?"

Foote closed the door behind Mannie. "I'm not taking you with me." His hand came up as Mannie opened his mouth. "I'll feel better if you're here."

"Yes, sir."

"Since when did you start calling me, Sir?"

"Since it started to feel like war."

Chapter Twenty-Six

LIZZIE AND DUKE WALKED ALONG the wall of the city, made up of trucks and storage containers. There were gaps, they weren't going to keep anyone out yet, human or otherwise, the wall was beyond symbolic at this point. The council had decided to fill up the gaps when Mr. Ray had convinced enough of the people to move inside the new city zone.

Betsy had called this boiling frogs, before she left. "You can't put frogs into a pot of boiling water, or they'll jump out. But if you turn up the heat a notch at a time…"

They were walking toward the next major gap in the wall, and the silence was beginning to crawl under her skin. Lizzie reached for Duke's hand and he pulled it away.

Duke stared straight ahead. "You wanted to talk. Talk."

"Duke."

"Lizzie?"

She wasn't going to put up with his shit. This was exactly what she was trying to avoid. Awkward silences and damaged relationships. What had possessed her to think she could separate sex from the relationship stuff? Was she really that hard up? Or just lonely?

His pace was swift. She had to hoof it to keep up. The sun faded on the white-tipped mountains, turning them a calm shade of pale pink.

"Hey, look at that," Duke's head gestured up ahead.

Someone with a rifle sat in a lawn chair in the middle of the street, right at the gap. "A nut?"

"Let's go see."

A teen-aged boy, lanky and tall, but still smooth cheeked, greeted them. "Howdy, folks."

"What's up, dude?" Duke raised his eyebrow.

"People aren't supposed to come around here. Dangerous."

Duke's attention perked up.

"What's dangerous?" he asked the kid with the gun.

"Same as everywhere: Utah Independents, coyotes, cougars, wild dogs. This part of town seems to be where the dog packs have run to."

"Why's that?"

The kid shrugged. "Who knows? More bodies?"

"Who's got you out here?"

"Mr. DiSilvio's orders."

"Seems like a pretty chill assignment," Lizzie said, motioning to the lawn chair and the bottle of beer.

"Yep."

"Let's go." Lizzie wrapped her arm around Duke's bicep and tugged him further down the street.

"You folks have a good evening."

"You, too," Duke said, letting Lizzie lead him. Up ahead in the distance, he saw the shimmer of a gas camp lantern. "Hhhhmmm… There's another one."

"This is weird."

"Why's it weird?"

"Guards on a side street. Spaced just evenly that people don't get past them? I thought the purpose of the wall was to keep out the bad things, not lock us in."

"Your paranoia must be exhausting." He stopped. "I'm tired, Lizzie. Say what you wanted to say already."

Lizzie kept hold of his arm. "It was nothing in particular. Just wanted to hang out."

He pulled his arm from her grip. "Lizzie, either just be my friend or let me be. I can't handle it."

The sound of dogs barking caught her attention. In the distance they were answered with coyote howls.

"See? The Guard's just trying to protect us."

"With a wall. Which reminds me. Let's go to the club, everyone calls The Wall, even though the management tried to rename it The Safety Dance. I'll buy you a beer. Maybe you'll meet somebody."

"With my ex-um… my— With you on my arm?" He shook his

head. "I don't get you, Lizzie."

"Let's go. I'll work on the just friends. One of the guys... That's me."

"Yeah. Whatever. You're one of the guys. It better be good beer."

As they reached the former University campus Lizzie couldn't help but laugh out loud at the birther propaganda littering the walls. Do you love him? Take him for a test drive.

That one had to be the funniest one she'd seen yet. "Hey, Duke, can I step on your gas pedal?" Shit. When would she learn to think before she spoke?

"You already took me for a spin, Lizzie. Besides, your tank is already full." His words were joking but his expression was flat.

She winced and said, "You're going to have to lighten up, if you're going to meet somebody."

"Then just shut up. Let's go find somebodies."

As they approached the club, 80's pop music reverberated down the street. Duke paused. "If they start playing Wang Chung, I'm leaving." But he waited for her at the door.

Lizzie scanned the crowd and pulled Duke inside. He scowled. She kissed him on the forehead. "Come on."

"This is stupid." He glanced around, his eyes flitting from place to place, person to person, then back to her. "I was never good at this."

"I'll help." Lizzie's eye settled on a girl clinging to the wall on the other side of the room. Her long hair was simply parted and her eyes seemed wary and aware without being nervous. Like she would know what she was looking for when she found it.

There was a tall table near her with three empty chairs. Lizzie guided Duke by the arm. "I'll buy you a beer." She sat him down where she thought there might be good odds on Duke seeing the girl. "Don't leave."

Lizzie squeezed through the crowd to the bar. The Wall had become a really happening place. Not long ago she would have had to flash fake ID to get into a place like this, but the Provo Council thought lowering the drinking age was good for moral. Drunk teens procreated more, obviously. She didn't really want to be here, but she wanted to somehow set right what had gone wrong.

The bartender nodded at her. "What'll you have?"

"A DARK BEER and a SPRITE WITH LIME."

A few minutes later, he returned with a dark brown pint glass with a gentle layer of tan foam puffing over the top and a glass full of carbonated clearness. "WE'RE OUT OF LIME!"

"THANKS."

She took a drink from each, figuring that might allow her to get across the dance floor without getting beer or soda on herself or others.

The song ended, some crappy old dub step mix, and in the moments of dullness, silenced by the previous sound she hurried across the floor to Duke. She put the pint in his hand and clinked the rim on hers. "To love." She drank.

"To love? Fuck." He chugged half of it.

"Yeah." She smiled. "See anyone?"

"Nope." He glanced around at the crowd. "Place is empty."

"Anybody interesting?"

Duke's eyes focused on her. "Besides you?"

"What about her?"

"The one with the long plain hair? Closer to my own age."

"Okay, old man. Cause 24 is so much older than 18."

An hour later, Lizzie had managed to introduce him to the long-haired girl, Aubri. She'd been happy to join them—even remembered Lizzie from her work assignment day.

"That's right, you were the receptionist," said Lizzie, surprised the girl had even noticed her.

Aubri gave her a smile of pity. "I felt so bad for you—you looked upset."

"Yeah. But enough about me—this is Duke."

Once Aubri sat down Lizzie made an excuse to leave, and disappeared for a bit.

When she came back Aubri was gone.

"What? Did you run her off that quick?"

Duke pulled a napkin out of his pocket with a phone number and Aubri's name. "I told her the truth."

"And that is?"

"You and I just broke up. You're trying to set me up with someone, but that I'm still in love with you."

"Shit. That truth. And she still gave you her number?"

"She left it for you."

A crisp, cold wind tugged at Zach's jacket as he glanced away from Nev, down the row of soldiers, with wives and girlfriends hanging around to say their goodbyes. Will and a few other soldiers stood alone.

Nev clung to him. He wasn't used to that. "This doesn't feel real. I'm going off to war and kissing the woman I love."

"It's not war," she said, but she didn't sound convinced. "Yeah, it's freaky. But everything's going to be fine."

He kissed the top of her head, and left his face there, breathing in the slight scent of her shampoo. "Logical, thoughtful response," he muttered.

"Zach Riley," she warned.

He placed his arms on her shoulders and held her there, trying to take in every element to keep in his head. He'd kept a vision of her in his head for years. The woman in front of him was several years older, and even prettier he decided.

"What?"

"Just thinking about what a wonderful adult you are. I still got a long way to go."

"I only pretend to be one better than you do." She pulled him back toward her.

Nervous excitement twitched in his muscles. "I love *you*, Nevaeh."

"Love you too, goofball."

He released her and knelt on one knee. "Nevaeh, will you marry me."

For a moment, she looked like the proverbial deer in the headlights. Then she glared at him. "Stand up."

He stood, feeling empty.

"No. I won't marry you. I told you. Not now. When and *IF* I am ready, I will tell you."

"Nev—"

"What? Do you want me to promise to marry you so you'll come back from the war?" She sighed and her chest shook. Now she held him at arm's length. "I promise if you die, I will wish I had married you. But that's not going to happen. Back off. Maybe we need this time and space."

"Okay," he said, backpedaling quickly. 'Space' was not the word he wanted to hear.

"Don't give me those puppy dog eyes. And don't try again." She yanked him back and hugged him fiercely. "I love you, Zach Riley. And that will have to do for now." Her arms tightened enough to take his breath away, then she released him and walked away.

Zach wanted to run after her. Instead he stood waiting until she was gone in case she turned around. He wanted her to know she was his focus. But she started to jog and turned the corner at the end of the block. His hands shook so he knelt down and started messing with his gear, tightening the straps on the pack.

The whistle blew for formation. Zach lined up in the front row of his platoon, relieved to be focused on standing at attention. Colonel Foote strode by to inspect. When he reached the end, he turned to face the men. "If I call your name, fall out to the front of the formation."

"Benson. Cantrell," he barked. "MacLane, Riley."

Zach slid out of attention like everything was cool. He lined up facing the platoon as Benson was doing. Benson was one of the few pre-pandemic soldiers in the militia and besides Foote, the only officer.

"2nd Lieutenant Benson. You are hereby promoted to 1st Lieutenant." Foote didn't pause. "Cantrell, MacLane and Riley, you are all promoted to the rank of 2nd Lieutenant."

As soon as Lizzie got back to the census office, a cubicle in a room down from the mayor's office, the phone rang. She stared at it for a moment before lifting the receiver. "Yes?"

"Lizzie Goodin-Guerrero?" a woman's voice asked.

"Yeah."

"It's Flo. At the hospital."

"Flo." Lizzie's heart skipped a beat. "What's wrong?" She sat down, just in case.

"Nothing really urgent. I'm calling on official business. I'm looking for a picture of a man. Mr. Frank Lorenzo. I was told you might have one. He died today and we'd like a picture for the obituary."

"I'm sorry," Lizzie said automatically as she flipped through her list. "Frank? Yeah. Just a few days ago. I'll e-mail it to you."

"Thanks, Lizzie. How's your boy doing? And your baby?"

"We're all fine," she said. "Thanks, Flo." After she put down the phone and e-mailed the file, she printed out Mr. Lorenzo's picture to take down to the stadium after work. The walls there were covered with memorials, and pictures of people who were unaccounted for.

She typed up her notes and entered the morning's information into the database before calling it quits for the day.

She grabbed the scotch tape on the way out the door and headed for the stadium. It was good to concentrate on work and not worry about complicated things. She hoped Duke would make it back to just being her friend, but either way, she was a lot more free than she'd been for a long time.

Her steps sped up as she approached what had become her personal shrine. The lost people on the walls were her reason for being alive. Helping make sense of the dead. Some of the photos and notes had fallen to the floor. She traced them to their previous locations and added new tape. It was a puzzle. A puzzle that kept her interested, just like the stories people told her. She knelt to pick up the next photo and stopped. Frozen.

There he was. The face she'd etched into her mind and sketched on so many sheets of paper. The face that belonged to the body dumped out near the middle of nowhere. Lizzie stared at the photo. A guy leaned back against a couch, a laptop on his lap and a haze of beard on his chin.

Her eyes searched the picture-crowded wall for the location it had fallen from. The tape residue on the photo was rectangular. She found the empty little wad of tape. There was a note underneath it. Help me find my cousin. He survived the disease and then disappeared.

A phone number followed the message, but no name. "Shit." Her phone was in her hand, though she didn't remember taking it out. She started typing the number... Then she thought better of it. Maybe have Glen check it out first. Instead of calling, she switched to camera and took a close up photo and e-mailed it to herself and to her father.

Then she headed hurriedly from the wall, deciding that her apartment would be a better place. She called Duke. "Hey, I found him. The guy. Come on over."

There was silence on the other end, then, "Lizzie. I'm kinda busy. I'll call you back later."

Heat flashed to her face. "Busy? Already?"

"Not like that. Give me a break. Talk to you later." The line went dead.

"Shit. I didn't mean it like that either!"

She hit Rachael's icon and let it ring. When voice-mail answered Lizzie left a message that she was headed home early. After she hung up she hurried home, feeling that someone was following her the whole way.

As soon as she got in the door she dialed Glen's number on the safe phone and left him a message with the number and a request to track it.

Lizzie's fingers chased each other. She flattened them against her legs. Don't get crazy. She sat down on the couch with her laptop. Maybe she could ID the phone number herself. Glen wasn't the only one who could use a computer.

She typed in the number and a list of search results popped up. At the top: Jenny Laurents, Provo, Utah.

She pasted the name into the search bar and a Facebook profile popped up. She clicked on **Friends** and started scanning down. There he was in a business suit, looking much more professional than when she'd found him under a flock of carrion birds. Her dead guy—Lou Laurents, She clicked his image then clicked **About** with shaking hands. Lou was the managing partner of an Internet Service Start-up called *FTL LTD*. A super geek.

What had he done to have pissed someone off that bad? Enough to off him after the end of the world, the end of law.

The door opened and Lizzie screamed.

"Lizzie," Rachael said, "It's me and Saj. You okay?"

Lizzie breathed. "Yeah. Fine. I need to make a call. But I'm a little freaked out."

"Saj," Rachael suggested, "Go put the toys in your back pack away in your room."

Saj stared at Lizzie, measuring the likelihood that she was going to yell at him.

"I'm sorry, Saj." She knelt and smiled. "You want a hug? Sissie's bein' a little weird."

He gave her a quick hug. When she hugged him back he sneezed, leaving a goober of snot on her shirt. "Oh, Saj. Sorry you're still a sickie."

"Yup. Saj sickie," he said and ran off to his room.

"Even sick he so damned cute." Lizzie stood, feeling her belly shift. "You want something to drink?"

"No. Tell me what's up," Rachael said. "I've got news, too. I hope yours is better than mine."

Coldness swept across Lizzie. "Mine's relatively good news. Tell me yours first." She collapsed into the couch.

"Despite Mr. Ray's promise..." Rachael stared at Lizzie, fear in her eyes. "A man came around today to schedule me for an appointment. To meet with an OBGYN."

"An OBGYN. That's weird."

"I don't think it's optional."

"Shit. Don't know how much longer I can handle this, Rach."

"Sissie!" Saj ran toward Lizzie, his little legs capable. "Bath?"

"In a minute, you can have a bath." She scooped him up into her arms and nuzzled him under the chin. "I remember praying for someplace to feel safe. But I never imagined it being this, this.... Stifling and scary."

Rachael nodded.

Saj always made Lizzie feel better, but her resentment and anger ran deep today. "It's like fucking Sunday school." She saw Rachael's lips tighten. "Sorry. I know. Don't talk like that in front of Saj. Unless I want to hear those words coming back at me."

"He heard it from me today, too." She sank into the chair, her head in her hands.

"You? Fuckin' A, Rach," Lizzie joked. "We might loosen you up, yet."

Rachael pulled her knees up to her chest, curling in tighter, hands wrapped around her head.

Lizzie realized she recognized the body language. She remembered something similar as she slipped down the road before her visit to the psych ward.

"Saj, you want a bath with Mama?" As she heard the words, she saw Rachael shift. "I mean, Sissie."

"You're his mama now, Lizzie." Rachael's voice came out low and clipped.

"You want a bath, Saj?"

"Bath," Saj agreed.

Lizzie set him down. "Go get naked." He trundled toward the bathroom as Lizzie knelt in front of Rachael. "We'll figure it out." She gently tugged Rachael's arms from her eyes. "You love, Saj. I know. I do, too." She released Rachael's arms. "My baby's a girl. I'm pretty sure. I don't want her growing up without any rights. You should come jump in the bath with Saj. He'll cheer you up."

Rachael shook her head. "Don't want to be cheered up. But I'll come with you. I don't want to be alone."

Lizzie headed for the bathroom. "If we keep our voices normal, think Saj'll notice any difference?"

"If you're stressed out, kids know."

"Okay. We'll just play in the bath." Lizzie headed for the bathroom. "I was beginning to think I wouldn't miss the old world."

"What's your news?"

"After Saj goes to bed."

PART III

Breakdown

Chapter Twenty-Seven

MANNIE COULD HEAR THE VOICES rising inside the small office. He was supposed to have an appointment with DiSilvio about supplies, but when the secretary had tried to ring him, the call had been rejected.

She gave him a pained smile sharing his discomfort. "They've been arguing on the phone all morning since the convoy left. Then Mr. Ray came over."

"Maybe I should go." He stood.

"I'd rather you didn't." Her eyes shot to his as her cheeks colored. "If Mr. DiSilvio wants you and you've gone…"

Mannie sat down, not wanting to cause her distress, if that's what she'd really meant. He glanced down at her nameplate on the desk—Dolores Winters. "Ms. Winters?"

"Mrs. Winters. Widowed. I—" She stopped abruptly.

Mannie slid back in the faux leather chair. "Wasn't married myself, but…"

"You lost her." It wasn't a question.

Talking about Isabel had triggered his last drunken disaster. He said the first thing in his head to move on quickly. "How long were you married?" And immediately regretted asking the question in the same theme. "Sorry."

"No. I don't mind. Nobody really wants to talk about the people we've lost. It's healthy not to…" She twisted the ring on her finger. "22 years. We were high school sweethearts. Three kids. All grown. Gone now." She said, her voice still a pleasant tone. A swift intake of breath was the only thing that implied she was uncomfortable. "I've got one grand-kid. She's two." Now she was beaming. "She's what I have left."

"My daughter found me and brought me an adopted grand-kid. Keeps me mostly on an even keel. And she's going to make me a double grandpa in about six months."

"Congratulations," Dolores smiled.

"Thanks."

"I miss Alex."

"I miss Isabel."

"Could we...?" She glanced away and took a deep breath. "I mean, I've never been this forward. But I've never been through an apocalypse. Would you like—"

Mannie felt his face warming. "I would like—"

Her phone buzzed. She sighed, pressing a button. "Yes, Mr. DiSilvio?" Her voice was perfectly pleasant, but the hardness of her face reminded him of Isabel when she talked to her father. He had never realized how much his daughter despised him.

"Is Guerrero here?" DiSilvio's voice barked.

"Yes, sir, he is."

"Send him in."

"Mr. DiSilvio will see you now," she hit the end button. "Good luck," she whispered with a slight smile.

"Maybe we'll continue this conversation when things aren't so crazy."

"No maybe," she said, "Please make certain we continue the conversation."

"Okay."

"And don't wait until things aren't crazy. We may not have that long."

Thanks," Mannie said, holding the glimpse of her pleasant smile in his head as he turned to walk into the maelstrom. He felt good, a bounce in his step despite what he was heading toward. He half expected Mr. Ray to come barreling out of the door. When he didn't, Mannie turned the knob and walked in.

"I need you to help us settle something, Guerrero." DiSilvio's face was red with anger.

Mr. Ray seemed calm and pleasant. He nodded in greeting. "Hello, Mannie."

"We need power," DiSilvio continued. "Electrical power we can guarantee. These recent brown- outs prove that. Our crew headed to the solar plant from the south is the first half of what we need. Badly."

"We do not need it badly enough to start a war," Mr. Ray's voice rose.

Mannie had never heard even a hint of anger or reproach from Mr. Ray.

"There has been enough death," Mr. Ray said.

"We may not have another option," DiSilvio's voice matched the new mayor's in level. "If we can't get the solar power from Delta, natural gas becomes our only choice."

Mannie stepped in between them. "I think you're both right. I don't think you're going to start a war diverting the solar plant. Getting the Olmsted going will relieve some pressure, but hydroelectric can only keep some of the city going and until we get melt off they're not even running to capacity. Doctor Packard assures us that we should have years' supply of Natural Gas. Though I'm curious. Are we really the only city trying to run off that supply?" Mannie looked to Mr. Ray. "That may be the direction Mr. DiSilvio's war comes from."

DiSilvio glared at Mannie. "Not my war. But you're right." The lights flickered, then went out. "What the hell?"

In a matter of seconds they flashed and came back to full life as the generators turned on and took over.

DiSilvio punched his phone. "Winters? Get the power plant on the line." He punched it again. "Well, that didn't take long."

"That seems entirely too coincidental," Mr. Ray said. "How long since the convoy left? When will they reach Delta?"

Mannie considered what Mr. Ray said. It was very soon after the last black out. Packard said it should be stable until they got the solar online—could it be sabotage? Mannie looked at his watch. 1400 hours. "Shouldn't take more than a couple hours. If they left on time, they should be there." He punched a channel open. "TOC to Murder One. Colonel Foote?"

"Mannie. Looking for an update?" Foote's voice sounded strange from the small speaker on the manpack radio.

"Yes. But also," Mannie glanced from Ray to DiSilvio, "Our power is down here again. So whatever you're going to do... We'd appreciate you getting to it."

"Are you thinking we could see some action out this way? I was planning on using this as a training exercise, not live fire. These boys aren't ready. "

Mr. Ray raised his index finger. "Foote. Take your time. We've got things under control here. Do what you think is best."

DiSilvio shrugged. "Yeah. A well-trained militia is an even higher priority than power."

"All right. I'll report anything significant. Foote out."

Mannie pushed the button and turned to the other two men. "Well?"

Mr. Ray spoke first. "Let's head to the Provo gas plant. Then out to the Olmsted Station Powerhouse. See how soon they'll be back online."

"I'll call Simmons," Mannie said, "and have him get us an escort together."

Mr. Ray blew air out his mouth. "They can meet us there. I'm safe with you two."

"Might not hurt to be armed," Mannie suggested. "If you think it might not just be a coincidence..."

"Good idea," DiSilvio agreed, crossing to his desk. He pulled out a pistol, holster and belt and strapped it on.

Mrs. Winters looked worried, but competent as DiSilvio gave her directions. She flashed a smile at Mannie as the other two exited. "See you soon, Mr. Guerrero."

Mannie drove them all in Rubi. The Provo Power Plant was only about five minutes away and thankfully, no one said a word, leaving Mannie to worry through this latest development.

Simmons' SUV squealed into the parking lot before them. Simmons, in full riot gear and three similarly equipped men fanned out as Mannie pulled up to the door.

Mr. Ray was shaking his head. "Tony. I really don't see the need."

"Mr. Ray. We've made enemies with our success. I'm afraid this is literally a power struggle."

"There's no one left to do this."

"The independents?"

"I'm going in. Maybe take a look around the perimeter?" Mannie left them to their conversation and hustled to the control room. The heavy metal door screeched when he tugged it open. There was no one in the room.

Then the door across the room opened and a young man hustled in. "The power is out, sir."

Mannie hesitated, then spoke calmly. "I know. That's why I'm here.

"The pipes were flowing. Just like usual. Then nothing."

"What do you mean, 'nothing'?" Mannie probed.

"Nothing. It stopped. No flow."

"All at once?"

"Uh, yeah."

Something didn't jibe with the kid's story. "How many minutes?"

"I, uh, I'm not sure."

"Okay. Off the record. It won't leave this room."

"What?" asked the kid.

"Johnson? Did you fall asleep?"

The kid collapsed like the air had been let out of him. He was a good kid, but couldn't lie for shit.

"Yeah." The corner of his mouth turned up and his eye twitched. "I don't know how long it took."

"Can the computer tell us?"

Johnson's face lit up. "I think so." He spun and clicked away with the mouse.

Mannie stood behind him peering at the screen.

"It stopped in 1.78 seconds. No gradual drop off." He spun back to face Mannie. "Somebody shut it down."

"How far does your data reach? Can we get info on where the flow stopped?" Mannie asked, grimly.

"Hhhmmm…" Johnson refocused on the screen. "Not sure. I'll see what I can track down."

"You do that. Here's my phone number. If the phones stop working I want you to run the information over to Mrs. Winters at Mr. DiSilvio's office. She can get it to me. How long will the generators in this building last?"

"Beats me."

"Find out. Do what you can. Thanks, Johnson."

"Mr. Guerrero," Johnson asked, "you're not going to report me falling asleep are you?"

"Will it ever happen again?"

Johnson shook his head quickly. "No. No, sir, Mr. Guerrero, Sir."

Mannie laughed out loud. "What should you have done when you got sleepy?"

"Stayed awake?" the kid offered tentatively.

"You're a bundle of laughs. No, kid. Tell someone. None of us are super human. Ask someone for help. Worse thing that happens is you get a talking to. Nobody's gonna shoot you for asking for help. Better to lose some pay than make a mistake."

Mannie clapped him on the shoulder. "All right. Get back to work. Your secret is safe with me." He strode back outside, surprised that his knee wasn't hurting him. He swung himself up into Rubi. It felt good to be needed.

He had a suspicion he knew where the shutdown had occurred. North. Now to find out for sure. His friends at Fort Williams, the Independents, the Boise folks or somebody else?

Mannie drove Rubi around the buildings. He could see in the distance that the two were continuing their argument. He pulled up and hollered out the window. "Tony? Mr. Ray. Come on. Let's go to the Olmsted. I'll tell you on the way what happened."

Zach scanned the flat and mostly empty ground around the plant. He would have laughed if things weren't so damned tense. The men were all wound up, ready to shoot anybody who got in their way.

It wasn't really that big a deal. They were flipping a switch. Sending power in another direction. Who would care? The people in California would be frustrated when they lost power, but they were a long ways away, and must have better options nearer and more convenient than this solar plant. They didn't need this many soldiers to flip a switch. DiSilvio was paranoid: convinced the rest of the country was going to come after him and everything he had in Utah.

Lt. Benson waved everyone back, then emptied several rounds into the doorknob.

Zach flinched. Stupid fuck. If Provo needed this functional, they wouldn't want the doors swinging open to the wild. Was Benson going to shoot out the windows, too?

Benson, motioned two men forward, one swung the door open while the other rushed in.

"All clear." Came a voice from inside.

The rest of the squad pulled in tight inside the door.

Benson glanced around at the men. "Riley. Samson. Go down the hall and check it out. If there is anyone alive in here, I want to know about it. Call back when you've cleared a room.

"You ready, Will?" Zach asked his partner. Not waiting for an answer, he crept down the wall ducking under the window in the door so he was on the handle side. When Will reached the other side, Zach turned the knob, throwing it open. Not like anyone but a deaf man could be unaware of the onslaught of the Provo regulars. Will slipped in through the open door, his gun at the ready.

Zach counted to three and then followed him in. Where had he gone? Will came out from behind a bookcase. Their guns pointed at each other.

"Shit." Zach lowered his gun. "We're not careful, somebody's gonna get hurt." They were playing army like in grade school, but their guns had live rounds. "All clear, Benson!"

They continued into the plant, alternating teams to clear the way before them. Between the nerves and the exertion, Zach could feel his undershirt soaked with sweat under the layers of winter gear.

Benson ordered Will and Zach forward for their second turn.

This time Will threw the door open. Zach spun in with his back to the wall and froze.

A guy stood there, dusty and bearded, but a hunting rifle held at his waist, like in an old west movie.

Zach's finger felt sweaty on the trigger. "Drop it. Now!" Zach had no idea if he could actually fire at the man if he refused to drop it. He knew if he pulled the trigger he couldn't miss.

"Drop it for God's sake," screamed a female voice from around the corner.

The gun drooped and the man slumped. He set the gun on the floor.

"Kick it over to me," Zach ordered. Had the guy been thinking the same thing as Zach? Can I kill in cold blood?

Zach's squad rushed inside surrounding them, guns ready. As Zach stooped to grab the rifle. Will smashed the man against the wall.

"Samson," Zach yelled. "Gently. He's unarmed."

"Maybe." Will let him go and stepped back, slapping his hands together.

The girl walked out with her hands up. She looked much younger than the man, but maybe the beard just made him look older.

"All right," Zach said. "Pull your pockets inside out." He kept his rifle ready as the captives complied quickly.

Benson pulled a couple backpacks from where the girl was hiding, and started pulling things out and throwing them on the floor. Zach could tell they were neither enemy soldiers nor plant personnel. But he stood silently guarding them while Benson came up with the same conclusion. After a call to Foote, they continued. An hour and a half later they had found no additional people and had been over the facility twice.

Chapter Twenty-Eight

THE SUN SLIPPED BEHIND THE hill as Mannie followed DiSilvio and Ray up the rise to the Olmsted Station Powerhouse. They were arguing as usual. Mannie's phone buzzed and everyone stopped. The screen read "Provo Power calling". He motioned to the rest of the crew to continue on. "This is Guerrero."

"Johnson here, Sir."

"Go ahead."

"Shut off occurred at Leroy Field, Uinta County, Wyoming at 13:42 hours."

"Doctor Packard said it should switch over to Clay Basin?"

"It didn't switch."

"Thanks, Johnson. Who knows, you might get a commendation."

"No, please, Mr. Guerrero, Sir. It would be too, uh…"

"I'm kidding, Mr. Johnson. See if there is any way to override the flow without going local."

"Yes, sir. I'll try."

Mannie closed the connection and hurried into the building. He found Ray and DiSilvio talking with the watchman. "The engineers knocked off after a setback, but, when I heard about the shutdown, I called them back. They should be here any minute. Feel free to wander the grounds."

He seemed relieved when they turned their attention to Mannie.

"Well?" DiSilvio rounded on him. "Was that a personal call?"

Mannie was instantly pissed off. "Sir?" he answered vainly

keeping the pique from his voice.

Mr. Ray stepped in, "Was it information we need?"

Mannie took a breath and responded to Mr. Ray directly. "Shutdown at Leroy Field, Wyoming. No switchover."

"Leroy Field?" DiSilvio asked. "You're sure. And it's shut down, not just run out?"

"As near as we can tell," Mannie said, still speaking directly to Mr. Ray, "it didn't slow down, it just stopped. I'm guessing someone up there shut us down. Beat us to the punch."

Mr. Ray's mouth twitched almost into a smile. "Just like we're planning to do to California."

Mannie nodded. "And how do you think they're going to feel about that?"

"Well," DiSilvio rubbed his hands together. "We've learned something the hard way. We'll gradually lower the power transmission, they'll just think something's gone wrong."

"Doesn't mean they won't come check it out," Mannie countered.

"Nope. But it might mean they come not realizing that there is anyone behind the shutdown."

Mr. Ray had a dark frown on his face. At least he felt some pain about what the 'troops' might get used for.

Still. DiSilvio's plan was probably a good one. Provided there weren't troops from California or Dugway or something there already. He should check with his contacts at Dugway and Ft. Williams. Did they still have power?

"Shall I contact Colonel Foote?" Mannie asked. It wouldn't do any good to make plans hinging on a power plant they didn't control.

"Yes. We'll inspect the perimeter while you do that," Mr. Ray said with a hint of a smile.

Mannie smiled back at him. Mr. Ray was all right. They wandered off as he headed back to the Jeep. He pulled the radio out of the charging stand and thumbed the recall button. "Colonel Foote?" He sat in the seat leaving the door open. It was chilly, but not as bad as a week ago. At least they didn't have to worry about keeping people from freezing to death.

The radio buzzed and he held it to his face. "Mannie?"

"Yeah. Status?"

"We've got control. Couple of vagrants were the only occupants. None of the men managed to get more than bruises from tripping on their own damn feet."

"Good training exercise then?"

"Should be back in Provo tomorrow. Planning on leaving a crew with Benson to continue training and defend the facility here."

"I'll pass that on. Has Packard figured out how to switch the system over?"

"He's growling and muttering in the other room, so I'd guess he hasn't yet."

"Provo would like you to lower the feed gradually when you shut things down. So it seems like the system is failing."

"Smart thinking. I'll pass that along. Any luck with the power?"

"Not yet. Check in tomorrow?"

"Right. Foote out."

Mannie sat there wondering what Zach was thinking about his first action.

A car pulled up behind him. A man jogged up the hill. The lights of another vehicle flashed back and forth up the hill. A loud explosion echoed off the walls of the canyon.

Was it a gunshot or an electrical explosion? Mannie jumped from the car, pulling his Sig from its holster, and spun as several more explosions and ricochets followed. Gunfire. From at least two different weapons and directions. He ran up the hill heading in between the two locations of fire.

More shots. Then quiet. As he crested the bank, he ducked behind a tree, evaluating the area for threats. Over by the river, he saw a man down, dark blood stained his shirt. It was Mr. Ray.

DiSilvio, crouching beside the body, looked up and spotted Mannie, then his eyes shifted to the ridge above. He pointed.

A man with two rifles stood with another man in front of him.

DiSilvio raised his pistol and fired. The guards fired their rifles.

One of the men ran as the other dropped behind the ridge. Mannie stared, his weapon remained cold and unfired. Odds of a hitting something with a handgun at this distance were slim, and he'd recognized one of the men. Duke Madison.

Mr. Ray is dead.

Lizzie stared at the text from her father and tears blurred her eyes. Mr. Ray was her last hope for Provo. Rachael's voice rambled on. But Lizzie didn't hear her words, until a single phrase pierced her bubble of shock and snapped her back to reality.

"Mr. Ray is dead," Rachael repeated to herself. Then she sprang into action. "With DiSilvio in charge, you and I are both going to be broodmares." She grabbed Lizzie's shirt. "How many can we save now? You, Saj, Me. Maybe. If we go now."

If we don't... Lizzie knew the answer. It struck her as weird for a moment that she was hesitating and Rachael was being impulsive. "But what about Dad? Nev and Jess?"

"Your dad and the boys will be fine. Nev and Jess? They're gonna think we're crazy and try and stop us. All of them are."

She was right. "Let's go." Lizzie stood and wiped her tears. "Once we're out. One of us can double back."

"No. We can send messages. Shut up and go." Rachael shoved her none too gently toward the bedroom. "Get Saj."

Lizzie stumbled forward. She began stuffing Saj's things into a bag. Pacifier. Snuzzie Bear. Children's meds.

Saj sat up in bed crying, a stuffy-nosed ordeal. She poured out a dose of the cold meds, checking the package to make sure they were the sleepy kind and not the stay awake wired kind. She teased his mouth with the spoon, like he was getting a treat, and then poured the sludgy pink liquid into his mouth. His eyes momentarily looked like fire. A 'you're going to pay for this when I get older' look. She pulled him into her arms and carried him into the living room. "Saj, you gotta be good. Gotta be quiet."

Rachael came out of the kitchen, dragging a pack. She smiled a tight smile at Lizzie and nuzzled Saj's chin. "I need to go home and get my gear and then we can go."

"Okay. I'll give you fifteen minutes. Then I'll meet you outside the library." Lizzie handed Snuzzie Bear to Saj and lay him down on the couch. "Rest, Sajiboy." She guided Rachael to the door. "What're we going to drive?"

"No cars yet. If we're walking it's easier to make excuses and slip past checkpoints. We'll find a car outside the wall."

"I'm going to go through the house here and the stuff I packed. Try to let my paranoia do some good." She hugged Rachael. "See you in about 25 minutes."

"Just don't over pack," Rachael said, her jaw tight.

Lizzie shut the door behind her and leaned her head into it. She wanted to tell the others. But if she did, they would keep her here, keep her safe. She took a deep breath and got to work, setting the timer to tell her when fifteen minutes had passed.

Saj toddled up to her in the bedroom almost immediately. "Saj. You should be sleeping."

He sniffed and scrunched his forehead. "Not sleep. Rachael go."

"And we're gonna go, too." Lizzie kissed his forehead and smoothed out the scrunch. "Can you get your snow coat on?"

Saj stared at her, his face still serious. He put his hands on his hips, looking like Rachael. He glared at her not moving.

"Now," she said, more sharply than she'd intended.

He looked for a moment like he would cry, then his face set with a stubborn expression that was probably a mirror of Lizzie, and he sat his butt heavily on the floor, looking like something a bulldozer couldn't budge.

Obviously, she just needed to wait for the sleepy meds to take effect. How long would that take? She turned back to her packing.

Zach stood uncomfortable in the meeting room of the Delta Solar plant listening to Colonel Foote making plans with Benson. His promotion to 2nd Lieutenant had lasted all of two days. Technically from the morning of day one to the evening of day two. He hadn't even got to wear his first bars and Foote had already given him a second. Now Zach was Benson's rank and he could tell that was a cause for resentment. Beside him, also ill at ease, was new 2nd Lieutenant Will Sampson.

"As acting Captain, Lieutenant Benson, you will be in charge of two platoons here." Foote stared down at the map of the area. "I want the first platoon to return with me."

Things weren't turning out the way Zach had planned. He didn't want to be stuck out here in the frozen desert while Nev was back in Provo. He hadn't imagined when he signed up that he'd be anywhere but Provo.

"But that's my platoon, sir," Benson said.

"It's Riley's now for the time being." Foote pointed to a spot southwest. "In addition to holding the plant, I want you to send a squad south and find a place to make the highway less passable.

"Sir?" Benson asked.

Foote's voice lowered to a hiss. "Benson, you are my second in command because of your military seniority. I have yet to be impressed. Do your job well and I might be."

"Yes, sir." Benson straightened up.

"I better be able to—" A static pop interrupted them and Foote punched his radio. "Crows TOC. Foote here." His face blanched. "Major? You're certain? You're there?"

Zach was really glad to be in the first platoon and under Foote's command instead of Benson's. Foote was a hard commander, but never petty—he gave respect when it was earned.

Zach's phone buzzed and he pulled it out. There was nothing on the screen. Dammit. It was his other phone, Lizzie's line from Glen. He slid his main phone back in and pulled the offending phone out. **Ray is dead. LZ** was all it said. *What the hell?* He hit the question mark, send, thumbed the ringer off completely, shoved it back in his pocket, and looked up. Foote stared at him with steel eyes as he continued his radio conversation. He knew, too. Then it was Lizzie being stupid.

The cords in Foote's neck were taut and the muscles of his jaw worked as though he were grinding granite between his teeth. Finally he put down the radio. "Mr. Ray has been shot. Everything is under control. I need calm leadership from you men. No doubt, some of the troops have already heard the news via cell phones." His eyebrow raised at Zach.

The men shifted. Benson stood with his mouth open, like he was catching flies.

"We know nothing other than that fact. DiSilvio's sent the bodyguards out to chase down the killer, but he's escaped into the woods near the Olmsted Station Plant."

Oh, god. Zach knew he should have been there. He'd seen the potential, the lax security. But no one thought such a thing could happen. Foote was still talking. Zach's ears perked up when he heard the power was out in Provo again. Was Nev okay? Lizzie?

"Riley. Listen up. I need you here and now."

"Yes, sir." Zach snapped to attention, pushing his worries and fears aside for later. He didn't want to give Foote any reason to second guess promoting him. He received a curt nod from Foote as he refocused his attention on his commander.

"They expect to have limited power up by morning. Your family and friends are going to be scared. I need you to set an example for the men. Come on. I'm going to address them."

Zach followed them out dumbly. He couldn't help but feel like he personally had failed. Mr. Ray was gone. And he had been out rescuing a solar plant from vagrants.

Chapter Twenty-Nine

LIZZIE APPROACHED THE LIBRARY GOING up the street in between the busier Freedom Avenue and University Way. The streetlights were dark and the street empty. When she could see the library down the alley, she tugged Saj's pack off and set it with hers in between two dumpsters. Saj looked like a little marshmallow man wrapped up in his puffy winter coat, happy to be outside. Frost blew from his mouth and his rosy cheeks glowed.

She hurried them past the Brigham Young statue in front of the library, as if he was going to sound the alarm, heading toward the back of the building.

The power outage was the perfect ally for their escape. Everyone would be too busy worrying about the lights and Mr. Ray to worry about a couple kids. And the darkness would conceal them.

She leaned against the far corner, where she could see Rachael coming. Saj bent down and rubbed his mittens in the snow. Life was so blissfully uncomplicated for him. He dropped his mittens, shoving his hands into the snow.

"Saj. Put your mittens back on."

"No," he said, not even looking at her.

Lizzie grabbed the mittens. Lizzie spied Rachael on the other side of the street. "Saj. Let's get Rachael." She scooped him up and attempted to pull his mittens back on. His little fingers balled into fists. "Fine. No mittens." She wrapped her arms tight and jogged to meet Rachael. She waved Rachael back. But Rachael continued toward them her arms wide.

When she got near Lizzie hissed, "Your pack. Who wears a pack to the library at night? Let's get off the main streets." She gestured for Rachael to head in the direction she'd left her and Saj's packs.

Recognition dawned in Rachael's face and she hustled in the direction Lizzie pointed her.

Lizzie made a beeline for their packs. "Okay, Saj," Lizzie pulled the straps over his arms, "we've gotta hurry."

"Let's play the quiet game, okay?" Rachael asked, helping Lizzie into her straps.

"No," Saj stated loudly.

Rachael flashed Lizzie a look of alarm.

Lizzie knelt down and looked Saj straight in the eye. "We're going to play Secret Spy, okay, Sajiboy?"

"Saj. No boy."

"How about Sajispy? Will you play??"

He nodded. "Saj play."

"Good. Saj play," Lizzie agreed. She stood up and took his hand in hers. "Let's go."

Saj moved forward all hunched over like he was sneaking. Lizzie held her laughter, happy that he was playing along. Why hadn't the meds kicked in? She remembered as an ADHD kid that sometimes meds had the opposite side effects. He didn't seem sniffly anyway.

Twenty minutes later they'd crossed outside the wall, sneaking under a semi-trailer that hadn't been collapsed. Lizzie hurried forward.

"Okay," Rachael said. "New game. Find a car with keys."

"Oh, shit. Glen said he programmed the phones with the ability to get into older hybrids if they haven't had the security updates."

"How does it work?"

"Hell if I know," Lizzie pressed the app titled Jumpin' Jack. "I guess we walk and push until we find a car whose lights flash when we hit a button."

They found a parking lot full of cars, neatly parked. It must be Collectors stash. They'd been driving cars that could drive near the city for easy access later.

"Okay," Lizzie said, "Pray if you do that sort of thing." *Come you lucky sevens, babe.*

Lizzie pressed the button and she heard a sound a slight beep.

"Over there." Rachael pointed. "I saw a flash."

"Woo hoo!" Lizzie hollered.

"Wooo!" Saj echoed.

Rachael hustled him over to the car. She pulled the door open. "No car seat."

"This is an effing escape, Rachael. We're not driving fast. You won't put us in the ditch." Lizzie tossed her bag next to Saj.

"Okay," Rachael said, "Keep praying." She pushed the start button. The car started; its lights flashed on, reflecting off the snowflakes and the billboard on the wall of the building. Then an orange charge light flashed on the dashboard.

"Kill the lights," Lizzie said.

Rachael twisted the knob.

"Okay, try again."

Rachael pushed the button. Nothing happened.

"Damned thing's supposed to start on gas."

Rachael pushed the button. The car rumbled, shook and the engine stopped. Lights raked across the wall.

"I said, no lights," Lizzie barked.

"The lights are off," Rachael complained. "Shit."

Lizzie whipped her head around, catching the flash of headlights in the rearview mirror. "Start it," she urged. "Let's go."

Rachael pressed the start button. The engine kicked over again, but didn't start.

"Again. Try again."

Rachael pressed, nothing happened this time. She opened her door. "We can hide."

"No. They're close. I'll get them to follow me." Lizzie shoved the door open and jumped out. She jerked the back door open, unsnapped Saj from the car and hugged him fiercely. He was finally drowsy. "Sissie loves Saj."

"Let's stick together, Lizzie," Rachael pleaded.

"Go, Rachael," Lizzie hissed. "Take Saj." She lifted the sleepy boy into her friend's arms.

"No. I don't want to leave you."

"Rachael, please." Lizzie held both Rachael and Saj, kissing them. "I love you. Now, go. That way. I'll catch up. Somehow. Meet me at the *Out N Back* in Orem."

Rachael hurried away down the cross street, searching for an escape route.

Lizzie kicked off her rubber boots, and tossed her coat. As soon as she was sure Rachael was getting away she swayed down the road back the way they'd come. Humming *The Final Countdown,* she pulled her shirt off, unsnapped her bra and let it fall. Old tricks are the best tricks.

The lights stopped a block away. Lizzie lumbered around the street corner, heading the opposite direction from Rachael and Saj.

"I see someone," called a voice behind her.

Lizzie heard running footsteps. She kept up her pace, breathing deep so she wouldn't notice the chill air.

"Oh, my god." A male voice said, following her. "It's a naked woman."

She swayed some more.

"Hey, lady. Come here."

Lizzie swung backwards, not seeming to see him, and then continued on her way.

"Where are the others? There was a kid."

"How should I know? I'll get this one."

"NO." The voice came with a forceful pop of static. "Find the one with the kid. Now. Leave the crazy one for later."

Lizzie spun, her breasts exposed to the cold. Through her bangs, she watched him. *Come on, buddy.* The collector stood in the snow, half-raising his gun at her, he took a long hard look at her naked body, then backed away and went after Saj and Rachael. He followed orders.

"Shit," she muttered, hustling after them. "Mother-" She scooped up her shirt and bra, shoving the bra in her pocket and pulling the shirt over her head. "-Fucker." She grabbed her coat and stopped long enough to slip into her boots. She continued to swear under her breath as she buttoned up the coat. Now they were after Rachael and Saj, the two people, along with her father, that she loved the most.

Lizzie barreled around the corner and dropped behind a parked car. "Shit." Lizzie pulled herself up so she could see what was happening through the tinted glass and the lights of the street lamps. A van had pulled up and collectors stood on either side of Rachael, with guns leveled at her and Saj.

"Come with us. You're endangering the child," one collector said, shoving his gun forward meaningfully.

Did they just threaten Saj!? Lizzie clamped her hand on her mouth to keep from screaming at him. Saj and Rachael needed her free if she was going to mount a rescue, or she would be latched onto that dumb fuck's back clawing his freaking eyes out right now.

Saj whined and twisted.

"It's okay, Saj," Rachael cooed and held him close. "Don't shoot, I'll go with you."

Right before she got into their van, Rachael turned. "RUN, LIZZIE," she hollered.

Lizzie slumped against the car, hot tears burning her eyes. She couldn't run, it was all she could do to stand here watching them, but they didn't bother taking the time to find her. The slider door on the van slammed shut, taking Rachael and Saj away—leaving Lizzie. She collapsed down into the snow beside the car.

Stupid Lizzie. Stupid. Crazy didn't go as far as it used to. Must've seen a lot more crazies since she'd pulled that last time. She sat there until the cold bit into her.

They were safe. Provo was safe. Maybe she should just go back, at least she would be with the people she loved. And her baby would be safe. She rested her hand on her belly.

"No!" she said into the darkness. Then she screamed it, "NO!" Provo was not for her.

She rolled to her side and shoved against the cold, frozen pebbles in the gravel. Using the car for balance she stood up and ran back to where they'd dropped their backpacks.

Lizzie had everything she needed. Extra clothes, food, flashlight, batteries, trail mix and Snuzzie Bear. Rachael still had almost all of Saj's gear with her. But Lizzie had Snuzzie Bear.

She trudged down the street. Then she had a thought. The car was out of charge; maybe all it needed was a jump start. Which meant she needed another car with a battery that had a charge. She popped the hood on the Honda they'd tried to commandeer and opened the hatchback.

No jumper cables. So she picked up the jack and threw it as hard as she could against the window of the Nissan pickup on the other side. It broke with a satisfying crunch. She opened the door and shoved the seat forward. Jumper cables.

She flipped the hood latch, realizing she needed tools to disconnect the battery. Another look behind the seat remedied the problem—tools. In minutes she had loosened the battery from its harness and set it on the ground. She checked the battery connections three times to make sure red went to positive and black to negative. Chad had left the lights on in his car once and had reversed the polarity of the connections, the resulting arc melted the post off his father's battery. His father had ripped him a new one while Lizzie stood uncomfortably beside him.

Once she connected the battery, she sat in the seat of the Honda for a moment, trying to think calm, positive thoughts. Then she pressed the start button. It growled, stumbled, hummed and kept going. "Thank you."

They had nearly reached the edge of Orem, the city north of Provo. Saj would be better off with Rachael in Provo, for now.

"Shit!" Will slammed on the brakes.

Zach had been snoozing, now he was jolted wide awake. The caravan had stopped. A train was stopped on the tracks where they crossed the highway. The train had machine guns mounted on it. And they were manned.

"Jesus fuck," Zach muttered. "Who-the-hell's army is that?"

Behind them, the rest of the vehicles screeched to a stop.

Foote was in the Hummer in front of them. Zach jerked his door open and raised his hands, jogging forward to talk to Foote. Foote rolled down his window, but stayed inside.

"This an interesting turn of events, Lieutenant," said Foote.

"Yes, sir." Zach's heart pounded as he scanned the view in front of him. The train snaked off in the distance, in both directions. Even if they successfully fought these guys, they would still have to get the train off the tracks to get to Provo. "What do we do?"

Foote sighed heavily. "If they were going to attack, they'd have done it by now. We wait. I'm pretty certain they're going to tell us who they are and what they want." He punched the button on his chest radio. "Guerrero. We need to talk." His attention returned to Zach. "Walk back along the caravan, tell them no one moves and nobody even shows a weapon. If they need to take a leak, do it by the side of the road, but nobody makes a move without my authorization."

"Yes, sir." Zach waited a split second, hoping for more communication. Foote waved him off.

When Zach returned, Will's eyes were big and his hands alternated gripping and loosening on the steering wheel. "Foote says we wait. Stay put unless you need to pee. No weapons."

"I can stay put. Damn near peed myself already."

"Sorry. You don't get to stay put. We give everyone behind us the same message. Alternating vehicles. I'll take the evens, you take the odds."

Zach hustled down the line of vehicles, calmly repeating Foote's orders to every other vehicle, while Will did the same on the other side.

When he reached the end, he jogged back to Foote's command

vehicle and stood at ease, waiting. The window of the Hummer was rolled up and Zach could tell something besides the train was wrong. The window rolled down.

Zach stepped back as the Colonel opened his door and got out. "The men have been informed, Sir. Any news on the Mr. Ray's shooter?"

Foote shook his head. "Nothing new. The bodyguards came back this morning with nothing. They think it's two shooters, though."

"So not just a single nut-case?"

"Probably not." Foote's face had become an impenetrable mask. "Provo is a mess. Still no power. The candlelight vigil for Mr. Ray got out of control last night. Three houses are smoldering embers." He spit on the ground. "Some people are running, leaving in the chaos."

Lizzie. Was there any way Lizzie hadn't run away again? Better get in touch with Mannie. If Lizzie had run off into the wilderness with his baby again...

Foote shoved past Zach. "Well, the proverbial shit just hit the fan."

"Sir?" He turned his attention to the train. An armed group of men headed toward them. They wore a variety of clothing, most of their heads were topped with straw hats or Stetsons. Not what he thought of as Independents.

Chapter Thirty

THE LITTLE HONDA DROVE WELL through the snow. Lizzie used her phone to tell her where Camp Williams was. What do you do when you're in trouble? Call in the Army. She drove west the way her phone suggested, but somehow the street she'd picked went over Highway 15, the way she knew she could get to Camp Williams. She took the next exit and swung around the off-ramp. When she tried to take the right turn at the end of the curved off-ramp the car kept going straight and slid. Her seatbelt ratcheted as the car veered slowly, horrifyingly sideways down the embankment and settled gently into a pile of snow.

Lizzie pushed it into reverse and stepped on the gas. She could hear and feel the tires spinning, but it wouldn't move. "I won't give up, Snuzzie. I'll rescue them. You'll have your Saj back soon." She hugged him close as she swung the door upward and stumbled up toward the road. She was out of the suburbs and into the countryside. The sky was no longer clear, with scattered snowflakes, now the snow was thicker and the sky was socked in.

Lizzie kept close to the center stripes of the road, following one after another—they pulled her forward. Her flashlight kept the next few stripes in view, everything outside her little pool of light was darkness. She realized her teeth were chattering. Her hastily abandoned, then reclaimed, clothes had returned to her damp. In the freezing night, they refused to dry.

Without shelter she'd die out here. Maybe she should go back to the car and run the engine and heater until morning.

Snow thickened the air, so the only sounds were her feet and breath. It had been a long time since she'd seen a mailbox. Half of her brain said turn around, but the other half kept her moving. Finally, around a bend she spotted a mailbox and a twisty driveway. She stumbled toward it, leaning on the mailbox when she reached it. Up the drive in the distance she saw a picturesque barn and a rustic two story house. She forced herself on, up the driveway. It fascinated her that she could not feel her feet, and yet still keep walking.

Lizzie tried the front door knob of the farmhouse. Not even knocking first. It was locked. She needed to be somewhere warm. The power was probably still out—the darkness of the night was far too complete. There wasn't even a city glow on the night horizon. But even if this house wasn't warm, it would be out of the wind.

Around back, she found a woodpile stacked right up to the back door. She opened the old-fashioned wooden screen door and tried the knob. It turned. She took a deep breath of the chill outside air and stepped inside, not sure what smells she would encounter.

It was a summer kitchen, with an old fashioned wood stove. A row of white-painted cupboards lined what would have been the side of the house and a sliding door led into the main living area. She let her breath escape. There was a hint of decay, but not as strong as the rank stench of a corpse. If there were any, they would probably be in the main house.

She shone her flashlight around the room. It was neat and tidy. Herbs hung for drying by the stove. Glass canning jars glowed red or green or yellow in the light of her flashlight. A cork board covered with photos of family and friends filled her pool of light as she scanned the room. She yanked open drawers until she found a book of matches and lit a candle with its bottom melted and stuck to the bottom of a pickle jar. A makeshift lantern for someone used to losing power. The glass reflected a decent amount of light on the walls.

There were already a few arm-loads of wood near the stove. Her shivering hands pulled open the firebox. One of the family's she'd babysat for had a stove like this—one of those Bellingham "back-to-sustainability" hippie families. At the time she'd thought they were weird living in a cob house, made of mud and straw. She joked about the big, bad wolf to the kids and had them completely terrified one night. Funny, the parents had still called her back to babysit after that.

This one looked similar to the one she had used at the Bellingham Hippie house. She rolled up sheets of newspaper like twisted sticks and stacked them inside. She built a little lean-to of kindling from the bin next to the stove and then put a small piece of wood on either side. She made sure the draft was open and leaned some small pieces of wood on her fire-starter setup. She pulled a long fireplace match out of a mason jar nearby and lit it on her pickle jar lantern. The match head fizzled into flame and she held it to the newspaper. The paper caught quickly and she soon had a respectable blaze to warm her hands over. She made sure it would keep going, stacking other chunks of wood inside and closing the door within finger's width to help with more draft.

"Thank you," she said aloud, she didn't know to who. Yes she did. It wasn't God. It was the Departed—the people whose house had saved her from freezing to death. The people who weren't lucky enough to make it, but had left their things behind—things to be grateful for. She glanced at the corkboard. A color-crayoned picture of two stick figures in front of a house said: *Thanks for letting me stay with you Gramma Emily and Grampa William.*

It wouldn't take long to heat up the small kitchen, but she'd do well to have some blankets and pillows if she was camping here for the night. She added another couple skinny chunks of wood to the stove, and closed and latched the door. That would keep it going, while she explored the house.

She slid aside the door that led to the rest of the house and the unmistakable scent of death hit her like a wall. "Damn," she stepped back into the kitchen, coughing, and slid the door shut.

She found a dish-towel and rubbed one of the flowery herb bunches, lavender, over it. Then she wrapped the dish towel over her nose and mouth and tied it behind her neck. She clicked her flashlight on and slid open the door once more. The house was frigid after the fire warmed kitchen. She stepped into a dining area with rustic wood furniture. Through there was a living area with a big hearth and a fireplace Lizzie could have climbed inside. There were no bedrooms on the ground floor but she found a circular stair with a hand carved rail and climbed it, pretty certain of what she would find. Seeing death hadn't gotten any easier.

Her breath caught as she reached the top of the stairs. On a rustic bed lay bodies. Hollow cheeks and skin stretched taught over a bald head. Long gray hair pulled back in a braid on the other. A cotton nightgown with blue flowers draped the woman, and her dry and bony arm lay across the man's chest. Lizzie didn't think she'd ever be that calm and peaceful, even after she was dead.

"I'm going to borrow some blankets if I can find them," she said, her heart pounding. It felt right to talk to them. She crossed to the closet and opened it to find stacks of blankets and quilts.

Returning to the kitchen, Lizzie spotted a big awkward rocking chair. Setting the stack of bedding in it, she dragged it toward the sliding door. Heat caressed her when she opened the door. She shoved the chair through and slid the door shut.

She pulled the cloth from around her face, breathing in the faintly smoky air of the kitchen, and tucked the thickest blanket over the wood of the rocking chair. The candle burned slow and the stove's heat had made the room quite pleasant. She found a can labeled, *G'ma's Peaches*, spun off the ring and popped them open with a can opener. She stuck her fingers in the cold juices and pulled a slice into her mouth. They were heavenly. She added a bit more wood to the fire and settled in, wrapping the rest of the blankets around her.

Emily would make a great baby name, she mused. *Thank you, William and Emily, for the use of your house.*

Chocolate. Hot chocolate would be good.

Lizzie wished she had a body to lean into as she prepared her hot chocolate. Duke was strong and smelled good. Rachael was soft and comforting, like a mother—better at it than Mama had been. But Lizzie didn't exactly feel the magic with Rachael either. That thing with Nev was long over, despite a few niggles of petty jealousy. And Zach— well, the thing with Zach had never been. Just a drunken mistake. So whose body did she want? Her mind flashed briefly to Aubri's pretty cheekbones—but that was absurd, she didn't really know the girl—and Aubri was for Duke, anyway.

She sat in the rocker with her cup of cocoa, pulling her legs up to her chest. Even if she knew who she wanted right now, it didn't matter. She was alone. She always ended up alone. Maybe she needed to learn to be happy alone before she could be happy with someone else. It sounded like something she'd heard on a talk show or something. But it suddenly made a lot of sense.

She rocked, lifting the cup to her lips. Lost in thought so long the chocolate had grown cold. It tasted lovely on her tongue. The warmth from the fire made her cozy. *I need to learn to be alone and to be with someone. Really be there, not wanting the opposite of whatever I have at the time.*

She thought of Rachael and Saj, wondering if they were okay— what would the collectors do with them? Were they in jail or just back home? Lizzie pulled out her phone and pressed the power button. Wishing she had an extra battery. Maybe Glen would have some info.

The phone turned on but its efforts to connect to a network or

Wi-Fi were in vain. Shit. She was going to have to leave if she was going to get any signal. She set it on the windowsill maybe it would get signal there.

The warmth of William and Emily's home made it hard to think about going back out into the cold—bodies and all. If she did go, which direction should she go? Back toward Provo or further away? *I'm not going back just to let myself get caught.* She was free now, and when she returned to *The Shitty*, she was going to be free and in control. Every person in Provo who wanted to leave with her would leave. But first she had to reconnect with them.

She looked out the door, spying a hill that looked tall enough to reach a signal. Tomorrow. When she wasn't so tired.

When she opened her eyes again snow had built up on the windowsill. She stood and wrapped the blanket around and walked to the window. The snow had stopped falling and the clouds had cleared for the moon. Its light caught falling flakes as they passed, invisible from the gray sky to the contrast of the trees and dark hills in the distance.

She retrieved her phone. It said thirteen new texts, but it wasn't connected! Maybe they'd come through last night, cascading down like the blizzarding snow. One flake would lay her low. The answer to the questions, "Would anyone miss her?" seemed clear. She started replying, but realized again that she had no service. Her phone had downloaded as it could, leaving her this overwhelming mess of love to drown her. But until she got solid service back she could not say a thing in return.

With a happy sigh she started through the messages. Tomorrow she would go find service and one of those USB booster packs to run her cell off of batteries. She settled back into the blanket. The last message was from her father. It was short. "Lizzie? It's your dad. I love you. Hope you're all right. Wish you had come to me before you left. I need to talk to you. Call me ASAP." She checked which phone it had come from, the scrambled one or his Provo phone—the secret one. What wouldn't he want to talk about on that line? *Shit.* It was going to be a long night. She'd better get some sleep and head out first thing.

Zach stood frozen as Foote straightened his coat, flattening it down between his handgun. The men from the train were approaching.

"Sampson, you're with me. Riley, keep the troops chilled out. If they'd wanted us dead they'd have started shooting a long time ago."

"Yes, sir." Zach wanted to go along, but being left in charge was a sign of Foote's respect. Still, if this was just a ploy to take out the leaders, he was going to take the rest of the men in shooting.

The two parties met half way and hands were shaken, introductions made.

Zach allowed himself to relax a little. What they did they want? Where these people behind Mr. Ray's death? He stayed still and calm, watching. For the sake of the men behind him he tried to appear to be patiently waiting while his brain raced. He flashed through scenarios; their defensive position was crap, but if they retreated they boys on the train would have to come after them.

Finally, Will and the Colonel turned and headed back.

Zach was poised to react. If they were shot in the back…

But nothing happened.

The Colonel seemed more relaxed as he motioned Zach over. "They say they're not interested in undoing what Mr. Ray and the city did, but want to continue the work of collecting and fortifying Provo.

"What are their demands?"

"It's a *friendly* takeover apparently," Foote said, tight lipped. "They say nobody will get hurt if we go along peacefully and we can all re-enlist under the new order in pretty much the same rank and position. They say nothing will change except who's in command."

Zach knew what Foote was thinking. None of their supposed soldiers were up for an armed confrontation. He was too good a commander to let it get to that if there was a peaceful way out. "Nothing will change?" Zach asked. "Do you really believe that?"

"That is a chance I have to take, because the alternative is not an option, Riley."

"So what's next, sir?"

"We can go forward, but leave our weapons on the train. They promise re-enlistment bonuses."

"Why would we do that?"

"Implication seems to be that someone needs to take over after we let our leader get killed."

"But, sir," Zach said. That one had hit too close to home.

"Riley," Foote growled, "Major Guerrero has a mission for you. Get TOC on the radio."

Did Foote know about Lizzie? "Yes, sir," Zach said. So Mannie was a Major and in charge of Tactical Operations. He stepped a few strides away and punched the radio call button. "Crows TOC. Crows TOC, this is Murder Two."

Static popped. "Murder Two this is Crows TOC, Zach?"

"Major Guerrero?"

"Yeah. Lizzie's out of bounds."

"Shit." What he was afraid of. "Sir."

"Colonel's willing to send you out on a dual purpose mission."

"Permission to speak frankly, sir?"

"Zach. It's Mannie. Tell me."

"I'm needed here. We… I can't keep pulling Lizzie's bacon out of the fire while everything else goes to hell." There was silence on the other end. "Do you copy, TOC?"

"Roger, Murder Two. I'll do what I can from here."

"Murder Two out." Zach released the talk button. His hands were shaking. He tensed them into fists and then stretched them back as he walked back to Foote and Will. "I'm staying with you, sir."

Foote gave him a long, hard look. Then turned back to Will. "Lt. Sampson, you're going to be taking a message to Benson."

Will looked perplexed. "Are they going to let us drive away?"

"I don't know," Foote said. "It's nearly dark enough now. Get some men and have them push the last jeep back along the road until they can't be seen from the trains. If anything happens, start it up and drive fast. They've got vehicles on the other side of the track, but I don't think they're going to move the train until morning. Riley, get him going and then report back to me."

Will and Zach hurried to the rear of the line.

Foote was right, from the last jeep, Zach couldn't see the train. He explained Foote's plan to the men nearby. They seemed happy to be doing something, anything.

"Will?"

His buddy still looked nervous. "See you in Provo in a couple days."

"Yeah," Will said, his jaw set tight. "Be careful."

"You, too. Everything's gonna be fine. Nobody wants a war. They just want our stuff." Zach was skeptical that it was really that simple, but it wasn't like that was going to change anything. "Go." Will hopped into the last jeep and pulled it out of gear. Zach pointed at the vehicle and made a pushing motion with his hands at the men who stood poised to push. The heaved into it and the vehicle started to move. "Good luck, my friend."

Chapter Thirty-One

THE NEXT DAY WAS QUIET, leaving the countryside asleep, blanketed in snow. With the sun providing light, but still behind the hills, Lizzie plunged forward through several inches of new snow. Someplace nearby there was signal.

She turned on her phone and walked back the way she thought she'd come. A few minutes later she found a Y in the road. Which way? They were each coated with a clean layer of soft, downy snow. No signal. She started along the street to the right; pretty sure it was west, unless she had gotten completely turned around.

Her phone buzzed at her hip. She jerked it out of her pocket, careful not to let it fall. New voice-mails.

The first was another from her father. "Call me. I have to talk to you."

She tried calling him back, but the phone wouldn't connect. She wandered around in wider and wider circles, hunting for bars. When her foot stepped down into a ditch, she decided to continue along the road. In a few hundred more steps her phone jumped from no bars to two bars.

She stopped walking and called her father.

"Lizzie?"

"Daddy. Are Rachael and Saj...?"

"They're okay. Under house arrest for now."

"Shit! This is insane. We are grown adults. They can't make us stay. This is worse than the breeders! Is Duke around? Maybe he can get them out?"

There was no answer.

"Daddy? Are you still there?"

"Yeah." His voice was soft, quiet.

"I thought I'd lost you."

"Elizabeth."

"What is it, Daddy? Just tell me."

"Duke shot Mr. Ray."

Lizzie's mouth worked like a dog-person and nothing came out.

"Elizabeth, I'm sorry. I saw him run. With two rifles in his hands."

"Duke's no assassin."

"Lizzie."

"He's not, Daddy."

"How do you know that?" Her father paused again.

"I know." But even as the words escaped her lips she wondered. Had she been fooled? It had certainly happened before. "Tell me what you saw."

She heard him take a deep breath. "We were out at the Olmsted Power Station, north of Provo. After the shots, there were two people on the ridge. I saw Duke clear as day."

"Duke told me he was going hunting up north."

"I'm sorry. It was a specialty rifle, not just for shooting deer. Elizabeth, come home—Saj needs you."

"Don't use Saj against me Daddy." She had to be strong for Saj now. Her voice dropped to a whisper, husky with tears. "One day, he will understand."

"Lizzie, don't—"

"Bye, daddy. I love you." Tears dripped on the phone as she ended the call. She tried Duke's number, the Glen line first. It went directly to voice-mail. "Lizzie. Call me. Now."

Then she tried the Provo-network phone—the one she was certain their spies would be listening on. "Hey, Duke. Just want to know how the date went with Aubri." She heard the jealousy in her own voice, even if it made no sense.

She opened Maps on her phone and GPS pinpointed her location. The freeway entrance was to her left. Where would Duke go? The house with the dead guy in the foyer? He'd presented it like it was a backup location, but it was in The Shitty. No way. And she had the feeling that even that secret place he shared with her might be a ruse. Duke kept a lot to himself—even from her.

North, she decided. Into the more deserted lands. To find him, she needed a vehicle. She needed to drive.

Lizzie hurried back to the farmhouse. In the garage was an old Ford pickup. She looked up over the edge of the open window and breathed a sigh of relief. The keys were in it and it was an automatic transmission.

She pulled the door open and tossed her pack inside. The garage door was not electric, she found the cord, and yanked so hard that both feet lifted off the ground. The door creaked upward. She tried it again and it came up most of the way. Snow piled up where the wind had blown it into a wall up against the door, but there wasn't much to break through before the snow became a thin blanket on the drive.

Lizzie crossed her fingers and climbed in. "William and Emily please let me borrow your truck—and let me be able to do this for once." She twisted the key and the truck coughed. The gauge read Full, but the truck was old.

She cranked it again. "Come on, baby." The engine growled to life, loud in the enclosed space of the garage. "Thanks." She patted the dash. "Good girl." She popped it into reverse and busted through the snow drift, swerving a bit as she backed down the driveway, narrowly missing a few trees. She kept it together and didn't give up when she was out on the road and slowly making her way toward the freeway— thrilled to actually be doing it.

Her phone buzzed. She stopped, letting the truck idle in the middle of the road. A text from Duke on the GlenPhone. **14388 S. Bridgefield Dr. Draper.**

Lizzie punched in the address. **Im 20 min away. Driving.** She texted.
You driving???

Yes. She'd rather not be driving in the daylight—rather not be driving at all, really.
Drive careful.

She shoved it back into drive, nudging the gas to get it moving. The rear of the truck swung on the icy road and she let out an embarrassing squeak. Good thing nobody was around to see. That seemed to really be helping. She didn't have her dad or Duke looking over her shoulder, judging her driving abilities. She straightened out the truck and rolled down the road with something that could almost be called confidence. She kept in the grooves of other tire tracks, trying not to think of who could have made them.

Ten minutes later, her phone buzzed again. She slowed the pickup to the speed of to a slow walk. "Yeah?"

"How close are you?"

"Dunno."

"Okay. Take the Draper exit, go right and then left almost immediately. Pull in and park at the state liquor store. I'll meet you there."

"I'm not here to drink with you, Duke," she joked.

"Cute. Now shut up and drive."

By some miracle, she made it. Ahead someone was running toward her. Her first instinct was to drive the other way, but then she recognized Duke. She ignored a handicapped sign, parked and jumped out. They caught each other at the halfway point and hugged hard.

"We're both outlaws now, Duke. How did we get into this mess?" He might be a killer, but he was all she had. And whatever happened, there had to be an explanation or a reason.

"Let's get indoors." Duke released her and guided her up the street to a super-sized two story home.

"You like the place?" He gestured at the solid oak door and porcelain tile entryway. "No dead guy and no basement, but the neighborhood's nice. This one has solar heating and electric. Not sure how long it will run…" He stared at her. "I wasn't sure I'd ever get to see you again."

"Yeah, being an assassin on the run is hard on a friendship." Lizzie watched him carefully, but he didn't get the hurt look she'd expected. Worry crept in at the edges of her certainty.

"I didn't do it, Lizzie. I know they think I did. It was Travis."

Immense relief lifted her heart, and then it sank again with cold dread. "But he's locked up."

"A ruthless willingness to kill folks is useful these days, obviously it got him sprung. What's happening back in The City?"

"Tony DiSilvio, has taken over, I think." Lizzie looked him straight in the eyes. "My dad saw you."

"Yeah, DiSilvio and his guards shot at me when I tried to take Travis back. They were in shoot first, ask later mode. So I ran." Duke's eyes shone like a cornered wolf. "I told you I was going hunting. But it wasn't deer. I found out he was on the loose and I wasn't going to wait around for him to hurt you."

Lizzie continued to watch him. How could she tell if he was lying?

"You believe me, don't you?" His earnest worry that she wouldn't was genuine.

"Duke. Don't be stupid." Lizzie lay her hand on his shoulder. "As much as everything didn't work out… I know you. I never for a minute thought you shot Mr. Ray. Now if DiSilvio had been shot, I might have wondered."

He huffed and gave her a humorless smile.

"That was a joke."

"But is it?"

"What?"

"He's not a joke. I've been thinking a lot being out here alone. Maybe I'm just paranoid."

"No. He wigs me out, too." Lizzie shivered thinking about the new laws requiring women to be barefoot and pregnant—DiSilvio was behind it, she was certain.

"I should have shot Travis. I had him in my sights. But I couldn't do it. Not like he does. Cold blood. So, I told him to drop his gun, he did. And I forced him back toward the plant."

Duke's eyes seemed to look through Lizzie back into that night. "Then the shooting started. He ran. I went after him. His gun is stashed at the safe house. Not sure if it can clear me, but I'm hoping."

"Duke, you're not a killer." Lizzie touched his cheek. "At least not like him. I couldn't kill him either."

"But he needs to die." Duke sucked air through flared nostrils, then blew it out. "Enough politics. God, it's good to see you." He sighed, obviously glad someone was on his side.

"What are your plans?" she asked, yawning suddenly.

"My plan is to get you to bed—" He shook his head at her arched brows. "Not like that. How's Aubri."

"What do you mean? Why would I know?"

"Come off it, Lizzie. Don't tell me you didn't talk to her again."

"Why would I?"

"God, you can be stupid. You should stop running away sometime, long enough for you to catch up to yourself."

"Whatever. I am tired," she said, unsure she wanted to go down the rabbit hole he was leading her into, right now. "This pregnancy is a killer for energy. Speaking of pregnancy, where's the bathroom?"

He squinted at her. "Down the hall to the right. There's a clean bedroom across the hall. Bed's probably been made for a year."

Lizzie walked down, her fingers fidgeting. Yeah, she'd thought about Aubri. But what did that have to do with anything?

When she came out of the bathroom, she could hear music coming from the room next door. It was slightly ajar. She knocked. "Duke?"

"Yeah, come on in."

The lights on the bedside glowed, their shades covered with t-shirts to keep the light low. The windows had cardboard duct-taped over them. "Paranoid much?"

"Not feeling particularly safe in this country. Some people actually think I killed their demi-god."

Lizzie sat on the bed. "Just because you're paranoid, doesn't mean people aren't out to get you."

"You sound like you lived that."

"Yeah. Can I take a nap here? I don't really want to be alone."

Duke nodded and Lizzie lay down, slipping under the comforter. She lay her head on the pillow facing away from Duke.

She closed her eyes and tried to breathe long and slow. But her brain was racing. It wouldn't let go. Finally, she rolled over and found his bemused stare. "What did you mean by the comment about Aubri?"

He put down the map he was studying. "Listen, I don't want to sound like the cliché guy who got dumped, but it's kind of obvious you're a lesbian, or at least bi. You looked at Aubri, the first night you met her, the way I wish you would look at me, for even a second."

Lizzie bit her lip. "I may have experimented with girls, but—"

"It's not an experiment. It's your normal."

Tears misted her eyes. She'd spent so long trying to have a "normal" relationship with a guy, she'd never stopped to consider that her normal would be different. Which was stupid. She'd never been mainstream.

"I'm about ready to tuck in. You going to sleep in my bed?" he asked, after she was quiet for a long time.

"If it's okay."

"Don't worry. I am good with it all, now that I realize what's been going on."

Lizzie scooted forward to give him room to lay down. "You can have the cold side of the bed."

Duke laughed behind her. "Some things never change."

"Taking care of myself."

"Yeah." Duke walked around the bed, tugging his t-shirt off his head. She examined him from her new perspective—a perspective she'd really had all along. She admired his beauty and his physique— he wasn't ugly to her. But lust didn't factor into it. Sure her hormones still made her somewhat horny. But she could take care of that herself if she really needed to. She didn't need to have sex with him to prove she was normal.

Duke pulled back the covers and backed into her. She wrapped her left arm around his chest, tucking her right arm up against his warm back. He shivered in front of her. "So, this doesn't turn you on? Being in bed with a lesbian?"

"Whatever. 'Think of me as one of the guys,' right?" Duke grunted. "Go to sleep."

"You first." Lizzie's left hand snaked down across Duke's belly, he wiggled in front of her.

"Lizzie, don't ruin it."

She laughed. "Just teasing."

He snorted. In a matter of seconds his breathing was deep and even.

"Thanks," she whispered, "You're a true friend."

Chapter Thirty-Two

LIZZIE WOKE TO AN EMPTY bed. She sat up and swung her feet to the floor, wiping the sleep from her eyes.

There was a knock on the front door. Her heart pounded. Who knew they were here? "Duke," she hissed. "Where are you?" Maybe Duke had turned her in for some kind of revenge. No, revenge wasn't his style. Maybe he'd gone for a walk and locked himself out. Yeah. She pulled on her jeans and slipped out the bedroom door, as the doorbell rang and the knocking repeated even louder.

"Shit," she muttered. "Who is it?" she called, as if this happened every day.

The knocking turned to banging and it sounded like someone leaned into the doorbell. "Open the fucking door or we'll shoot it open." The voice was not Duke's.

Lizzie gritted her teeth. Her brain fast forwarded through the scene playing out in her mind. "Just a minute. I'm getting dressed."

She pulled on her jacket, slipping down the hall to the back of the house. She poked the curtains apart so she could see a tiny hairline slice of the backyard. She saw movement. *Damn.* Out of options she went back to the front door.

"I'm alone. And I'm pregnant." Maybe that last would get her some preferential treatment. Seemed to be the only thing sacred in this new world.

She slipped the slider catch chain out of the slot, turned the deadbolt and then undid the latch on the door knob. Then she turned it and opened it up. "Yes? Can I help you?"

"Stay out of the way." The lead guy growled, shoving her aside. His machine gun ready at his hip, he slid into the room, motioning other armed men in after him.

The cold air gusted in with the men. They streamed down the hall, nervous as hell. They looked straight out of a video game.

Lizzie was glad she'd put the jacket on, the cold air sliced through the thin material. She went to close the door.

"Leave that open," The leader ordered.

"It's cold."

"I'm not worried about the cold right now."

Lizzie hauled an old afghan throw off the back of the couch.

"All clear," came a voice from down the hall.

"Post someone at the back door, K-Rod. Pierson, front door. Everybody else, follow the tracks." He'd been checking Lizzie out as he gave orders. He cleared his throat and spoke more softly. "Okay. So do tell why a pregnant girl is out here all alone in renegade country."

Lizzie tried to think of something clever to say—but she was all out.

A soldier slid past him onto the porch.

"Let's try this again." The leader shut the door, and sat on the couch, affecting a smile that was meant to put her at ease. "I'm Lieutenant Carillo. Have a seat."

Lizzie sat on the couch, wrapped in the blanket. The leader was hardly older than Lizzie; he was Hispanic, but he pronounced his name like a gringo. Was it because he'd run out of patience correcting people, or because he was totally out of touch with his roots?

"Lizzie. Gooden-*Guerrero*," she said, emphasizing the Spanish pronunciation, the way her father taught her.

His eyebrow raised. Without saying anything more he walked back to the door and opened it. He whispered something to the kid he'd called Pierson. Then he closed the door and moved to the recliner against the wall facing Lizzie and the door.

"Well. I guess we got lucky. Your father's worried about you."

Lizzie's guts twisted, the beginning of tears in her nostrils. "Is he with you?"

Carillo shook his head. "We're in contact with him."

Lizzie stared at him doubtfully. Had her father really sent the army after her?

"I don't like the implications of you being here, Ms. Goodin-*Guerrero*. Our intelligence report from Provo suggested a dangerous murderer and traitor was holed up here. And now we find you. Alone. Were you involved in his actions at the Olmsted Power Station? Did you help him escape? Where is he?"

She bit her lip and said nothing.

There was a knock at the door. Lizzie started. Carillo's mouth was a grim line. "Come in."

The door opened and two more soldiers in white and gray camo came into the room stomping off their boots on the rug.

"Duke Madison's not here," Carillo continued, "Got folks following the track out the back door. No sign of him your way?"

"No sign," said the first soldier.

"Waters?" Carillo motioned the other soldier toward him. "Go through the bedrooms. Anything that might give a clue, bring it to me."

"Bring the girl to our temporary HQ. We'll bring her into Provo when we find Madison. I'm not willing to spare the man-power."

Lizzie had no interest in being this guy's trophy. None of the guns in the room were pointed at her, but she didn't feel like she had much choice, for now.

Lizzie slid open the window. The screen was in tatters so she didn't have to pull it out. She didn't see a way to climb down, but saw a way to climb up. An abandoned two-story apartment building made the perfect temporary HQ for these Army numbskulls. They thought they were so clever making a second floor apartment their personal prison ward. Who would have thought a pregnant girl would ever escape out a window with a two-story drop.

She swung across to the neighboring window, which still had iron bars encasing it. She hung precariously between them for a moment, then got a firm hold and swung the rest of the way. She stood there with her feet on the bottom cross bar, staring into the empty room. Thank God it wasn't their main office or something. She would have to be careful.

Once out onto the roof, she longed for her backpack and a proper coat. The February air was still too chilly to only be out in a jacket. She looked out over the roof's edge. There were men coming and going at the front of the building, but not the back. She could climb down unseen.

Climbing buildings while pregnant. *Crazy Lizzie, what the hell are you doing?* She was good at crazy—and running away. Those were her special talents. She went to the back wall, and considered her route.

She had trouble putting her dad out of her mind. Gone since she was three, and now he was suddenly allowed to be the over-protective father? That didn't fly with her.

She could see a way down. It involved more window bars, the drainpipe, and a small overhang on a first-floor extension. She tested the edge of the roof under the gutters. The slant wasn't too bad, but falling most of two stories would not be good for the baby, or her.

She walked along the edge of the roof to the corner, where she had the best chance of getting down safely She swung and shimmied her way down to the overhang, not even stopping to check the windows for activity. If they spotted her, they spotted her, but if she was fast enough, they might not.

She slid on her butt down the asphalt shingles of the overhang, then hung from the gutters, with her legs dangling. There should only be a short drop.

Come on, Crazy Lizzie, jump.

A bolt holding the gutter in place snapped, and the whole apparatus groaned under her weight.

She squeezed her eyes shut and let go.

Her feet hit the wood of a small garden storage bin, and the thud was loud. She swore silently, waiting in a crouched position to see if anyone came to investigate.

No one came. Other than distant barking, the night was quiet.

Lizzie breathed for a moment, then slid into the shadows, moving as quickly as she could. Her heart pounded with elation.

When she'd gone a few blocks, she reached for her phone and found nothing, then she remembered the soldiers had taken both her phones. Her jaw clenched. "I won't cry about my god-damned phone." But without the phone she was cut off from everyone. How was she supposed to arrange a meetup with Rachael to help them escape? Her entire plan—not that it was much of a plan—hinged on her being able to contact Rachael.

Now I'm finally really alone. And really fucked.

Lizzie stumbled. Snowflakes swirled around her as another storm whipped up. Her flashlight flickered. It had seen better days. She'd found it in the storage bin along with a pair of wicked looking garden clippers that she thought would make a good last ditch defense.

In her efforts to foil pursuers she had become somewhat lost. She walked down another country road with a noticeable absence of mailboxes. Freezing; and dressed entirely wrong for the weather. She should have stayed in the old Farmhouse instead of chasing after Duke. Stupid Lizzie.

There had to be another house, or a town. She was somewhere between Provo and Salt Lake City; it should have been wall to wall suburbia. Her head was swimming. How long had it been since she'd eaten? She had to get food and shelter soon, or she was going to be just another secondary casualty of the plague.

A light flashed ahead. She waved her flashlight back and forth. Was it reflecting off something? Her pace quickened. Maybe a car to take shelter from the storm. Maybe...food.

Her flashlight blinked and went out.

The light in front of her remained steady. A crazy laugh escaped her throat and strangled off. Now she was seeing things.

Up ahead the light swung, as though turning away from her.

"Help," Lizzie croaked, but the weather swallowed up the sounds.

She ran forward, waving her hands with difficulty. Her arms seemed almost frozen. "Help me, please." She didn't care anymore about collectors, renegades, independents, zombies or aliens. As long as there was food and warmth.

The light pointed directly in her eyes.

"Hallo?" A gruff voice broke through the storm. It sounded familiar.

Lizzie's throat tightened; she tried to answer. No. Tears flowed down her icy cheeks.

"Lizzie?" Arms encircled her.

"Mama?"

"No. It's Duke. Thought I'd never find you."

"Duke?" She collapsed. "I didn't tell them, Duke."

"Come on you gotta help me—you're too heavy to carry." Duke's strong shoulder steadied her, supporting her under her arm.

She wanted to tell him to fuck off, but she didn't have the energy. He helped her to get her feet under her. They clumped down the street together. When she stumbled he pushed her on.

A red brick wall rose out of the snow in front of them, he guided her around the building.

Lizzie relaxed as she saw the back door, propped open with a flattened cardboard box. Duke pulled it open and kicked the box inside. The warmth bathed her. But then it was too warm and, as the feeling returned to her fingers and toes, everything started to burn like it was on fire, but still frozen at the same time.

Duke guided her to a couch and wrapped a blanket around her. He scrabbled at her clothing. Lizzie batted him away.

"You need to get warm and dry," Duke's voice was tough. "Let me help you."

His hands were insistent and Lizzie gave up. She was so tired. The floor tilted to the side; her stomach lurched. "Water."

He placed a dixie cup of water into her hands, and Lizzie let out a little cry as it jostled her painful fingers. The pain was worse than anything she'd ever felt. She imagined her fingers were frozen solid and a feather's touch would shatter them like glass.

She sipped the water gingerly, and the pain began to subside.

Before she passed out completely she said, "You found me. How?"

Chapter Thirty-Three

LIZZIE LAY IN THE WELCOME warmth of Duke's friendly arms. He had found her after hearing about her capture and escape by listening in on radio communications. Lizzie wasn't the kind to put much stock in miracles, but this was pretty close to an honest to goodness miracle.

And he had something she needed very badly—his *GlenPhone*.

She held the precious device in her hands for a moment before calling Rachael. This one didn't have her saved voice-mails, but it provided the crucial communication she needed to set her shoot-from-the-hip rescue plan in motion.

She dialed.

"Lizzie," Rachael's usual calm had been replaced by a tone bordering on hysteria. "There are troops driving through town, I am pretty sure they're Independents. They're taking over."

Shit. How many groups were involved here? The men who had captured Lizzie were not Independents, they were true Army. She'd heard them say something was happening in Provo that they needed to stay out of until the dust settled.

"Okay, Rach. Relax. No one is going to hurt you or Saj. Remember, to these nut-balls you are the future."

"Okay. Okay" Rachael was taking deep breaths. "You're right."

Lizzie's brain flitted from thought to thought. Could she give good enough directions to Rachael to get her to the safe house? It didn't seem likely. She could walk there if she was in town, but she hadn't written down an address for the obvious reasons. It was a secret.

"Have they taken the militia? DiSilvio?" She hesitated asking about her dad. If he'd been killed in the fighting, she didn't want to hear it.

"I don't know. They are making everyone stay indoors and prohibiting anyone from gathering in groups. I can hear shouting outside. I'm not really sure how many militia were left. Most of them went off to the solar plant."

"Rachael, stay where you are. See if you can get Jess to come to you. Nev, too. Anyone else you know and trust, who might be looking for a way out?"

"Not sure." Rachael's voice clipped off in a half-sob.

"Okay. You'll be fine. Stay indoors. Start gathering as many people as you can. Tell them to stick to the back alleys and only come in ones and twos. Keep your *Glenphone* nearby. As soon as I have a meeting place, I'll call and we'll get everybody the fuck out of there."

"Do you really think we can pull it off?"

"Yes, Rachael. Bye." Lizzie hated to cut her off, but she had a rescue to plan. Which was the crux of it. So far her plan wsa to have Rachael bring everyone to some not-yet-determined location, and get them the fuck out. It was pretty lacking details. She put the phone in her pocket and turned to Duke.

"You sure you know what we're getting into?" he asked. "We're free now. If we go back, we might not be."

"Absolutely," Lizzie said, snatching the map of Provo from his hands. "You don't have to come."

"Of course I do. They're my friends too."

The truck jostled Mannie back and forth. His knee was giving him shit like a nagging wife.

At this point, he knew they were probably heading into a trap. He never should have let DiSilvio convince him to leave. The sneaky bastard. If he was behind all this, Mannie would personally wring his scrawny neck. But it wasn't like he had a choice. Provo was in chaos without Mr. Ray, and even more so without the power back on. If they were going to convince everyone that things could return to normal, they had to have their power back.

But that wasn't possible now. If there were Independents poised to, or already in the process of taking over Provo, there was no returning to normal. He could turn the transport around and go back. But looking around at the riff raff of the militia he had with him, he doubted any of them would make a difference. The only thing they were likely to do well was die.

The only thing to do now was go forward. Turn the lights on, even if it was just for the new upstarts to see their victory more clearly.

He tried stretching his knee out far enough to give himself some relief and ended up kicking the militiaman across from him. The young man sprung awake, hands scrambling for a thankfully absent weapon.

"Sorry," Mannie hissed. "Damn leg."

The kid focused on him, backing down from red alert. "No worries."

Most of the kids were sleeping. At least that was like the real military. Those who weren't looked wired. Trigger-happy was another phrase that popped into his head. This was a fucking recipe for disaster. These raw recruits were as likely to shoot each other as take out the enemy. All the more reason not to tell them this was anything more than a routine mission to flip a switch.

Why the fuck wouldn't DiSilvio listen to reason?

Mannie snorted. He hadn't listened to Mr. Ray who'd been his boss and his friend. Why would he listen to Mannie or Foote? The asshole had delusions of grandeur. Calling himself the Redeemer— more like the Pretender.

The troop transport rattled. Middle of fucking winter. And they were in green fatigues. They'd stand out like a sore thumb. Clown costumes for a troop of clowns. The truck ground to a halt. Mannie's radio popped. "Murder Six. We're here."

"Roger."

The men were jumping to their feet, wired. "Okay, no body do anything stupid. Be alert, but do not shoot any civilians." He hopped to the ground. Pain lanced up his leg. "Do it like you trained."

They moved in, cheching the doors, which opened. Then they disappeared inside. Mannie limped forward gripping his AR-15 comfortably ready. He hadn't wanted to be ready for this ever again. He paused. Listening carefully as his men, his kids went to work.

"Major?"

Mannie heard the word, but it was a few moments before he realized the word was directed at him. They'd walked right in to the power plant, no problems, no opposition. Part of him would be happy if this wasn't a trap. None of these kids would die. The other part of him, comprised mostly of ego, realized that the only reason this wasn't an ambush, is nobody fucking thought they were a threat worth neutralizing. "Yes. What is it?"

"We found the controls to switch the power across."

"And?" Mannie stared at the uniformed kid in front of him. He didn't even look like he'd finished puberty. Had he lied or was Mannie just old enough to think that 18-year-olds were still little kids?

"Wanted you to know, Major."

"Shit, kid. I'm no more Major than you are an experienced soldier."

The kid's eyes fell.

"Look. Sorry. I didn't mean anything by it. Switch it over. On my order. Then let's get back to Provo and see if there is anything left."

Lizzie had chosen the Provo River Parkway as the best way to get close to Provo undetected. It was a strip of forested city park land that ran like an avenue up to the walls of New Provo. At least most of the way. They would have good cover to mount their rescue from here and then make a quick getaway. Lizzie wondered if this had been one of her father's parks before his duties moved more to larger issues.

"Drop your weapons."

Lizzie glanced at Duke. Evidently, they were not the only ones who had considered the ease of access southward through the park.

Duke shrugged, but didn't drop his rifle.

She fanned the darkness with her weapon. "Why?" Lizzie asked, taking her cue from Duke.

"Why?" The voice laughed, a touch of madness in it. "Because you're surrounded. But it's your lucky day, this ambush isn't for you. If you drop your guns, you can be on your way."

"Then we'll just keep walking," Lizzie offered.

"Not with guns in your hands."

"You're probably just one guy trying to scare us."

"Seriously?" The bushes rustled to Lizzie's left but she still didn't see anyone in the dark. "Guys. Say something. Sound off names."

From all around Lizzie heard voices.

"Simpson. Jones. Williams." The list continued. She heard at least a dozen voices and names. Some of the voices were female. So, not the Provo Militia.

"Shit." She set her rifle on the ground as Duke did the same.

"All right, put your hands in the air. Real high."

They did as they were told.

"Evening, folks." A young man with a toothpick in his teeth came out from behind the tree. "What's a nice couple like you traveling around armed to the teeth."

"Who are you waiting to ambush?" Lizzie retorted.

"None of your business, little lady."

"And it's your business, old man?" she watched the young man, barely sporting a patchy brown beard. He'd probably been growing it for years.

They were under guard in a small clearing next to a parking lot off the greenbelt. The good news was the power had come back on. Under the single light post, Lizzie could see a half dozen cars littering the lot, which clearly hadn't been worth collecting.

The man holding the gun on them was sweating despite the cold.

"I'm not the bad guy you think I am." He said, sounding like a whiny child. "Not that I'm a particularly good man, but I've done what I needed to survive."

Lizzie nodded. Maybe she could win him over. "Most of us have."

Sensing her strategy Duke asked, "So, what's in store for us after this? Line us up and shoot us? Buddy, we are no different from you. What's to stop them from putting you in this position one day?"

"Well, at the moment, I'm not going to do anything except keep you here. Boss' orders."

There was movement out in the dark woods. Lizzie sensed that more people had arrived, but no fighting broke out. Must be more Independents. She heard some whispers and then someone approached where Lizzie and Duke were being held.

"Lizzie?" A woman's voice said softly. A familiar voice. "It's Kylie."

"Cougar woman?" Lizzie asked, incredulously. How did this woman keep showing up in her life? "Should have known you would be behind this."

"Right. More like beside it. I think you give me too much credit. I'm here on personal business. Need to make certain things happen. What the upper echelons do is their business." Though Lizzie and Duke had already been searched, Kylie patted her down for good measure.

Lizzie jerked away. "How the hell do Independents have upper echelons—didn't you say they're an anarchy?"

Kylie snorted and settled against the hood of the nearest car. "More like an army of stray cats and dogs." She stared out into the parking lot as though waiting for someone. "Some of us don't take to herding well."

A man with a spotter scope in his hands came into the clearing. "He's coming," he hissed.

Lizzie glanced over at Kylie, who held a finger to her lips. Her crossbow nestled in her hand and her rifle leaned up against the car in front of her.

Three men entered the parking lot, coming toward the woods and Kylie's crossbow.. Lizzie opened her mouth to shout a warning, but Kylie's crossbow drifted in Duke's direction. Lizzie's mouth hung open. Seconds stretched into centuries.

Lizzie recognized a face—skin-headed now instead of blond surfer dude hair, but instantly recognizable.

Travis.

Duke's eyes went wide. He stood up, grabbed the rifle from the startled man who'd been holding it on them and raised it to his shoulder.

Travis stopped and stared.

Duke fired just as answering muzzle flashes spewed from Travis' gun.

A rat-a-tat echoed through the parking lot Lizzie ducked and flattened herself behind the car. It shook as bullets hit it.

Duke didn't take cover. He kept shooting, but then bullets rocked his body. Blood spurted from his shoulder. Lizzie flung herself to her feet and barreled into Duke, taking him down behind the other car.

"You stupid son-of-a-bitch," she yelled.

He plastered on a smile. His eyes rolled upwards.

"Duke!" Lizzie tore his jacket open. "You're bleeding all over the place."

"Did I get the asshole?"

"I don't know. I don't care. You stupid fuck. Who do you think you are? Arnold fucking Schwarzenegger?"

"You're pretty."

"Somebody help me, please," she yelled. The gunfire had stopped. There were other voices of pain.

Two of the boys in army surplus gear ran over with a medical kit. One spread out the kit, as the other pushed her aside. "Pressure here," he ordered and the other guy pressed the bloody spot on Duke's chest.

The confrontation had paused, but wasn't over.

"Drop it, Travis." Kylie yelled. "We've got you covered."

"What the Hell? Dickhead shot me."

"Travis," Lizzie spat the name out. She scooped up the fallen rifle; stood, aimed and fired at Travis' stomach. He fell backwards.

Kylie jerked the rifle from her hands. "He was mine, you little bitch."

"He was mine first."

"He killed my son. I wanted him to stand trial." Lizzie saw the raw grief on the woman's face and knew her pain.

"Sorry." Shoving aside Kylie's attempt to stop her, Lizzie ran back to Duke, collapsing to her knees by his side. His hand grasped for hers, she held it to her. "I'm so sorry I dragged you to Utah, Duke." This was all her fault.

"Yeah, me too. But I'd be a hell of a lot sorrier if I'd never met you." He grinned, his teeth bloody. "Wouldn't've missed it for the world."

Damn. She wished she'd been able to come up with something more than just friendship for Duke. He deserved it. He'd saved her life, helped her through some really dark spots and what had she done? Spurned him. Friend-zoned him.

Duke laughed, spitting bloody phlegm. "Stop being sorry, Lizzie. Just be you."

The two medics backed off.

"No. No. No. No. Save him!" She threw herself across him, wrapping him in her arms as if she could confuse Death until he left him alone.

"They can't." Duke squeezed his eyelids together. His whole face scrunched up in pain. Then he breathed. His mouth shaped like an O, his breath came out in bursts. "Can you do something for me Lizzie?"

"Sure." Lizzie's fingers touched his face. The blood on her fingers left red marks on his skin.

His eyes again squeezed shut as he dealt with the pain. "Tell Aubri I'm sorry. Will you give her something?"

Lizzie swallowed the lump in her throat. "Of course."

"You've got to promise."

"Don't die and you can give it to her yourself."

His body convulsed. "Promise," he groaned.

"Fine. I promise."

"Come closer," his voice was barely a whisper.

"Give her this." His hand rose toward Lizzie, but it was empty. He kissed her, pulling her head into his. His kiss was hard and full of life at first and then his hand fell away and his lips softened.

Tears spilled from her eyes onto his face. He stared up at the sky with empty eyes.

"Goddammit. Why do I always have to fuck things up so totally?" She kissed his lips.

"He's gone." The medic said.

"I know." Lizzie pushed herself to her feet and crossed to Travis. The other medic bent over him. By some miracle he was still alive. The medic was still frantically laboring over him, though his gut was destroyed. Kylie's son, and Mr. Ray might get their justice after all.

Travis sneered through his pain. "Come to kiss me too, darlin'?"

"Shut the fuck up," Kylie said, crouching off to the side and kissing a small pendant around her neck. "For you, my boy."

The medic started an IV and handed the bag of fluids to the other soldier to hold high.

"Was that your stupid boyfriend?" The voice rattled with liquid. "I had to take him out. Didn't think he'd make it so easy."

"I should have killed you when I had the chance, you evil son of a bitch."

"You still don't get it." Travis grimaced.

"Get what, asshole?" Lizzie shook him by the shirt collar.

"Let go," the medic ordered. "You're gonna kill him."

"I'm the gun," Travis muttered, as his head lolled. "Just the gun," he cackled.

"What do you mean?" Kylie stepped forward, pushing Lizzie. "Let him go. I need to know what he means!"

Travis reached up and squeezed Lizzie's breast roughly with his bloody fingers. "Nice tits."

Lizzie shoved him away from her. "Fucking asshole"

Travis' head thudded against the ground. He leered at Lizzie as his eyes rolled up in his head.

The medic moved in, checking his pulse. "He's dead," he said, shocked.

Kylie cried out in rage.

Chapter Thirty-Four

ZACH HAD FALLEN INTO A half-awake stupor until the transport slowed, rolling back into Provo, passing through a gap in the finished wall of vehicles.

Well-armed men dressed more like soldiers and less like cowboys than the Indies back on the train stood ready. Inside the ring of the wall, the streetlights glowed, so power was back on, at least.

All troops were coming back to Provo, by order of Colonel Foote. It was the only reason Zach had come back without a fight. If Foote was still in charge, there was hope.

Zach stood up from the bench on the back of the transport vehicle. He felt weird without his rifle, they had taken it away—a temporary measure he was assured. It had been a part of him much of the last few weeks and especially the last few days. Not having the weight of it, made him feel too light.

He didn't know how he felt about the new government, though they were taking extraordinary measures to make it seem like business as usual, but he knew what he wanted. He swung himself down to the ground. His eyes scanning, looking. Then he saw Nev, standing in the glow of a streetlight, her arms wrapped tightly around herself. His feet hit the ground and he ran to her.

Nev stepped forward tentatively, tears of joy flowing down her face.

She met him halfway and jumped up into his embrace. He spun her round and round; refusing to let go or set her down.

"I love you, Nevaeh."

"Shut up and hold me, Zach."

Mannie pulled the door open, not bothering to knock.

Colonel Foote stood in an at-ease stance, facing out the window overlooking the square. "Mannie?"

"Sir," Mannie replied. Foote didn't look back.

"We've got some things to do."

"Like quit?" Mannie said.

"No. I'm not a quitter. I'd fight if I thought it made any sense."

Mannie stared at Foote in disbelief. "You're working with them?"

Foote nodded, his lips pursed. "With Mr. Ray gone, what else are we going to do? They don't seem to be interested in changing much."

"But that's my concern. What are they interested in then?"

"Control of our resources, I think." Foote put his hand on Mannie's shoulder. "We don't have a lot of choice."

Mannie's jaw clenched. Switching allegiance wasn't his style. But the idea of allegiance to DiSilvio grated on him. "What about DiSilvio?"

"They've taken the title of Governor back from DiSilvio." Foote returned to his desk and straightened a stack of papers. "Still have the same paperwork to do. Our rank is the same. We report to the same people. We get to do as we've been doing, but we're part of the new Provisional government."

Mannie chuckled. "The *new* New Provo Provisional Government?"

A smile lightened Foote's face for a moment, then his frown returned. "Back to the message I just got."

"Yes, sir." Mannie saluted him. Looked like he was switching allegiances, for now.

"One of the squads of Independents is bringing in your daughter and two bodies. Their man is holding Elizabeth in custody."

"Shit." Mannie sat down hard on the wooden chair. Worry and relief conflicted in him. He was worried about her status as a prisoner. Worried she would blame him for everything, after all he'd interfered with her plans by sending Carillo and Zach after her. If her boyfriend died because of him, she probably wouldn't be in the forgiving mood. But immensely relieved that she was safe."

"I'm sorry."

"What the hell is going on?"

"They're charging her with obstructing the law." Foote grimaced. "Duke Madison, too, but apparently he's paid his debt to society."

"Help me," Mannie said, "please."

Lizzie walked back into Provo surrounded by guns. If Kylie couldn't make Travis pay for her son's death—Lizzie would do so in his place. Her strides lengthened as she saw Saj on Rachael's hip, feet slipping in the slush. "Saj!"

A hand held her shoulder to keep her from running away from her escort, but they didn't stop Rachael from running past them and throwing her arms around Lizzie's neck.

Saj squirmed in Rachael's arms, twisting around. "Sissie," he cried.

Lizzie smothered him with kisses. "Don't worry, Sissie will be okay."

Tears filled Rachael's eyes. "I'm so sorry, Lizzie. We waited for your call as long as we could."

"I won't let you down, Rachael. We are still on. Be ready."

One of her guards did not like the sound of Lizzie's cryptic message and shoved her in the shoulder. They pushed her on, leaving Rachael behind, hauling Lizzie's ass to jail for a second time since she'd arrived in Utah.

Her plans were not over, just postponed.

The empty jail cell held nothing of interest. The last cell she'd been in had more character. No magazines this time, but at least this one had a toilet in its own little room. No door, but a semblance of privacy.

She sat back down on the bed and blew out a long suffering sigh. The mattress, with its tough, plasticized cover, sank almost imperceptibly, solid and hard beneath her body. The one amenity was a rocking chair. She scoffed at it. What a ridiculous piece of furniture for a jail cell.

After a minute she went and sat in it, rocking herself to keep from going completely loco. The last time she'd been locked up it had been nearly half a day and had felt like two. A few hours were already feeling like a few years. The soldiers promised to tell her dad she was here. Why hadn't he come to spring her yet? Was he mad at her? She heard them say he was back in town, along with just about everyone else.

Except Duke.

Fresh tears sprang to her eyes.

The door, with its skinny wire reinforced window clicked. Someone was coming.

The door opened and a woman stepped in. Blood rushed to Lizzie's head. Aubri. Not who Lizzie expected.

"Hi," Aubri said, letting the door close behind her. "Heard you were coming back."

"Hi." Lizzie could think of nothing else to say. So lame...

Aubri came toward the bars of the cell. Lizzie stood without thinking and walked to meet her.

"I'm worried," she said. "People think you aided Duke in escaping and they think he killed Mr. Ray…"

"He didn't," Lizzie blurted.

"I know." Aubri sighed, her hands grasped the bars about head height. "At least I figured he didn't. He's not the type."

Lizzie folded her arms across her chest. "No. He wasn't." Aubri wasn't accusing or judging, she was just stating the facts. Lizzie tried to relax, and unfolded her arms. She put her hands on the bars underneath Aubri's.

Aubri's hands slid down until they made contact. "Are you okay?"

Their faces were so close that Lizzie could not keep both of Aubri's blue-greenish eyes in focus at the same time. "I don't know. I don't know anything."

Aubri's face pressed in between the bars, even closer. "Can I help?"

"Uh, Duke said I was to give you something. I promised. Haven't been good at keeping promises." Lizzie's face moved toward Aubri's, her lips opened and breath escaped as her head banged into the bars.

Aubri broke into a pleasant, melodic laugh. "Did you really just bang your head on the bars?" she asked.

Lizzie giggled; when had she ever giggled? "I'm kind of a klutz."

"What did Duke make you promise?" Aubri asked.

Lizzie pulled back slightly, fresh tears pricking her eyes.

"Aww, honey, tell me later. It isn't fair. Duke was a good guy. And a great friend, I bet."

"The best." Lizzie swiped at a tear slipping down her cheek.

The door opened. Aubri and Lizzie pushed away at the same time.

Aubri gripped the bars tightly as a uniformed militia man came into the room.

Foote nodded to Lizzie and turned to Aubri. "I need to ask you to leave."

Mannie stood behind him looking pensive.

"Doesn't she get a lawyer?" Aubri asked, not letting go of the bars.

"Does she need one?" Foote asked.

"Aubri. This is Captain Foote. And my dad, Mannie." Lizzie turned to them, "This is my friend, Aubri."

"Colonel Foote, Lizzie," the older man corrected. "And your father's a Major now."

"Oh." Aubri looked flustered. "Pleased to meet you."

"I'll be okay," Lizzie said. "Come see me later and we can continue our conversation."

Aubri looked ready to fight, fire in her eyes. "I'll be right outside."

"Thanks," Lizzie smiled at her.

Aubri let go of the bars and smoothed her shirt. Lizzie watched her curves walking away. She looked back at Lizzie once more with a slight smile, before closing the door solidly.

Lizzie turned back to Foote.

"We don't really have any sort of law other than running with the old rules, which seem to me to still be in force. But if you want someone else here, some sort of legal counsel, in addition to the three of us…"

Lizzie shook her head. "No. this is fine. I'd say the interested parties are represented."

Her father seemed sad. He still hadn't spoken.

Foote motioned to the bars. "Would you feel more comfortable with the cell open?"

"Yeah."

Foote put a key in the lock. He turned it with a loud clank, then slid the door aside. He motioned her toward the rocking chair.

Her father sat on the bunk and Foote remained standing.

Lizzie sat in the chair, rocking to calm her nerves.

Foote began. "Can you explain what happened out there?"

Lizzie stared back at him. "Can you explain what happened here?"

"Lizzie, please," said her father. "This is serious."

"Oh, I understand that." She tugged at the cuff of her shirt sleeve, where a small spot of blood had found its way past the coat she'd been wearing when Duke died in her arms. The soldiers had taken her ruined coat, but missed this small speck.

She kept staring at the speck. There had been so much blood. It could belong to either Duke or Travis. "You were chasing the wrong man. Duke was there when Ray was shot, but he didn't shoot him."

Foote laced and unlaced his fingers together. "Seems awfully coincidental."

"Whatever." Lizzie turned away. "What are you charging me with? Because it seems to me, that my being in Duke's vicinity when you were looking for him, is about as coincidental as Duke being there at the time of the shooting."

Foote grimaced. "I'm not interested in charging you. I want to find out the truth."

"And I gave it to you."

They stared at each other for a long time. If Foote thought he could stare her down, he was sorely mistaken.

Foote stood stiffly. "I want you to write a statement. And I will release you into your father's custody, as of now."

Lizzie thought of half a dozen smart ass answers, but kept her mouth shut. When the time came, her father's custody would not hold her back. But the window for rescuing Rachael and Saj was temporarily closed. From what she had seen as they escorted her back, guards on the wall had tripled, and they all seemed to be rocking some kind of 24 hour energy juice. Then there was Aubri. Lizzie didn't even know yet if Aubri was willing to leave. But she couldn't be happy with all the breeding bullshit and confinement of women either.

Lizzie was still of the opinion that Provo was not for her. But for right now, she and Provo were at a stalemate.

Foote took her silence for agreement, turned on his heel and strode outside, opening the door with a clang. Lizzie doubted she would have had the same lenience if her father wasn't his favorite pet.

"Well, Elizabeth. Things are certainly not boring around you." Her father's cheek twitched. "I'm sorry about Duke"

Lizzie nodded. "So, I'm free to go?" She motioned to the door.

"Yes."

She stepped out of the cell. Outside the bars the air felt clearer.

She turned to her father. He pulled her into his arms.

"Lizzie. You scared the shit out of me." She could scarcely breathe as he held her. Then he let go. "I love you. Don't know that I can stand to lose you again."

Lizzie wrapped her arms around him and hugged him tight. "You're not mad at me?"

"I'm glad you're safe."

"Could you give me a few more minutes to talk to Aubri? If she's still waiting."

Her father shrugged. "Invite her over."

"Uh, okay." She glanced away, certain that he could see right through her. She stepped to the exit, half expecting it not to open. It did and she rushed out.

Aubri looked up. Her eyes lit up. She hadn't been expecting Lizzie to walk out.

"I'm free. For the moment. I mean, I don't have to stay locked up. My dad is my jailor and he suggested I invite you to come over to—" Lizzie stopped talking as Aubri's smile grew into a grin.

"Do you want me to come over?"

Lizzie swallowed. "Yeah. I'd like to talk."

It seemed her release to her father involved being at his place for now. Which meant less privacy. Which could be awkward. But Lizzie was happy not to have bars between her and Aubri anymore.

They headed outside to Mannie's jeep. Lizzie walked after her father, exquisitely aware of Aubri close beside her. Aubri's hand brushed her's every few steps and each time it was like electricity.

When they got to Rubi, Lizzie said, "Aubri, meet Rubi. Rubi, Aubri. She's really not as scary as she looks."

"Are you talking about me or the jeep," Aubri asked, arching her delicate eyebrows.

"You obviously."

Aubri opened the door and held out a hand to help Lizzie up. She couldn't decide whether to be offended or charmed. Aubri was much taller than she was and the step up to the Jeep was high. She decided to be charmed and held onto Aubri's hand as she climbed in after her.

"Aubri, what do you do around here?" Mannie asked as they settled in the vehicle.

"Communications. I connect people." Aubri squeezed Lizzie's hand.

When the Jeep rocked backward and then turned out of the parking lot Lizzie leaned into Aubri.

"How'd you and Lizzie meet?"

Aubri flashed Lizzie a grin. "Trying to connect people. We met at the club."

"I'm glad you kids have someplace to go to meet new friends—give you some sense of normal."

"Yeah," Lizzie agreed. "Normal."

The End

If you finished STRAIGHT INTO DARKNESS please leave an honest review on Amazon and Goodreads. Reviews are the best way to help an author find their audience.

If you want to find out when NO MAN'S LAND is coming, author appearances, and special offers, please sign up for the newsletter at www.desertedlands.com.

ROBERT L. SLATER

Acknowledgments

I'd like to thank my family first and foremost: Elena, Cail, Tanner, Daen, Sheridan, Ian and Miranda, Mom and Dad, James, Michael and Megan.

And all the usual suspects: Sam, Alex and all the rest at Village Books, the Heinlein Forum, my WATTPAD Followers, My Google+ers, My Facebookians, My Twitterfans, and ALL MY STUDENTS!

My friends, fans, and critiquers: Amanda J. Hagarty, Andrea Kinnaman, Jesikah Sundin, Betsy Childs, James R. Wells, Brian Soneda, Christopher Key, Kayti Nika Raet, Donald Drummond, Mark Leslie, Virginia Herrick, Pam Beason, Joannah Miley, Selah J. Tay-Song, Michael Sarrow, Peter Rust, Jim Kling, Katie Kindland, Alberta Hendrickson, Dave Straub, Tina Shelton, James Hagarty, Alice Acheson, Tsena Paulsen, Janet Godsoe, John Seltzer, Kathy Brown, Hope Musick, Tonja Myers, and Tamar Clarke. The Fanily: Eddi, Katie, Nicholas and William Vulic. Brian Lenius, Chris & Christine Perkins, Joe Collins, David Miller.

My Beta-readers: Ilana Halupovich, April Murphy, Ashley Sheppard, Betsy Childs, Caitlin Botha, Chris Drye, Cleo Martini, Denica Rodriguez, Emily Hester, Gareth Bateson, Hannah, Heather Icenbice, Jim Phillips, Kim Carter, Lee Meyer, Mattias Ahlvin, Pete Thibadeau, Priscila Martinez, Robert Wright, Ruth Simms, Samantha Murphy, Sheron Hughes, Thomas Huntley, Tshepiso Ngaleka.

I am certain I have forgotten people. My apologies, and know that I appreciate your support. Yes, Chuck Robinson, it takes a Village to publish a book!

About the Author

Growing up in the Pacific Northwest, Robert L. Slater wanted to be an astronaut or a rock star. At 42, he gave up those dreams to become a writer of science fiction and fantasy, where he can pretend to be both.

Like some of his characters, he has a propensity for speaking in lines from 80s movies, drinking Mountain Dew and eating pizza. He loves music as a listener, a zealous fan, a guitar player, and a singer/songwriter.

After nearly 20 years as a schoolteacher, and 35 as a teenager, he is beginning to have a hint of insight into young-adulthood. He has been in that hood a long time!

Robert can be found on various social media: Twitter - @robertlslater
Wattpad - @robertlslater
Facebook - Robert L. Slater
Google+ - RobertLSlater1

He posts regularly on the Deserted Lands Blog at www.desertedlands.com/blog
and irregularly on his personal blog at www.robslater.com/blog

www.ingramcontent.com/pod-product-compliance
Lightning Source LLC
Chambersburg PA
CBHW051257210726
48287CB00002B/544